ACCURSED SON

ERIC AVEDISSIAN

BOOK 1 OF
THE MARTYR'S VOW

ACCURSED SON
BOOK 1 OF THE MARTYR'S VOW

First edition. December 12th 2022
Copyright © 2022 Eric Avedissian
Written by Eric Avedissian
Cover design © 2022 Jessica Moon and Chad Moon
Cover art © 2022 Francois Vaillancourt
Formatting done by Mandy Russell

Published by Shadow Spark Publishing
www.shadowsparkpub.com

TABLE OF CONTENTS

CHAPTER ONE.. 1
CHAPTER TWO... 12
CHAPTER THREE... 23
CHAPTER FOUR... 28
CHAPTER FIVE... 35
CHAPTER SIX... 41
CHAPTER SEVEN... 46
CHAPTER EIGHT.. 56
CHAPTER NINE.. 62
CHAPTER TEN.. 69
CHAPTER ELEVEN.. 82
CHAPTER TWELVE....................................... 90
CHAPTER THIRTEEN.................................... 101
CHAPTER FOURTEEN.................................. 108
CHAPTER FIFTEEN....................................... 123
CHAPTER SIXTEEN...................................... 135
CHAPTER SEVENTEEN................................. 143
CHAPTER EIGHTEEN.................................... 151
CHAPTER NINETEEN.................................... 160
CHAPTER TWENTY....................................... 167
CHAPTER TWENTY-ONE............................... 178
CHAPTER TWENTY-TWO................................ 185
CHAPTER TWENTY-THREE............................ 193
CHAPTER TWENTY-FOUR.............................. 204
CHAPTER TWENTY-FIVE............................... 214
CHAPTER TWENTY-SIX................................. 227
CHAPTER TWENTY-SEVEN............................ 236
CHAPTER TWENTY-EIGHT............................. 242
CHAPTER TWENTY-NINE............................... 248
CHAPTER THIRTY... 259

CHAPTER THIRTY-ONE.. 269
CHAPTER THIRTY-TWO.. 277
CHAPTER THIRTY-THREE....................................... 287
CHAPTER THIRTY-FOUR... 297

To author and critic Ara Baliozian.
Your letters gave me perspective and
brutal honesty when I was a young
writer searching for my voice.
Here's to the outcasts and dissidents
wherever they are.

AT DEATH'S DOOR A MAN WILL BEG FOR THE FEVER.

Armenian Proverb

"TRY AS MUCH AS POSSIBLE TO BE WHOLLY ALIVE, WITH ALL YOUR MIGHT, AND WHEN YOU LAUGH, LAUGH LIKE HELL, AND WHEN YOU GET ANGRY, GET GOOD AND ANGRY. TRY TO BE ALIVE. YOU WILL BE DEAD SOON ENOUGH."

William Saroyan

CHAPTER 1

THE DAMNED FAMILY

If most people knew the particulars of my career, they'd crawl back into their stuffy cubicles or retail hells and thank their lucky stars they don't have to do what I do for a living.

For me, every day is the same. Only the bodies change.

Today it's Mr. Haroutunian's turn.

When I'm done with him, the former grandfather and insurance salesman sprawled on my porcelain table will look fabulous. That's my unwritten guarantee.

My name is Armand Tarkanian, and I embalm corpses.

Not the greatest gig, but it's the only one I know.

Of course, Mr. Haroutunian won't look fabulous if I don't focus on the work, so I manipulate the hose and soak him thoroughly, wetting his face, ears, and mouth. I clip the hose to the table with a suction cup and wash the rest of the body, giving Mr. Haroutunian one last shower. My gloved hands then massage his hairy arms and legs, easing the rigor mortis until those gray, lifeless limbs are pliable.

Feature-setting comes next. Plastic eye caps resembling pointy contact lenses slide over Mr. Haroutunian's eyes, pinning them closed. I inject needles into the gums and wire his jaw shut so his mouth doesn't flop open. He almost looks serene, like the old gent is napping.

I make a small incision above his collarbone with a scalpel and dissect the fascia with surgical instruments called aneurysm hooks, until I locate the jugular vein and carotid artery. I cut into both, then slip one end of a flexible tube into the carotid artery and attach the other to an embalming machine. A second tube runs from the jugular vein into a nearby sink. The machine clicks softly as it pumps a solution of formaldehyde, humectants, plasticizers, and dyes through Mr. Haroutunian. His blood cascades into the sink like a gurgling cranberry juice river.

Mr. Haroutunian's pale skin blooms into a pinkish, life-like hue—though he remains quite dead.

It's a beautiful and slightly disturbing transformation. I'm like a magician resurrecting the dead, except my magic is a cheap illusion. Smoke and mirrors. I preserve inanimate flesh for burial or cremation, nothing more.

Death isn't pretty until I make it so.

Uncle George stands behind me, supervising my work like a teacher peering over a mischievous student's shoulder. Drawn-faced, with hollow eyes and a wiry mustache, he resembles an old-timey silent movie villain.

"I knew Haroutunian from church," Uncle George says in the driest way possible, a dull monotone he's perfected. "We went way back. His viewing and funeral are tomorrow. The family spared no expense. Flowers have been coming in all day."

I wipe the front and back of my hands on my polyethylene gown. "Since they spared no expense, maybe a bit of a pay raise is in the cards?" I nudge.

"You know money is tight, Armand," Uncle George tells me. "We all have to make sacrifices."

I pull the nitrile gloves from my sweaty hands and drop them in the trashcan.

2

"Sacrifices *are* all I make." I sound exhausted, defeated. "Day in and day out, I'm burning my candle at both ends while you handle things upstairs. I could work in the office with you."

"The office?" Uncle George stares at me like I sprouted another head. "Upstairs is not for you. What I do is delicate. Administration and bereavement counseling. It's a skill—not a thing you learn in your," – he makes a series of dismissive hand gestures — "school classes. You're either good with people or you're not. And Armand, you're not good with people. No. You belong here, in the embalming room."

"If I can't grow here, then what's the point?" I tell him. "Thirty-six years I've been cooped up in this town. Doing the same job isn't healthy. I want to leave Fresno and discover what else is out there."

Uncle George's face wrinkles like he's sucking a lemon. "Leave your family? This is where you belong." He levels a stare my way. "I pay for your student loans, and I put you up in my house. Your life is pretty good here. A little gratitude won't kill you."

"I've given you nothing but gratitude," I reply. "I've given you respect. All I want is for someone to listen to me."

"You're just having a bad day," Uncle George tells me.

"Bad day? I'm broke! Between you charging me rent and paying my student loans from my salary, I'm practically an indentured servant," I reply.

"I pay you just fine."

"Not enough to save. How can I buy a car or leave Fresno?"

He dismisses my concerns with another hand wave. "You know what your problem is, Armand? You want to work in the office, you want to leave Fresno, and you want to get paid more. You can't commit to one thing."

"I've been committed to this," I say. "I've been committing the hell out of this for years."

"And you'll continue to commit," Uncle George's voice is sharper than the scalpel I used to cut open Mr. Haroutunian. "As long as you're a Tarkanian, you're a team player."

"Yes, sir," I reply, then attend to the best and deadest insurance salesman in Fresno.

If only I had picked the garden trowel during Agra Hadig, my life would've been different.

When an Armenian baby gets its first tooth, the family drapes a veil over the teething baby's head and showers it with pelted wheat. After much fanfare, the bewildered infant is placed in front of a series of objects and is made to choose one. The first thing baby picks determines their future profession.

Choose money, and you'll be a banker. Pick the hammer, and you're a builder. Scissors predict a tailor or seamstress, while a knife foretells a surgeon or doctor. Grab a book, and you're a teacher, or a pencil for an exciting writer's life.

That's the Agra Hadig ceremony. Fatalism at its finest.

My mother once told me that my father wanted me to follow in his footsteps and become a farmer, so he carefully positioned a garden trowel in front of me. But someone casually discarded a toy motorcycle on the floor, and that's what I picked instead.

Dad seized the motorcycle from my stubby little baby hands and forced me to select something else. He said no son of his would suffer the vulgar indignities that comes with riding a motorcycle. My second choice was a knife, and as far as the family was concerned, fate chose me for Uncle George's funeral home.

Aunt Miriam folds grape leaves over the rice, pine nuts, and tomato paste filling. She wears her *Kiss Me I'm Armenian* apron and dominates the kitchen, cooking recipes passed down from her grandmother to her mother to her.

She raised me after my mother died. Aunt Miriam is the closest thing I have to a mother now, a matriarchal presence drowned out by Uncle George's patriarchal bullshit.

My cousin Samantha pulls the string cheese apart into thin strands from a tightly knotted bundle. Samantha looks like a walking commercial for Hot Topic. Between the shiny crimson nail polish and her black and purple dress, it's a miracle that she's been able to cultivate this aesthetic for herself with such a conservative family.

I help with the lamb chops and making the rice pilaf. Traditional Armenian meals take hours to prepare but are *so* worth it. With my relatives, food goes hand-in-hand with angst. We sling guilt and denials over dinner and complain about each other without any end.

"Armand! You're getting so skinny!" Aunt Miriam chirps in the same cheek-pinching baby voice she used with me when I was four. "Don't I feed you enough?" I smile because I like the attention, but the act is getting old.

"I can never get enough of your lamb, Aunt Miriam," I say. As the lamb broils in the oven, its heavenly aroma is enough to make me weep.

"Thanks for helping out, Armand," Aunt Miriam replies. "Your Uncle George thinks cooking is woman's work and won't lend a hand in here even if you paid him."

"I don't mind. Helping out in the kitchen relaxes me," I confess.

Aunt Miriam hums a song I don't recognize. Her entertainment has always been Armenian, so this song surely is as well. Aunt Miriam loves singer Charles Aznavour and old episodes of *Mannix*—whose star, Mike Connors, was born Krekor Ohanian, right here in Fresno. But that tune? It's different, unlike anything she hummed before.

"What's that song?" I ask her.

"Just a folksong my grandmother taught me."

"What's it mean?" Samantha asks. Her grasp of Armenian is probably as bad as mine.

"It's a blessing. So that we are protected from evil spirits," Aunt Miriam replies.

"Is that a problem? Evil spirits crashing our family dinners? Is *that* why we can't seem to get rid of Dikran?" Samantha quips.

Aunt Miriam raises an eyebrow and gestures at Samantha with a wooden spoon. "It's no laughing matter. Besides, Dikran is your brother. Don't be mean to him because women are smarter than men." She looks at me and gently pats my cheek.

Samantha retreats with a smirk and goes back to her string cheese. Aunt Miriam laughs and resumes her song. It feels like a sad and ancient melody, one that conveys hardy perseverance. How very Armenian.

"Stir the pilaf," she instructs Samantha while I stab the lamb chops with a meat thermometer. A strong odor of cumin, parsley, and paprika fills the kitchen.

"How are your studies, kiddo?" I ask Samantha.

She shrugs. "I'm stuck on funeral service law and ethics. Too many different laws and ethics. *It's hard.*"

"Just wait until you're studying embalming and restoration. Whatever you may have seen downstairs doesn't prepare you for actually getting your hands dirty and doing it yourself. *That* is where it gets hard."

"How long did it take you to get used to the smell?"

"Who says I have?"

Samantha swallows. "Shit."

"Samantha, language. Stop scaring her, Armand." Aunt Miriam scolds.

I chuckle. "If she wants to study mortuary science as my apprentice, she's going to have to suppress her squick factor."

"Squick factor?" Aunt Miriam asks.

"It's what I call the gag reflex when you're dealing with a decedent," I reply.

"Enough! No more talk of the dead. Both of you! We're preparing food," Aunt Miriam says, wooden spoon in hand.

"Get over your squeamishness and study hard," I tell Samantha. "I know you can do this."

She smiles. "Thanks, Armand. Maybe you can show me the ropes?"

"Whatever you need, I'm here," I say, then mutter under my breath, "Forever… Apparently."

The interior decorating in the funeral home's dining room is fifty years out of style. Nobody cares except me. Flowery oriental rugs, lace doilies, and polished brass blended with Pine-Sol scented wood. It's like living in a rummage sale. We sit around the large mahogany dining table, all formal-like. Uncle George, shirt halfway unbuttoned, takes his place at the table's head and eats his lamb and pilaf like a debauched monarch.

Dikran, my other cousin, reeks of cologne and wears sweatpants and a T-shirt printed with the logo of some famous gym, even though he never works out. He devours his food just as noisily and with little regard to etiquette as his father.

Head down, I eat in silence like I do every night. Knife in hand, I cut the lamb and pop a piece in my mouth. It's succulent and juicy, with a hint of parsley. Chewing sounds, slurping, and the clinking of silverware fill the room instead of pleasant conversation.

Finally, Uncle George shatters the calm.

"I have a job that'll get you out of the embalming room for a while." Uncle George pulls a folded paper from his pocket and hands it to me. "Your first pick-up. Retrieve a decedent from the coroner's tomorrow."

I unfold the paper and read the name. "Maddie Hinkle? Dikran's the runner. Why isn't he going?"

"It's time for Dikran to branch out. I'm taking him under my wing and showing him the business side of things," Uncle George beams as he reaches over and squeezes his son's shoulder.

Dikran, his mouth full of rice pilaf, nods.

"The business side? But I'm the one who studied mortuary science," I remind him.

Dikran swallows his food. "And we're grateful for your hard work, but I'm not interested in embalming. That's your thing. You deal with the bodies. I'll deal with the business."

The idea of asking my asshole cousin for a raise in ten years makes me lose my appetite.

"Does this extra responsibility come with extra pay?" I ask.

"No, but you'll have a chance to get out of that freezing room and get some fresh air," Uncle George says. "Work hard and prosperity will come."

"Will this so-called prosperity let me afford a car?" I wonder aloud.

"You'll take the company car," Uncle George says.

"You mean the first call minivan that reeks of death? That company car?"

"You can borrow my car," Samantha suggests.

"Have you ever tried getting a corpse into a Honda Civic hatchback?"

"Point taken," Samantha says with a grin.

"Don't be so cynical, Armand. You're lucky you even have a job." Dikran flashes a smug and flaunting smile, the kind you only make if you're a privileged fail-son coasting on your daddy's hard work.

"Educate me on how lucky I am with my predetermined existence," I say.

"Listen, cousin. If you weren't doing this, you'd be on the farm with Uncle Hagop. Just take care of the stiffs downstairs and stop complaining, okay?"

"Respect the decedents, Dikran," I warn.

"I *do* respect them, cousin. I just don't spend all my time with them like a weirdo. Get a girlfriend, Armand, you'll feel better. Don't you want a special lady in your life?"

"Like you're a real ladies' man." Samantha quips.

"I'm doing better than Armand here," Dikran replies. "Besides, he should be living in that farmhouse with his father instead of leeching off my parents."

"I'm not leeching off your parents." My voice cracks a bit. "I'm doing everything I can, but it's not enough."

"Then do *better*," Dikran says. "This family's needs are greater than your own."

Aunt Miriam throws down her fork and crosses herself like she's at church. "*Amot!*" She cries; the Armenian word for *shame*. "This family is cursed! I've heard the stories from my mother. She knew we're cursed."

"We're not cursed," Uncle George reassures her.

"Yes, we are! We're forsaken. There's something not right with this family," Aunt Miriam laments.

"That's an understatement," I mumble into my plate.

"Enough arguing, you two." Uncle George reaches into his pocket and slides the keys to the first call minivan across the table to me. "Armand, pick up the decedent tomorrow morning. Family helps family, you know?"

I bow my head and accept my uncle's request, my fealty absolute. If you don't respect the patriarch in the Tarkanian household, you'll get an earful. Or worse.

"Sure, Uncle George." I tell him, each sickening syllable sticking in my throat. "Whatever you say."

After dinner, I wash dishes with Aunt Miriam. She grips a shammy with calloused hands and dries each plate carefully.

"I understand your frustration, Armand, but Uncle George wants what's best for you," she says.

"Uncle George wants what's best for Uncle George." I submerge another plate into the soapy water. For a second, it's like I'm washing Mr. Haroutunian again.

"We worry about you," she says.

"You don't have to worry. I'm not going anywhere. Ever."

"Don't talk that way. We're family."

"You called us a cursed family—that's what you said at dinner—what was that about?"

She looks away from me and keeps drying dishes.

"And I suppose you're not going to tell me," I say.

Aunt Miriam shakes her head and sighs. "Some things are better left unsaid."

"I wish more things were left unsaid around here," I reply, and excuse myself.

I head up to my room, change out of my shirt and slacks, and crawl into bed. Hours later, I still toss and turn, despite my exhaustion. The sheets are cool, but I'm smoldering under them. I get up and pace around my attic room, floorboards creaking under my bare feet.

Inside I'm bursting.

It's late by the time I change into a pair of shorts and a T-shirt and go out for a night run. Night running cleanses your soul and provides a release to pent-up frustration. The dimly-lit streets cloak you from the day's problems.

Tonight is different. I run so far and fast that my legs burn, and I don't care. If I collapse, if my heart explodes, or if my lungs pop, Uncle George would probably still want me to return to work.

I run farther than I ever have, down side streets and main boulevards, the humid night air warm against my skin. My breath rattles like an engine, conking out and restarting, spluttering to life, then turning over. I hurl myself headlong into the night, my stride quickening, my sneakers bounding on the asphalt. I rush through intersections without looking—If a car hits me, it'd be a spectacular conclusion to a wasted life, a commemoration of my failed dreams.

I run for so long that time dissolves. I make it all the way to Fig Garden and then head towards Muscatel.

I don't care where I'm going, or even if I'll ever stop. Despite my belabored breathing and sore muscles, I push myself—digging deep, my feet pounding the pavement.

My ankles hurt and my hamstrings burn.

I propel myself forward—I'm like an animal, some kind of primal screamer—a thing in the darkness running for its life.

Mid-stride, my body gives up and I double-over. I'm hyperventilating. Perspiration glazes my skin and drips down my face.

I collapse on the curb, my head in my hands. My tears mingle with sweat.

I can go no further.

Yet I want to keep running.

CHAPTER 2

IT'S A LIVING

I'm driving the unmarked first call minivan – a jet black Dodge Grand Caravan – to the morgue, System of a Down's "Chop Suey!" blasting through mediocre speakers.

My head pounds like a crazed drum solo, a rapid staccato migraine.

Uncle George, Dikran, the funeral home. Banes of my existence, pains in my ass.

"Who does Uncle George think he is?" I grip the steering wheel harder while ranting by my lonesome. "Where's Dad's anger at George for leaving the family farm to ruin? Why guilt me out over this? It's not my stupid farm."

By the time I see the Toyota pickup switch lanes at the red light in front of me it's all over. I mash my foot on the brake and the minivan's tires screech.

Time slows.

The minivan rams into the truck's rear. Metal crunches. Glass shatters. I'm hurled forward. The seatbelt and airbag stop me from eating the steering wheel.

Adrenaline fuels my pulse. I quiver and blink before a defeated groan escapes my lips. At the edge of my vision, the smothering airbag descends like a blurred horizon. My head races with possible scenarios: Did I kill anyone? Am I injured? How badly is the truck damaged? What will Uncle George do to me now? I get out of the minivan on wobbly legs. I expect the worst and survey the damage.

There's no leaking coolant or burning smoke, only two cracked headlights, a slightly crumpled fender, and dented front bumper. The pickup has a very minor indentation on its rear bumper and broken tail light.

I close my eyes, hold my breath, and exhale. When I open them, two men get out of the truck. They look first at their vehicle, then at the minivan, and then at me. Both eye the truck's rear bumper. The driver is short and stocky, while the other is more mountain than man.

I almost piss my pants.

"I'm sorry," I hear myself say. I feel like this is lawsuit territory, and I'm picturing an enraged Uncle George taking more money from my paycheck to cover the damages. "It's my fault. I didn't see that you had stopped."

The shorter one turns to me. "You never admit you're at fault for an accident," he says. He has a thick accent. "You injured, my friend?"

"No. You?"

"We are fine."

"I think we should exchange insurance information and wait for the police."

The short one shakes his head. "For this?" He laughs a bit. "No need. It'll be more of a hassle to deal with the insurance companies, and I'm sure that this winds up looking less than stellar for you and…" he looks at the minivan and then at me, "your mother's car?"

"It's a company vehicle. I'm on my way to the morgue, and I'm running late." I hand him one of my business cards.

The stranger eyes my name and asks, "Tarkanian? You are Armenian, no?"

"One hundred percent," I reply. After all, you can't swing a dead cat in Fresno without hitting an Armenian.

"Armand Tarkanian, as in the Tarkanian Funeral Home?" he asks.

"The funeral home is my uncle's," I reply. "He's the funeral director. I'm an embalmer."

The stocky guy flips my card to look at the back before sticking it into his pocket.

"We too are Armenians. I am Berj Manoogian." He flashes a crooked smile and I notice the glint of gold teeth shining in his mouth.

We awkwardly shake hands. His accent is pronounced, like he's fresh off the plane from Yerevan. I get a good look at him—he has no neck, a thick forehead, and a bulbous nose. Berj points to his massive associate, "This is Gor."

Gor is a monster of a human; well over six feet tall with broad shoulders, a hairless scalp, and piercing dark eyes. Shaking hands with him will surely crush my fingers, so I politely wave. He shrugs and walks around the minivan.

"Will your engine start, my friend?" Berj asks me.

"I think so," I tell him, and walk back to the minivan and get in. I turn the key in the ignition. The vehicle struggles to come to life but eventually does.

"Sounds like you need a mechanic," Berj suggests.

Uncle George is gonna kill me, I think.

Motorists behind me lean on their horns, so I wave them around. Rubberneckers pass me, each taking a gander at the worst driver in Fresno. A blue Honda, a white Mazda, and a couple of bikers with black leather jackets covered in patches all cruise around my damaged minivan.

"You said you are an embalmer at a funeral home?" Berj asks. "You handle the bodies?"

"I probably won't be after my uncle finds out I crashed the first call van," I tell him.

"My friend, we all make mistakes from time to time. I am a reasonable man. Let me help you. Armenians should watch out for each other."

It's the first time in a long time that I feel like my Armenian heritage has just saved my bacon. I don't know if a non-Armenian would be as altruistic given the circumstances.

"That's generous, Mr. Manoogian, but we should exchange insurance information. My uncle would want to know who he's dealing with. The minivan is in his name."

Berj shakes his head. "If he's anything like my uncle, I'm guessing things aren't going to go well. I'm sure we can settle this one Armenian to another. Let me help you get your car fixed. I know a mechanic that owes me a favor or two. His garage will accommodate you right now and have your van back to you in a couple of hours."

"I'm broke and can't afford to repay you," I admit. "And there's a dead body on ice waiting for me at the morgue. I've got to get it back to the funeral home before my uncle murders me."

Berj and Gor look at each other and chuckle.

"I think, my friend, we can arrange a deal. I'll loan you the money for your repairs right now, and we can just resolve it later." Berj tells me.

"Okay, what's the catch?" I ask.

"No catch."

"I can't repay you, Mr. Manoogian."

Berj holds up his hand. "You are Armenian; I can do business with you. We'll find a way for you to pay back the loan."

He says something to Gor and the massive, hulking man walks over to the pickup, reaches in, and pulls out a yellow envelope. He gives it to Berj who opens it, takes out a stack of bills, and hands them to me.

"Use it to fix your minivan," Berj tells me. "Go to Aram's Garage on South Orange Avenue. Tell him Berj sent you. I will call you later to make sure you're doing okay."

15

"Mr. Manoogian, I can't accept this. It's generous, but my uncle handles these decisions."

With three thousand dollars of multiple Benjamin Franklins staring up at me, I wonder if my luck is about to turn around. I've never held that much money before in my life. Each pristine bill is crisp and free of creases, like they're fresh from the mint.

A moment later, the pickup truck, along with Berj and Gor, is gone. I don't know what happened. I sit in the first call van with a pile of money in the passenger's seat beside me, feeling like a conman about to light out of town after a heist.

The minivan struggles a bit, but I get it going and head towards South Orange Avenue to get it fixed.

Aram's Garage has car parts, automobiles in various stages of repair, and shifty-eyed mechanics everywhere. It feels like the kind of place that you imagine a chop shop looks like, but it's not like I've been in many garages to make that assessment—maybe it was just the adrenaline from the day.

A rakishly thin man emerges from underneath a Ford Explorer wiping his greasy hands on his overalls. He's in his late twenties, with long stringy hair and thick stubble on his chin.

"Can I help you, pal?" he says, droopy-eyed.

"Berj sent me," I say like I'm knocking on a speakeasy door. "He told me you'd fix my minivan today."

Aram examines the damage, whips out a pad and pen, and does some quick calculations.

"He give you the cash for it?" Aram shouts over a shrieking pneumatic drill.

"He did, but I'm not sure if …"

"It's enough." The situation feels very clandestine, like I'm a spy. Or a criminal.

16

I hand over the money Berj gave me along with the keys, and Aram lets out a sharp whistle. Other mechanics drop what they're doing and get to work on the minivan while I wait in a dingy office. I say office, but resort for cockroaches is more accurate. I pace while I wait and contemplate how I'll repay Berj. My heart races faster as the accident consumes me. To my surprise, Aram comes into the office a short while later with the keys to the repaired minivan.

The headlights, fender damage, and bumper look brand new. I marvel at the shiny, painted and polished metal.

"This is a fantastic job," I tell Aram. "Thanks."

Aram wipes his sweaty face with a rag and shakes his head.

"No more words, man," he says. "You got what you came for. Have a nice day. Oh, and one more thing."

"Yeah?" I reply.

"Forget this place. You were never here."

"No Yelp review," I joke. "Got it."

Aram gives me one of those I'm-pretending-to-be-amused smiles before walking away.

Almost everyone who works in Fresno's death care industry knows Chief Pathologist Dr. Lorraine Martindale. While I've never met Martindale before, Uncle George has spoken of her so often it's like she's one of the family. Her office is cold like my embalming room and scrubbed just as clean.

A middle-aged woman in a white lab coat and thick-rimmed glasses, Martindale is all business. She scrutinizes my paperwork while I wait with my hands behind my back and the car accident on repeat in my brain.

"Tarkanian Funeral Home," Martindale says as she signs the release form. She clicks her ball-point pen and peruses a list of funeral homes for my place. She checks it off when she finds it. "You're late. I had her put back in cold storage."

"Sorry," I apologize. "I got delayed."

"Haven't seen you around, Armand. Your uncle still running things there?" Martindale says without looking up from her paperwork.

"You know Uncle George. You'll have to pry his job from his cold dead hands."

"George Tarkanian may never die," she says. "He's indestructible. Ornery and indestructible."

"That's the truth."

"We could've done anything we wanted with our lives, but this line of work called to us, right?" Martindale stares at me expectantly.

"Before my mom died years ago, death was a mystery— a spooky thing I didn't understand," I tell Martindale. "I thought with laughable innocence, 'What better way to conquer my fear than immerse myself in it?' I went to mortuary school, and fortunately for me, death was the family business. I realize now, after embalming hundreds of bodies and sending them to their final rewards, that I know all about dead people. It's the living ones I don't get."

She smirks. "The living ones do seem to get themselves into trouble."

Martindale walks over to a nearby shelf, pulls down a cardboard box, then hands it to me. The box is labeled with the deceased's name and contains her possessions: clothing and a damaged purse, a broken cellphone, twenty-five dollars in bills with a handful of change, lipstick, and a wrapped tampon.

"Maddie Hinkle's stuff?" I ask. "Doesn't seem like she was big on possessions."

"It's all we have. Early twenties. Found face up on the ground near a dry riverbed. She wasn't carrying much."

"What happened to her?" I ask.

"Post-mortem toxicology tests and liver specimens detected cocaine and its primary metabolite benzoylecgonine. Probable overdose." Martindale points to a slim man in the autopsy room. "He doesn't think so."

The man is wearing a gray suit with a thin navy tie. He runs his fingers over his thin mustache and removes his mirrored aviator glasses. The man looks at me, adjusts his necktie, and walks over. The way he acts makes me think he's a cop, but I don't see a badge, uniform, or gun.

"José Alvarez, private investigator." He extends his hand, and I instinctively grasp it. He has a firm handshake. Warm with a vise-like grip.

"Mr. Alvarez is working on a case involving Miss Hinkle. He doesn't believe it's an overdose even though our tests conclude it is."

"I have my suspicions," Alvarez says. "Nothing for you to concern yourself with, mister ..."

"Tarkanian. Armand Tarkanian. From the Tarkanian Funeral Home."

"Armenian?" Alvarez asks.

I nod. "Unfortunately."

"You seem disappointed."

"It's not easy growing up Armenian."

"My parents have a nice Armenian who lives next door. Great guy, that Mr. Kasbarian." He waits for my reaction. I smile awkwardly and wonder why everyone who knows at least one Armenian in Fresno thinks we're all related.

"We try to be good neighbors," I snark.

Martindale enters a walk-in cooler and exits pushing a body bag on a stainless steel gurney.

Alvarez turns his head toward the body bag containing what I assume is Maddie Hinkle.

"That her?" I ask.

"Yeah. A real shame to get the candle snuffed out so young," he replies. There's something almost hammy about Alvarez, like he's every film noire PI incarnate. I'm sure that if it were permitted, he'd be smoking right now.

Once again, I can't help myself and dig a bit, "What do you think happened?"

"A hiker found Miss Hinkle miles from where she lived and worked." Alvarez eyes me, like he's gauging my reaction as if I'm a potential suspect.

"What a shame," I say.

Martindale wheels Maddie Hinkle outside to the minivan. Alvarez follows closely.

"So why did George send you and not Dikran?" Martindale asks. "He's the runner, right?"

"Uncle George is training Dikran to take over the business. He thinks Dikran will make an excellent funeral director," I reply.

Martindale snorts as we load Maddie Hinkle into the van.

"Yeah. I'll bet," she mumbles.

That made me smirk, if only for a moment. I make sure Maddie Hinkle's body bag is secure and slam the rear doors shut. Before I leave, Alvarez stops me.

"Excuse me, Mr. Tarkanian." Alvarez produces a pen and notepad like he's a reporter from some old Republic Pictures serial and clearly doesn't plan to take no for an answer. "Do you mind a couple of questions?"

"I don't mind. Fire away."

"Where's your funeral home?"

"Tarkanian Funeral Home. We're on Ventura. Big Victorian house."

"When's the viewing and funeral?"

"I'm embalming her tonight, so I'd guess the viewing is tomorrow night with the funeral the next morning."

"Can I get your card, Mr. Tarkanian?"

We exchange business cards. Alvarez reads my name and title aloud, then flicks it over and stuffs it into his jacket pocket.

"Nice meeting you," Alvarez says in a way that makes my skin crawl.

"Likewise."

Alvarez looks at the bumper of the first call minivan for a moment but doesn't say anything.

By the time I get home and situate Maddie Hinkle in the walk-in freezer, everyone has eaten lunch. Aunt Miriam feeds me leftover lamb chops and rice pilaf. When I'm finished eating, Uncle George approaches and gives me shit for being late.

"What the hell took you so long?" he asks. "I send you out to pick up the decedent and you take three hours?"

"I was delayed. It's okay, though. She's in the freezer downstairs," I explain.

"That's not the point, Armand. I give you a simple assignment and you leave us stranded with Haroutunian's viewing and funeral. I had to dress him, and Dikran and Samantha had to help because you weren't here."

"I'm sorry."

"What delayed you?"

"There was some private investigator asking questions and stuff," I say. "What am I supposed to do, just ignore him?"

Uncle George grinds his teeth. "A private investigator is not the police. You don't need to talk to them. You do your job and do what your family asks you." His eyes burrow into my soul. "I give you a break and you screw it up. You have a responsibility to us, Armand."

Uncle George makes his proclamations like the prophets of old. What the patriarch decrees must be followed.

"Yes, sir." I leave Uncle George red-faced and head downstairs to the embalming room.

My mind spins as I contemplate recent events. The accident. The garage. Alvarez. My heart beats faster, and I wipe my perspiring forehead. As my fingers wrap around the freezer's door handle, my cellphone rings. Maddie Hinkle will have to wait.

"Is this Armand Tarkanian?" The voice on the other end of the line is unfamiliar for a moment.

"Mr. Manoogian?"

"Call me Berj. We are friends, you and I," he says. "How are you doing? Aram tells me you visited him. He fix your vehicle good?"

"It's been a hell of a day. But Aram was great. Repairs usually take a few days."

"He is resourceful, that Aram." There's a pause for a moment. "You know Donut King on Ventura? Be there in thirty minutes. Can you do this?"

"I don't know, Berj. I've got embalming to do ..."

Berj makes a dismissive noise on the other end of the line. "My friend, you know what the best part of a corpse is?"

"What's that?"

"A corpse isn't going to get up and walk away. It'll still be there when we're finished." Berj chuckles like he's in on some kind of joke. Gallows humor, I think it's called.

"It's just that I'm under pressure here," I say. "I mean ... I guess I can make time for you."

"Ah, how generous."

"I didn't mean any disrespect," I add.

"I know, my friend. Donut King, in thirty. We can talk about you repaying my debt, yes?"

"Sure."

"Good man," Berj says, before hanging up.

Chilly air blows through the embalming room, prickling my skin with gooseflesh. I open the door to the refrigeration room and peek inside. Maddie Hinkle lays undisturbed on a shelf, stretched out beneath a white sheet.

"You're lucky," I tell the cadaver. "For you, the hard part is over."

CHAPTER 3

DONUT KING

Located in a decrepit strip mall about a mile from the funeral home, Donut King sits nestled between a laundromat and hair salon. One of those twenty-four-hour donut joints with a wide glass case containing every donut imaginable, it reeks of burnt coffee and its tables are guaranteed sticky.

We are the only customers.

I crave a Bavarian cream donut, but my wallet is running close to empty. I obviously don't want to come across as destitute, so I pool together some spare change and order a small black coffee. Muzak blares from speakers in the ceiling—the boring notes grating on my already frayed nerves. I walk to the back of the shop and sit down at the table with Berj; Gor stands nearby and watches me.

Berj bites into a glazed donut, and his gold teeth sparkle. I squint and notice markings etched into them.

"My teeth fascinate you?" he asks.

"I've never seen gold teeth like yours before," I admit.

Berj nods, takes a swig of coffee and swishes it around his mouth before swallowing. He gives me a big toothy smile so that I can get a better look. "They are protective glyphs. Talismans from a bygone age," he tells me. "Magic."

Berj reaches into his jacket, pulls out a rectangular package wrapped in brown paper with a small cloth bag hanging from it, and sets it on the table in front of me.

"What's that?" I ask. My stomach flutters, and my mouth goes dry. "God, you don't want me to sell drugs, do you?"

"What?" Berj looks at me for a moment, confused, and then chortles. "Sell drugs?" He looks over at Gor. "He thinks we are drug dealers, Gor!" The hulking man gives a half smile, perhaps the maximum amount of humor he can show.

Berj caresses the package lovingly like a baby. "It's a legitimate business opportunity for you, my friend," he says. "It's come to our attention that you have a young woman named Maddie Hinkle in your possession. I would like nothing better than to see her laid to rest. Respectfully, of course."

"How do you know Maddie Hinkle?"

"Through a mutual acquaintance."

Berj nonchalantly slides the brown-wrapped parcel across the table towards me, and I notice a tiny cloth bundle fastened to the package with twine. "If you help us with this, we'll call off the debt." I reach out and pick up the bundle. It smells like incense, a pungent fragrance you'd sniff in a really old church.

"We'd like you to place both this package and cloth bag inside Miss Hinkle and sew her up so that she's buried with them," Berj says like it was the most normal request in the world.

"No, I can't do that," I tell him. "You're asking me to sacrifice my reputation. It would be such a violation of everything I …" I pause for a moment. "Look, Mr. Manoogian, what you're asking goes against all respect for the dead. You want me to bury a woman with this inside of her? What's in it?" A headache forms at my temples.

Berj waves dismissively. "Does it matter?"

"Yeah, it kinda does," I say—my tone bordering on irritated.

"Some twigs, incense, cloves, spices, a few ritual components to facilitate Maddie's transition into the afterlife," he says.

"That's it?" I ask. Berj nods. "How about I hide it in the casket? No one will ever know it's there."

"No. It must be inside her torso."

"Inside her torso?" I repeat his ghoulish words. "I could throw the package away and tell you I buried it with her."

Berj smiles and light glints off his gold teeth. "Maybe, but I think that you'll do the right thing. Besides, you need the money."

"Absolutely not," I say. "It's illegal. If I'm caught, I can go to prison. My uncle's funeral home will close. This could ruin my whole family."

"If Maddie Hinkle is buried with this box and bundle in her, the debt will be called off, and we will hire you for future work. Two thousand for this job." Berj gives me a bit of a shrug. "If you don't want to, that is also fine, we can call your uncle tomorrow and settle our debt through him. I guess that he is like my uncle though…" Berj makes a face. "My uncle was a bit of a jerk."

"You're serious?"

Berj reaches into a pocket, pulls out a small envelope, and puts it on the table.

"You have to slip this parcel and bag inside her, and stitch her up again," he tells me. "You can handle that, no?"

My eyes fixate on the envelope. Two thousand dollars, for a thing that no one would ever know about. Two thousand dollars to not have Uncle George on my case. I can't lie, the thought of getting two thousand dollars for doing something utterly reprehensible oddly tempts me.

Berj leans across the table and locks eyes with me. "We're trusting you. I think you're the right man for the job. Do this for us, and your debt is paid. Do a good job, and we might call on you again. It's that simple, my friend." He slides the parcel so close that it rubs against my arm.

"I guess I can help," I offer, my voice small.

"This is good, Armenian helping Armenian." Berj says. I understand what he's saying. Armenians are persnickety about doing business with outsiders. We like to keep things familiar and intimate. He looks over at Gor. "See? What did I tell you? The Tarkanian boy would be smart."

Gor regards me with a nod.

Berj claps his hands, rubs them together, and takes a big bite out of his donut as he leans back. I spot a nazar around his neck, an amulet of concentric glass circles that safeguards the wearer against the evil eye. Gor is also wearing one.

They're amulet buddies.

"Nazar and talisman teeth? Color me intrigued," I say wryly.

Berj looks pleased that I know what the amulet is. "There is an unseen world, accessible to those brave souls who know where to look."

"I get it. You're superstitious. New Agey. Crystals and meditation. It's cool." I quip.

"No," Berj replies. "Not new—very old magic." He bites into his donut and chews.

"Magic? There's no such thing."

"Oh, but there is." Berj leans forward. "I think that there is magic in you, Mr. Tarkanian."

"No magic for me, just dissatisfaction. I live with my uncle, aunt, and cousins in a depressing funeral home."

"No talking with the dead?" he asks.

I chuckle. "If I could, work wouldn't be so boring."

Berj lets out a hearty laugh, "Right you are." He grins. "The dead always talk. Maybe you choose to ignore them."

"Look, Mr. Manoogian, I'm an embalmer in my uncle's funeral home. That's all I am. That's all I'll ever be. I'm stuck in Fresno until the day I die. I've spent years of my life embalming cadavers, setting their features, and dressing them for burial. In all that time, not one of those lifeless bastards has given me so much as a '*hey, what's up?*'"

Berj plucks a business card from his pocket and slides it across the table.

"Take the package and my card," he tells me. "I'll be at Maddie's funeral. If all goes as planned, consider your debt canceled. Maybe you can take some of this payment and buy yourself something nice—at least you won't have to scrounge for donut money."

My cheeks flush as I take the envelope and put it into my pocket. "Yeah," I agree.

"Armenians help out Armenians. It is our way," Berj says as he downs the last of his coffee and stands up. He pats my shoulder as he walks past; then I'm alone.

I pull the package and cloth bundle towards me. "This is crazy."

Before he died, my grandpa imparted me two maxims; never believe outsiders and cling steadfastly to your heritage.

"Trust only your people, Armand," he had rasped (the result of a lifetime of smoking). "Armenians are all you have."

I sit there for a while and mull my grandfather's words before standing up. The idea of installing a mystery box supplied by a magical gold-toothed Armenian dude into a cadaver doesn't sit right with me, but explaining the fender-bender to Uncle George makes my skin crawl even more.

I quickly tuck the package under my arm and head home.

CHAPTER 4

THE DEAD SPEAK

Maddie lays on the table, mouth open and eyes white as the moon. Her pale skin, which once must have bloomed pink with youth, has a waxy and lifeless rigidity under the halogen lights.

During my first embalming in mortuary science class, my nerves almost made me quit. The rumbling nausea, pungent stench, and the traumatic shock of a lifeless bare body still hasn't left me.

This isn't just any garden-variety corpse, however.

Maddie Hinkle is special.

She comes with some pretty big strings attached, thanks to my ineptitude and greed. I nervously eye the package Berj gave me. The strange cloth bundle reeks of cloves and spices like a potpourri for the deceased.

I suit up. Embalming gown, nitrile gloves, shiny black welling-tons. After slipping the respirator and plastic safety glasses over my face, I'm finally ready.

"It's showtime," I tell myself with a heavy sigh.

Using a scalpel, I cut through the stitches holding Maddie's chest together and peel back the Y-shaped incision. The section of the rib cage that the coroner severed is moved, and I spray it with dehydrating liquid. I take out the plastic viscera bag containing Maddie's vital organs – a disturbing meat and blood stew floating behind a hazmat label – and wrap it in a towel.

I suction out as much of the blood as I can with an autopsy aspirator, and then dry the torso cavity with dehydrating chemicals. I've always hated this part. Things can get messy if you're not careful. One time I accidentally punctured the intestines and what oozed out made me gag for a half hour.

I gingerly coat the torso's insides with a preservative powder and thank the funeral gods for such small miracles.

After a few deep breaths, I wedge the package and cloth bag into Maddie Hinkle and wiggle it around inside her to make sure it fits. Part of the stubborn package snags on a piece of her ribcage. I push down, and, with a little finesse, the package is snug inside, but there's no way that I get the viscera bag back into her.

I sew the Y-incision shut with a waxed suture and curved needle; a bit of gel makes the tight baseball stitch waterproof.

I don't know why, but I'm longing for that motorcycle I'd grabbed during my Agra Hadig. If only I had that bike, I'd leave Fresno behind and Uncle George could eat my dust.

My mother always told me to be careful what you wish for. She said things change when you least expect them, and that life twists and turns and leads to defining moments you can't ignore.

My defining moment comes in the form of this dead woman.

Without warning, something inside me shifts, and what was once in disarray snaps into place. The room's temperature plunges to a bone-chilling cold, and the overhead lights flicker.

My heart races.

I sense someone behind me.

I turn around.

A shimmering and translucent Maddie Hinkle stares back at me from several feet away. Gossamer garments cling to her skinny frame and her hair billows around her. She hovers inches off the floor, her toes not touching the linoleum tiles beneath her.

My heartbeat quickens. I shut my eyes. When I open them seconds later, Maddie Hinkle is three feet in front of me, her mouth locked in a terrifying ghostly scowl. She's an aberration and shouldn't logically exist.

Yet the spirit does exist and its uncanny presence real.

"Get away from me," I hear myself say, but the words catch in my throat, and a messy croak is all that comes out.

"Help," she says, her voice scratchy and distant. *"He killed me. Help."*

I back away and bump into the table where Maddie Hinkle's body lays inert. "Killed you?"

"Help me," the spirit repeats.

"Help? You're dead."

"Find them. Stop them." Maddie Hinkle gets closer, and her ghostly body melts into me. Icy pain tingles from my head down through my spine, numbing my legs and freezing me in place.

Then, Maddie Hinkle shows me how she died.

I am a part of Maddie. I see the world through her eyes.

She's outside, miles from civilization. But not alone. The night presses in, like it's following her.

She runs. Her legs feel like they are slogging through mud. Her lungs burn, and her heart nearly beats out of her chest. Sweat beads her brow. Maddie scrambles down an embankment. The sultry air feels like it's going to suffocate her.

Her go-go boots snag on a gnarled branch. She falls to the ground. She peels them off and continues barefoot. Rocks and brambles scrape her skin as she sprints headlong into the night.

Her pursuers are gaining. Their voices carry on the wind behind her. Flash-

light beams stab the darkness. One of the men shouts in a language Maddie doesn't understand. The rest follow him.

Her joints ache as she runs for her life.

The men close in, their flashlights blind her. She glimpses leering faces in the gloom. A figure in a dark suit and silver bolo tie advances. Maddie trembles when she realizes who the man is.

"Please. I didn't do anything," she stammers. "I won't tell. I didn't see anything."

The figure places a cigarette between his lips.

"I'm sorry. I just had too much to drink," Maddie sobs. "It won't happen again."

The man quietly clicks a lighter. The flame dances beneath the cigarette as he inhales. His face, obscured in shadow, shifts in the flickering fire. He takes a long drag on his cigarette. Smoke swirls above his head like a cancerous cloud.

"Such a pity." His voice is deep and hazy. "You are beautiful, yet so careless. It is not polite to gossip. You're a talker."

The magnitude of his words washes over her.

"No!" she cries. "I won't talk. Not ever."

"I'll make sure of that."

Maddie trembles.

"Please. Oh, God. Please," she whispers. "Don't. I'll do anything you want."

The man flicks his cigarette to the ground and crushes it beneath his leather boot. He peers at Maddie and begins chanting in some strange language. She recoils at the oddity of each word, the cadence is guttural and alien, the tone harsh and unsettling.

Maddie sinks to her knees and clasps her hands over her ears to muffle the chanting as the others join in, each repeating a strange phrase.

The leader raises both arms in front of him. His fingers extend. The men speak faster as their leader's voice transitions into an otherworldly rasp.

Maddie's neck snaps back. A deluge of live frogs, rushing up her esophagus, spews from her mouth in a torrent. As they squirm, she tastes and feels the earthy wet sliminess of each frog. Maddie is suffocating. So many frogs. An unseen force propels their tiny bodies forward. Musty and earthy and rotten. All Maddie tastes is decay and death.

She convulses, her limbs go numb, and she falls to the loamy earth. Her head cocks to one side, her arms and legs askew. Blackness folds around her, but frogs keep coming and the man in the bolo tie looks down and smiles.

The vision ends and I tumble backward to the floor, clutching my stomach. It takes me a moment, but I pull myself upright. The ghost vanishes, leaving me with the real—actually dead—Maddie Hinkle.

I peel off my gloves, splash water on my face, and warily approach the body. She lays motionless, her flesh still pallid despite the blush. A far cry from the living, once breathing girl whose death I just experienced.

My head aches as the disturbing events replay in my mind, but they're foggy—like fragments of a dream that slip through your fingers after you wake. Frogs emerging from the frightened woman's mouth. The disturbing chants. A shadowed man. And an incorporeal floating spirit.

"What the fuck just happened?" I ask no one in particular.

Maddie Hinkle was undeniably dead. I tell myself that the graphic death I just witnessed and the phantom visitor were just figments of my overworked brain. Late-night hallucinations and nothing more. On the other hand, the sudden chill, the woman's voice echoing in my head, and the frogs that I can still taste paint a different picture.

I drape a sheet over the cadaver before the sound of footfalls coming down the stairs distracts me. My heart almost stops when the door opens and Uncle George and Alvarez walk into the room.

"Armand, this is Mr. Alvarez. He's a private detective looking into this young woman's death," Uncle George says.

"We've already met," I tell him. "At the morgue. Like I told you." Even in the state that I'm in, I can't help but get that dig in.

Alvarez notices my protective gear, "Hope I'm not interrupting."

"Not at all," I say, checking my watch; how late do private investigators work?

The detective asks if I was the only one who embalmed her. I tell him that I worked on Maddie alone.

"Getting her ready for tomorrow, huh?" Alvarez points to the sheet. "May I?"

I nod warily. I can't shake Maddie Hinkle's ghost from my mind. After a few deep breaths, I lift the sheet, and Alvarez leans in for a closer look.

He wrinkles his nose and readies his cellphone. "Have you noticed anything unusual with the body? Any strange discoloration of the hair or nails?"

"No," I reply, walking over to Maddie Hinkle's body and double-checking her hands for him. "Nothing like that."

Alvarez snaps a few photos of the cadaver's hands and then slips the phone into his jacket pocket.

Uncle George leans over and touches Alvarez's shoulder.

"How about I show you where we'll hold the viewing?" he says to Alvarez, guiding him towards the stairs. "It's up here, in our memorial chapel. We call it a chapel because it's respectful for all people, you know?"

Alvarez gives me a nod. "Thanks, Armand. I'll be in touch if I have any more questions."

After Uncle George and Alvarez leave, I sit down on the clean tile floor and hyperventilate.

After several minutes, when I'm able to get my feet back under me, I double-bag Maddie Hinkle's vital organs, seal it with thick tape, and place them in my duffel bag.

It's late when I drive the minivan to an empty field outside of town, and start digging a hole. The dry earth yields to my shovel and the night is uncomfortable and cool, but I have a job to do. This evidence

33

needed to find a new home underground, miles away from me.

When the hole is two feet deep, I unzip the duffel bag and take out the viscera bag. I put it down near the edge and ponder whether I should add another foot to the hole. Before I even realize it, a scruffy dog with knotted fur and chocolate brown eyes is sniffing at the bag. It tears the plastic visceral bag open with its teeth.

"Hey! Get out of there!"

I wave the shovel around, trying to spook the animal.

The dog ignores me and roots around in the bag. A moment later it emerges with Maddie Hinkle's heart between its teeth.

"Give me that!" I advance towards the beast.

The dog sees me and bolts, carrying the lifeless organ in its teeth. I give chase, following it as closely as I can until it comes to a stop and sits down.

"Nice doggie. Drop the heart." I extend my hand towards the animal's mouth, and the dog's teeth clench tighter. If the situation weren't so dire, I'd be laughing my ass off.

"Your defiance is duly noted but misdirected," I say, realizing that I'm addressing an animal. "Let go of the heart, and I won't feed you to Dikran."

I'm about to pounce on the dog when it clearly tires of the game and swallows the heart—the whole thing—with an undignified squishing noise.

"Stupid dog," I mutter. "Look what you did."

The pooch licks blood and pulmonary muscle fragments from its gore-splattered lips and stares at me with what I can only describe as innocent wonder.

Before I can adjust to the madness of the scenario, the animal *smiles* and runs away. A lone feather flutters from the dog's fur to the ground.

I don't know what was more distressing at this point; the loss of Maddie's heart, the mystery feather, or that a dog could smile.

CHAPTER 5

ROUPEN

My brother Roupen's bookstore next to Fresno City College provides him the perfect clientele; young, affluent readers crazy for books. Roupen always says that used bookstores smell like heaven. He loves the mixture of old, yellowed paperbacks, cherry tobacco, and sandalwood that seeps from every corner and crevice.

Of course, a few handsome men in his store didn't hurt, either.

Roupen straightens his glasses and flashes one such specimen a friendly smile. My brother is a shameless flirt, which is how he met his partner, Brent, a professor of journalism at the college. Three months after their first date a year ago, Roupen asked Brent to move in and the two have been living together ever since.

"Brent wants to drag me to Sonoma for some wine tasting thing," he tells me as he dusts the shelves. "He says that there's this B&B out there that serves high tea in the afternoon. I told him no thanks. The last time I had an afternoon tea party, it was with my stuffed animals and I was seven."

Roupen is thirty-three now and came out to me when we were teenagers. When he was twenty-four, Roupen took me to his first pride parade. I felt completely out of place, but Roupen was so relaxed and happy, like he finally found his people. Why would anyone take that joy away from him? That's when I resolved to always be in Roupen's corner. Mess with him and you mess with me. This includes family members too casual with their bigotry.

"Don't you want a vacation? I'd kill for one." I look through the fantasy literature stacks.

"I'd have to close this place," Roupen says.

"Hire some part-time help? Like a student?" I suggest.

"Students are unreliable. All they do is play on their phones." Roupen huffs. "Speaking of unreliable, how is our dear Uncle George?"

"The guy who puts the 'mean' in Armenian? Same old tyrant. He doesn't listen to me. Says I should shut up, keep my head down, and suffer." My fingers caress the spines of a few books, and I take a deep breath. "Something happened to me today."

"Oh? You finally met someone? A special lady, perhaps?" he asks, interest piqued.

"What? No. I saw something weird in the embalming room."

"Dikran screwing one of the corpses? Sex with a stiff?" Roupen asks.

"No. Gross," I say. "I might not be that surprised, but no. I think I saw a ghost."

Roupen furrows his brow and walks over to the counter near the door. "Can I get you something, maybe? Coffee? Tea? Lithium?"

"I'm serious. I was embalming this woman's body, and her ghost appeared and showed me how she died." I stick my hands in my pockets and lean against a bookshelf.

"Are you feeling delirious? Do you need to lie down?"

"Roupen, I'm fine."

"This is probably because you're over-worked," he offers.

"I know it sounds nuts, but I swear it happened. I actually felt what the girl went through. I saw how she was murdered," I say.

Roupen might not believe me, but he's never one to shy away from a good story. "Murdered? How?"

"Frogs." I say. The memories are getting hazier, but I can't forget those frogs.

Roupen smirks.

"Was it Kermit, with the cleaver, in the kitchen?"

"Roupen!"

"Sorry, but that shit's insane. Have you told anyone else about your supposed uncanny brush with the supernatural?" He gives me a concerned look.

"Who am I going to tell? Uncle George? Aunt Miriam? Dad?"

"Ain't that special?" he says. "My big brother has ghostly visitations and I'm his confidant? I'm honored."

"Screw you."

"Can I tell you what I think?" Roupen asks.

"Always."

"I think you're a psychological mess. You work too much, you have no social life to speak of other than hanging out at your brother's used bookstore, which, while it is the best in town, is not really 'getting out' so to speak, and you have an asshole of an uncle and an even worse father. You always bitch about Uncle George and Dad and complain how conservative and unyielding they are." Roupen looks around for a moment, finds his cup of coffee, and takes a sip from it. "Weird things happen. Unexplained phenomenon. Bizarre encounters. My money is on stress-induced trauma from living with Uncle George."

"I'm not *that* bad."

Roupen stops me. "Armand, Sylvia Plath would take one look at you and be like '*that* guy's got daddy issues'."

I groan. "It's definitely not trauma."

"Maybe a therapist could help," Roupen suggests.

"No way. You know the Tarkanian's number one rule. Never tell outsiders our problems. Uncle George and Dad would lose their minds if they found out."

"What do you care what this family thinks? I learned to stop giving a shit years ago."

"What else could it be?" I ask.

"Maybe you accidentally inhaled embalming chemicals and hallucinated or something? Maybe Dikran pulled some kind of elaborate prank?" Roupen frowns. "Scratch that, Dikran is an idiot. Maybe Samantha did?"

"Those two? Really?" Roupen doesn't buy it either, I can tell from the look on his face.

"Let's suspend our disbelief and imagine that a certain dead girl spoke to you…" My brother points at one of the overstuffed armchairs—I make my way over and slip into the old piece of furniture.

"This feels comfortable."

"I know. So, why would a ghost come to you, of all people?"

"I have no idea, but what's to say that girl didn't have unfinished business here? Doesn't the Armenian church believe in all that supernatural life after death stuff?"

"Everlasting life in Heaven, not traipsing about a funeral home scaring the shit out of the embalmer," he tells me.

"She wanted to show me something. Wanted me to do something," I say. "It was like someone else's dream, except I was forced to watch it." Maddie Hinkle's presence still permeates me even though some details of the vision faded; her words reverberate in my skull: *Help me. He killed me. Help. Stop them.* "Roupen, I swear I'm not delirious—I felt a shitload of frogs spill out of her mouth. I felt every one of them squirming up my throat. It was terrible."

"I've heard about having a frog in your throat, but this is ridiculous."

"It's not a joke, Roupen. It's like some kind of supernatural magic killed Maddie Hinkle." My throat is sour, and my stomach lurches queasily.

"Who?" Roupen asks.

"That's her name," I reply.

Roupen makes an *ah-I-understand* face. "So, this dead girl gives you a vision, shows you how she died, and now you're supposed to avenge her like some kind of hero?"

"I have no idea." I let myself sink into the chair and stare at the ceiling.

"You, my good sir, need to get laid because this bookshop is a stress-free zone."

"How's Brent?" I ask, changing the subject.

"Overworked as always."

"When are you marrying your boyfriend?"

"Boyfriend? Ugh! How gauche. He's my *life partner*. Boyfriend sounds so *Sweet Valley High*." Roupen grins. "I don't need a piece of paper from the government to tell me we're right for each other; I knew it from the moment we met."

"How'd you know?"

"Brent has this sort of cool detachment—an unshakable confidence. The first time I saw him, he was so intimidating. I felt my skin get flush, I got chills, my mouth was dry. I didn't know how to approach him. I was a mess."

"What'd you do?"

"I summoned the nerve and complimented his clothes," Roupen says. "He was rocking a blue sweater. It was all I could think of, but it was my in. We talked about books for a while. The next night we got coffee. The rest you know."

Roupen's face always lights up when he tells me that story.

"You're a lucky man," I say.

"It'll happen to you, too. Somewhere out there, the right woman exists."

"Sure. A woman who thinks that being an embalmer isn't morbid? A woman who isn't bothered that I'm indebted to a stingy uncle? Face it, Roupen. Nobody like that exists."

"I'm *sure* the right woman is out there, bro."

"Hey, my romantic concerns aside, I need a favor. A book. Something on spirituality, the occult, or parapsychology," I say.

"Why don't you go to the library?" Roupen says. "Fresno still has a library, right? It hasn't been closed due to budget cuts?"

"I need the book now," I say. "If what I'm dealing with is a ghost, I'd like more info. Maddie Hinkle gets buried tomorrow, and I need to find out all I can about the spirit world."

Roupen points me to the right section where I methodically pull books off the shelves and look at the covers. *Treadgore's Compendium of Spirits* and *A History of the Occult* seem like good starting points. The creased and torn cover of *The Encyclopedia of Ghosts and Hauntings* catches my attention. I scoop up all three and bring them to the counter.

"Wait? This is what you're going with? Don't you remember the ultimate spirit guide?" Roupen asks.

"What are you talking about?"

"When we were kids, you had this book about spirits, a bit juvenile if you ask me."

"*Madame Opal's Guidebook to Seances and Psychics.*" I remember the book. Madame Opal was a hack medium who toured the country in the early 1970s. She had a popular following with the gullible and desperate, including children. Kids bought into the magic and the mystery, along with the whole line of Madame Opal's products—from Ouija boards, crystal balls, and seance kits. Mom bought me the book when I was ten, after I begged her for it in Kmart.

"I need that book! Do you have a copy?"

"No, but you still do, you spooky weirdo."

CHAPTER 6

GHOSTS OF THE PAST

The family farmhouse stands like a faded ruin outside of Fresno. Two-stories, pitched roof, and peeling and cracking white paint; it's a nearly empty husk of memories—a mausoleum for my family's history. My father sits on the wrap-around porch, nestled in a rocking chair and overalls, the very model of a man satisfied with his misery.

His head turns towards me as I approach, every crag and crease of his wrinkly face moves slowly, like one of those *really* old Galapagos tortoises.

Condominiums grow from the grounds where crops once were, the open space has been claimed in the name of progress. The farmhouse is out of place next to these new buildings, a blemish amidst modernity.

"Why are you here?" Dad says from his chair.

"I'm looking for a book." I climb the stairs to the porch. The steps creak under my weight.

Dad sniffs. "Ah. Well, I didn't throw anything out."

The damp and musty mildew smell inside the house makes my eyes water. It's as if nothing has changed since I left. Everything is how I remember, only dustier. A leather sofa, armchairs, and varnished tables fill the living room. The cheap oil paintings depicting scenes from Armenia share wall space with crucifixes and religious iconography.

I ascend the narrow staircase, past ancestors who stare at me through old family photographs, trapped in black-and-white for eternity. Stepping into my bedroom is always like traveling back in time. A Fresno Grizzlies baseball cap rests on the nightstand, and my old boombox sits on the floor nearby with an Eric Bogosian CD still inside. The tricolor Armenian flag with faded red, blue, and orange stripes, hangs on the wall.

Roupen's bed is stripped of sheets, and his half of the dust-covered room is bare. Dad gutted everything, shoving Roupen's belongings into boxes that are now at the back of the closet, where he wished his youngest son had stayed.

It's as though Roupen had never lived here.

I realize that my father wasn't exaggerating when he said he hadn't thrown anything out. There are boxes of toys, books, and clothing within reach. Everything from my childhood must still be here.

After a bit of searching, I find the book in a box of old graphic novels. Madame Opal's picture on the back cover stares up at me. The book is scuffed and the pages have yellowed with age, but it is intact, even after all these years. I close the box up again and stand up, pushing it back under my bed with my foot. It's strange being in this room again. Every time I wind up coming here, I swear to myself that it'll be the last time.

I walk over to the window and look down at the weed-clogged back yard. The desiccated remnants of the grape arbors form a wall between this ancient and decaying Armenian world and new condominiums. The dead grapevines, brown and still clinging to the warped wood, resemble a ghoulish topiary maze.

Grandpa Garabed would sit out in the arbor with me when I was a kid. Back then, the arbor grew big, vibrant leaves and round grapes. Roupen and I once played there, darting through the arbor, hiding in the cool shade of the grape leaves.

"Don't trust nobody. The odars, they are not Armenians. They are not like us," Grandpa Garabed told me once. Why I remember this memory now is beyond me, I suppose that if life is going to be a disaster for me, why not go all in?

"What are odars?" I had asked.

"They are not Armenian. They are the strangers."

It was the first (but not the last) time that I heard the Armenian word "odar."

"My friend Tommy is not Armenian. I think he's Irish or something," I had said to him. "He's always nice to me."

Grandpa Garabed loomed over me that day and blotted out the sun like a massive hairy giant.

"You must not be friends with him! Ever again!" His words stung and numbed my small heart. "There are plenty of Armenian children for you to play with."

I protested, but Grandpa Garabed had grabbed my shoulders and squeezed them in his gnarled, arthritic hands. "Armand! You will obey your elder. You have no need for odars. You must have Armenian friends. Nobody gives a shit about us Armenians. We must stick together."

I saw pain in my grandfather's eyes that day, but it had taken me years to figure out what the pain was from. The deep wrinkles etched in his face held sadness and tragedy. He had passed his anguish and resentment to his son and then to us—each generation poisoned by mistrust and old hatreds.

I never saw my friend Tommy again after that. Like all good Armenian boys, I repressed everything, tamped it down inside, and pushed it to the back of the closet just like Dad did with Roupen's stuff.

I leave the house and walk to the minivan. Dad gets up from his rocking chair and ambles towards me.

"Did you find what you were looking for?" he asks.

"Yeah, I got it."

The old man gets a far-off look in his eyes.

"You should spend more time here with your family," Dad says.

"I spend more time with the family than you do."

Dad's muscles stiffen, his mouth forming a menacing rictus. "Yet you don't give a damn about them."

"This isn't about me not caring about them, I clearly do." I say. "This is about you not doing the same."

"He made his choice."

"Being gay is not a choice."

"Isn't it?"

"No, Dad. It isn't," I say.

"Amot," Dad groans. "He's doing it to spite me. Everything that boy does is to spite me."

"Dad, Roupen is your son. You've got to love him."

"Love?" Dad draws the word out slowly. "Don't talk to me about love. You didn't love me when you turned your back on me and moved in with Georgie."

"There wasn't a future here," I say looking past him at the house. "Mom died. This place was going under. There *still* isn't a future here."

Dad bares his teeth like a cornered animal. "And now you play with dead bodies all day like a sick person. You never wanted to be in the funeral business. You always talked about traveling, not about funerals."

"I made my choice," I tell him.

"Do whatever you want. Living in that fancy old house with those people. Work in a freezing room. Embalm those stiffs. Keep lying to yourself, all right?"

"I know what this is about. You're jealous of Uncle George."

For a moment, Dad looks down at his shoes. He clenches his fists and releases the rage he's bottled up for decades.

"You're damn right I'm jealous!" he erupts. "He lives in a big house with his family and has a thriving business. I'm here, alone, the father of a queer and of a coward. Two useless boys who don't want anything to do with me."

Not wanting to engage Dad's tantrum, I get in the minivan. My father is still ranting as I turn the key and the engine roars. I see him hobbling down the porch steps towards the car, but I don't wait for him to get near. My foot mashes the accelerator.

In the rearview mirror, the farmhouse and my angry father grow smaller and smaller.

CHAPTER 7

REST IN PEACE

Samantha assists me in preparing Maddie Hinkle's body.

I use a photograph Maddie's family provided as a reference for applying the makeup. The photograph shows Maddie in a pink prom dress, smiling like some fresh-faced innocent. The fact that her parents didn't have any recent photographs of their daughter tells me a lot. Were they estranged? Did Maddie leave the nest early and strike out on her own?

Jesus, I'm starting to sound like Alvarez.

My attention shifts to the makeup kit and the cadaver before me. I dust Maddie's cheeks with rouge, brush her eyelids with eyeshadow, and apply peach lipstick to her lips. Samantha styles Maddie's hair after washing and brushing it, and uses a curling iron to make the dead girl's tresses wavy.

Samantha removes the dress that Maddie will be buried in from its plastic cover, a pretty and tasteful black number accompanied by leather high-heeled shoes. Using scissors, Samantha cuts along the back of the dress. We slip Maddie's arms through the sleeves and place the garment over her body, pulling the fabric so that it fits properly.

"She looks amazing for a dead chick." Samantha slips stockings onto the cadaver and then the shoes. "It's weird though."

"What's weird?"

"She doesn't really look like a drug addict, know what I mean? She just doesn't look like the type," Samantha says.

I attach Maddie to a harness and we hoist her into a casket, which Samantha wheels to the elevator. The casket heads to the funeral chapel, where we position it where her loved ones will pay their respects.

"Has that private eye been around yet?" I ask.

"Yeah. I saw him earlier. He wanted to know if I noticed anything strange about the body," Samantha tells me. "I don't like that dude. He's intrusive as fuck."

"What did you tell him?"

"Nothing. What's there to say?"

You'd be surprised, I think.

I go upstairs, take a shower, and don my suit and tie. I fasten my nametag to my lapel and then head back downstairs.

Uncle George, Dikran, and Samantha are waiting for me. We all wear black, channel solemn respect, and say as little as possible.

Flower assortments are heaped by the casket; great billowing wreaths and bouquets with cloth sashes declaring "In Sympathy" and "We Miss You." Soothing music plays through concealed speakers, plenty of violins and piano that get you crying. Boxes of tissues and comfortably cushioned chairs are placed strategically around the room.

This staging is always the same, more or less. Offer them a place conducive to grieving and spending time with the departed.

Yet something at Maddie's viewing feels a little off, and it has everything to do with a package currently taking up residence inside her.

I fill a paper cup from the water cooler and sip nervously.

"You look like shit," Uncle George whispers. "What the hell happened to you?"

47

"Long day," I tell him.

"Well, get it together. We're working here," he hisses.

Maddie Hinkle's parents enter the funeral home. Mr. Hinkle has a bald spot, a suit rumpled from sitting in a car for a while, and a noticeable paunch. Mrs. Hinkle sports a gold crucifix and a black dress. Her eyes are probably red and puffy behind the pair of sunglasses she wears. Uncle George approaches them. He offers his condolences and guides them to the viewing chapel, where they silently pause in front of the casket.

They stay there for a minute, holding hands, their sobbing muffled, two people who lost their daughter.

More attendees file in. Members of the Hinkle family from as far away as San Bernardino County arrive. They are sad-faced, moist-eyed mourners in black sport coats and sundresses. Breezy blondes with tattoos and long fingernails, men with pierced faces and bulging muscles, and mourners who look like they'd be at home at a race track instead of a funeral home, all take turns in front of the casket to say their goodbyes.

Berj arrives in jeans, a white shirt, and red necktie. He approaches the casket and shakes hands with Maddie's parents. I assume he's offering them his condolences because his tone is soft. He looks towards Maddie and tilts his head for a moment before turning away and mingling with some of the people there. Finally, he walks over to me.

"She looks good," Berj tells me. "I would like to thank you for making sure that everything is in place." The subtext is as obvious as his gold teeth. Berj clasps my hand and gives it a firm shake before making his way towards the door.

A man in a purple jacket sobs and wipes his eyes with tissue as he chats with Maddie's parents. Every once in a while, he looks ruefully at the casket. After saying something to Maddie, he sits on one of the folding chairs and puts on a pair of sunglasses, hiding his grief as best he can.

"Wow," I say to myself. "Poor guy."

"Yeah," Alvarez agrees.

"Jesus," I jump a bit after being caught off guard. I know that Alvarez has been kicking around, but I wasn't expecting him to be lurking behind me. His eyes sweep the room as if he's searching for something out of place or someone who shouldn't be here.

"A little jumpy there, Mr. Tarkanian?" His voice is gravelly, like he's been chain smoking since he was five. He's got deep bags under his eyes.

Alvarez looks how I feel.

"Who's the guy in the purple jacket?" I ask.

"Stuart Newkin," Alvarez volunteers. "Maddie's boss. They all say he's a gentleman, but the seedy side of the business tells me that he's not what he seems. They never are …" He reaches into his coat pocket and pulls out a toothpick.

As I continue watching Stuart's misery, a stunning woman enters the room. Her aura is magnetic and her presence ethereal—she has tawny brown skin, black shoulder-length hair, and a velour dress that might be a size too small. She admires Maddie's photographs and then stands next to the casket for a few minutes.

In that moment, I understand what Roupen had explained to me about meeting Brent.

I wait for her to step away from other people and then I take a leap of faith. "She really was beautiful," I say to her.

"Yes, she was," the woman replies.

"I'm terribly sorry for your loss." I'm shaking as I stare into her eyes.

"Thank you. How do you know Maddie?" she asks.

"I work here. I prepared her for…" I'm the stupidest man on the planet. I'm trying to flirt with a woman at a funeral. "Embalmer. I worked on her. I'm Armand. Armand Tarkanian."

"Yvonne. Yvonne Hudgins. Vonnie." She says as we shake hands. "Maddie and I worked together."

"You worked with Maddie? What did she do?" I ask.

"We're both dancers." I see her face twist a bit. "Well, you know."

49

"Dancers?"

"Strippers."

"Ah. I see."

"It's always that reaction. A pause, an internal battle with your moral superiority. A looking down upon those lowly ladies who flash for cash," Vonnie says.

I caught myself. "Hey, no judgment here. Whatever pays the bills, right?"

"Exactly. It's a job, like anyone else."

"Did you know each other for a long time?"

"About six months, I guess? I kind of took her under my wing and showed her the ropes. The younger girls always look for mentors. She showed a lot of promise."

I gesture towards Stuart. "He seems to be taking it hard."

"Stewart. Poor guy. He's a mess." Vonnie shakes her head.

"Were they close?"

"Stewart is close to all of us. He's a good man. Never lays a finger on us. But Stuart is a good man in a shitty business." She looks a Stuart and sighs.

"Well, if there is anything that I can … we can … that the funeral home." And there goes any semblance of me not being an idiot. "Just call. I mean, let me know. Let. Us." I clear my throat and take a step back.

Vonnie's eyes narrow a bit, and she gives me a bit of a half-smile. "All right, Armand. Thanks."

I guess that she has years of experience gracefully shooting down advances. While I'm contemplating my life as a tongue-tied celibate, Uncle George squeezes my shoulder.

"What was that?" he asks.

"What was what?" I feign innocence.

"You and that Black lady."

"I'm consoling one of the mourners," I reply.

"This isn't a singles bar. You're not here to pick up women. Approach the mourners if they approach you. You are here to nod, provide tissues, and tell people where the restrooms are. This is *their* time. They're grieving. Leave them alone."

"At least I'm trying. Dikran and Samantha aren't doing anything."

"Exactly. They're doing what they're *supposed* to." Uncle George turns and walks off in a huff. I watch him go and then realize that my mouth is incredibly dry. Anxiety again. Fantastic.

We transport Maddie Hinkle's body to Everafter Memorial Gardens Cemetery in a black hearse and, beneath swaying sycamore and cypress trees, we lay her to rest.

During the service, Alvarez is a fly on the wall, observing everything at a great distance. He must've smoked a pack and a half of cigarettes over the course of the service.

On my way out of the cemetery, I cross paths with Alvarez. Sure enough, he's assembled quite the little pile of butts. I flash him a disapproving glance and he seems a little bit less tough-as-nails-sleuth and more of a normal and embarrassed adult. He clears his throat a bit.

"I'll be sure to clean them up," he says. I nod and keep walking but come to a halt a moment later.

"Mr. Alvarez?"

"Hmm?" He doesn't sound like he's paying attention.

"You saw where they found her body, right?"

"Maybe, who's to say?" He says with a shrug as he pops a Lucky from the pack and fishes in his pocket for a lighter. He clicks it a few times and gets a flame going.

"Did you find any frogs where she died?"

He freezes for a moment.

"Why would you ask me that?"

"Did you find any frogs?"

"Yes. Quite a few. The police think that they were from a nearby pond or stream."

"But there wasn't a pond or a stream for miles, was there?"

"How do you know about the frogs?" Alvarez gets uncomfortably close. I can smell his aftershave through the burnt smell of a hundred cigarettes.

"I think I saw how Maddie Hinkle died," I say.

The detective's mouth falls open and he stares at me.

"You saw her die? How, exactly?" he asks.

"A vision. I saw her in a vision."

Alvarez relaxes and his shoulders go slack. He rolls them like he's trying to get rid of stress. "I get it, Mr. Tarkanian. You work with the deceased, so you're morbid. This isn't the time or the place."

"I'm not joking," I tell him.

Alvarez shakes his head and makes a noise of disgust as he takes a step back and then walks away.

He didn't clean up his butts.

I look back over my shoulder at the service. Maddie Hinkle will be at rest, taking Berj's care package with her.

When we all get home, Aunt Miriam feeds us roasted chicken kebabs and rice pilaf. Uncle George gripes about my behavior at the viewing while Dikran talks about Maddie Hinkle's attractive cousins.

Uncle George turns to me. "I saw that private investigator talking to you? What did he say?"

I scoop more rice into my plate. "I don't know, wanted to know about Maddie's fingernails or something."

Uncle George makes a grunting noise.

Samantha pipes up. "The guy is a total creeper."

Uncle George grunts again and goes back to his food. He seems satisfied, and with the patriarch happy, everybody resumes eating in silence like we always do.

After dinner I wash the dishes, and thank Aunt Miriam for the meal.

"Oh, a letter came for you today," Aunt Miriam says as I'm going up the stairs. "I put it on your bed."

"Thanks, Aunt Miriam."

"Armand?"

"Hmm?" I hear her turn off the tap. She comes out of the kitchen and stands at the bottom of the stairs.

"Do you know the story of Ara the Beautiful?" She looks up at me and folds her hands.

"Is this one of your folktales?" When Aunt Miriam wants to drive home a point, she reaches into her treasure trove of ancient Armenian lore.

"Queen Shamiram of Assyria became captivated with Ara the Beautiful, the king of Armenia. Shamiram wanted to take Ara as her lover, but he starkly refused. Some people can't handle rejection, and so Shamiram sent her army to capture Ara. Armenian forces clashed with the Assyrians and then suffered a humiliating defeat."

"Armenians get defeated even in their folktales? Defeat really is our brand."

Aunt Miriam ignores me. "Unfortunately, Ara was killed in the fight. His body was brought to Shamiram, who hides it in her palace. She prayed so that the gods would resurrect him. The gods sent an Aralez, who licked his wounds and gave him life. Aralez can do this, they have the power to heal fallen soldiers."

"Quite a story."

"It is about hope. If you pray hard enough, your prayers will be answered," she says.

I descend the stairs and kiss her on the cheek. "Thanks Aunt Miriam, but it always feels like my prayers are wasted. Nobody's listening."

She smiles sadly. "Maybe you are just not listening to the answer."

Exhausted, I go to my room, undress, and don my pajamas. I noticed the envelope on the bed and open it. Inside is a thousand dollars and a note. It is brief:

A welcome bonus for a job well done.

Berj, I'm sure.

I count the money for several minutes, holding each bill to the light for any evidence of forgery. The Benjamins are legitimate so I tuck the money into my nightstand where the other two thousand still hides and retrieve *Madame Opal's Guidebook to Seances and Psychics* next to my lamp. I open the book and a curious folded piece of paper slips out from behind the cover and flutters to the floor. I pick it up, turn the paper over in my hands, and unfold it. My hands tremble as I read:

My hokis,

I'm writing this because one day I might not be there for you. If you're reading this now, I'm so sorry Armand that I couldn't stay—if there was anyone that I would have moved heaven and earth to stay for, it would have been you and your brother. I love you both so much. But the doctors found cancer, and I've been sick for a long time and just couldn't tell you until now. You're a smart boy, so you probably already noticed I haven't been myself these last few months. But I don't want you to be afraid. You and your brother are both very strong in your own ways. Look after Roupen. He is headstrong and fearless, and that will get him into trouble. He follows his heart and you follow your mind. He admires you so much hokis, he will listen to you (I hope!).

I know that your father and grandpa have been rough on you, but I think that you've been made strong by this, maybe stronger than you realize. I know you've been sad lately. I understand you're nervous a lot of the time and that you worry so much about all the things

54

that might be or could happen. You're a sensitive boy, more than you admit, but try not to worry so much! You are not alone.

I will always love you, my Armand. My handsome boy.

Tsavt tanem.

That means "let me take your pain away." We should take away pain from the ones we love. Practice that throughout your life.

Goodbye, hokis. Live well.

Mom

P.S. – Please practice Armenian, I know that you don't speak it well, but you should!

I learned years ago that the word "hokis" was Armenian for "my soul." It's the sweetest and most endearing thing a parent can call their child.

I must have been 19 and was working on the farm with Dad that summer when I read the letter for the first time. I went into the house to cool off. Aunt Miriam had already been by to drive Mom to the hospital. I found the note on my bed. I remember reading it a few times before any of the words made sense—it was like a veil had been pulled down over my eyes, smothering my vision and obscuring everything.

I must have hidden the note in *Madame Opal's Guidebook to Seances and Psychics*.

Finding Mom's letter releases long-dormant memories in a messy storm. A queasiness coils itself in my gut. What, I wonder, would my mother think about my unusual side venture? She'd be disappointed, surely. Nothing screws you up like disappointing your mother, at least in my family.

But the thrill of having three grand supersedes parental guilt. For the first time, I feel powerful and in charge.

This time, I answer my own prayers.

I close the nightstand drawer and then my eyes. Madame Opal can wait.

CHAPTER 8

FRESH MEAT

Donut King is once again devoid of late night customers. I stare into my coffee cup. The half-eaten Bavarian cream donut, which I could finally afford, tastes like sugary guilt. Gor gazes deeply into the display case, going over the rows of donuts, trying to figure out which one he wants. If Donut King sold 'human baby' flavored donuts, that ogre would probably buy a dozen.

"My congratulations again," Berj says to me. "Your debt to us is paid. And you did such a good job that I gave you a bonus! You got it, yes?"

"Yeah, I did," I reply flatly. "Thanks, Berj. What happens now?"

"Now you have an opportunity to make some real money for yourself, my friend!" Berj removes another package and tiny cloth bag from his jacket, almost identical to the last one. "Any fresh meat?"

"We got another decedent in this morning," I tell him, feeling gross at how dismissive he is of the dead. "An older man, but he hit his head and died."

Berj stares at me. "This is not a problem, yes?"

"Well, no autopsy means getting your little care package inside him will involve cutting him open and pulling out organs," I explain.

Berj shrugs.

"I'm not a butcher. It'll be a messy job. There'll be a lot of blood," I say.

Berj thinks for a moment and scratches his large chin.

"I have every faith you'll perform this task like a professional," he says. "And so you will be compensated well."

"If I get caught, I'm looking at criminal charges for abuse of a corpse."

"We will give you four thousand then."

"It's not about the money," I tell him.

"Oh? Well, then, if it's not about the money, then I'll keep it!"

"That's not what I meant."

He pushes the package towards me.

If I had any decency, I would've shoved the package back to Berj and told him and his pet monster to fuck off to wherever they came from. But I don't have much decency. I need to buy some wheels and escape my family. Get a car, hit the road, and don't look back. That takes money. I lean forward, fold my hands, and tell Berj I'm in.

Berj leans close. "Armand, you're a very reliable man, I like that. Armenians should help out Armenians. I think you're doing the right thing. I can't get some odar to do this task. Best that someone smart and competent do it, you know what I mean?"

Odar. The word sends a real and cold chill down my spine. It roughly translates to non-Armenian or outsider, and it's one way we Armenians distinguish ourselves from everybody else on the planet. I've always bristled at the word and its negative connotations.

Berj smiles, those gold choppers on full display as he reaches into his pocket and pulls out an envelope. He slides it across to me, and I take it.

"Thanks, Armand. You're doing a god's work." He gets up and walks towards the door, tapping Gor on the shoulder. The mountain seems disappointed that he didn't get a donut, but follows behind his boss.

After they leave, I head into the restroom and wash my hands. I feel like there's blood on them. The money is nice, though. I'm up to seven thousand dollars, minus a Bavarian cream and a small coffee.

Now all I had to do was cut open some rich old guy.

In life, Franklin Waterhouse was a giant, a business tycoon of notable wealth with a well-to-do family. Now he's just a giant cadaver.

Waterhouse looks every bit his sixty-seven years. His jowls fall backwards towards the table, hanging in full glory from his round cheeks. Wispy grey hair adorns his chest and ample stomach. Cutting through all this will be challenging.

I use a scalpel and make an incision in Waterhouse's diaphragm, beneath the ribcage. I want to avoid dealing with those pesky ribs, so I cut south of them, right where Waterhouse's belly rises like foothills on a great, flabby mountain range.

A grotesque odor hits me when I breach his stomach. Waterhouse's innards reek. I gag and nearly vomit inside my face-mask. And then there's a chill. An all-permeating cold hangs over the room. It's happening again.

There's a voice behind me. *"What are you doing?"*

I turn. Mr. Waterhouse's perturbed spirit stares at his earthly remains.

He's like Maddie Hinkle, a ghost in a white gown, floating above the floor. Waterhouse's spectral eyes are filled with a mix of revulsion and curiosity.

My stomach lurches—part from the smell, part from the spirit from beyond the veil of life deciding to haunt me.

"*I asked you a question, young man,*" the spirit says. "*What are you doing to my body?*"

"You don't exist," I say to the ghost as I take a couple of deep breaths. "You're not here."

"*I am Franklin Pierce Waterhouse and I definitely am here.*"

"Oh my God," I say, my eyes widening.

The spirit shrugs. "*What?*"

"You used all three names? Rich people are just the worst." I sigh and stand up straight, my nausea under control. "You aren't here, you're there. See? Dead." I point to the cadaver.

Waterhouse's spirit scrutinizes my handiwork.

"*Wait, what are you doing to me? Please don't do that.*"

"You're dead. Shut up." I reach into the cavity with gloved hands and remove his liver and slip it into a bag. I start fishing through the body to get to his lungs.

The spirit starts wailing, going full-on banshee.

I turn around and look at the spirit. "Really? That's what you're going with?" He stares slack-jawed as I slice out his heart and wrap the organ with the liver. I place them all in a duffel bag. There's just enough space for me to fit the package inside his rather large body.

"*Young man,*" Waterhouse leans in close, "*I don't know what you're doing, but I assure you my family didn't request that ...*" I start stitching him closed, trying to make the incision as invisible as humanly possible. "*I'll make you a deal.*"

What kind of deal could a spirit make?

"*I won't haunt you forever, but in exchange...*" The ghost reaches his translucent hand towards my shoulder and a bone-shaking cold rips through me. Franklin Waterhouse shows me his murder.

"What is it this time, Monty?" Waterhouse grouses at the gangly twenty-something in front of him. Waterhouse sits in his favorite chair on a patio overlooking a massive swimming pool and well-manicured yard.

59

"The guys are going up to Aspen this winter. They're renting a chalet and going skiing; I need a few grand for the trip," the young man says.

"A few grand? You blew through the money I gave you for Vegas?" Waterhouse asks.

"Luck wasn't with me at the keno tables."

"Keno? What the hell were you doing playing keno?"

"Gambling. People do it."

Waterhouse grinds his teeth. He's livid. "Damn it, Monty! How many times have I told you not to carelessly blow your money? Just because I have it, doesn't mean you get to spend it all."

"I'm not spending carelessly," Monty says. "I'm just having some fun. I need to blow off steam. Life is stressful, you know?"

"Stressful? What do you know about stress? When I was your age, I was working at my family's company. Long hours. Hard work."

"Yeah. Right. Hard work. You were the boss's son."

"And I had to work twice as hard for half the respect because of it. You wouldn't know an honest day's work if it came up and kicked your scrawny ass. Your generation is too soft and fragile for any real work," Waterhouse grumbles.

"I don't want to work in broadcasting, okay?" Monty says. "I need money for Aspen."

"Haven't you listened to a goddamn word I've said?" Waterhouse snarls.

Monty's face tightens. He reaches into his pocket and pulls out Waterhouse's checkbook. "Five grand is a good start. Call it a Christmas present."

"It's August, you jackass. And how did you find my checkbook?"

"It's not hard, is it, Dad?" There's an edge developing in Monty's voice.

"Stepdad. I married your mother. You're the trash that came with the deal."

"Don't quibble. One check and you won't see me until college starts."

Waterhouse snatches the checkbook from Monty's hand and gets out of his chair, walking over to a nearby table. "College. What a joke. Pulled strings and got you into Stanford. All you do is drink and waste time with your tennis buddies."

"Make it ten grand then, old man. Okay?"

"I ought to have my head examined." Waterhouse writes the check and hands it to Monty. "Take the damn thing, you little shit."

"Thanks," Monty's voice deepens. "About that head of yours." Monty swings at Waterhouse, stunning the large man who stares, dumbfounded, at his stepson.

Monty sharply knees his stepdad in the groin. Waterhouse groans as he doubles over in pain. Without hesitating, Monty slams his stepdad's head onto the stone table twice. I feel the impacts—there's a cracking feeling the second time that comes with a sharp, brutal pain. Waterhouse falls to the patio, face contorted, eyes rolled back.

Monty puts his sunglasses on and stands over Waterhouse's body as the old man's life fades.

My senses reel as I catapult through blackness, back to the embalming room.

Waterhouse's spirit nods. *"You know what to do,"* he says, then vanishes.

"Well, not really. What *am* I supposed to do? Should I call the cops?" I shake my head a bit and look down at Waterhouse's corpse.

My job takes precedence over a ghost's wishes, so I get to work.

I shampoo Waterhouse's thinning hair, stuff cotton in his mouth until his cheeks look full, and finish setting the features and makeup to Waterhouse's face, giving his pallid cheeks a colorful tint. Without Samantha around, dressing Waterhouse is a bit challenging, but I manage in the end; penance, of a sort. I place Waterhouse back in cold storage.

After removing my mask, gloves, and gown, I pick up my duffel bag and go outside.

Carefully, and without drawing attention to myself, I take the minivan and bury the duffel bag's contents near a raisin farm just outside of town.

The soil there is rich, and the air is sickly sweet.

CHAPTER 9

ABRACADABRA, A MISSING CADAVER

Alvarez looks like he hasn't slept in days.

He's standing in the front parlor talking to Uncle George.

"Armand, can I have a minute?" Uncle George asks. He's never this polite unless there are other people around. "You know Mr. Alvarez."

"Good to see you again." I take Alvarez's extended hand and shake it.

"I was just telling your uncle here that someone exhumed Maddie Hinkle's body last night."

"Wait, what?"

"Her body was removed from her grave and is missing," Alvarez clarified.

"Someone just took her and left? Who would do such a thing?" The surprise and shock in my voice are definitely real. 'Stolen corpse' was not on my Wednesday bingo card.

"We analyzed the security camera footage from the cemetery. The tapes were all static, as if someone erased them. Did either of you see or hear anything unusual at the funeral? Maybe see any suspicious characters?" Alvarez asks.

"No. Not at all. Just a pile of cigarette butts," I reply. Alvarez shoots me a look, but it feels more like one of embarrassment than warning.

"I'm appalled, detective," Uncle George chimes in, before his inevitable sales pitch. "This is not reflective of the quality and procedures at Tarkanian Funeral Home. We take our work very seriously here."

"Mr. Tarkanian, you're a busy man, with things to do." The detective fishes in his pockets for his smokes. "Maybe, if it wouldn't be too much trouble, could I borrow your nephew here so that he can explain a few things about sending off the bodies to the great beyond?"

There's something almost hammy about how he talks. At times Alvarez sounds like he would have been right at home selling something on a radio in the 1940s. He lives that whole 'private dick' lifestyle; hardboiled, edgy, and unapologetic. A poor man's Bogart, toothpick in his mouth, five o'clock shadow gracing his chin. He's on the case.

Alvarez gestures at me with the unlit cigarette. "Would you mind accompanying me to the cemetery?" Alvarez asks, looking for opposition from my uncle. "There's a CSI team there now."

"I'm just the embalmer. I don't know how helpful I'd be," I tell him.

"Armand, Mr. Alvarez is here to help clear up this mess. Go with him." I realize that Uncle George is genuinely worried that this whole thing could hurt the business.

"Yes, sir."

Alvarez squints at me. "Good man." He leads me down the steps of the building. No sooner than hitting the sidewalk, Alvarez lights a cigarette.

"You left a mess. Could you not flick your discarded butts everywhere after you smoke?" I wonder if I can keep him on the defensive and out of my less savory pastimes. With Maddie's body apparently missing though, there's nothing to even find under the ground that would lead back to me.

"Yeah, it's a filthy habit," he says as he takes a deep pull on the cigarette. We walk in silence for a few minutes. I guess we're not taking a car. "You know what I think is weird?"

"What's that, detective?"

"That thing you said about the frogs. How'd you know that?"

"I told you," I say.

"You did indeed. You a psychic?" I find a bit of mockery in his voice, but he probably can't help himself. He doesn't strike me as the kind of guy that believes in that sort of thing.

"No. I don't know what I experienced, only that it's never happened before. When I was embalming her, Maddie Hinkle's spirit appeared and showed me how she died." He doesn't say anything, he just lets me talk. "I … she was in the woods, I'm not sure where. There were some people chasing her." I try my best to remember anything else about the events.

"Part of me thinks that you got some kind of dumb luck and you guessed it, like how hard could it be to guess that there were frogs in a forest, right?" The question's subtext is clear: Armand Tarkanian, fraud or not?

I rub my eyes, trying hard to remember. Unlike Waterhouse's vision, which was sticking around a bit more, that first time was still hazy.

"She was barefoot." I say. "She was wearing go-go boots, she took them off because she fell. She was barefoot!"

Alvarez looks at me and seems to give me the tiniest benefit of the doubt.

"The frogs. They fit into this how?"

"It's how she died. Several men chanted something at her; they just did that and then the frogs came out of her mouth."

"Chanted?"

"Some kind of spell, I guess?"

"One problem with that theory. The police found no other footprints at the scene," Alvarez says. "Only Miss Hinkle's body and a plague of frogs."

No footprints? How could that be? Did these spooky bastards magically cover their tracks somehow?

"She was found miles from the Neon Oasis, a divey strip club where she worked. Can you explain that, Amazing Kreskin?" Alvarez asks.

"Her ghost didn't show me how she got there," I tell him.

Alvarez produces a notepad and flips through a few pages black with ink. "The police don't have much to go on here, this is the sort of thing that probably goes unsolved." He flips a few pages and hands me the notepad. I look at him and then take it.

Maddie Hinkle. Name in purse. Why so many frogs. Cigarette butt. Why did she take off her boots? His notes might as well have been a script for my vision, and they reminded me of the smoking man. Who was he?

"I'll need more to go on than your alleged supernatural chat with Miss Hinkle," Alvarez says. "The facts are the body is missing and exactly zero cops are going to buy that the embalmer is talking to the victim's ghost." He narrows his eyes. "I wouldn't be banking on me believing you either … a far more plausible explanation is that you were literally there and saw it happen." he says, giving me a different spin on my story.

"I wasn't."

"That I believe."

"What if I gave you a different story?" I see the graveyard up ahead.

"Of Maddie? I'm all ears."

"No, Franklin Waterhouse." I say.

"Fat rich guy?"

I wince a little bit. "A bit of respect for the dead, please?"

No small irony there.

65

"Fine. *Hefty* rich guy."

"He showed me how he died. He was murdered," I say.

That piques Alvarez's interest. He takes his pad back from me, and whips out a pen. "That one has no evidence of foul play as per the Fresno PD. Why do you say that?"

"He showed me. I saw his stepson, Monty, in a vision. He and Waterhouse were on the patio, near the pool, arguing about money."

Alvarez frowns. "Franklin Waterhouse died in his driveway. A slip and fall. Hit his head."

"No, he was murdered. His stepson smashed his head against a stone table and made it look like an accident. Right before he died, Waterhouse wrote a check to Monty. I'll bet he cashed the check."

"How do you know this?"

"Waterhouse showed me." I catch myself. "I mean, his ghost showed me. Look detective, I get how crazy this sounds, but they don't really drop off a locker full of evidence. Why don't you just go check it out? Monty killed him and must've dragged the body to the driveway," I say.

Alvarez tucks the notepad back into his pocket. "Why would he do that?"

"Maybe because he's a spoiled little shit. Maybe he thinks he gets an inheritance? I don't know, I'm only telling you what the ghost showed me."

"Is it possible you thought you saw something? A hallucination? A mirage?"

"Mirages occur in the desert. I was in the embalming room," I reply. "Sure, it's possible it was a hallucination, but I'd bet a few thousand dollars that what I saw was real."

Does Alvarez think I'm bullshitting him? I'm not sure, and I don't think that I care. This is how the pieces of fate seemed to be playing out for me recently, and I'm completely powerless in their motions.

"Something weird is happening here," I say.

"Mr. Tarkanian, you don't know the half of it."

The modern casket is more than a mass-produced sarcophagus with hinged lids and an attractive appearance so your loved one can look comfortable. These boxes come in a wide variety of external materials including lacquered woods like pine, poplar, and mahogany. Those with a bigger budget can bury their loved ones in metal ones — stainless steel, gauge steel, or copper.

I've studied the brochures Uncle George has in his office and pointed grieving families toward our casket showroom, so I know my caskets.

Maddie Hinkle's casket is durable wood, but you'd never guess that by looking into her grave.

The casket's lid is destroyed, as if it had exploded open. Dirt and soil are scattered around the grave, as are fragments of the burial vault, an outer shell containing the coffin.

Alvarez shines a flashlight into the hole, and illuminates the casket. There's no sign of Maddie Hinkle's body. A crime scene investigation unit is processing the scene, photographing the grave, tagging debris, and searching for possible evidence—one of them looks over at Alvarez and glowers.

"Yeah, allowed to be here, Jack," Alvarez says to the guy. The other guy rolls his eyes and keeps working. I guess there might be some tension between detectives like Alvarez and police forces, but that's beyond my knowledge, and I don't think that Alvarez is going to share.

"Like I said before, there were no footprints leading to the grave. We did find these, however." A set of uneven streaks in the mud leads away from the burial site.

"Looks like somebody got dragged?"

"That's what I thought. It gets more unusual, though." He kneels beside the lines. "No footprints."

"No footprints for Maddie either in the woods, right?" Alvarez nods and gives me a small shrug. A piece of shattered concrete sits next to his foot. I point at it and Alvarez looks down.

"That's part of the burial vault," I tell him. "It's a concrete box with a stainless-steel interior that a casket rests in. They're used to prevent the ground from settling."

"Whoever wanted the body must've been really dedicated because the top of this box is shattered, along with the casket lid." Alvarez pulls himself to his feet. He looks over the CSI guy. "Hey Jack, any idea why someone wanted Miss Hinkle's corpse?"

"We're interviewing the groundskeeper and the cemetery's management now. Got any theories, hotshot?" Alvarez shakes his head. "With all that leeway that the chief gives you, you'd think you'd be more useful." Jack produces a short snorting laugh.

"Tell you what, Jack, I got a little something that'll make sure you get your birthday bonus." Alvarez gives me a brief look. "I'll tell you about it later."

He's talking about Waterhouse, I'm sure of it.

"Is there anything else, Mr. Alvarez?" I ask, barely holding it together. The detective looks at me and then shakes his head.

"Thanks for your time Mr. Tarkanian."

"Not a problem, detective."

CHAPTER 10

THE WORMS CRAWL IN

After two minutes inside the Neon Oasis, I already feel like I need a shower, and not the sexy kind. Night brings the perverts out. Men wearing windbreakers and tight shirts. Deviants dripping with gold chains and drenched in aftershave. Weirdos in sunglasses ogling every woman.

I find myself in a wasteland of leering, drooling, and hooting. An underground kingdom of nocturnal fetishists and women grinding against metal poles envelops me. Dollar bills are the currency of choice, slipped between spray tanned asses and Lycra G-strings.

But I'm not here for the dancers. Not the living ones, anyway.

I'm here for answers about Maddie Hinkle. If I can find out more about her life, maybe I'll know more about the horrible vision she showed me.

My heart races as I pay my cover charge and head for the bar.

Stuart is there, nursing a cocktail. He runs his hands over his wrinkled velvet jacket and Hawaiian shirt, a look that both suits him and screams "downtrodden lounge singer." I slide up and sit next to him.

The bartender, a tall blonde with icy blue eyes and pocked skin caked in foundation leans in close. She doesn't say anything. "Whiskey and Coke," I order. She pours the drink, takes a bottle of Coca-Cola from the fridge, then fills the cup the rest of the way.

"Twelve," she says.

I slide a twenty across the bar to her. Feeling kind of cool and flush with green, I wave my hand at the change. She smiles and gives me a wink.

I sniff the plastic cup and take a sip. The drink is strong. I cough a bit, hitting myself in the chest with the palm of my hand before clearing my throat. I sip the drink again and give the bartender a thumbs up. She smiles again and goes to serve other customers.

I realize that Stuart is looking at me.

"This is my first time in a strip club," I say.

"Congratulations," Stuart replies. He looks like he's trying to pin down why he recognizes me. Finally, he hits the bar with an open hand.

"You were at Maddie's funeral," he says.

"That's right."

"You guys gave her one hell of a sendoff. Real classy." He looks down at his drink. Reliving the memory seems painful for him, he doesn't want to relive that moment of his life.

"It was the family," I say. "We really don't …"

"Don't be modest!" Stuart puts his hand on my shoulder and gives it a squeeze. He's strong, and while he's not physically imposing like a bouncer, it is clear that he could handle himself in a fight if it came to one.

"I'm Armand," I tell him.

"Stuart. Stuart Newkin."

We shake hands.

"I'm sorry about your loss, Stuart. While I didn't really know her, it is very clear to me that she was well-liked," I say.

"Of course she was. Hard not to like Maddie." Stuart downs what's left of his drink. "Vee!" The bartender leans against the back counter at the opposite end of the bar. She pushes herself off and comes over. "I'll have a Blue Label."

"Let me get it for you," I offer. Stuart smiles and shakes his head. I hold up my hand and take out my wallet. "I insist."

The bartender, Vee, leans across the bar. "Eighty-five." I blink, pull out a crisp hundred, and put it down in front of her. Vee's second wink is different from the first, it's slower and sultry. She pours Stuart a few fingers of Johnny Walker Blue Label. I make a mental note of what to drink when I'm as rich as Waterhouse.

"Pay is good at the funeral home?" Stuart asks. He almost certainly suspects that I have a side gig after flashing that kind of cash for a drink. "Thanks … Armand." I guess an eighty-five-dollar drink is the thing that gets your name remembered. "What was I saying?"

"Maddie." I remind him.

"Shit, yeah. Good kid." He raises his glass to me and I do the same. "These girls, all come here broken or broke, damaged or escaping something. Some got addictions and personal problems. I'm not big on judgment here. Except Maddie. She was different."

"How?"

"I don't know," Stuart recalls. "She made you feel special. Like you're the only one in the room, you know? Maddie was a sweet kid. She was like an angel in this place, and she wasn't like a lot of the other girls. No thugs chasing her, no debts to pay off, no weird addictions keeping her strung out. She just showed up one day and wanted to dance, Vonnie took a shining to her too."

Vonnie's name makes me sort of freeze for a moment. I wasn't quite expecting him to bring her up.

"Wait, I'm sorry to pry, but you just said *no* drug issues?" I ask.

"No way. She was no addict. Maddie *hated* drugs." Stuart's giving me a weird look.

"Sorry, the coroners said that she OD'd—that's all."

71

"Maddie always declined when a client offered her anything, and it's a regular pharmacy in here some nights," Stuart tells me.

"Is that right?"

"Mhm. Like I said, regular angel that one."

I raise my glass. "To angels among us and the spaces they leave when they depart." I toast. Stuart smiles and clinks my glass with his.

"Good words."

"You don't work in a funeral home for years without hearing an assortment of good words," I say. "So, you own this place? It's nice."

"Me? Nope. I manage it. I don't actually know who owns it."

"Really?"

"A paycheck is a paycheck, man. It could be coming from the devil himself, but it shows up in my account on time, and that's all I care about."

"Is it hard to make this place work if you can't contact your boss?" I ask.

"Piece of cake. Money comes in, money goes out. I just make sure everything runs properly and that the deposits get made."

Ghosts. Mystery packages. Missing corpses. Strip club with a non-existent owner. This whole mess is a smorgasbord of strange.

"You have way more trust than I ever get at my place of employment," I say.

A techno version of the *Bonanza* theme song starts to play over the speakers. Stuart shrugs a little and looks over his shoulder at the stage. I look down at my drink and take a sip.

Vonnie, the woman I met at Maddie Hinkle's viewing, struts across the stage in a pink buckskin cowboy outfit—its fringes sway as she moves. A pink Stetson sits on her head, and white leather cowboy boots adorn her feet. Vonnie's bare midriff reveals a diamond belly ring that catches the strobe light.

She straddles the pole, arches her spine with gravity-defying, acrobatic perfection, and flashes the front row a broad, toothy smile. I'm captivated. Vonnie slides to the floor and crawls her way to the edge of the stage. Twerking on her knees, she seductively unfastens her top and bares her chest. Dollar bills fill the air like confetti.

"I … uh," I grunt.

I turn back towards Stuart who smirks at me.

"Mhm," Stuart says. "Thanks for the drink, Armand. You're a good guy." He offers his hand, which I shake, and he gets up. He walks towards the end of the bar and says something to Vee who looks at me and smiles. She nods. Stuart gives me a wink, and then disappears into an office near the bar.

I sit for a bit, stewing in my own brain, when someone's hot breath tickles my ear.

"Thanks for the drink," I turn and find myself staring at Vonnie.

She blinks, recognizing me. "You!" She has a sort of confused half smile.

I look at the drink she's holding. Some kind of amber liquid. "But …" I spot Vee. She gives me a bit of a smile and starts cleaning glasses.

Vonnie also turns and looks at Vee, who has an I-don't-know-what-you're-talking-about look on her face.

"You're welcome," I say. "That was quite the dance," I add, stumbling through the conversation like I'm drunk. She closes her eyes and snaps her fingers a few times.

"Armando?" She asks.

"Armand."

"Close enough. So, what brings you from your nice little funeral home on the right side of the tracks to a place that is *very* much on the wrong side of the tracks?" She sips her drink, wincing at its strength.

"I was hoping to ask you something," I tell her.

"Seems weird. Because we're in a strip club." She arches an eyebrow.

"It's about Maddie."

She pauses, takes another sip of her drink, and puts the glass down on bar.

"Two hundred bucks," she says.

"I'm sorry?"

"That's what my time is worth. Take it or leave it."

I reluctantly reach for my wallet.

"Not here." She yanks my arm. "Follow me, stud."

Vonnie walks over to Vee and tells her that she's taking a break. Vee nods. She says something that I don't hear. Vonnie laughs and shakes her head. She comes back, grabs my hand, guides me through a beaded curtain, down a hall, and out an exit. The door dumps us out into a dimly-lit alley that leads to a large parking lot.

"Where are we going?" I ask.

"My place. It's not exactly the Taj Mahal, but it'll do."

Her place is a 31-foot-long 1980 Airstream Excella II trailer and it sits near a single dangling lamp in the parking lot. Vonnie fumbles with her keys a bit as she tries to get them into the lock of the prefabricated silver door.

Inside, wood paneling and linoleum flooring reign supreme. There's a small kitchenette with a cabinet and refrigerator, a foldaway table, a credenza, lounge seats, and the strong smells of incense and cheap perfume. There's a small bathroom with a shower, toilet, and sink halfway down the hall. A bedroom lies just behind an accordion door. As curious as I am about the soft light and what might be in that room, I can't really see.

"Sit," she says. "Want something to drink?" Vonnie doesn't wait for an answer. She reaches into the refrigerator and pulls out two Coronas. She deftly manipulates a church key over each. The bottle caps pop off. Vonnie hands me a beer. I sink down into a lounge seat. She walks past towards a chair and offers to clink bottles as she goes. The two bottles come together and we swig the beer. It's cold and bubbly. I forgive her for the lack of lime.

She takes a drink and then lets the edge of the bottle sit right under her lower lip. She blows softly, filling the silence between us with the low note of a mostly filled Corona bottle.

"I need to know about Maddie Hinkle." I sink deeper into the chair.

"Come on. In all seriousness, I remember who you are. You're the guy from the funeral home. We talked, like, once. You figured out where I worked and now you're here for a little, you know, extracurricular fun." Vonnie cradles her beer and grins.

"I assure you, I'm not here for *that*."

Vonnie pouts. "Black women not your thing?"

"No, it's not that," I stammer like an awkward school boy. "You're totally beautiful. Totally. I think you … uh." I feel myself floundering badly with the right turn the conversation has taken. Vonnie doesn't look insulted or upset though—a little amused maybe.

"What do you want to know about Maddie?" Vonnie asks.

"Was she into recreational drugs?"

"Maddie? Hell no. She was clean."

"Yeah, that's what Stuart said. Were Maddie and Stuart dating?" I ask. My hands tremble a bit—Vonnie has a weird effect on me. My mouth goes dry and I can't concentrate. Roupen was right about meeting The One, I guess.

"Damn, you ask a lot of questions. You sure you're not a cop?"

"I'm a mortician," I reply.

"A mortician? That's what *every* girl wants to hear."

"Look, I just … I think I know how Maddie died."

The look on her face becomes inscrutable.

"This better not be some kind of fucked up game morticians play." Her voice is low.

"No!" I say. "No. So you and Stuart both say that Maddie was not into drugs, but when I went to pick up her body, the coroner said that she had overdosed."

She raises an eyebrow. "If you know that, why tell me? Why not go to the cops?"

"Truthfully? Let's say I want to avoid entanglements with the police." I look at my bottle and then take a drink, between the Corona and my drink at the bar, I am starting to feel warm. "Did Maddie get into any trouble when she was here? Maybe with a cop?"

"Trouble?" Vonnie swallows a mouthful of beer. "Maddie was sweet. She was from some nice neighborhood and came here to escape some domestic abuse or shit at home. She kept all that toxic shit that might have existed inside her. Never dwelled on it. Didn't let it get her down. Most guys liked her. There were a few creeps, though."

"Like who?"

"I don't know. Creeps. Men that are too handsy for their own good. They'd pull some shit and the bouncers would break it up. Ass-holes like that don't stick around too long. Maddie stayed with me. Poor thing needed a place to crash, better with me than some douchebag."

"Maddie lived here?"

"Uh huh. We slept in the same bed." Vonnie winks at me and I nearly choke on my beer. My mind fills with suggestive images of Vonnie and Maddie. Vonnie anticipates my reaction, reaches over, and lightly slaps my wrist.

"Mind out of the gutter. It was nothing like that. Strictly platon-ic. Maddie was like a roomie. I have some of her stuff. Wanna see?"

I nod.

She gets up, walks over to a closet, pulls out a plastic shopping bag, and plops it down onto my lap. The bag contains a pair of red high-heeled shoes, a few T-shirts, jean shorts, a set of keys to who-knows-what, and a romance novel.

"This is everything?" I ask.

"She was a 24-year-old stripper from Fresno. She must've stashed her Rembrandt elsewhere," Vonnie snarks. "Yes. It's all she had."

I try to imagine the stories behind each item, how Maddie came to acquire them, what value she placed on them, whether or not they made her happy.

"Her body went missing," I tell Vonnie. "Someone dug her up and took her from the cemetery."

Vonnie's eyes widen. "Jesus Christ. You shitting me?"

"Obviously, that's super hush hush," I say flipping quickly through the pages of her book.

Nothing.

"Places like this aren't run like charities," she says. "This club is a front for some kind of criminal activity, places like this are *always* fronts. There's always someone on the take. Always a dirty cop. Always something just beyond sight." She takes a swig of her beer. "There are a lot of sick motherfuckers out there. I've probably danced for a few of them—but I don't know anyone that's digging up bodies for kicks. That feels like the kind of shit that would get around."

"I think I want to figure this out for Maddie," I say, looking at all that was left of Maddie's things. When I look up, I find Vonnie staring at me.

"Mind if I ask you a question?" she asks.

"Knock yourself out."

"If you're trying to help a dead girl – and don't get me wrong, that's nice of you – why aren't you working on yourself? Why are you so unhappy?" I blink and she continues. "I'm good at reading people. You seemed like you were uncomfortable in your own skin at the viewing. Like you wanted to be a million miles from that funeral home."

"I do."

"That's it? You're not going to regale me with tales from the funeral parlor? How did an Armenian embalmer become so enamored with a dead chick he seeks out a stripper's help to solve the murder mystery?" She polishes off her beer and puts the bottle on the floor next to her chair. "And here I thought Armenians love talking about themselves. They'll tell you their whole life story unsolicited."

"That's not me. Sorry. There's not much to tell. Third generation Armenian-American. Born in Fresno and probably will die here. I work for my insufferable uncle, and my father is disappointed with me. That's my life in a nutshell."

Vonnie laughs. I like how she sounds. "I figured you were this nervous, anxious dude. Run away and not look back, right?" She leans forward in her chair. "Looks like I was right. You gotta live a little," she says.

"I'm all ears if you've got suggestions."

"You can come pick me up, Sunday afternoon. Maybe I can teach you how to talk about yourself."

My heart shoots into my throat, and my lips pull back into a smile that I have no control over.

"Uh, yeah!" I say.

There's a banging and the trailer door bursts open. Vee, the bartender, rushes inside.

"What's wrong, sugar?" Vonnie asks. She's already rising to her feet. I do the same.

"Vonnie! Oh, my God!" Vee cries. "Stuart is dead!"

Stuart Newkin lays in his office, eyes bulging, arms stretched outward.

What's crumpled on the shag carpeting isn't really Stuart anymore, at least not physically. The dead man is a withered husk, with gray wrinkled skin and white, oily hair. There's no mistaking it's Stuart; the Hawaiian shirt and velvet jacket are a dead giveaway. Unnaturally aged and desiccated, Stuart's body is about as ugly as his fashion sense. Worms, too many to count, wriggle from Stuart's open mouth, spill down his chin, and roll over his teeth. The long, white worms, blind and alive, feast on Stuart's tongue. These aren't maggots; I've seen my share of maggots over the years. What nests in Stuart's face are segmented worms, pale like alabaster, slippery and alive.

My stomach does cartwheels. I dash from the office to the nearest garbage and puke my guts out. I slowly straighten up and look at Vonnie who waits outside. Her eyes widen.

"What the fuck is that?" Vonnie points towards Stuart's office. A half-dozen dancers and bouncers mill around near the office; no one is dancing and the music is long dead.

"I don't know," I tell her. *Of course* I knew. Whatever supernatural hocus-pocus killed Maddie Hinkle also did this to Stuart Newkin. At least he had an expensive drink before he went.

I feel robbed of that money now.

The Neon Oasis is an active crime scene, and I'm in the middle of the shit storm.

The police show up and prohibit everyone from leaving. They question us separately and seal off the property with yellow crime scene tape. It's not long before my good friend Alvarez shows up and ducks under the tape. He doesn't bother extinguishing his cigarette when he comes in; he just starts exploring, leaving an acrid cloud in his wake as he goes.

He frowns when he sees me. "What the hell are you doing here? Wait. Don't tell me. You smelled a fresh cadaver."

"We've got to stop meeting like this," I tell Alvarez.

"Back to my question. What are you doing here?" he asks, closing the distance between us. He's inches from my face and not amused.

"Clearly I'm having a little fun ogling nearly naked women," I snark.

"Oh, feel free to ogle, but it's *so* peculiar that you're ogling women in the same place Maddie Hinkle worked. You get how that's weird, right Mr. Tarkanian?"

"I'm trying to find out what happened," I say after a moment.

Alvarez takes a step back and pulls the finished cigarette from his lips and fishes out his pack. He puts a new one between his lips, using the old cigarette to light the new one before dropping the butt on the carpet and stamping it out with his foot.

"You really need to travel with an ashtray or something, detective," I say. Lung cancer was going to do in Alvarez, *for sure*.

"What happened here?"

"Looks like you contaminated a crime scene by crushing a cigarette into the carpet."

"Mr. Tarkanian…"

"I don't know. I didn't see him die. I wasn't here."

"Where were you?"

"He was with me," Vonnie interjects.

"You? Uh, Miss Hudgins, was it?"

"Vonnie."

"Maddie Hinkle's roommate, right?" Alvarez asks.

"Armand was in my trailer with me," Vonnie said.

"Hot," he says with a wry grin. He wraps his arm around my shoulder. "Gotta borrow your boyfriend here," he says to Vonnie. Neither Vonnie nor I have the chance to protest before he drags me outside. The air is warm but clear. I didn't realize how much the club smelled like death and smoke.

"I went snooping around Waterhouse's place after we talked," Alvarez tells me. His voice is low and serious. "I found traces of tissue embedded in the table on the patio and blood on the flagstones at Waterhouse's place. Then I searched Waterhouse's checking account and discovered a check written to his stepson and cashed the day Waterhouse died. The cops put out an APB on Monty. It didn't take long to find him. He confessed. You were right."

I feel vindicated and must've shown my cockiness when Alvarez shakes his head.

"Look, just because your so-called visions may have led to an arrest doesn't mean you're correct about Maddie Hinkle," Alvarez says.

"You are intrigued though, right? Maddie with the frogs? Stuart with the worms? Admit it, detective. You can't explain this, and it's *real* weird."

"We have a missing body and one fresh dead guy in a strip club—from the looks of him, he ain't so fresh."

"Yeah, that's going to be hard to make look good …"

"Hang on. There's no guarantee Newkin is going to wind up at your funeral home. The chances of you even seeing this worm-riddled stiff are astronomical."

That's where Alvarez is wrong.

With the way things are going for me, astronomical seems like the right odds.

CHAPTER 11

A WALK IN THE DARK

After Martindale performs the autopsy, Tarkanian Funeral Home receives Stuart's body for what will obviously be a closed casket. She tells me she never saw anything like this before in all her years as a forensic pathologist. I say as little as possible, apart from the odd grunt or head nod, and transport the withered corpse home.

Stuart lays on the embalming table, his face frozen in a startled scream. His body is open like Maddie's was, but the organs are desiccated beyond recognition and crumble when I touch them. Alvarez stands in a corner of the embalming room. He grills me about my visions.

"Martindale had a time clearing the worms away," Alvarez says. "The innards were unidentifiable. Stuart here is about as hollow as a chocolate Easter bunny."

"I've seen my share of dead bodies, but not ones belonging to people I talked to an hour earlier," I tell him.

"What were you *really* doing at the club?" Alvarez asks. "You're not a detective. This isn't Hardy Boys bullshit here."

"Hardy Boys? Update your references, old man." I nonchalantly lean towards the cadaver. There's more than enough space in Stuart's torso for one of Berj's little care packages.

"You know what I mean. Whatever it is you're seeing, whatever otherworldly visions you're getting, I should know," he says.

"Okay, I'm not a detective, but I get visions from dead people, visions you're treating as clues."

"Not clues. Signs, maybe. You were right about Waterhouse's stepson and the frogs at the Hinkle crime scene. Can you summon up some vision and tell me how our boy Stewart bit the dust?"

"It doesn't work like that. The spirits come to me. I don't crack open a Ouija board and start chatting."

Alvarez's shoulders slump and he rubs his eyes. He looks tired, like he's under pressure.

"Well, whenever you communicate with the great beyond, let me know," he says.

"Did the coroner say why Stuart looks like roadkill?"

"Advanced necrosis or something like that. It was as if all the blood was siphoned from him."

"Exsanguination? How could that even be done so quickly?"

"Don't know. Let's see if Stuart's body goes missing."

"Maybe we stakeout the cemetery," I suggest. "See if anyone digs him up."

"This isn't Scooby Doo, Mr. Tarkanian. It's an active police investigation, and you're not part of it. Hell, I'm barely given information, and I got hired to look into it."

"I'm not part of it? The cops arrested someone based on information I gave you from talking to a dead millionaire. I'd say that makes me part of it."

Alvarez thinks for a minute, then groans. "Pro bono consultant. Information is confidential. Terms are non-negotiable, deal?"

"Deal," I say. "You and me. Partners."

"Here's news for you, *partner*. Franklin Waterhouse? Gone."

"How?"

"Same as Maddie Hinkle. Big hole, lots of debris. It was like someone ripped open the casket and removed his body."

"I want to see his grave. Maybe there is something there that can help."

"You're a consultant, not an investigator."

"Then let me consult. I know things about the dead."

"That's why you're valuable to me. Stay here, out of the way. The last thing I need is the only guy with any magic woo-woo that seems to be yielding anything to get himself killed." Alvarez leaves me alone in the embalming room with my thoughts.

I'm playing a dangerous game, cooperating with a private eye while desecrating bodies for profit. By keeping Alvarez close, I had hoped he wouldn't suspect me. So far so good. But I need to be careful and extinguish several fires all at once.

My phone rings. I peel off my gloves and answer it. Berj.

Speaking of fires…

Five minutes after midnight and Donut King is deserted. The same kid as usual is working behind the counter, out of sight, scrubbing coffee stains off the tile floor.

Berj walks in, winks at me, and saunters to the counter. He orders a small coffee and then sits down across from me. Gor, as usual, explores the donut shelf.

"You gonna eat that?" Berj's eyes are on my Bavarian.

"Nah, something is wrong with the taste," I say. "Did you have anything to do with the grave robbing?"

Berj blinks. "What grave robbing? I know nothing of grave robbery." He scoops up the donut and takes a few bites, his gold teeth sparkling as he eats.

"That's not an answer," I observe.

Berj wipes his sticky fingers on his pants, reaches into his jacket and pulls out another wrapped package and cloth bundle.

"Four grand for…" he pauses for a moment as if he's trying to remember something, "Stuart Newkin?" he asks.

"How did you know Stuart Newkin died?" I ask.

"Mutual acquaintances."

This guy has a lot of mutual acquaintances.

"Did you have anything to do with the disappearances of Maddie Hinkle or Franklin Waterhouse?"

"What? No! Anyone could have dug up those bodies. They might have just gotten up and walked away, right?"

"Answer me," I insist.

"Armand, I like you. You're doing a good job, but if I were you, I'd be grateful that I'm being paid very well instead of getting arrested by the police. Think how shameful it would be for your family if they found out that you were desecrating the bodies of the loved ones of those people who pay your uncle's bills."

Nausea creeps through me as a chill runs down my spine. I swallow the lump in my throat.

"See? We have a working relationship. It is about loyalty and trust. You cannot work with someone and not have trust," Berj says.

I retrieve the package and place it on the seat next to me. "I guess Stuart will go missing, too."

Berj inhales and leans forward. "Armand, my friend, we have a good thing going, but you better be careful. It's a dangerous world and you want the right people looking out for you." Something tells me that he's not the "right people".

"A detective is sniffing around," I tell him.

"Detective?"

"A private investigator. A real Sam Spade character," I say.

"He'll find nothing." Berj seems very confident of this. I think that he has no idea that I'm talking to Alvarez, which is good. "Cheer up! You don't know how important this task you're doing is for us."

"Are you ever going to tell me what is going on?" I ask. "What are these packages? Who is 'us' exactly?" He raises an eyebrow at the last question.

"You'll find out soon, if you're lucky," Berj says.

"Or unlucky."

Berj smiles, and his gold teeth catch the light like a mirrored disco ball. "This is why I love you, Armand. Your humor is so self-deprecating. Be good, and don't do anything stupid."

Berj and Gor leave. The unknown package next to me has a date with Stuart's chest cavity. I decide that Alvarez will have to continue to be kept in the dark about my activities; his investigation might be dangerous though, so I need to keep him close.

I pick up the mystery package and take it with me back to the funeral home.

Stuart's spirit appears later that night, after I stitch the package inside him. Same chill, same floating. The initial shock of seeing ghosts has worn off—though the cold is still bone-chilling.

The spirit's lower lip trembles when it views the corpse.

"*Is that me?*" He points to the body under a sheet. Stuart's voice is barely a whisper.

"Ignore it," I say brusquely. "Tell me who did this to you."

His translucent fingers reach out and pull the sheet back, a feat both repulsive and fascinating. I hold up my hand and the ghost stops.

"Stuart, you don't want to see what you look like. Better for you to remember yourself fondly," I say.

"*What have you done to me?*" Stuart asks. His mouth falls open and his hands clench into fists.

"Me? Nothing. But, whatever killed you wasn't kind. I'm sorry."

"No, you're not," the ghost snaps. *"You did something. This feels…
wrong."*

"Focus, man. I want to help, but you need to tell me what happened."

Stuart's spirit hovers high over the table, almost touching the embalming room's ceiling. I know what's coming next and I brace myself.

The ghost dives into me and a thousand icicles – cold, unpleasant, and agonizing – machete their way through my flesh.

Here we go, I think as my vision shifts into Stuart's last mortal memory.

He's in the Neon Oasis, standing behind his desk in a cluttered office. The room feels hazy, like a filter over reality. Things are hard to read, colors look wrong, everything distorts. It's like something is actively making the vision harder to see.

"We told you the envelope was pretty fucking light last month. Now you insult me with this shit? Another light month!" The voice feels familiar but is muffled and difficult to understand.

Stuart's heart sinks.

"I told you over the phone that clients haven't been coming to the place as much now that the Tangerine Pegasus opened. That place has a free buffet and more shows than we do," Stuart says. "If you want more customers this place needs more in the budget—we could maybe do a few renovations, fix it up, then get a boost in clients."

"Renovations? This is what you suggest? You think putting a fucking salad bar in here will get the people in?"

"Chicken wings," Stuart corrects.

"Wipe that smirk off your face, you prick!" The man is seething.

"Sorry, boss. Ever since Maddie's death, guys are reluctant to come here," Stuart says. "It's like this place is cursed or something."

"Cursed? I'll give you cursed." The other man reaches across the desk and

grabs Stuart by the lapels, dragging him over the desk and pinning him down on the ground with a knee. "Are you skimming off the top?"

"No! I'm not. I swear."

The man keeps his knee on Stuart's chest, pushing down with surprising strength. He reaches into a pocket and pulls out a pack of cigarettes. He takes one, lighting it with a butane lighter. The hiss is familiar.

Maddie Hinkle's killer.

The man's face is lit by the lighter's flame for a second before the light vanishes. Shadows swirl around in unnatural ways. Stuart's memory should be clearer than this, but it isn't.

The man blows smoke in Stuart's face as he reaches into his jacket pocket and pulls out a small ceramic idol of a man with an animal head—he waves the idol in Stuart's face. The strip club manager's vision wavers and all sounds snap to dead silence.

"Stuart, Stuart, Stuart." The man runs his fingers over the idol. While still distorted, all Stuart can hear is the man's hypnotic voice. "What are we going to do with you? I took a risk hiring you. Business isn't slow. You're taking my money."

"Yes," Stuart says. His voice is slow and mechanical.

"You have been talking about Maddie to other people, haven't you?"

Stuart swallows. "Yes."

"This is wrong. You never discuss employee business with outsiders."

"Yes."

"Here I was, just wanting to collect my money and I find out you kept information from us. You didn't think I'd check? That I wouldn't learn about it?" He continues waving the idol.

"No," Stuart replies. "I thought I could get away with it."

"You have made your employer very unhappy. Those who act selfishly will be punished."

"Yes," Stuart says. Tears are rolling down his cheeks despite the placid subservience.

"The time for second chances is over," the man says. "You've disappointed me."

The man stands up, dusts himself off, and then reaches down. Strong hands pick Stuart up and then wrap around his neck. An ancient prayer fills Stuart's ears. It is all he can hear. His body convulses. Sharp pain rips through him.

He screams, but no sound comes out.

Blood splatters across the room and he sees the other man smile, ear to ear—a mouth full of gold teeth.

Then, everything goes dark.

Stuart's spirit is gone and I'm sitting, alone and shivering, on the floor.

"Fuck."

The man who entrusted me to do his dirty work *is* the murderer. I debate calling Alvarez and reporting the entire thing, exposing Berj and whatever black magic he wields.

Then I come to my senses.

I pick myself up, wash myself off, and leave the parcel inside Stuart Newkin's corpse.

CHAPTER 12

THE UNGRATEFUL DEAD

We hold Stuart's funeral the next day, a spectacle featuring strippers, bouncers, and eccentric characters. Berj is respectfully dressed in a black suit and tie. Pomade-slicked hair and sunglasses make him resemble a gangster from an old movie.

"You throw a hell of a funeral," Berj quips. He gives me a golden smile.

I bristle at his voice but don't say anything. Thankfully, he doesn't stick around for long.

Vonnie comforts her co-workers. She pats down her black dress and takes a tissue from her purse and hands it to a crying dancer. I give her my condolences.

"How are you holding up?" I ask her.

"Not as well as I could be. Stuart was a good guy. I wish it didn't happen this way. He deserved better than this."

I take a deep breath, "I think I know who murdered both Maddie and Stuart."

"How do you know?"

"A bit of a long story, to be honest. Now's not the time. Has business been slow since Maddie's death?"

Vonnie thinks.

"Now that you mention it, I guess so, yeah," she tells me. "Things haven't been the same, but it hasn't been that long, so it's a bit hard to say? I guess some dudes are scared to come by. Stuart tried advertising, running these goofy promotions, even hired a new DJ, but the crowds have largely stayed away."

I stand there not sure how to handle the elephant in the room. "So…"

Vonnie's eyes are so brilliant and fathomless, I almost forget what I want to say.

"What is it?"

"I guess we're taking a raincheck for Sunday?" I ask.

"God no, I need a bit of boredom in my life as soon as possible."

"Great," I say before I realize what she said. "Wait…"

She winks at me as she walks away. My head swoons, so I take a moment to step outside and get some air. Despite there being no air conditioning outside, the air feels fresh and clear. Well, mostly clear. Alvarez's pungent cigarettes distract me.

"Good to see and smell you, detective," I say.

Alvarez nods. "Mr. Tarkanian."

"You really should smoke less. It's going to kill you."

"Everyone keeps saying so. I don't buy it."

"Stuart Newkin's spirit appeared last night. I saw his murder."

"Okay, I'll bite. Who is it?"

"That's the thing. I didn't get a good look at their face, but he talked about how Stuart had been skimming money from the club. That's why he was killed." There was truth in this. For whatever the reason, I couldn't see much of anything. The more I think about it, the more I'm sure that something about how Stuart died made it harder for me to see the vision. Can a ghost's vision be blocked? Is there a spiritual equivalent of a lead box?

"The club is owned by a dummy corporation with a weird name." Alvarez consults his notes. "Spandaramet Enterprises."

"You know where they're based?" I ask.

"Right here in Fresno. It's some kind of trucking company on Van Ness Boulevard. Business records say it was created about ten or eleven years ago."

"A trucking company and a strip club. Interesting business ventures."

"You mentioned something about skimming money."

"That's what the murderer said. He said that Stuart was skimming money off the top."

"Anything else?"

I close my eyes and try to put myself back into the time and place of Stuart's death, but it's difficult. "A few things ..." I say. "The guy is strong. Real strong. There's some kind of little figurine that he's waving around." I'm exhausted and rub my eyes. "It was so much harder to see this time than any of the others."

Alvarez is taking notes and when I stop talking he looks up at me for a moment before snapping his pad shut and slipping it into his pocket.

"Mind if I ask you a question, detective?"

"Sure thing," he says.

"I'm trying to understand why these ghosts keep showing me how they died. It's like they want me to help them. I've seriously given some thought to the idea that I'm just losing my mind, that I've gone straight off the deep end, but I don't think that's the case. What do you think is happening to me?"

Alvarez doesn't say anything for a moment. "I've been around for more than a few weird cases. Serial killers. Bank robberies gone wrong. Husbands murdering wives and wives murdering husbands. Crimes that make you wonder if we'll ever escape the darkness of these days and into the light of whatever comes after it ..." Alvarez fishes a Lucky Strike from the pack and lights it off the tail of the one he just finished. "I don't know if you've gone crazy. Maybe you're just *very* lucky at making guesses, but I don't think so. Maybe these spirits, these people, came to you because you're the only one that could help. Hell, maybe they're cursing you for fucking up their embalming"—I wince—"but whatever the case might be, it seems your lot in life. And since the Fresno P.D. doesn't have a paranormal ghost-hunting division, you're shit out of luck. You do what you gotta do, and if that means helping some restless dead, then I guess that's what it is."

If Alvarez wouldn't throw me in cuffs the second he found out about my extracurriculars, I think that he might have understood the situation I was in. Some of it was my own making, but other parts weren't. I wonder what side of the fence Alvarez would have fallen on. Jail or help?

"Thanks, detective."

"No problem," he says as he starts going down the stairs away from the building.

"Why not go to the cemetery with me tonight and see what happens?" I suggest. He turns around and snorts.

"I've got more important things to do than camp out in a grave-yard."

"Like what? Cases more interesting than grave robbery? I want to know who's pilfering corpses of people I embalmed."

"*America's Got Talent* is on," he says.

"You're fucking kidding me," I reply.

"Mr. Tarkanian?" He looks back over his shoulder.

"Yeah?"

"You're being followed." He sticks the cigarette between his lips and keeps walking.

I stand there for a moment, wondering if he was talking about the police. Did I have a tail? Is that what they're called? Tails? I don't know, but if I take much longer Uncle George is going to lose his shit later. I turn around and that's when I see them. Two burly and strong-looking guys, sitting on top of their motorcycles in the parking lot across the street. They're wearing black leather jackets covered in patches. One of them leans over to the other and they both start up their loud motorcycles and peel away.

Roupen is behind the counter of his bookshop, engrossed in a collection of essays, eyes focused on the pages, mouth moving as he reads. If there was a Zen-like state for readers, my brother has found it.

"Can you recommend any good books?" I ask.

Without looking up, he replies, "Try Barnes & Noble. We only sell used shit that nobody likes."

I yank the book from him. "Are you doing anything tonight?"

"I *was* going to do some reading," he says. "Oh, wait. I can't. Some dick grabbed my book."

I toss the book on the counter. "Brent isn't around?"

"He's teaching a graduate class."

"If you're not busy, maybe we could hang out. Like we used to. Before everything went to hell."

He smirks. "What did you have in mind? Remember I don't do bowling. Or anything remotely involving golf."

"Then you're in luck, my brother. How would you like to stake out a cemetery?"

Roupen blinks and leans backward. "Are you turning into a creep? Should I call somebody? Because I can call somebody."

"I think someone is robbing graves, and I want to catch them in the act," I say.

"Can't we have a nice quiet night at home?" Roupen's tone mocks my suggestion. "Make popcorn, watch a movie? *Nope.* My creepy brother wants to go to a cemetery and watch crimes happen."

"I know how crazy this sounds …"

"Do you? Because it sort of feels like you don't."

I sigh. Roupen is encumbered with common sense and rationality even though they both need to be checked at the door for what I have in mind. My intuition is telling me that these grave robberies pointed to Berj. Call it my curiosity or stubbornness, but when someone steals corpses I embalmed, it feels personal.

"The police are investigating, and I'm worried that the funeral home will wind up in the crosshairs," I say.

"How?"

"Because all the cadavers that have gone missing came from Tarkanian Funeral Home. Me, Uncle George, Dikran, Sam. We'd all be suspects."

"Why should you be worried? If you had nothing to do with it, then you'll all be fine." Roupen takes his book and puts it on his chair. He checks his watch and then walks over to the door and flips the sign to read CLOSED. "Right?" He looks at me and I clear my throat. "Right, Armand?" He repeats.

"I maybe might not want those bodies to be found," I murmur.

"Say what?"

"Okay. This is going to sound bad." I look around for anyone lingering in the store, then tell Roupen everything. I tell him about Berj, the accident, our arrangement with the cadavers, the empty graves, Alvarez's investigation. Everything.

When I'm finished, Roupen looks at me. "So, you got roped into some kind of weird and potentially illegal scheme because you're too scared to tell Uncle George that you rear-ended someone's truck?"

I frown a bit. "Well, when you say it like that …"

"You're officially the dumbest person on the fucking planet." He rubs his eyes. "You literally pulled the crown off Dikran's head, shoved him out of the way, and said 'no, no, this belongs to me', and then you put that crown on and started doing illegal things."

"Yes," I admit. "Look, Roupen, I'm in over my head with Berj. I have no idea what to do. I can't just quit because this guy has me by the balls. He's already killed people, and the only way out is to make sure that he gets caught but doesn't rat me out."

"Well, you gotta have faith," Roupen says, and begins singing an off-key rendition of George Michael's "Faith" while rolling his shoulders.

"Roupen?"

"Yes, my idiot brother?"

"Roupen."

My brother looks at me and sees that I'm serious. He ceases the impromptu choreography and sinks into his chair.

"None of this is normal. It's batshit crazy. I'm talking to ghosts, which is also crazy. I see how these people die. I want to … I need to find out why this is happening," I tell him.

"Fuck it," he says after a long pause. "Fine. What do we need?"

"Thanks, Roupen. You won't regret it."

"I already do."

It's night when we arrive at Everafter Memorial Gardens Cemetery. Velvety shadows cloak the statuary and monuments. There's something that makes the statues of cherubs and angels seem deformed and terrible. In the gloom they become goblins and demons.

It takes us no time at all to hop the fence and make our way along the rows of headstones and sad-looking trees. We hurry along a small path deeper into the cemetery, keeping our heads down and moving with caution, like spies raiding an enemy compound.

Dragging Roupen along is probably a terrible idea. Why I thought it was a good plan is beyond me, it's also feels like a reminder of why I shouldn't be allowed to come up with plans.

Still, Roupen being Roupen, takes it all in stride.

"You know I do this because you're my brother," he whispers as we crouch alongside a cenotaph.

"Duly noted," I say. "Best brother ever."

We prowl through the night, past weeping willows and a large pond, toward a sloping hill near Stuart Newkin's fresh grave. Sod covers the burial plot.

"Looks undisturbed," Roupen says.

"We're early. Let's hide and wait."

Roupen squats behind a tombstone, and I stretch out underneath a gnarled sycamore tree several feet away.

It's not long before a bright light stabs my eyes. I squint and hold my hand up to block the beam.

"Mr. Tarkanian," Of *course* Alvarez would show up and crash my plan.

"Detective," I reply.

"You're trespassing," Alvarez reminds me.

"Weren't you watching *America's Got Talent?*"

"Yeah. The weird dancing kid got kicked off."

"Perry?" Roupen shakes his head, disappointed. "Damn it, I was going to watch that! I do loves me some Perry."

Alvarez turns and shines the flashlight at Roupen, then back at me. "Who the hell is this?"

"My brother," I reply.

Alvarez sighs and his flashlight clicks off. The light disappearing makes the night more oppressive than it was before. My eyes need to adjust again. I can hear Alvarez walk past me and I'm pretty sure I hear him fishing for a cigarette. He snaps his lighter then exhales.

"Smoking's going to kill you, detective," Roupen says. "You should try chewing gum or candy."

"Shut up, Armand's brother."

"Right-o," Roupen says.

We sit in silence, unsure of what will happen. Whoever dug up Maddie and Waterhouse was going to come for Stuart. I guaranteed that would happen.

"Shh," Alvarez pipes up. He shushes us, but we've been sitting in silence and smelling his cigarettes for close to an hour. "Did you hear that?"

There's a sound, like cracking wood or shifting dirt. We look at each other and start creeping closer towards the grave.

Soil shifts in the burial plot, and a pair of hands rip through the dirt, straight up like a cheesy horror movie. Stuart's body burst from the surface, his lifeless face turned up at the sky. His eyes are closed, and muffled groans come from his stitched shut mouth.

"What the *shit?*" Roupen asks, horrified.

Stuart heaves himself up and balances on two wobbly legs. Alvarez pulls a gun and starts advancing towards the corpse. "Sir, I need you to stop right there."

"Alvarez! What are you doing? Get away from it!" I cry, but it's too late. Stuart turns to Alvarez. The detective advances towards the shambling figure.

"I need you to put your hands on your head." Alvarez has a moment to get a shot off when Stuart's corpse takes a hard swing at him, catching him in the chest and knocking him backwards into a gravestone. He hits the stone at full force and doesn't move after that.

Stuart turns and staggers away. I can see the hole from Alvarez's bullet in the corpse's chest. Stuart's arms dangle and flop around as he starts to move away from his own grave.

Roupen and I race towards Alvarez. I check for a pulse and see that he's still breathing.

"Come on, Roupen. Let's go."

"Go? Are you out of your mind?"

"Got any better ideas?"

"Literally *anything* other than what you suggested. I gotta call an ambulance for the detective."

"It's getting away!" Stuart starts moving faster. "Let's go Roupen, it's now or never." I hear my brother curse as he starts jogging alongside me while calling for an ambulance at the same time. We give chase as the thing heads towards the low fence surrounding the graveyard. With all the skills of a dead and zombified Olympic gymnast, Stuart vaults over the fence and lands upright on the opposite side. My brother and I hop the fence, as easily on the way out as on the way in. Stuart races down the street.

For a corpse, Stuart runs like lightning. I match his pace, though Roupen has a bit more difficulty keeping up. My brother swears at me, his footfalls as erratic as his breathing.

Stuart takes a turn into a cornfield near the outskirts of town—I can hear Roupen, still keeping pace, but just barely. Stuart crosses into a dirt lot where a lone warehouse sits on a vacated street. It moves towards a door lit by a single spotlight, lifts one of its dead hands, and bangs on the metal door. Then it stands there silently under the harsh light. Roupen catches up and we crouch down, eyes trained on the building.

"What is this place?" Roupen asks. I shrug and put a finger to my lips.

The creature teeters on its dead legs like it's waiting for something.

The rusty door opens with a loud creak. A man in a T-shirt and jeans answers the door and steps out of the building. He walks around zombie Stuart a few times, and we can hear him talking to someone— the words are hazy and unclear. The man pulls a gun from a concealed holster, puts it under Stuart's chin, and fires. The top of the dead man's head flies off in a wet burst of skull and brains. Roupen and I duck for cover; my brother covers his mouth with his hands.

The once-animated corpse is animated no more and collapses into a heap.

After wiping his nose on his sleeve, the man lightly nudges Stuart with his foot, and starts laughing.

We watch as other men step out of the warehouse; they're also laughing. They spread a tarp on the ground, pick up the now re-murdered Stuart by his arms and legs, and drop him onto the blue plastic sheet.

"What the actual fuck is going on?" Roupen whispers in a panic as we watch from our hiding place.

One of the men produces a large hunting knife and slices open Stuart's belly. He reaches inside and retrieves the wrapped package I put there. The knife-wielder barks some orders and the men obediently wrap up Stuart in the tarp. Two men carrying shovels drag him away.

Once the men disappear back into the building, I'm brave enough to move again. I retreat a bit and then dry heave behind some bushes while Roupen sits there, stunned. I grab him by the shoulder and drag him away.

We don't say anything for the rest of the night.

CHAPTER 13

SUBTERRANEAN DREAM CASTLE

On Sunday, Vonnie meets me at Forestiere Underground Gardens, a network of subterranean rooms, passageway, and courtyards in the middle of the city.

The story goes that Baldassare Forestiere spent forty years meticulously constructing his underground gardens, replete with unique stonework, Roman arches, and labyrinthian corridors. Fruit trees give the place a surreal and almost whimsical atmosphere, and the many sloped passageways lead to atriums that are budding with vegetation and life.

Vonnie and I laugh like teenagers in the cavernous stone structures, inhale the fresh citrus of lemon trees, and marvel at what it must have taken to build this place.

"Isn't this something? One dude worked for years and made all of this," Vonnie says.

We walk beneath an archway into a courtyard with a fruiting lemon tree.

"Forestiere built underground to escape the heat," I tell her. "He didn't use any designs or plans. He worked on each section as he imagined it and labored on it for the rest of his life."

"That's crazy."

"Sure. Until you walk through the final result."

"Why would anyone go to the trouble?"

"It's his legacy," I say. "He wanted to leave something behind, something that told the world he existed."

"What about you? You have some legacy you're working on?"

"Me? I don't think I'll have a legacy," I confess.

Vonnie raises an eyebrow. "Oh? Who's stopping you?"

"If I'm lying, my family. Truthfully, it's me." It feels strange to say out loud what I've started to realize is true.

"You could make your own legacy." Vonnie reaches up and gently caresses a lemon tree's green leaves. "Dig a castle underground, like this dude."

"That's just copying someone else's thing."

Vonnie smiles. "The world needs more imaginative subterranean dream castles."

Our fingers interlace, and we draw each other near, exploring the spaces underground as the spaces between us grow smaller. My heart beats faster, not out of fear but in elation.

Vonnie laughs.

"What's so funny?" I ask.

"I was thinking about how we met. I'm always meeting guys at the club. They see me shake my ass and they just fall in love with me. Then they ask for my number or stalk me." Vonnie puts her other hand on my forearm and her head on my shoulder.

"I didn't stalk you," I remind her.

"This is the first time I met someone at the club I actually want to go out with," she says.

"We met at a funeral home, not a club," I remind her. "And I'm happy you agreed to go out with me."

"You should be. I don't give this sweet ass away for nothing." Vonnie grins. "So, embalming. What's up with that?"

"What would you like to know? Ask me anything. I'm a ghoulish compendium of the grotesque."

Vonnie laughs. "Okay, hotshot. Take me through the whole embalming process."

"I start out with a decedent on the slab," I begin, like a professor teaching a class. "I wash them thoroughly, running my fingers through their hair and scrubbing the follicles using a strong shampoo. I'm like a stylist for the recently departed. I lather, rinse, and repeat. I put plastic caps in their eyes so that they don't sink in. I won't even describe what we do with a trocar, but let's just say it's a lot like puncturing a septic tank with a spear."

She winces, still smiling.

"Since a corpse with its jaw agape is unsettling, I insert tiny wires into their gums with a needle injector and pull their lips together. This ensures that they won't complain about the service," I tell her.

"Uh huh," Vonnie mumbles.

"Next I mix the embalming chemicals," I continue. "A horrid cocktail of preservatives that gives them a healthy 'I'm not dead' glow. I insert a tube in their carotid artery and pump them full of embalming fluid while another tube bleeds them out into a sink. I can stop if you want."

Vonnie shakes her head. "No. At this point, I'm enthralled. Go on."

"After I drain them, I dress them up in their Sunday best because the family wants to show them off in a really expensive box. That collection of guts, bones, and flesh they casually neglected in life still decomposes inside, albeit slowly. Then we bury them, and I get paid. Aren't you sorry you asked?"

Smiling, Vonnie nods.

"That's not what I expected. And that doesn't bother you?" she asks.

"Why should it?" I reply. "It's only a job, nothing more. Forget about me. Let's talk about you. What's your story?"

"It's a sad one. It's not the kind of story that people want to know. But it is the kind of story you might expect from someone who winds up stripping near an airport in Fresno," she gives a bit of a shrug.

"I'd like to know, if you want to share."

She pauses, sizes me up, her eyes wandering over my face.

"A few years ago, I was married, had a kid, and worked at a grocery store in Atlanta," she begins. "My husband served in Afghanistan. Operation Enduring Freedom. A few months after his deployment, my house caught fire in the middle of the night. Faulty wiring, I was told, and the alarms didn't go off. My son Jason and I tried getting out, but we were trapped in the flames. I couldn't see shit. There was too much smoke. I heard Jason crying in his room, but I couldn't reach him. It wasn't my fault. I tried. It was too dark. The lights weren't working."

Her voice is a dull monotone now, as if her pain overtakes her. "The fire consumed everything. Jason screamed. That's the last thing I remember. My boy screaming for me. I passed out and woke up in the back of an ambulance. They told me afterwards that Jason didn't make it."

Vonnie's head sinks to her chest. "He didn't make it," she whispers. A lone tear rolls down her cheek.

"Jesus. That's terrible," I say. "Nobody should have to deal with that much pain."

"Truthfully, the pain came later." Her grip tightens a bit. "Mostly I just felt numb. Parents, shitty or otherwise, always believe that their kids will be around. We expect that they'll be the ones burying us and not the other way around. You ever see a child's coffin?"

"Unfortunately."

"The size threw me off. It was so small. Coffins feel like the sort of things that should be large. Adult-sized, right?" Her voice cracks and she clears her throat. "After the funeral, my husband blamed me for what happened to our son. We fought constantly. He started drinking. Then, we were over. I left Atlanta and wandered out west like some kind of zombie. I don't even remember how I made most of the trip. I did some shit, Armand, and I barely remember it. Maybe that's for the best. I wound up working in Vegas, Reno, Lake Tahoe. Nobody cared about me, and I didn't either."

"Look, if you need to talk …"

She smiles. "You're a good guy, Armand. I like you—but I don't need saving." She pats my arm. "I sometimes wish I was back in Atlanta in my old life, but that's gone, and I can't go back. I learned the hard way to survive. I'm nobody's damsel in distress, and I won't ever be."

"I agree," I say. "You're one of the strongest people I know."

She punches my shoulder, which stings a bit. "In my line of work, you have to be." We walk in silence, not uncomfortable silence, but the kind of silence where people are processing things. "So, is now a good time?"

"For what?"

"Idiot," she laughs. "You told me that you knew who killed Maddie."

I had completely forgotten. Things had been so weird the last few days that I'd spaced out.

"You're not going to believe me, but I want to be honest with you," I say, stumbling over my words. "Vonnie, I like you. You're neat." She looks at me and mouths the word *neat*. "You're the first person besides my brother who listens to me. What I'm going to tell you will sound insane, but it's true, and I'm asking you to just hear me out, okay?"

Vonnie nods. She holds my hand. "Whatever it is, you can tell me."

I exhale.

"I see dead people," I say.

"Yes, Armand. You're an embalmer. That's your job."

"No. I mean, I can communicate with dead people." She starts

105

to say something but I stop her. "I'm not kidding. I have full blown visions of how they died. I saw how Maddie died. I saw how Stuart died. Hell, I've seen how some old rich dude that we buried died. I helped that private eye solve the guy's murder." The look on her face is impossible for me to read, but the flood gates are open, and I keep talking. "Maddie and Stuart were both killed by the same guy with some kind of weird magic."

"Armand," she says. "There's no such thing as magic."

"You saw Stuart, Vonnie. Did that shit look normal to you?"

She frowns a bit, knowing that she couldn't explain it and that it made not a shred of sense. "All right, go on."

"I think the owner of the Neon Oasis wanted Maddie and Stuart dead." Vonnie's eyes widen and her mouth falls open. "Stuart was skimming money off the top, and Maddie must have known about something. But it's not only that, the owner is the one doing some weird magical shit."

Vonnie says nothing, purses her lips, and releases my hand.

"You don't believe me," I say.

Vonnie folds her arms. "Okay. Let's assume you're not delusional. What do you want me to do? I'm a stripper. I shake my tits for drunk men. I don't have the broadest skillset in the world to help you with your magic villain."

"Maybe you can find out more about the guy who runs your club."

She laughs so hard she snorts. "Are you fucking for real, Armand? You just told me this guy magically murdered two of my friends."

I open my mouth to say something and then close it again. I'm spent. I'm trapped in this situation with no escape. I'm trapped by a family that won't let me get away. I'm just trapped. I sink my face into my hands and rub my eyes. I feel Vonnie's hands on my cheeks and then her lips on top of my head.

"I think you're probably crazy," she says to me. "You need help. Serious psychiatric help." She offers me her hand. I take it and she pulls me up to my feet. "But then again, I'm not a bastion of reason."

She looks off towards the distance. "I need a little bit of time to process this."

"I am not crazy! I swear that I can see and hear the dead speak."

"I'm not talking about that," Vonnie says. "You've got some serious family issues that you need to sort out. Like, pronto."

I laugh, and for once, feel like I might have someone in my corner that cares more about me than they do about "what the family would think."

She leans in and kisses my cheek softly. "I had fun, Armand. Give me a little bit of time to sort this stuff out, okay?"

I nod.

Vonnie says good bye and leaves; I sit back down and sigh. I'm not sure how long I've been sitting there, but when I look up, I see that I'm not alone.

"What do you want?" I ask. "Come to gloat?"

From its matted fur and the gleam in its eye, I can tell that it's the same mongrel that ate Maddie Hinkle's heart. It whines and walks over, sniffing its way to my hand. Its tail wags furiously and it lets out an overjoyed bark. Before I can react, it licks me, coating my hand in viscous doggy slobber.

"Ew, gross." I wince. "Thanks a lot, asshole."

The dog barks again, wags its tail a little faster, and then turns and sprints off into the underground maze. I wipe my hand on my pants, and head home. For the rest of the night I can't shake the feeling that things aren't as bad as they seem.

Unfortunately, my newfound optimism is premature and misplaced.

CHAPTER 14

CHILDREN OF
SPANDARAMET

My morning jog burns off some of the tension I wake up with.

You're barking mad if you're running in the Fresno summer. It's a good sign that a person has lost their mind. The sun scorches everything and makes life outside miserable. Imagine a sauna filled with lava and fire; that's Fresno during the summer months. In the shade. Being outside in athletic wear is one thing, but the bikers following me around were wearing black leather.

Fresno attracts all kinds of weird.

My runner's high keeps me going even though my legs burn, but the euphoria dissipates when Dikran greets me outside the funeral home.

"Out for a run?" he asks, smoothing his necktie.

"Nope, just trying a new look. I think it suits me," I say.

"Where were you yesterday? I had to work because you weren't around."

"I was on a date, with a real human woman. Try it sometime."

"Who? That Black chick?"

"Her name is Vonnie."

"Listen, what you do on your own time is your own business, but if you're going to continue seeing some *sev*, this family won't like it," Dikran says. He uses the Armenian word for "black." I've never hated Dikran more.

"I'll add racist to your long list of personality traits," I reply.

Dikran thrusts his head towards mine so all I see is his scowling face, flaring nostrils and his dull angry eyes.

"Cut the bullshit, Armand. You know my Dad doesn't like them."

"Don't threaten me," I say.

"I'll do what I want. This is my family's house. There'll be more shit if you keep seeing that girl," Dikran thrusts his hands in his pants pockets. "If George or Uncle Hagop find out about her, you'll really get it."

"I'm an adult and can see whomever I want," I tell him.

"Not in this family you can't," Dikran replies.

"Why *do* you assholes always try to take away things that make me happy? You come at me with this traditional Old-World bullshit. Always."

"Know your place in this family." Dikran has a smarmy, shit-eating grin. I ball my hand into a fist but relax when a car pulls up.

Alvarez gets out. He's smoking, his suit is wrinkled, and he's got a soft brace around his neck.

"Morning, Mr. Tarkanian."

"Hello, detective," Dikran pipes up, trying to be the alpha. He clearly thinks that Alvarez is here to talk to my uncle.

Alvarez looks at Dikran for a moment with a blank look on his face, "Who're you?" My cousin shrinks, his shoulders slumping. It's hard to look cool when you're blanked like that. "Sorry, whoever-you-are, but I need a word with Mr. Tarkanian, if you don't mind."

Dikran looks at me, and I give him a shrug. He glowers as he turns and goes into the house.

"More family?" Alvarez asks me.

"My cousin."

"You looked like you were going to pop him."

"The thought had crossed my mind. How are you feeling?" I ask.

"I'm fine, all things considered," he says. "The hospital discharged me this morning."

I start to apologize. "Look about the other night …"

He shakes his head. "I woke up in an ambulance, and you guys were gone. They patched me right up. Even got some morphine out of the deal."

"Detective, I'm sorry…"

"Save it. Stuart Newkin's body is gone. I don't know if the thing that attacked me was him, but all traces of whatever it was disappeared."

"Evil magic," I mumble.

"Same as with Maddie Hinkle?" Alvarez says, fumbling for his pad and pen.

"Yeah."

"Of *course* it is." Alvarez sighs and shakes his head. "Up until the other day, I would've thought you were clinical, but I'm starting to become a believer."

"Up until a few weeks ago I thought the idea of conversing with spirits was crazy, yet here we are. Stuart's boss killed him."

"Do you have any proof?"

"I have what the vision revealed."

"Anything else?"

"A name. Berj. Berj Manoogian."

Identifying Berj was dangerous, but having him get arrested might free me from this downward spiral.

Alvarez takes a few notes, then flips back a few pages. "Same guy registered as the contact for Spandaramet Enterprises. Know anything else about him?"

"Not really," I lie. "I've bumped into him at Donut King from time to time."

"Bump into?" Alvarez's voice trails off and his eyes narrow.

"Donuts. Coffee."

"Why didn't you mention him before?" Alvarez asks. "No bullshit, Armand."

"Armenians don't trust outsiders. Non-Armenians screwed us in the past, so we're naturally cautious. Going outside of Armenian circles can get you kicked out of your family, if not the entire community, depending on the patriarch." While everything I say is true, it's tinged with omissions and personal bias.

Alvarez scrunches up his mouth. "I don't get it. You Armenians have some weird hang-ups. If you want to keep being my consultant, no more bullshit like this. I trusted you by going to graveyards and I got my ass kicked by a dead dude. We're well past 'we need to learn to trust before we learn to love,' you understand?"

"Absolutely, detective."

"The police still have no idea what is going on, so if we get our hands on Berj first, that'll be good. Me and Berj need to have a chat," Alvarez says. He turns around and walks towards his car. "Thanks for telling me, Mr. Tarkanian."

"Thanks for believing me."

Will Alvarez save me from Berj? Can this nosey P.I. bring the weight of the Fresno Police Department down on these black magicians, whoever they are? He has influence with the department, I'm sure. Maybe if he gets the police involved, then these ghosts that have been showing up will disappear from my life forever, and I can finally rest in peace.

I'm already on my second cup of coffee when Berj and Gor walk into the Donut King. A duffel bag rests on the seat beside me, waiting for its suspicious cargo. After a handful of these clandestine meetings, I'm becoming an expert at transferring illegal cargo and not attracting attention. Or so I like to think.

Whether it was good fortune or dumb luck, Berj called me the same day I talked to Alvarez. The time and place were as usual, late at night, at the Donut King.

Berj orders himself a coffee and a cinnamon donut and sits across from me. Gor leans against a nearby wall and folds his arms like the threatening monster he is.

"You seem a bit on edge tonight, my friend." Berj sips his coffee.

"There was another incident at the cemetery. Another body went missing." I scan his eyes for any reaction.

Berj looks surprised and I realize then that he's a good liar. He reassures me that everything is fine and then surreptitiously passes another wrapped package and cloth bundle to me.

"It's so strange that these bodies go missing. I don't know why, and I don't care. But you're doing a good job, and if you keep it up, you're going to be rich," Berj says.

I force a smile. "We don't have anyone at the moment."

Berj chuckles. "Someone's always dying, Armand. The first person who drops dead, you put that in them." He points to the unmarked box.

"Sure thing," I say. My stomach goes all sour and lurches.

Berj finishes his donut in three greedy bites, downs his coffee, and leaves the shop. I put the package in my bag and leave. Berj and Gor climb into their truck and then head down Ventura Avenue. I walk over to the van and toss my duffel into the trunk.

That's when Alvarez pulls up. He leans over and opens the passenger side door.

"Get in," he orders. "We're following him."

"What are you doing here?" I close the trunk of the first call minivan.

"You *literally* told me that you meet him at Donut King, right? Well, this is the closest one to your house. You know I'm a detective, right? What did you think I was going to do? Wait around until you felt like cluing me in on other details? Get in."

I get in his car and a strong cigarette smell overwhelms me. Alvarez peels off down the street. Without Berj and Gor's truck in sight, it's safe for him to make up the distance.

"What's in the bag?" Alvarez asks.

"What bag?"

"The one you had when you exited the donut shop."

"Gym clothes." I don't know if he believes me.

After a while, the truck is in Alvarez's sights; he slows down and keeps his distance. Berj continues driving through Fresno's streets, past warehouses and abandoned lots. Eventually, Alvarez pulls over and lets Berj and Gor disappear down another street.

"Aren't you going to follow him?" I ask.

"No, I think I know where he's going," Alvarez says.

I crack open the car window, letting some fresh air wash over my face.

"Look, Mr. Tarkanian. I buy your mystic woo-woo stuff, I do. It's weird, but I buy it." He lights a cigarette. "But you're not clear of this, and you're not telling me something. That's fine. I'm a P.I and work with some pretty shady people sometimes." He pauses for a moment and takes a long drag. "I don't think you're a mastermind criminal or anything. I get the feeling that you're just some poor idiot that got suckered into this whole mess."

"Look, detective …" Alvarez starts his car up again and pulls off the side of the road and drives down the street at a leisurely pace. "You're right." I say. He looks at me and nods.

"Let's see what these magical assholes are doing, then you need to tell me what the hell is happening, because I'm sure that you know more than you're leading on," Alvarez says.

As we turn another corner, Alvarez kills the headlights of his car. We meander further down the road. He pulls the car over so fast, it nearly jumps the curb.

"This is where we walk," he tells me.

Warehouses surround us, large metal and cinderblock structures fronting Van Ness Avenue. Berj's truck veers into a parking lot near one warehouse that looks abandoned. The air outside has a coppery, raw smell, a reeking miasma of rotting organs. I've encountered this before.

It's the stench of death.

Out of the corner of my eye, I detect formless shapes moving in the dark. A faint rustling fills the air around us. I swallow hard.

A foreboding dread hangs in the night, and despite the moon being out, things are cloaked in shadow.

"Something's not right." Alvarez walks back to the car. I hear a heavy thud and see him struggling with an unseen assailant. I turn. A sharp pain radiates from my neck. My body sails through the air and hits the ground. The world turns sideways and spins for a moment. Faces leap out of the gloom.

Alvarez hits the pavement next to me. His eyes go wide. Someone slips a canvas bag over his head. I try screaming, but no sound comes out. Instead, the rough scratchiness of canvas scrapes my face, and all goes dark.

The first thing I realize when I regain consciousness is that my hands are bound behind my back, and the canvas bag is still over my head. The air around me burns with sulfur and sage.

I'm sitting in what feels like a metal folding chair. I groan a bit and realize that I'm not alone. Someone yanks the hood off and bright lights blind me for a moment. My vision blurs and then comes into focus. I'm in a warehouse, I think, with Alvarez. He's also tied to a chair with a bag over his head.

Several sinister shapes linger nearby.

"Whatever this is. Whoever you are, I'm nobody, right?" I stammer. Talking is hard with this level of headache.

"Nobody? Really?" Somebody moves close, but beyond my vision.

"I'm an embalmer from the Tarkanian Funeral Home," I say. "There's been a mistake. I only want to leave here in peace."

Gor steps out of the shadows. "Peace? There is no peace for you. Not now."

He punches me hard in the gut. I double over and start coughing. The pain is unreal, but, at the same time, the thought that crosses my mind is, "That's not what I expected him to sound like." Gor's voice is not a deep rumbling engine of sound, it's softer and nasally.

Me getting my ass kicked wakes Alvarez up. "You guys fucked up. I'm Detective José Alvarez and I'm ordering you to let us go."

Gor hits Alvarez in the face. I hear some part of the shamus's face crack when the fist connects. Berj steps into the light and leers at us.

"I'm aware of your profession, detective, though, I suppose that 'private investigator' is more accurate. I donate generously to the California Peace Officers' Memorial Foundation and to the Fresno PD, and I don't think I've *ever* heard your name come up. But, it is important that we honor the memory of the brave men and women of law enforcement, right? Nobody lives forever. You certainly won't." Berj pulls the hood off of Alvarez's head. His nose is broken. "I am Berj Manoogian."

"What do you do here, Mr. Manoogian?" Alvarez fights against the restraints.

"Business, Mr. Alvarez. I think, though, that a better question is what are *you* doing here, trespassing on my property?"

"Untie me and I'll show you," Alvarez says.

"I'm afraid I can't do that, Mr. Alvarez," Berj replies. Gor laughs from the shadows nearby. Berj turns his head and looks at me. "I'm surprised at you, Armand. Were you not happy with our arrangement?"

Alvarez turns and looks at me, he doesn't say anything, but it's clear that he's having one of those "I hate being right" moments.

"You didn't tell the private detective what you've been doing? Well, I'm happy that you listened to me when I told you that Armenians have to watch out for each other, my friend!"

"I kept my word," I murmur. "He doesn't have to know."

"What haven't you told me, Armand?" Alvarez looks angry, I don't blame him. I turn away, I can't bear to look at him. Waves of discomfort bubble in my gut.

Berj picks up on my reticence.

"Someone can keep secrets," he says. "Us special types need to stick together." My eyes snap up—did Berj *know* that I could see the dead? "I think it's time I enlighten you as to the reality of what is going on." Berj turns and shouts something in Armenian; I don't understand what he says. His assistants turn our chairs around.

What Alvarez and I witness in that cavernous warehouse leaves me cold. The inside of the warehouse has been converted into a massive temple. Two statues of winged sphinxes flank the room. Stone stelae marked with the cardinal directions, just eight feet from the floor, each adorned with ancient symbols. A large statue of a woman towers above all else. She's cloaked in flowing robes and a ceremonial headdress. In one hand, the stone figure holds a spear; in the other, she clutches a human skull. The statue overlooks an altar surrounded by smoking bronze braziers. Overhead, a tapestry emblazoned with two golden eagles and a star—the emblem of the Artaxiad dynasty—hangs on the wall.

A dozen shirtless men, their faces painted to look like skulls, stand next to the altar. Leering statues adorned in jade and marble peek out from niches around the room, and the torchlight casts eerie and macabre shadows everywhere.

"This is the Temple of Spandaramet, Goddess of Death, and we are the Children of Spandaramet," Berj announces like he's unveiling a new Disneyland ride.

"Who are they?" I ask, and tilt my head towards the men surrounding us.

116

"These are my disciples," Berj snaps. "The Children of Spandaramet will build a new Armenian empire on the bones of this decadent nation. For now, though, we are growing … and with any organization's growth comes the need for money to finance our expansion."

Alvarez whistles. "I imagine that enormous stone statue of a chick in a crown costs a pretty penny. Tell you what. If you surrender now, this stuff could be placed in a museum while you rot in jail."

"Oh, I'm not going anywhere, detective," Berj says. "You, on the other hand …"

"Cut the bullshit," Alvarez struggles with the ropes. "You're crazy."

"I expect people will say that," Berj shrugs a bit. "But the spirits have shown me so very much. I know what is coming, but there is still much more to learn. So much more to do."

"How is this possible?" I ask Berj.

He turns towards me and I get a chill that runs up and down my spine like electricity.

"My family was slaughtered by the Ottoman Turks in 1917, except for my great-grandfather, who escaped from his village and hid in the mountains. While in hiding, he stumbled upon a cave with vast subterranean tunnels stretching for miles. There, deep underground, he found salvation and the tools for vengeance." Berj looks up at the large statue of the woman. "In those caverns, my great-grandfather uncovered a treasure trove in lost artifacts and writings, including a book."

"What book?" I ask.

"*The Book of the Obsidian Way*, a tome containing rituals for human sacrifices, incantations, and forbidden ceremonies. True magic. Real power. My great-grandfather made an unholy pact with Spandaramet." His voice shifts from a dull monotone to an almost frenzied cadence. "He used the book to summon the death goddess. Spandaramet taught him necromancy and ancient magic. My great-grandfather wanted his people to use *The Book of the Obsidian Way* to repel the Ottomans and reclaim their lost empire." An unmissable malevolence fills his eyes.

"This story have a point?" Alvarez pipes up. Gor hits him across the face.

"Offended by his blasphemies, his fellow Armenians turned on my great-grandfather," Berj continues. "Fearing for his life, he escaped to Syria, taking *The Book of the Obsidian Way* with him. It has been in my family ever since."

Berj retrieves a large polished lacquered box with an ornate, arabesque design. He opens the lid with a bit of dramatic flourish, revealing a worn leather-bound book.

"Big deal. You can get those on Amazon," Alvarez says. I turn away so that I don't have to see Gor hit him again, but I hear it.

Berj smiles. "When Tigranes the Great ruled the Kingdom of Armenia, the Armenians proved triumphant in battle, culture, and influence. Tigranes's ancient blood courses through my veins. My world is one of revenge against those who have wronged my family and the Armenian people."

"You're just a cult leader," Alvarez says.

"Precisely. And the Children of Spandaramet will use *The Book of the Obsidian Way* to get back our usurped kingdom." His voice has a stone-cold confidence.

"Except the old kings aren't in charge anymore," I say. "Neither are your old gods. Armenians are Christian. We're all about Jesus now, right?"

Berj rolls his eyes. "Just because a nation adopts a new religion doesn't mean the old gods are gone. They're waiting patiently for the right sacrifice."

"Tell you what, Jim Jones, if you surrender and let us go, I'll drop the kidnapping charges." Alvarez twists his wrists against the restraints.

Berj removes the old book from the box and holds it with reverence.

"I'm afraid the time for cutting deals is over, Mr. Alvarez."

"Killing us will only raise more questions. You think the cops won't look for us? They'll track my cellphone to this place," Alvarez says.

"Your cellphone has been destroyed, along with your vehicle." Berj flips through the book, each page brittle and ancient.

An uncomfortable sensation ripples through my body as my anxiety seizes me. I realize that nobody knows where I am, and if I died, nobody would ever find me.

"Don't do this. Don't kill me." I rasp.

Berj's lips curl into a toothy, gold, and disturbing smile.

"Kill you? I don't intend to." His words hang there ominously. "You will watch the detective die."

The men with skull-painted faces seize Alvarez, cut him free from his chair, and drag him up the temple steps. Alvarez tries kicking and punching his way free, but he's tossed onto the altar while someone tightens leather straps around his wrists and ankles.

"You're a bunch of grown men playing dress up," Alvarez shouts. "That's what you all are." He spits blood on the nearest cultist.

"Detective, you can't even begin to understand the powers you are dealing with," Berj warns.

"Can you?" I ask. "Do you know what you're unleashing?" Berj looks at me and smiles.

Attendants cloak Berj in a crimson robe and hooded headdress. The followers gather in front of the temple, while he ascends to the altar. Low chanting and the smell of burning incense fills the room.

But Berj isn't Berj anymore; he's a conduit for something ancient and wicked.

He raises his arms, thrusts his face to the heavens, and speaks to the goddess Spandaramet in an unwavering tone. A masked attendant hands Berj a sleek black dagger, which he points at Alvarez.

More words spoken in a strange tongue.

Chanting.

A foggy haze permeates my vision. The room feels heavy around me, the walls closing in. My heart beats fast and my stomach lurches. A sourness fills my mouth.

Alvarez screams.

I try to turn away, but Gor holds my head and forces my eyes open, making me witness the bloody spectacle.

Berj slowly pushes the dagger into the detective's chest. Alvarez emits a piercing scream unlike anything I've ever heard. Tears stream from his eyes and he keeps screaming as Berj's hands reach into his chest and move around like he's kneading dough. With zealous fervor, the congregation triumphantly raises their hands as Berj holds aloft Alvarez's still beating heart.

He places the heart into a stone vessel and lights it on fire. Flickering flames illuminate Berj's face like some kind of ghoul. Alvarez's isn't moving. His blood runs down the side of the stone slab. The detective's lifeless eyes stare right at me.

In my fear and panic, it's difficult for me to understand what happened, but I know—*I can feel it in my bones*—that it's something horrible and unmistakably evil.

Berj cuts me loose as his whispering cultists drag Alvarez's body from the altar and lift him onto a table at the far end of the room.

"You work for me." Berj says as he removes his headdress, revealing his pitch-black curls. "You see nothing, you say nothing. Maybe I'll cut out your tongue if you talk, maybe your genitals, but I don't want to. Someone with your skills can earn good money if you cooperate."

"Why did you kill him?" I ask through choked sobs.

"Your friend was a worthy sacrifice. Spandaramet needs blood to be able to live in this world. You, however, have better uses and you will help us," he says.

"Help you? I'm nobody. What can I do?"

Berj sets another one of those damn packages on the table near Alvarez's corpse.

"The only thing that you are good at, Armand," Berj orders. "He's already halfway open."

Seconds tick by in surreal silence as Berj waits for my response.

"I don't understand," I say.

"It's simple. Either you prove your loyalty by inserting the package and bundle into the good detective or I will cut out your heart and offer it up as tribute to the goddess. Now that she's been given one person in sacrifice, I'm sure she has a taste for it."

Slicked with sweat, my palms itch and my muscles tense as I look around. I haven't seen her, and I can't even be sure that Berj isn't lying to me, but the chill in my bones says that he's telling the truth.

"You could join him on the slab, my friend."

"What happens if I do this?" I ask.

"I spare you. You get two thousand dollars for your troubles and we let you leave," Berj wipes the detective's blood from his fingers on his robes. "Unlike you, it seems, I am still a man of my word. We made a deal."

"Just like that? No strings attached?"

"Oh, there are always strings."

The idea of being in debt to these monsters makes me shiver.

Berj hands me a knife and I absently take it. The wooden handle is warm and almost comforting. The jagged cut Berj made in the man's naked chest reveals sliced arteries where he removed the heart. I make an incision above and below the cut, looking through half-closed eyes. I reach into Alvarez's chest and remove only what is necessary so that the package will fit. I dump the organs into a plastic container beneath the altar.

I'm a reluctant mutilator.

Berj keenly watches me work through the lens of a small video camera. He pivots around, holding the camera like a gleeful father taking shots of his kids opening their Christmas presents.

I wedge the package and bundle into Alvarez's chest cavity and wipe the blood onto my shirt; woozy, I lean against the table after the task is finished.

"Is that what you wanted?" My stomach lurches and I feel like vomiting.

"Perfect!" Berj snaps the video camera off. "Just in case you get any funny ideas to go to the cops." He smiles pleasantly.

"Why me? Of any funeral home in Fresno, why mine?" I choke back tears.

"I told you, you're special. Like me. And we're Armenian." He says this again, as if it is a valid reason, but then I pick up on it—he *knows*. What was a suspicion before is now certainty in my mind. "Armenians should help out Armenians. I own you now. You do what I say and you'll be a rich man, Mr. Tarkanian. Stray from our path, and retribution will be swift, this I guarantee."

Berj cuts me loose, and then looks at Gor. "Make sure he remembers," he says to the hulking monster. Gor hits me in the stomach, then in the face. He strikes me repeatedly, each blow stings sharper than the one before.

The world fades to a deep, inky blackness and Berj's voice rings clearly in my ears: "Don't worry, Mr. Tarkanian. We'll call you."

CHAPTER 15

LEGION OF THE LAMB

Someone shines a light in my eyes as searing pain rips through my back and shoulders.

Through the haze, I see two scruffy pale guys in leather jackets standing over me.

"Hey, uh, you okay, buddy?" the short, bearded one asks.

"Let's just call an ambulance and get out of here," the wiry one says. A thick '70s pornstache hugs his upper lip. He removes his helmet, revealing a military buzzcut that would make a Marine Corps sergeant weep with pride.

"We ain't leaving him. That's not, uh, our way," the bearded one replies.

"He's just drunk."

"He ain't drunk, someone, uh, kicked him down." The bearded one leans in close and I see flecks of salt and pepper in his beard. Long, greasy hair cascades down his forehead. A crude necklace of fangs and animal teeth dangles over his shirt. "Pay no mind to Reece, mister. He's an asshole, but he, uh, means well in his own way." Rough hands help me up. "You're coming with us."

"Like hell he is. What are we going to do, Muskrat? Bring him back to the clubhouse?"

"Uh, exactly." Muskrat has me in a seated position now, my bearings are starting to make sense, but it's dark, and I'm in the middle of nowhere. "We care for those in need, and I think this guy has got a story to tell us once he, you know, gets all sorted out. Besides, Wanda'd be *pissed* if we, uh, let this guy die."

"Hank won't like it. Strangers are forbidden in the clubhouse, Muskrat." Reece warns.

Muskrat scratches his beard. "I'm not leaving him to, uh, die out here. Come on. Grab his legs. We'll put him in my sidecar."

I feel weightless as the two strangers carry me to an old motorcycle with a sidecar. They fold my legs and jam me in like they're storing an accordion. Muskrat fastens a helmet on my head and props me up in the seat.

"Relax, pal. We'll get you someplace, uh, safe," Muskrat says, all good-natured and kind. He slips on a brain bucket helmet and straddles his motorcycle. The hog roars to life, a thunderous hell-belch of industrialized fury—a gravelly, spluttering growl. Reece climbs onto his own motorcycle, and soon we're racing down the street. I bounce in the sidecar and feel myself drifting in and out of consciousness. Racing past the streetlights is hypnotic and my head slumps down. When I look up at Muskrat, my vision is so hazy that I can barely make out a skull on his helmet. Who are these guys? Will they kill me? I don't think so, but I don't know for sure, and I'm not even sure if I care.

I lean back and shut my eyes.

I wake up flat on my back on a pool table in a dimly-lit bar. The lights above me are turned off. There is a pleasant glow and electric hum coming from a Budweiser sign on a nearby brick wall.

I try sitting up, wince in pain, and collapse again.

"See? He's okay!" Muskrat says. He places a big hand on my shoulder. "You all right, uh, buddy?"

"We don't know who he is or why he was out there." I can hear Reece nearby.

"I know who he is," Muskrat says. "He's Armand Tarkanian, and he lives on Ventura Avenue."

A new voice joins the conversation, "Does he have a concussion?" The rich voice belongs to a bald man with deep umber skin, broad shoulders, and a horseshoe mustache. "If he does and he doesn't get to a hospital, he's fucked."

"My cousin had a concussion and he didn't get treated in time." The voice belongs to a woman. "He can't drive a car and doesn't know what Wednesdays are." I turn my head and a young woman with spiked hair folds her heavily-tattooed arms. Could this be Wanda?

"How's letting him crash on our pool table helping him?" the bald man asks. "I thought it was billiards night."

"Uh, shut up, Big Earl," Muskrat barks.

Spiky-hair takes a long drag on her cigarette. "You know Hank won't approve of this."

"I know that, Josie. But Wanda said to make sure he's okay and if he dies then he's, uh, not okay."

"Where am I?" I ask.

"He speaks!" Muskrat cries. The others in the room stop talking. Maybe they're suspicious of strangers, or maybe they just don't want to talk to the random guy who got his ass kicked by a cult.

Reece leans over me. "Buddy, what were you doing on the street?"

I rub my head. It feels like Gor is still punching it. "I was beaten up. Several men. Bad men."

"Who beat you up?" Reece asked.

"I...I don't know," I reply. "Can't remember."

"That's okay. You're safe now," Muskrat says.

My memories, fuzzy as they are, slowly come into focus.

"There was this one man. A leader. He…he murdered someone," I tell them slowly.

"Murdered? Who was murdered?" Reece leans over me, his eyes locking with mine.

I rub my forehead. The pain is gradually subsiding.

"He was…what do you call the Humphrey Bogart movie guys with the guns and raincoats?" I ask.

"Private eyes?" Big Earl offers.

Another puzzle piece slips back into place. I remember Alvarez.

"Yes! A private eye…a detective…was murdered. Murdered by a crazy cult. Then I think I got thrown out of a van. It might have been moving still, I'm not sure. Where am I?"

"That so?" The more reluctant of my two saviors sounds skeptical.

"In our clubhouse," Muskrat skips over Reece's interrogation to answer my question. "Want something to, uh, eat? Wanda has some chili from last night."

"He doesn't want food, idiot. He needs medical attention," Reece tells Muskrat.

"Uh, no, Reece. He needs sustenance. Wanda's, uh, chili hits the spot."

"No thanks." I try to haul myself to a sitting position and then off the pool table.

"Where are you goin'?" Big Earl asks. "You're in no shape to go anywhere."

"Seriously, dude. Stay put." Josie clamps the cigarette between her teeth and points at me. "Eat some of the damned chili. Muskrat."

"Sure thing, Josie." Muskrat hums a little tune as he disappears into what I imagine is a kitchen.

The place is a biker bar, with shelves of liquor, beer taps, and tufted leather stools. A jukebox lights up from time to time and a Medieval Madness pinball machine sits next to a Ms. Pac-Man arcade cabinet. Everyone in the room except me is wearing a black leather jacket.

I feel like this is the place you go to when you're looking for trouble—you come here to throw punches and wrestle on the sawdust-covered floor. Maybe you chuck a beer bottle at someone's head. It's a bar full of possibilities.

Framed photographs decorate one wall, but I can't see who's in them. In big white letters, just under the pictures, is painted: "Pugnare Malum, Salvificem Mundum." I stare at it for a moment, trying to figure out what it means, but don't get far.

"It means, 'Fight Evil, Save the World,'" a gravelly voice says behind me. An older man with grey hair and a wild beard approaches us. He's your typical biker grandpa. Barrel-chested, tattooed arms, clear blue eyes. He wheezes and hobbles over, his gait uneven.

"Who are you people?" I ask.

"Well, I'm Hank, and we are the Legion of the Lamb," biker grandpa says.

"I never heard of you."

"You on the up and up of secret orders?" Hank walks over and gets a closer look at me. "We were keeping an eye on you, but I don't think that making you aware of our presence was in the cards."

Of course. The bikers. It clicks. Alvarez was right; I was being followed.

"What happened to you, friend? You look like shit." Hank teeters a bit.

"I don't even know anymore—something about an Armenian death cult, I'm being blackmailed, people are turning into zombies, and now I'm hanging out with a biker gang." I survey the room. Not one of them is looking at me like I'm crazy. "And nobody here is surprised by any of this?"

"Do you want salt and pepper?" Muskrat sticks his head out of the kitchen door, breaking the awkwardness with more awkwardness. "Salt? Uh, pepper?" He holds up little glass jars and shakes them from side to side. "Yes?"

"Sure" The tension in my answer just evaporated. "Yeah, sorry," I mumble. "What was I saying?"

"Armenian death cult." Hank gestures for me to continue.

"Sorry, yes. They called themselves the Children of Spandaramet."

"That so?" Hank raises an eyebrow.

"Glass of, uh, water?" Muskrat shouts from the kitchen.

"Can I get a beer?" I ask. It's been that kind of day.

"M'ok!" I hear Muskrat open a fridge.

There's a sort of strange silence that hangs in the air for a moment, the assembled group seems to be rolling their eyes in unison. Hank chuckles.

"Muskrat is a good man, but not always the sharpest." Hank explains in a hushed voice. Muskrat returns holding a tray with a large bowl of chili, a spoon, the salt and pepper shakers, and a Budweiser. He puts them down at a table near me and smiles. "Enjoy!"

"Thanks." I limp over to the table and sit down. "It looks really good."

"You're damned right it does," says a voice from the kitchen.

A woman with short grey hair and pale skin inked with tattoos approaches. Her eyes light up when she gets closer to me.

"You must be Armand," she says. "I'm Wanda."

I look at her, dumbfounded. "How do you know my name?"

"I can sense things about people. It's my thing—a certain degree of clairvoyance. I can detect those who are touched and uncover information from beyond the Vale." She reaches into her back pocket and pulls out my wallet, offering it. "Also, it's on your driver's license, and we've been following you for a while."

I take my wallet, open it, and then put it on the table and eat some of the chili. I don't remember the last time I ate, it feels like a lifetime ago. "What do you mean by *touched*?"

"You got some weird power in that noggin of yours, young man," Wanda says. "You know what I mean, don't you?" She sits down across from me.

I nod.

"I can see dead people, and they are all about showing me how they died, apparently. This ability is new. It came to me recently. " I sip my beer.

"Well, shit my britches, you're a latent! That's very rare." She's fascinated.

"Dang it, Wanda. He's already confused and scared," Hank tells her.

He's not wrong.

"What's a latent? Why are they rare?" I ask.

"As you might have guessed," Hank starts, "people with gifts, or curses, depends on who you ask,"—Wanda looks at me and mouths "gift" Hank continues—"well, they're one in a million. They range from mild ESP and guessing what card you're holding behind your back, to full blown talking with the dead and moving shit with their minds."

"Ah," I say. I'm not sure I'm processing everything, but at least it makes sense.

"Wanda here is also touched, but she can't throw things across the room with her mind or anything." Hank says. "You've got quite a unique ability, shit like that could have and may have won wars and brought down empires in times past. Nowadays, maybe not, but there is never a shortage of people who want information from the dead. That's why hacks and fakers have a whole racket, tricking poor unsuspecting folks out of their cash."

Madame Opal, I think.

"This explains that death cult's interest in him," Reece says. His voice sounds like he's begrudgingly accepting that Muskrat was right, but he strikes me as the kind of guy who isn't big on admitting he's wrong.

"That's my bad," I admit. "I rear ended the leader's car, and he's sort of been blackmailing me about it since."

Reece, Josie, and Big Earl all laugh, and Muskrat looks at them for a moment before also chuckling a bit. Hank and Wanda aren't laughing though.

"You think that it's a coincidence that you, an embalmer with literal supernatural abilities, just *happened* to rear end a guy that turns out needed access to a funeral home so that he could get his hand on corpses? You're not *that* naïve, are you son?" Hank asks me.

"Well, when you put it like that..." I start to say before Wanda interrupts.

"Hush! You knuckle-heads have shit to do, don't you?" Wanda looks at the other members of the Legion of the Lamb who all salute in varied ways and scatter. "Look, my latent friend," Wanda says to me, "I'm sorry, but that's what you would call getting swindled. I hope you at least got something of use."

"A few thousand dollars," I tell her.

"Better than getting punched in the face."

"I got that too."

"I'll go get you some ice and start on breakfast. I make mean flapjacks, and I'm sure you can put a bit more food in you."

"Breakfast?" I check my watch and see that it's almost seven in the morning. "Shit, my family is worried about me. I gotta go." I start to stand up. Pain shoots up my back and down my arms. Hank puts an old gnarled hand on my shoulder and gently pushes me back down.

"Not yet," Hank says. "I'm going to level with you, son. You're a guest for now, but I want a bit more information from you before I'm sure it's safe to let you go."

"Wait. Are you going to torture me?" I ask.

"What? No." Hank gives me a weird look. "Why would I torture you? We just saved your life and gave you beer. Skittish much?"

"Sorry. It's been a weird week."

"The Legion of the Lamb doesn't sound like the kind of group that tortures people, does it?"

I mull it over. "No, I guess not. It is the weirdest name for a biker gang I've ever heard though," I admit.

"We're not a biker gang," Hank says. "Not how you're probably thinking. We're not one percenters."

"One percent what?"

"One percent of motorcycle clubs are outlaw biker gangs, which we are not."

"Then what are you?"

"The Legion is a brotherhood tasked with eliminating other-worldly entities and paranormal threats. We shield the innocent from dark forces that threaten humanity. Things the average Joe isn't meant to know. True malevolence from beyond this mortal plane. That sort of shit, you know?" Hank leans against the pool table. "People like Reece and Josie sort of came into this life, and it took them a bit of adjusting, but I got the feeling that you know what I'm talking about."

"Oh, I know." Flashbacks from Berj Manoogian's secret temple return.

"I'm gonna tell you something, Armand, that I think you need to hear."

"What's that?"

"I believe you. I believe that you see some wacky shit that you can't explain. I believe that you had your ass kicked by a cult of weir-dos, and I believe that there is more to that story." I close my eyes, realizing that he was right—I needed to hear that. "So, in exchange for the services rendered, what with not leaving you to die on the side of the road, you're going to sit your ass down in a chair, you're going to eat some flapjacks, you're going to tell my wife that she's a delightful cook, and you're going to share a bit of information. Sound good?"

I grin. "Yes, sir."

After eating, Hank slips me a card with that weird Latin motto and a phone number. "It's not a coincidence that we were following you. We know there's strange goings on around Fresno—people talk—and we figured that anyone on the diabolically evil side of things might want to go after someone like you." I pick up Hank's card and he continues, "Malevolent forces tend to go after people like you and lure them into the fold. Blackmail, bribery, all that jazz, until they have themselves a handy slave that can fucking raise the dead or pry secrets from the recently deceased."

"How long were you following me?" I ask.

"Wanda sensed trouble a month ago. An imbalance between worlds leaning towards you," Hank replies.

"Look, I've had a long night and just want to go home. I'm appreciative, I am, but do you mind if I go?" I ask.

"Sure, but if you're ever need our help, you know where we are." Hank says.

I thank everyone and get up to leave. As I leave the clubhouse, I see that dog. That fucking dog—I swear it's tormenting me. The animal barks when it sees me, sits, and extends one of its paws.

"Get out of here!" I shout at it. I'm not in the mood for the animal's antics.

The dog cocks its head to one side and barks again before sprinting away.

"Not an animal lover, eh?" Wanda chuckles; she insists on seeing me out.

"Not *that* animal," I say. "Is it yours?"

"I've never seen that critter in my life," she replies. "You're always welcome here, Armand. It's a crazy world, and if you ever want a bit of help unpacking that gift of yours, you know where I am."

"Thanks, Wanda, I appreciate it."

Exhausted, in pain, and full of pancakes, I walk home. It's a hike of several miles, but I'm glad to get out into the sunshine and fresh air.

Uncle George and Aunt Miriam come rushing to the front door when they hear me come in. Uncle George is about to admonish me, but after seeing what I look like, he stops. I'm sure that there will be a time for the guilt and the drama, but this is one of those moments where I thankfully get a reprieve. Aunt Miriam covers my face with kisses while I wince. Uncle George demands to know where I parked the first call vehicle. I tell him it's at Donut King. He tosses his spare keys to Samantha and tells her to fetch it.

"What happened? We were so worried about you, weren't we, George?" Aunt Miriam's embrace almost fractures my spine.

"You should have called us," Uncle George carps.

"What happened to you? Good God! Were you in an accident?" Aunt Miriam asks.

"I got jumped by some jerks," I reply. This is not a lie. "I'm fine, though, nothing is broken. Some good Samaritans found me, and took care of me."

"Found you? Were you in some sort of trouble?" Uncle George pries.

"I woke up on the side of the road, they must have hit me hard," I say. Flashes of Alvarez strapped to the ceremonial slab haunt me. "I don't remember what happened."

Uncle George, in a moment of extremely rare understanding, tells me to go upstairs and get some rest. My brain isn't working well, it's hard to think, so all I can do is agree with him and make my way up the stairs. My aunt and uncle are planning on speculating about this for hours. I get to the top of the stairs and go into my room.

I barely recognize myself in the mirror.

The corner of my left eye to about my jawline is swollen and purple. I have some cuts and bruising, and when I slip off my shirt I realize why breathing is such a pain in the ass. Several parts of my chest and ribs have the gross purple bruises. I toss my shirt into the wash, slip out of my pants, and go to the bathroom to take a shower.

When I get out, brush my teeth, and put on some clothes, I head back to my room. Samantha is sitting on my bed.

"Jesus, Samantha," I say, startled.

"Sorry!" she chirps. "Who did you piss off? You look horrible." She frowns and I see that my duffle was on the bed behind where she was sitting. "I just wanted to make sure you were okay, I found this in the car and figured it was yours."

"Did you open it?"

"What, and look at your dirty gym clothes? Ew," she says with a snort. Samantha walks past me to the door and then stops, holding the door knob in her hand. "I'm glad that you're okay Armand. I was worried about you." From her, I believe it. She closes the door behind her.

I open the bag to make sure that everything is still there, and then carefully stow it under my bed.

I need sleep more than anything else in the world right now.

CHAPTER 16

FUN WITH SPIRITS

Balancing the Dutch Bros Coffee in my arms, I open the door to Roupen's bookshop without spilling a single drop. The usual clientele fills the place—aging academics and students browsing for cheap textbooks.

Roupen is behind the counter, immersed in a novel, mouth sucking in air as he reads.

I set the coffee in front of him. He doesn't look up.

"What do you want, Armand?" Roupen asks.

"I thought we might talk." I push one of the coffee cups towards him.

Roupen continues reading. "This a peace offering? Get me some Dutch Bros and all is forgiven?"

"Something like that, yeah."

I realize that Roupen is looking at the book, but isn't reading it. "Armand, because of you, I'm aware of some pretty horrible things I didn't realize existed. I was happy in my blissful ignorance," he says.

"I know why you …" He looks up at me. "Jesus Christ, Armand, are you okay?"

"Let's say I'm regretting a series of life choices."

"Me too," Roupen frowns but immediately softens. "Your new friends?"

"Yeah."

My brother stares at his coffee and then finally pulls the lid off the cup and takes a sip. "Ooh, you sprung for the good stuff. Is your handsome detective friend okay?"

I look around to make sure no one is within earshot. "He's dead," I tell Roupen. "Murdered." I exhale. Thoughts of Alvarez's final moments play in my head—the blood, the screams, the helplessness—as vivid as when it happened.

Roupen covers his mouth. "Oh, my God. Was it a zombie?" He whispers this leaning forward.

"No, not from the undead. Someone else. I watched the whole thing go down."

"That's awful. Who was it?"

Deep in my mind, I hear distant drums thrumming. Alvarez on the stone slab. Frenetic worshippers. A pungent smell. Dancing flames. Wild rites from history's darkest corners. A Dagger. Blood. Silence.

"There's nothing you can do except forgive me," I say.

"Armand, what's wrong?" Roupen's eyes are wide.

"I didn't know that a dead guy was going to come to life—what you saw in the cemetery was only a glimpse of what I know. It's a cult that kills."

"I'm calling the cops." He whips his cellphone out. "You're filing a report."

I snatch his phone from him and put it down on the counter. "He owns them. These people have video of me with Alvarez's body. They'll frame me if this gets out."

Roupen raises his eyebrows. "Did *you* kill him?"

"No! But they made me put something in his body after they killed him. I guess the blackmail is to make sure I keep my mouth shut."

"What the fuck, Armand?" This is less question and more statement of disbelief on my brother's part.

"I know it looks bad."

"Looks bad? This *is* bad. My brother is being blackmailed to work for murdering cultists who reanimate the dead. Does it get worse?"

We sit there in silence for a bit. Roupen quietly sips his drink.

"Remember grandpa?" I ask Roupen.

My brother takes a deep breath. "Yeah. Good old Grandpa Garabed. May he rot in peace."

"Remember how he talked about the Armenian community back then? The church? The family? He seemed so comfortable with everything. Always reminiscing about how people knew their place. How Armenians interacted. The intimacy of tradition."

Roupen smirks. "I never cared much for those tales."

"He was afraid of change. Didn't like how Armenians left Fresno."

"What'd you expect? Garabed perpetually lived in the 1940s."

"Maybe that's how we all live. In denial."

When Grandpa Garabed died, a shadow lifted. We were spared his excoriation of youth culture and his bellicose pronouncements— Roupen and I had rejoiced privately.

"You think if he were still alive, we'd both be back on the farm? That I wouldn't be working for Uncle George?" I ask.

"I don't think anyone or anything would've kept us tethered to that place," Roupen tells me.

"Mom. She'd keep us there." Roupen looks into his drink as if the answer to that particular sadness lay somewhere in his extra double shot vanilla mocha coffee. "Embalming is even worse," I say, changing the subject. "Nothing suckier than dead people."

"Dead people who come back to life. That is objectively shittier than regular dead people," Roupen corrects me. "It's more exciting than watching an old family farm die, though, I suppose. At least you're seeing ghosts and chasing zombies."

I chuckle at that. I have to.

"Grandpa was a selfish prick who made our lives hell. I don't think that Dad and Uncle George are any different. It's all about appearances with them. Traditions. Reputations. And the more time that goes by, the more I realize that they're chains holding me down. Escaping this family is all I really wanted, but I was too scared to do it. I want to explore the world. Find myself. I've always been proud of you for being so strong, way stronger than I've ever been able to be." I say.

Roupen smiles at me, "You're being very Jack Kerouac right now. I dig it."

"I really want to get out. I feel like I need to leave. There's so much dark shit that's going down, but at the same time I have to protect the people that matter to me."

"Classic fight or flight, brother." Roupen hoists his coffee cup. "I'm sure you'll do the right thing and make Grandpa Garabed proud."

I almost snort coffee out my nose and Roupen gets a good laugh in. A young woman comes up to the counter and pays for a couple of books, before leaving. Me and my brother stop talking until she leaves.

"Want my advice, Armand?"

"Do I have a choice?"

"Embalmers aren't supposed to talk to ghosts. That isn't normal. Maybe it's for a reason?"

"You know my thoughts on fate. Not a fan."

"I know, but why not just help these spirits? You clearly weren't put on Earth to be some pathetic scrub working for our shitty uncle until our moronic cousin takes over the business."

"But it's my job."

"And that's why you've never been able to take steps for yourself." Roupen rolls his eyes. "It sounds like you're letting the Agra

Hadig do the talking, Armand. You're not some Armenian teething baby ritual. Be your own man."

My brother always has a unique way of seeing what other people don't. All our lives he's been the insightful one, and I needed his perspective more than ever. I finish my coffee, thank Roupen, and head back to the funeral home to see if fate blessed me with another fresh cadaver.

Usually there's one decedent in storage, ready for embalming. But our freezer is woefully empty, and nobody dying in Fresno puts pressure on me.

Berj wants the package planted, and without a fresh corpse, I can't deliver.

I stretch out on my bed and think about how one day I'd be lying on a slab, a lifeless hunk of decaying me. Another embalmer would work on me, draining my blood into a sink, pumping me full of embalming fluid and then they'd wash me and prepare me for my family to look at me and talk about how I never accomplished anything.

I grab *Madame Opal's Guide to Seances and Psychics* from where it sits on my nightstand. Madame Opal grins at me from the front cover. I crack open the old book and start flipping through pages. After a while, one passage catches my eye:

Communicating with souls from beyond is rare. Channeling—the act of acting as a conduit for spiritual possession—is a worldwide phenomenon. Mediums such as myself set themselves up as a willing vessel, and we welcome the spirit inside our souls. While this has its drawbacks – like having an actual ghost use your body – channeling gives spirits a way they can pull themselves back into this world for a little bit. But how does one contact the dead in the first place? Throughout the centuries, psychics, clairvoyants, and mediums—the shamans, seers, and magicians of old—communicated with the spirit realm by willful transference into the astral plane. This is the rarest gift. The seer concentrates and sends out a psychic message into the universe. The spirits then come to them, much like calling someone long distance, but without a telephone. If you practice hard enough, maybe the spirits will hear your message. Maybe you can summon the ghost of a long-dead relative by using your mind. But be careful. Some spirits can't take the hint and want to stay longer. They might try to channel with you. Set your boundaries and let your intentions be known up front. Once you're finished communicating, the spirit will leave.

I shut the book and put it on my nightstand; the writing is horrible. Madame Opal was gimmicky and cheesy back in the day, but people bought her books by the millions.

I close my eyes and clear my mind. I think about Madame Opal, who died years ago, and am forced to wonder if she was like me? Could she have been? Is that why she was so good at convincing people? I sit up on the bed, cross my legs, and focus. At first, there is nothing but my own mind but then I hear something at the back of my brain and feel a chill run down my spine.

"For what purpose do you channel my immortal essence?" Madame Opal asks in a thick Eastern European accent. It was different from Maddie, Waterhouse, and Stuart; it was more like a conversation you would have with yourself. But it felt like I was trying to grasp a fish in a pool of water. I open my eyes and sigh, trying to remember the feeling of what it was like when the ghosts had showed up to visit me. I put myself in that time and place—and I feel something else.

My father's disappointment. My grandfather, old and hateful of everything I grew up wanting to be. My mother's support. My aunt's affection. Emotions swirl around my heart and the chill deepens.

"Well?" The old psychic is staring at me from the edge of my bed.

"Madame Opal?"

"In life I was called that. In death, I am but a traveler in the ghostly realms."

"Knock off the drama, Opal. You were a celebrity mystic from Akron, Ohio. How are you here?"

Madame Opal drops the Eastern European accent, which changes to a mish-mash of Midwestern and tough-as-nails Western Pennsylvanian.

"*You channeled me,*" she says.

"But, I don't have your body, or anything." I say.

"*You don't need it, kiddo. A medium's ability is from their emotions and their soul. That's what calls out, it's not like a telephone book.*" She looks at the copy of her book and runs her ghostly fingers over the cover. "*You've had this for a while, and your bond to the book is strong,*" Opal looks back at me. "*It's not science, and if there are rules, I don't know them. A lot of it happens because it needs to happen, I guess. But a lot of it was related to emotions for me—you feel your way through it. Don't think about it.*" She shrugs. "*I don't remember how I did half the stuff I did.*"

"So, you *were* a medium?"

"*A decent one,*" she says. "*Others were better, but some of us didn't really go very deep into the practice. There were orders, and clubs, and all sorts of people who were into this sort of thing, and to be honest, I just wanted a paycheck and to make some people happy where I could. A book deal or eight didn't hurt.*" She laughs, but it sounds different from the Eastern European laugh I remembered from TV when I was younger.

"I need to know why I developed this ability. Why now? Why didn't I see ghosts when I was a kid?" I ask. "All my life I couldn't summon anything. The dead were dead. Then I start seeing and hearing spirits. How is this possible?"

"*Kiddo, you don't seek this gift. The gift seeks you. Maybe there was a recent trauma in your life that triggered it? How should I know? Like you said, I was a celebrity mystic from Akron.*"

"But, I don't want this responsibility!" I protest.

"*Tough,*" Madame Opal says. "*You're stuck with it.*"

"Do you know where it comes from?"

"*Sorry, I don't. Some have said that it is a curse, some say that we're touched by God, some people think that it's passed on from parent to child, could be anything. None of the reasons why, though, change the reality of what it is.*"

"And what's that?" I ask.

"*You're far from normal. And you don't have a say in the matter. Once bestowed, the gift cannot be removed. This is your life, kiddo, so you can either*

141

pretend that life isn't happening, or you can live the best life you can."

I cringe. Another person who doesn't know me already can tell that I'm letting life pass me by. Is it stamped on my face? "Some really awful people hired me for unspeakable things. If I don't do what they want, they'll kill me. Spirits keep showing up asking for help. What do I do?"

"You help them. Obvious, right? Help them rest in peace. You've got a rare gift. Don't throw it away because you're scared."

"When you've seen what I have, you got nothing but fear." She laughs. "What's so funny?" I ask.

"You're a funny kid," she says. *"Here you are talking about what to do about a magic gift that you've been given, and all you can do is whine about it. You sound like a child, so maybe you should start acting your age and do something other than blaming everyone for the hand you've been dealt."* She floated around my room and looked out the window down onto the street. *"You know what everyone always wants to do when they think that you're a medium?"*

"What's that?"

"They always want to talk to their loved ones," she says. *"Makes sense, right?"* She comes back over to the bed. *"But all they want to do is talk to people they talked to their whole life. There is no growth in that, that's why they bought eight books that basically said the same things in different ways. Kiddo, you better start figuring out how to break this mold that you're trapped in, otherwise you're going to just die, sad and pathetic, dwelling on the past."*

The past.

I look up at her. "Thanks," I say.

Maybe Opal wasn't as terrible a mystic as I thought.

CHAPTER 17

STRIPPING AND OTHER DANGEROUS OCCUPATIONS

A stench of cigarettes, alcohol, and sweat permeates the Neon Oasis. Rihanna's "Push Up On Me" blares from a shitty sound system, and cigarette smoke makes it hard to see the stage.

After I get myself an eighty-five-dollar drink, a quiet homage to Stuart, but also a solid "why the fuck not?", I walk over to the strip club's stage and sit down in the front row. A young frat guy repeats, "More titties!" in a sort of drunken chant.

As if summoned by this drunken idiot, three strippers appear on stage, strutting on high-heels. Vonnie is among them, clad in her pink cowgirl outfit. My heart practically bursts when she walks in front of me, squats down, and shakes her body rhythmically.

"Of all the gin joints in all the world, I had to walk into yours," I shout over the music.

She looks at me, does a double-take, and grins. "I'll catch you after the dance," she says with a wink.

When Vonnie finishes, she comes out to the floor and sits down next to me, still in her Stetson.

"You look like shit." Vonnie's hair spills over her face as she leans in for a better look.

"Thanks. I got beaten up."

Vonnie scans my face and her mouth falls open when she realizes I'm not joking. "Holy fuck, you okay?"

"No. I'm a complete wreck. Can I buy you a drink?"

"I'm working for a bit."

"After work then."

"I don't know. You did take a few days to follow up on our reasonably decent date."

"You think so? That's good to know, there's been a bit of a drought of good news lately."

"You're some pain in my ass, Armand," she says, giving me a hard pat on the cheek. I wince from the bruise and she blows me a kiss. "I've missed you. Stop by my place in about three hours."

"Sounds good." I get up and make my way to the door.

Three hours isn't really much time for anything, *maybe enough time to grab a cup of coffee and a donut*, I tell myself. I get into Samantha's Civic, which she kindly let me borrow (I told her that I was going to see a girl and she practically pushed me out the door), and drive over to a Donut King up the street.

I order a coffee and a Bavarian cream donut, and then I sit down at the back of the shop. It's not the same Donut King that I met Berj and Gor at; the layout is different, and the coffee tastes better here. Even the donut tastes slightly better—just a little though, I'm not about to start touting the joint as a wonder.

I sit in the coffee shop looking out the window, feeling my heart leap into my throat every time the bell on the front door rings from someone opening it. People come in, people leave—some stay, some go. I realize that it's a lot like life, this little donut shop that I sit in, the only way that anything good happens to you is if you get up, take a few steps, and make the order. Otherwise, you sit there under uncomfortable fluorescent lights near the open sign on the windows

144

until someone says that you need to leave. Better to leave on your own terms, I think.

Inside the Airstream, Vonnie removes her earrings and puts them on the credenza. She doffs her high heels and fringy pink vest. I try not to stare when Vonnie straightens her pink hot pants and bikini top.

"Beer?" She opens the fridge and pulls out a couple of bottles.

"Anything that'll make me forget the last 48 hours," I say. She opens one of the beers and offers it to me. I give her a bag with two donuts that she tosses on the counter. Vonnie's not in the mood for donuts.

"So? Out with it," she presses.

"Out with what?"

"Why are you stalking me at work? Don't you know that we have bouncers around here who enjoy kicking stalker asses?"

I chuckle and wince, holding my side. "Thanks. I needed a good laugh."

"What happened?" she asks.

My mood darkens a bit. "Vonnie," I start, unsure of what to say. "I really like you, I do."

Her face hardens. "But?"

"I need to be honest with you, the last 48 hours have been insane, and I'm really worried that you're going to get pulled into whatever shit show is happening right now."

"Look, Armand, I told you before, I don't need a white knight here. I can take care of myself. I'm a big girl," she says as she leans back in her chair. An uncomfortable silence hangs between us. Time ticks by, and I need to be the one who talks.

"Alvarez is dead." I say.

"Alvarez? That detective? Jesus."

"Murdered. Same guy that killed Maddie and Stuart. The guy moonlights as a cult leader. They're called the Children of Spanda-ramet."

"Spanda-what now?"

"Doesn't matter really, but they've got video of me with the body, and they said that if I go to the cops, I can expect to be in jail. Or dead. I'm not sure, they're sort of unclear about the specifics of their threats." I gulp my beer quickly. "Things are insane, Vonnie, I watched Alvarez get murdered. I got blackmailed, then got my ass kicked, then rescued by a gang of bikers who told me that they were on the side of good and wanted to stop this guy, then I summoned the spirit of a 1970s TV psychic …"

I slow down and realize that I must sound like I've lost my mind. Rather than looking skeptical, Vonnie waits for me to continue.

"And?" she asks.

"Well, then … I came here."

"Well that fell flat."

"I guess it did."

Vonnie takes a drink. "I don't think I can help. I'm a nobody, Armand."

"You're not a nobody. You're awesome, Vonnie." I fall silent for a moment, staring at my beer.

"Armand?"

"Yeah?"

"You got quiet."

"Sorry, I'm just thinking. I feel like I'm trapped in a no-win sce-nario, like every option is bad." I lean forward, and roll my shoulders back to try and knock out some of the stress. "But, I don't accept this, not anymore." I feel a wave of confidence followed me to Vonnie's place. "These guys have cops paid off, they're everywhere, they said that they summoned some kind of spirit and that it was hungry. I can't run anymore, they'll just find me and kill me anyways. Or my family. Or you. And then make me suffer. I have to stop them." I say, feeling some strength in my chest.

146

"Armand?"

"Yeah, Vonnie?"

"That was kinda hot," she says with a wink.

She doesn't say it, but also doesn't need to—Vonnie is in my corner, there's some strange bond that I feel between us, a comfortable flame that burns brightly. We both have our own traumas, and we both know that life will eat you alive if you let it.

"Thanks." I get up. "I should go. Need to return Samantha's car back to her."

"Let me see you out." Vonnie says with a laugh as she walks over to the door of the Airstream and opens it.

Berj, with that hulking bodyguard of his in tow approaches us in the parking lot. He's smug in his stride and wearing a shit-eating grin.

My heart beats fast and sweat slicks my palms. "What are you doing here?" I ask him.

"I'm taking over for Stewart," he replies.

"You're going to micromanage a strip club?" I ask.

"I own it, why wouldn't I?" Berj says.

Vonnie looks over at Berj and then at me.

"Strippers should never go home with a customer." He admonishes Vonnie like a parent catching his daughter after curfew. "For all you know, this guy could be a freak. You're not a freak, are you, Armand? Haven't done anything illegal recently I hope?"

"He's not a customer. He's my boyfriend," Vonnie replies.

Berj raises his eyebrows. "What? You and her? Not bad, Armand." He looks at Vonnie. "You're hot."

Vonnie smirks. "Thanks, but my name is actually Vonnie." If the situation weren't so serious I would have snorted with laughter.

Berj sneers and flashes his gold teeth. "I know who you are. You're a funny girl, Vonnie. Don't forget who signs your checks, though."

"You don't sign my checks. I work for tips. I pay you for the privilege of stripping," Vonnie says.

147

I mouth "Really?" at her.

She replies, "Yeah. It's a fucked up system."

Berj ignores her. Turning to me, his smile fades. "I thought I'd pop out and remind you that you should be back at the funeral home working."

"How did you know I was here?" I asked.

"Are you kidding? This place has security cameras everywhere. It's not how you say, rocket science. Anyways, go embalm someone."

"No cadavers came in." Alvarez comes to mind, and I say pointedly, "I only embalm people. I don't kill them."

"Is that right?" Berj asks. Then he shrugs, as if he's letting the matter go. "That'll change."

"You're on all weekend," he tells Vonnie.

She's is about to protest and Berj smiles. He gives her an *it-is-what-it-is* shrug and then walks away. Gor stands there for a moment longer before turning around and following his boss.

Vonnie and I stand next to the Airstream in silence as we watch the two men disappear into the club. She turns, heads into the trailer, and comes out a moment later with two fresh beers. She pops the caps off them and hands me one. Then we drink.

"Someone needs to knock out his fucking teeth." Vonnie's harsh words fill my ears like a sweet symphony. "Why agree to work for that? I mean, I didn't know he owned the club, I just work here. But you? You signed on the dotted line with that motherfucker knowing what he is."

"That's not what happened." I confess everything, about the packages Berj gives me, about stuffing them in the corpses I embalm, and how the cult owns me. "I needed the money, and I was too scared to own up to the car accident. I'm not particularly proud of it."

For the first time in a long time I've been able to tell someone all the details without them judging me. It's almost nine in the morning now though, I'm sure that Samantha is going to have some choice words for me later.

148

"You did something you're not proud of. I can relate. Besides, that creepy motherfucker knows we're together. So, if he wants to hurt you, he's coming for me. Shit, I kind of liked this job." She sighs. "Up until the people started dying and the insane cult leader for a boss part."

"We're together?" I ask, fixated.

"Focus, Romeo." Vonnie leans over and pats my cheek. "We need a plan."

"I say we let things run their course. Someone dies, I stuff them with the package, the cult is happy and leaves us alone."

"That's your plan? No plan? What happened to hot assertive guy?"

"If I don't deliver what they want, I'm as good as dead. Assertive guy doesn't want to be shot and dumped in a garbage bin."

With no new bodies for Berj, I'm stuck in limbo. The Children of Spandaramet need their fresh corpses, and I need to deliver.

"Well, so far he seems to be okay with you and me doing our thing. He apparently needs you for something," Vonnie says.

"Hank thinks that Berj knows I have some kind of gift and is just trying to suck me in deeper before revealing what it is," I tell her.

"Hank?"

"One of those Legion of the Lamb biker guys."

"Oh. This would be the biker gang that saved your ass?"

"Yeah. They battle evil, or so Hank told me."

Vonnie inhales.

"So, then we do your dumb plan for now until we come up with a better one?" She clearly doesn't like my plan at all. I think it's as good a plan as any for the moment. "Why don't you call those sheep bikers?"

I reach into my back pocket and pull out my wallet, fishing out the card that Hank gave me. I flip it over and then take out my phone. "You think that's a good idea?" I ask Vonnie.

"Armenian murder cult, man, that's your literal alternative," she says, rolling her eyes.

"Point taken," I say.

Before I could dial Hank, my phone vibrates. It's a text message from Samantha. I don't bother to read it, she must be pissed.

"Damn it, Vonnie, I gotta get my cousin's car back to her, can I call you later?"

Vonnie is opening up another beer. "Sure thing."

I get up and walk over to her, leaning in and giving her a kiss on the cheek. "Thanks, you're one in a million," I say.

"Don't you forget it," she says with a smile.

I arrive home about twenty minutes later, and find Samantha sitting on the porch. She sniffs and rubs her red eyes, removing some mascara in the process.

"Samantha, I'm really sorry, I just got tied up and …"

"Armand." She stands up, descends the steps, and wraps her arms around me. Her voice shakes. "I'm so sorry. Your dad died."

CHAPTER 18

FATHER AND SON

My father Hagop Tarkanian died alone in his living room. This man, who was a raging titan against the desires of his children, who raised me with gruff words and zero sentiment, was no more. I could practically hear his voice in my head, admonishing me for being upset.

Part of me believes it's a hoax, that he's at the funeral home right now, complaining about his kids with Uncle George and devouring Aunt Miriam's almond and date cookies.

But he's not.

He's really dead.

Samantha tells me that Uncle George got a visit from a police officer a couple of hours ago. She embraces me tightly, her tiny body shuddering against mine.

Roupen comes out of the house while Samantha hugs me. She gently lets go, and Roupen and I embrace. He pats my back a few times as if to say, "I'm here for you, bro," but my brother is strangely distant.

"You know, I wish I could be sadder about the whole thing, but I can't," Roupen admits. "I know it's terrible, but that's how I feel."

"He still loved you, I think," I say.

Roupen's pain is buried deep. Dad shamed him at every turn, and Roupen weathered it the best he could. Roupen won't ever get closure, but he has never needed Dad's approval before—why would he need it now?

"He loved having a son. He didn't love *this* son." Roupen points to himself. "Are you okay?"

"I don't know. With everything going on in my life, I am having a lot of difficulty processing another major event."

"I guess so … Come on, Aunt Miriam is fixing breakfast. A death in the family, and that woman just wants everyone to eat. Not that I'm complaining. How often do I get apple cinnamon pancakes?" Roupen says.

In the living room, Uncle George perches in his armchair, staring at the TV. His cheeks are red and his eyes are watery and big.

"Armand!" Uncle George slowly lifts himself from the chair and lumbers towards me. We awkwardly hug. His massive shoulders hunch over, like someone knocked the wind from him. "He's gone, Armand! Gone! I asked him to see a doctor. Begged him. He shrugged me off like he always did."

"Is he downstairs?"

"No. The coroner still has him. I sent Dikran to fetch him. Where did you go last night?" Uncle George asks.

"I was out with a friend."

"His mailman found him," Uncle George says. "Of all the people. The screen door was open and the mailman usually chats with Hagop. Today, something seemed off. He calls for Hagop, but gets no answer. He looks inside and sees him dead. To be found like that. Dying alone like that." Uncle George seems to be coming apart at the seams and can't focus on much. I take a step back and guide him to his chair.

Who knew? Uncle George is capable of human emotions after all.

We gather around the breakfast table and bow our heads in prayer. Aunt Miriam serves pancakes and coffee and we all eat in silence. In my experience, Armenians are squeamish about death. We avoid discussing it, along with illness, divorce, sex, or anything else worth talking about. We bury our feelings like we bury our dead, silently and showing only tears.

My family likes to smother grief with food. My father is dead, so we're eating pancakes like it's just another day.

"We'll invite the cousins from Chicago, but not the ones from Massachusetts," Uncle George decides after breakfast. "They can come to the funeral, not the forty days. That's our time. As intimate family."

In Armenian tradition, a forty-day mourning period follows the burial. Families wear black and visit the gravesite on the seventh and fourteenth days after the funeral. Immediately following the funeral, the family gathers for hogehats, a meal usually served at a restaurant. A brief repast to remember the deceased.

Uncle George outlines the funeral service, where we'd get the flowers, what the prayer cards would say, who would compose the obituary.

"You should do the embalming," Uncle George tells me.

"Why not give this to another funeral home?" I suggest.

"No! He must be handled by us. We are family. This is Tarkanian business. We alone must do this."

I can't believe his suggestion. Of all the cruel and clueless moves, this was his worst one yet.

"You want me to embalm my own father?" I ask, the words jarring to my ears.

"I can't do it. He was my brother. Dikran and Sam are unqualified. You are his first born, you should take responsibility and honor your father."

Emotional blackmail runs deep in this family, cutting through generations, creating silent rifts. The old terrorize the young through guilt and manipulation, using traditions and paternal fealty to bind us. No wonder I'm alone and trapped.

"I don't think I'm up to this." My voice trembles.

Uncle George clasps my shoulders with his hands and draws me uncomfortably close to his sweaty chest.

"I have faith in you," he says, letting me go.

That's all he tells me before settling back down in his recliner, which creaks under his weight.

"I have faith in you," he repeats with a wave of his hand.

That's it. The patriarch has spoken.

There is a dull pain in my chest and my breathing is belabored the more I stare at the embalming table. My father lies, there in ghoulish repose, a once-imposing figure now waxy and small. The room starts to twist when I put down my duffle bag near the table and don my gown and gloves—I feel panic sink itself into my chest.

I start crying.

There's no emotional buildup, no lone tear followed by a few more. It's an instant deluge, an outburst that I've repressed for years.

Dad is now insignificant and quiet, like a baby taking a nap. My sorrow temporarily abates, and I grasp the flexible shower head and turn it on. Water cascades over my father's head, shoulders, and abdomen. I wash him, dry him, and prep him for embalming.

This man, who raised me, who tormented me, who made me feel so weak and alone, lay pale and lifeless. He could harm me and my brother no more.

He smells like sour meat, freshly dead but already breaking down, slowly decomposing at the microscopic level. I curse Uncle George for making me do this as I fasten a tube into my father's carotid artery and connect it to the embalming machine. I run the other tube from his jugular vein, dangle it into the sink, and switch the machine on. My father's blood flows into the drain.

It resembles the blood of countless others I've embalmed, except they were strangers.

This is my father.

There's nothing I can do but watch this unfold. I discretely place the sheet over him and take a deep breath. I feel the chill creep through my bones, and I know what's coming.

"Is that how I look?" Dad asks.

Cloaked in a white frock, Dad's spirit peers inquisitively at his corpse. The ghost's eyes widen when he sees me.

"You? They're making you do this?" he says.

"I didn't want to," I murmur.

My Dad's translucent fist slices the air.

"George! That bastard. He never could stomach anything difficult. At the farm, he always passed his work onto other people. Your grandfather hated when he shirked responsibility." Dad grumbles.

"I'm draining your blood and pumping embalming fluid into you." I explain—my father always hated that I was an embalmer.

"Don't tell me. I'd rather not know."

"You don't have to be here. If you want to continue on to wherever you're supposed to go, feel free …"

He holds up a hand. *"No. I have something to say. First, I need to show you something."*

From my personal experience so far, nothing a ghost shows you is pleasant. Dad lunges forward, his form sinking into my body. I have a front row seat to Hagop Tarkanian's last night on Earth.

My father sits on the sofa, television blaring. He wipes his nose with his hand as his vision blurs slightly.

He's crying, but not at the TV.

He's holding a framed photograph of Mom, drinking in every detail through misty eyes.

My father is sobbing, but I'm not sure why. "I need you."

Tears fall onto the glass and the frame, and run down like rain on a windowpane. Mom is happy in the photo, she's young and carefree. Her playful smile reveals dimples on her cheeks. She's in her favorite sundress, the one he gave her for her birthday one summer when we visited Knott's Berry Farm in Buena Park.

My father's heart races and his left arm tingles. Numbness radiates down to his fingers. His jaw hurts. He drops the frame and the glass shatters when it hits the ground. My mother's beatific face stares up at him.

The pain in his chest grows severe, like strong hands gripping his heart. He starts to reach for the phone beside the sofa, then stops. He places his hand over his chest, grits his teeth against the agony, and leans back on a cushion. A wave of nausea and pain hit him. Dad looks up at the ceiling. A soothing calm washes over my father—no more misery, fighting, and sorrow. No more.

Darkness clouds his vision as the sound of the television fades, receding into silence as all around him vanishes into a comforting oblivion.

Snapping out of the haze, I stumble backwards and steady myself on the embalming table's edge.

My father chose to depart the world on his own terms. He could've called for an ambulance. Dialed 9-1-1 and had a slim chance to be revived. But he didn't want that. There was nothing in his life anymore; it was so empty and frightening for him, and he sought death. Hagop Tarkanian died lonely and miserable, missing the only person who loved him unconditionally.

"Now you know," he told me. *"We all end up with regrets. These things have a way of taking over your mind and your heart."*

We both stand there in silence for a moment.

"I think I owe your brother an apology. I was a terrible parent."

"Not exactly father of the year, no." I agree.

"I want you to have the farm. I left it to you. The house, what land I didn't sell to the developer. It's yours. I think that you can make the farm work."

I laugh, despite myself.

156

"You're out of your mind," I tell my dead father. I can see it clearly in him, the inability to let go. He couldn't let go of his wife. He couldn't let go of the farm. I narrow my eyes. "Maybe I'll sell the house. Would you like that? I'll sell it to a developer. A few townhouses on the last remaining acres of Tarkanian Farm. What a swan song that'd be, eh Dad?"

"Armand, we both know you won't follow through," Dad says. *"You're a goddamn Tarkanian. You'll go back to your old habits and live in the house with ghosts of your childhood. You're too nostalgic. And you don't have the spine. Like me, like my brother, like everyone in this family."* He laughs. *"Ironic that the son that I loathed the most in life for being a gay was the only one that was man enough to stand up for himself."*

"Fuck you, Dad. I have to get back to work now," I say, hoping he would take a hint. "We wouldn't want you rotting away, would we?"

Dad sidles near. The cold makes the hair on my arms stand up.

"Be kind to my body, son. I know that you might think that I don't deserve anything, but it's my only wish. I want to be buried with your mother. We have that nice twin burial plot, by the old sycamore in Ararat Cemetery."

"I know." Dad's corpse awaits my attention. I massage his arms while the embalming solution slowly fills his veins. "Goodbye, Dad." I say after a moment. "I hope that maybe you find peace wherever you wind up."

I look over and my father's ghost is gone.

Normally, Uncle George or Dikran would have been down here hassling me for the sake of it, but thankfully they've stayed away, a moment of serenity in a torturous life.

My cellphone rings. The flashing number is too familiar.

"Fuck," I mutter under my breath and answer it.

"Armand, my friend! Are we having a funeral tomorrow?" Berj sounds delighted.

"Berj. Uh, about the strip club …"

"Forget it. Water under the bridge, right? You get any fresh meat? I heard that you got a new corpse."

157

I tighten my grip on the cellphone. He must have someone at the coroner's office. These cultists were like termites; they got into everything. "There has been a death in the family. My father died."

"Excellent! Use that one."

"Thanks for your condolences." I restrain myself from telling this knuckle-dragging troglodyte what I really think of him. "Did you hear me? It's my father. I can't."

Berj sighs. "I thought we had come to an agreement, Armand. Armenians help out Armenians, right?"

"I'm not desecrating my father's body. Why don't we just wait for another cadaver?" I suggest.

"Hey, I understand. It's family. Family is important. So important that you'd do anything for them, like keep them alive, right? Now, you can do one of two things. Sew the package into daddy dearest's goddamn chest and bury him, or defy me and you will find out exactly how painful Spandaramet's wrath can be."

He doesn't say that the wrath is his. Is he going to send a spirit after me?

"Come on, Berj …"

His voice gets ugly. A primal snarl, more beast than human. "No, you little shit! You've seen what we're capable of, Armand. It'd be a shame if that funeral home were burned to the ground with your family still inside. Bad part about that is, you'd be responsible for their deaths. It's on you, my friend. You don't play ball with us, terrible things happen. We own you."

He hangs up.

My eyes fall to my father. I can't cut him open, remove his insides, and do what Berj wants me to do. The thought of my father as a mindless shambling undead gutted and splayed for a cult's amusement is just too much. He may have been a wretched, overbearing, bigoted asshole, but he was Dad, and family – as I've been told ad nauseam – matters. But then, Samantha, Aunt Miriam, Uncle George, and even my knucklehead cousin Dikran shouldn't pay for my sins.

I place the bundled package next to my father's body. My father's spirit is gone now and there are no prying eyes. My gloved hand reaches for a scalpel. The metal implement shines in the light.

I shouldn't do this, I think.

I flash back to Alvarez and how they cut him open. His tortured screams reverberate in my head. There's so much blood, his blood, cascading over the stone altar.

Berj wants his damn package. Spandaramet wants her glorious corpses.

My fingers grip the scalpel tightly. My father's body is nothing more than a helpless shell now.

I hold my breath and plunge the blade downward.

CHAPTER 19

PATHOS PANCAKES

I slice through the wrapped package and into its soft contents. White powder sticks to the blade. I drag the scalpel along the length of the package and open it up.

Cocaine.

Of course it's cocaine, I think. *What else was it going to be, chocolate chip cookies?*

The discovery just confirms my suspicions; Berj has been selling drugs. I've been transforming cadavers into human shipping containers for that asshole. I pick up the little attached cloth bundle and open it up; roots, herbs, and dried animal parts. Mixed together they apparently create powerful magic and reanimate the dead.

Rising from their graves, the shambling corpses traveled—a kilo of cocaine inside them—to their drop-off points. They were then shot, sliced open, and the drugs retrieved. As a reward for their service, they were given an unceremonious burial in a ditch.

The perfect scenario for anonymity in the drug trade. Zombie drug mules. They don't squeal to the cops, don't ask for a bigger cut of the action, and they operate at night when they're triggered.

My father looks blissfully unaware of my predicament. I wonder what he would say. Something mean, I'm sure … And I'd deserve it.

With gloved hands, I carefully retrieve the package and dump its contents into the toilet. It takes a few flushes and some plunger work before all the cocaine disappears, flowing into the sewers with a blue fragrant gurgling whoosh.

I finish embalming my father and place him back in refrigeration. The overwhelming feeling of regret hits me like a baseball bat to the face. I think about the cadavers I sliced open out of cowardice and greed. Berj's promises, Alvarez's death, my father's ghost— all stitched together into a horrible, death-soaked tapestry.

Dad is going to be buried *without* the package inside him. I will defile no other bodies for Berj. And the Children of Spandaramet will have my family in their sights. As I clean up the room, wiping down counters and making sure that there were no traces of cocaine, I mull over my options. Most of them point me to one solitary conclusion:

My life is over.

This funeral home, with all its stifling familiarity, is like a cage. The walls close in around me. I have nowhere to run, except outside, into the night. I peel off my gloves, pick up the little cloth package, and toss it into my duffel bag. I bring the bag up to my room. No one says a word when I grab the keys to the minivan and leave the house. They wouldn't have been able to stop me if they tried.

I drive around Fresno, window rolled down, and let the warm evening air sweep over my face as the minivan cruises over cracked asphalt streets. I pass the Tower District and its thrift shops, the artsy cafes, and the trendy bars. I cruise along the tree-lined roads in Fig Garden, and Cincotta's streets are clustered with working class homes and apartments. Without having planned to wind up there, I find myself sitting in the parking lot of the Neon Oasis. I park the minivan, walk over to Vonnie's Airstream, and knock on the door.

She answers, hair tousled and eyes half open. There's a blob of tomato sauce on her T-shirt and her legs are bare.

"Armand?"

"Hi Vonnie." I throw my arms around her.

"What's wrong? It's late."

I cry. Partially from exhaustion, partially from the misery of my life, and partially because I almost cut my father open to turn him into a zombie cocaine-delivery service. The ghosts had all asked for my help, and I had ignored them. Vonnie rubs my back. If there's one bright spot from all this insanity, it's Vonnie.

"My dad died." I say.

"Aw, babe," she pulls me against her tightly and wraps be in warmth. If anyone knew what it was like to lose family, it was Vonnie. "Come in," she leads me inside.

I sit down in my now-usual seat. "How does life get so fucking crazy, so fast?" I wonder aloud—I know that she can sympathize with my plight, but I don't expect her to say anything. "My old man was an asshole, he treated Roupen like trash, made fun of him for being gay, berated me constantly … and now that he's gone, it just hurts."

She gets up and grabs a beer out of the fridge, offering it to me. I take it and twist the cap off.

"Berj called while I was embalming my dad."

One of her eyebrows shoots up. "You embalmed your own dad?"

"My uncle refused to do it, said that my cousins weren't qualified. Said that I needed to be a good son."

"God, what an asshole."

"My family is rife with them," I say. "I was sitting there, looking at Dad and just, I don't know, couldn't do it. No more, just … over." I take a swig of the beer and close my eyes. "Remember how I told you these assholes were making me put packages into the corpses? How they told me not to open them?"

"You did?"

I nod.

"And?" Vonnie asks.

"Cocaine. They're using the corpses as drug mules, sending them to wherever they need to go, some place on the edge of town, where they get shot and cut open," I say. "I didn't want to desecrate my father like that. He might have been a bastard in life, but in death? He even asked me specifically to be kind to his body, so I just couldn't cut him open."

"Wait, you talked to him after he died?"

"Yeah, all he wanted was a bit of dignity in death." I drink more of my beer. American beer is utter pisswater, but I need this right now and take another gulp.

"Where's the cocaine now?" Vonnie asks.

"I flushed it," I say "Straight down the toilet."

"Okay. Why?"

"Because what else am I supposed to do with a kilo of coke?"

"Trade it for …" She closes an eye while she does the math. "Like, twenty-eight grand?"

"I'm not selling coke on the side, nor am I obeying Berj or the Children of Spandaramet or my family. Not anymore. I've had enough."

"You do realize you're a dead man, right? You could run, just get the fuck outta Dodge."

"They'll kill my family," I tell her. "I brought this on them. I was desperate and angry and shouldn't have agreed to this. My family, shitty as they can be, didn't do anything to deserve this kind of retribution."

"What can you do?" Vonnie walks over and sits on the armrest of the chair and rubs my shoulders.

"I can go into the club and tell Berj." I stand up. "Confess everything. Tell him I know it's cocaine."

"You'll be killed."

"I'll tell him to pay me more money because I'm assuming greater risk." I pace the floor, my heart pumping in my chest.

"He'll demand the cocaine back. Then he'll kill you."

"I'll give him baking soda."

"Oh, they'll figure it out, and then they'll kill you."

"Is there any scenario in which the cult won't kill me over this?"

"Probably not. You're pretty fucked."

"Well, step one is to bury Dad without their precious parcel of coke." I sink back into the chair. "Vonnie, do you mind …"

"Of course, I'll go," she says and gives the back of my neck a squeeze. "You should go clean yourself up a bit." She gestures to the bathroom.

I get up and close the little door behind me. It's small, not much room to move around, but there is enough. I run the tap and splash water on my face and look at myself in the mirror—for a moment, I don't even recognize myself. There is something different about the man that is looking back at me through the glass. Despite looking like shit, with a scraggily beard and bloodshot eyes, something's missing— but I can't tell what it is, and he can't tell me. I run my fingers through my hair, slicking it back with water and realizing that it was just a mess and in the way.

The guy in the mirror doesn't look like me. Not anymore. I am changing, like some kind of creature in a cocoon, and I don't know what I'll be after I hatch.

Vonnie is throwing on a pair of jeans and a tank top when I step out of the bathroom. She slips on a pair of flats and picks up her keys from the small credenza near the door.

"Come on, depressed guy. We're leaving."

"Can't I just crawl into bed? I can sleep for a few weeks."

Vonnie tugs my arm. "Nope. You need food. I know this all-night diner."

"I'm really not in the mood to eat," I whine.

"I'm buying you pancakes and coffee, and we'll sit there until we think our way out of this," she says.

Pancakes. Always pancakes. Why the fuck does everyone want to feed me pancakes?

We step out into the parking lot and walk over to the minivan. I'm so lost in my thoughts that I don't notice the leather-clad bikers on the other side of the parking lot until the van is pulling out on to the street. Was it the Legion? Or was I just seeing things now?

The Happy Place Diner glows like a flashy Art Deco beacon, the kind of place with humming neon and glass where you could see the people inside eating, or people could watch you eat. Brightly-colored booths, avocado green carpeting, and a black and white checkerboard floor right out of the 1950s, when carhops were fun, and small jukeboxes at each table were a thing.

Vonnie devours a short stack of pancakes and link sausages. She wipes her syrup-smeared lips on a paper napkin and gulps down some black coffee. I nudge my pancakes with my fork while chewing on some bacon.

"Heaven," she says between the pancakes and sausages. "What about those guys?"

"What guys?"

"The lamp something-or-others?"

"Legion of the Lamb?"

"That's the one. What about those guys?"

"I haven't called them. I still have their card, and I guess I know where they all hang out; it'd probably be easy enough to find them." I decide that pancakes were inevitable and I might as well get used to it—I pour cheap syrup over them and dig in.

"Did they seem like they were full of shit?"

I think about it for a moment while I'm chewing. "No, not really. One of them had some kind of power, like she knew that I had power anyways, so whatever that is worth." I pick up a piece of bacon and bite it in half. "I dunno Vonnie, it was a lot to take in. I'd just gotten my ass kicked pretty hard and Alvarez was dead. I don't think that I was processing much that day."

"Maybe this is your out?"

"What do you mean?"

"Well, you don't have many choices right now, right Armand?" I shrug and nod in agreement. "So, maybe these guys can help you—protect you or something?"

I lean back and try my best to sink into the booth. "Maybe."

"One way to find out," Vonnie says.

"Yeah, I guess so ..." I reach for my wallet and then stop. "Tomorrow."

"Armand ..."

"Vonnie, I want to bury my dad."

She smiles warmly, realizing that for all the different directions I was being pulled in, one was pulling harder than the others—family was family.

CHAPTER 20

DADDY DEPARTED

Dad looks serene. To the casual observer, he appears asleep; eyes closed, head resting on a silken pillow, hands folded carefully on his belly.

Like every embalmer, I prepared his body to fool the family into thinking their loved one is at rest. Only I know the truth though, he wasn't at rest before he died, and he's not at rest now.

Armenian families hold a wake – the Dan Gark – the night before the funeral, either at their home or at a funeral parlor. Since our home *is* a funeral parlor, it's that much easier to sort out.

Before the service, a thought burrowed itself into my brain and made itself comfortable. Embalming fluid is a designated carcinogen—it's the reason why embalmers have an increased risk of cancer, arteriosclerotic heart disease, and leukemia. We all learn this in school, but it's not the sort of thing that you really think about.

My job is literally killing me, bit by bit, day after day. Everything in my life seems like it's trying to destroy me.

I take a long shower and scrub my skin hard. After bathing, I shave away the excess stubble, leaving my goatee and then, before I realize what I'm doing, grab a pair of clippers and remove all my hair. The clumps of black hair fall into the sink and the more I take off the more I start to recognize myself. After I finish with the clippers, I take my razor and carefully finish the job.

"You look terrible with a shaved head," my father says, his ghost appearing behind me. *"Your hair was very good. You had classic Armenian hair."*

My father's dislike for my new look is a stamp of approval.

I wear my black suit and necktie, black Florsheims and a white pocket square in my breast pocket. Working in a funeral home, you get used to, and invest in, a proper somber wardrobe.

Relatives come from all over, far-flung and sad, their pale and dull faces as alien to me as their names. Aunts, uncles, and cousins I barely knew or had never met showed up at the funeral parlor dressed in black. These were old women with black veils, sunken-eyed men in large suits, and curious children clutching their small stuffed animals.

Dad floats next to me, criticizing everyone in the family without fear of repercussion. He's dead, so what can they do? Sue him?

"Wow. Aunt Gladys got fat. And Cousin Vahan's new wife is half his age. He must've come into some money," Dad quips.

"What are you doing here?" I hiss, hoping nobody sees me conversing with thin air.

"I thought I'd see what the fuss is about," my father's ghost says. He floats over to the casket and looks in. *"You gave me too much makeup. I look like a floozy. And what's with the suit? I hated that suit."*

Despite the critique, Dad's corpse looks good. His hair is combed, nails clean, pinstriped suit pressed and perfect. I approach the coffin and straighten the silk pillow under his head. The florist brought quite a few funeral wreaths and fresh cut flower sprays—chrysanthemums, mostly—for my father.

Roupen and Brent finally arrive. Roupen is chatty and sociable, while Brent stares uncomfortably at the casket. "Can I just say, brother, that I dig the new look." He says touching my freshly shaved head. "It suits you. Also, can I say, Dad is never more delightful than when his mouth is stitched shut." I laugh a bit but clear my throat.

168

"*That little shit*," my father glares at Roupen for a moment before sighing and wandering off.

Vonnie arrives not long after; she somehow always manages to look fantastic at funerals. She's wearing a black dress with a shawl draped over her shoulders. All eyes turn towards her when she enters. I hear muttered words, from old lips to older ears. People chatter about the unfamiliar Black woman and wonder aloud whether she's lost, or showed up at the wrong funeral.

Vonnie walks over and gives me a kiss on the cheek. I'm sure that public display of affection is going to rattle some of the older relatives. Clearly, Vonnie is not Armenian.

She leans in close, "Hot, I like the new look."

Vonnie eyes my bald head and flashes an impish grin.

"Thanks for coming," I say.

"Of course, Armand. I wanted to." Vonnie draws herself close and slips her arm around mine. "Besides, I didn't have any plans today, so I figured, why not, what's one more funeral?"

That tickles me. She knows exactly what to say.

Roupen slides over, Brent in tow. "Hello," he says to Vonnie. "I'm Roupen, black sheep of the family, gay book dealer. This is Brent." Brent waves awkwardly, and I can see why Roupen likes him.

She smiles. "Vonnie, just Black, sexy exotic dancer."

"Ooh! So you're why my brother feels the need to shave his head and be a bad boy," Roupen squeals. "Is he going to buy a leather jacket too? Either way, I very much approve of the influence you seem to be having on him."

Vonnie laughs, and Roupen takes her by the hand. "Let's go. Armand has filial piety to perform." Roupen gestures with a jerk of his head towards the slim man with a salt and pepper beard and curly hair who's making his way towards me. The priest, or Der Hayr – the "Lord Father" in the Armenian Apostolic Church – recites a prayer and mentions how devout Dad was, even though Dad hated attending church. I'm not totally paying attention, to be honest. The Der Hayr then passes around a small basket for special collection in Dad's memory.

"I'm sorry for your loss, Armand," he says, his accent thick.

"The Der Hayr asks for cash over my dead body. Literally. Do you believe that guy? What a crook," Dad hisses.

"Would you kindly fuck off?" I ask, a little exasperated. My father hasn't talked to me this much in the last five years. "This is a place of sadness and mourning. Let us grieve." The priest looks at me, gaping. "Sorry, father, not you … talking to my dad."

The priest slowly closes his mouth and then nods uncomfortably before backing up a bit and going to look for money from other mourners.

"Stop haunting me," I tell Dad.

"You're not grieving for me," Dad notes.

"You're *literally* talking to me. You grieve and mourn the departed, but you're still *here*."

"Fine," my father says finally. *"Hey, Armand?"*

"Yes?"

"Thanks for not cutting me up," he says.

"Yeah." I shrug. "Sure. Go be with Mom or whatever it is that ghosts do." I really do want him to leave. I want time to mourn him, and he's not letting me do it. Typical Tarkanian, in everyone else's business.

I'm so lost in thought that I don't notice the old woman in front of me. Her hair is blue and her skin reeks of lilac perfume. She touches my neck with cold, clammy hands.

"Oh, Armand. I am so sorry," she says.

"Thanks." I stare, trying to place her.

As if she sensed my ignorance regarding her identity, the woman speaks up, "I'm Cousin Bernice. From Glendale."

"Gotcha, Cousin Bernice." I say flatly.

"Your father looks so peaceful. God bless him. It's like he's sleeping," Cousin Bernice says.

"I couldn't well leave him looking like he was dead, could I?" I observe, peering over at my father, admiring my handiwork.

I feel lighter. It's as if I shaved off some familial burdens along with my hair.

"Yes, well …" She looks very much unsure of what to say in response to that.

Cousin Bernice smiles uncomfortably and turns around leaving me to my thoughts. I don't get to be alone with them long—Roupen and Vonnie come back over. They seem to have lost Brent, and my brother looks almost giddy. "Armand, did you tell the Der Hayr to fuck off?" Vonnie is giggling.

"No, I said it to Dad," I tell her.

Roupen puffs his cheeks a bit and frowns. "Dad? He's here? The guy can't even stop hassling his kids at his own funeral."

We load Dad's casket into the hearse and drive him to Holy Trinity Armenian Apostolic Church in downtown Fresno.

Holy Trinity, with its red brickwork masonry and metal domes, is indicative of Armenian churches from the fifth century. Three generations of my family have worshipped within these sanctified walls. We were baptized, married, and eulogized amid heady incense, Byzantine-inspired reliefs of saints and angels, and priests in sequined robes.

"You're not going to believe this, but I actually cried last night," Roupen tells me as we wait outside for the mourners to file past, each one drearier than the next. "Bawled my eyes out for that man in the casket. I thought, 'Why are you crying? He was horrible to you.' Then it hit me. I wasn't crying because of how he treated me, or even because I was sad. I cried because he wasted so much of his life hating what I was instead of knowing his son." Roupen chews on a fingernail. "I guess that it was just a sad way to spend a life."

"Dad hated lots of things," I reply.

"You seem distracted, and not in a 'we're-burying-my-Dad-to-day' kind of way. What's wrong?"

"Not really the time."

Roupen nods. "One of those things?"

"One of those things."

I excuse myself and head toward the church entrance, where I spot Vonnie. She smiles at me, and we enter the sanctuary together. I feel like the room gets strangely silent. I'm certain that between Roupen being gay and me being with Vonnie, we were officially the branch of the family that no one wanted to invite over for lunch. Uncle George is probably pissed.

"Is this her?" Uncle George murmurs to me when we get to the front pew.

"My girlfriend, Vonnie." I introduce her.

Uncle George and Vonnie shake hands.

"I'm sorry for your loss," Vonnie tells Uncle George.

"Yes, well," Uncle George stammers and shifts his weight uncomfortably. "Thank you."

Vonnie and I settle in the pew. "That's the most cordial I've ever seen him to a non-Armenian that wasn't paying the bills." I tell her.

The Der Hayr enters, commanding God's presence with him in all righteous fury and benevolence, while wearing a black tunic and an embroidered stole over his shoulders. He makes the sign of the cross and blesses the congregation in Armenian. We respond in kind, crossing ourselves.

The Der Hayr's sonorous voice reverberates off the church walls, deep and mighty, rumbling in a language I can barely comprehend. I understand a little bit of Armenian—but very little. My relatives excoriated me about not learning Armenian when I was younger and accused me of committing cultural genocide by not keeping the language alive—they eventually gave up trying to get me to learn.

The priest swings a thurible with heady frankincense back and forth. Smoke wafts through the air and drifts above us.

The Der Hayr addresses the congregation in English—he starts talking about Dad's life as a second-generation farmer, and of how much Dad loved his family. How Hagop Tarkanian cared for his wife and two sons. How he sacrificed everything to put food on our table. I sit there listening to it, but I feel divorced from the story being told—this isn't my father, and it isn't my family.

My father didn't hate Roupen, I'm sure of that; my father hated what Roupen represented. My brother was change, he was brave. He was what my father was not. I was so much like my father in so many ways, incapable of change and always making excuses for how I needed to stay the same as the world changed around me.

Roupen looks over at me and makes a strange face. "Stop being a weirdo," he whispers.

My stomach does somersaults. The incense is giving me a headache—it's getting hard to breathe with all this stifling smoke and the rattling cymbals aren't helping. I rise, politely excuse myself, and walk out of the church.

The humid Fresno air slaps me in the face. I sit down on the front steps, close my eyes, and inhale. I must have left right before the ceremony's end, as a few minutes later mourners start filing out. The Der Hayr walks over and pats me on the back, and then, after I stand up, he embraces me. He smells of cologne and frankincense.

"Take comfort your father is in Heaven now with your mother. It was a very good thing you did, handling his earthly remains. You are a loving son," he says.

"Thanks, but I really had no choice," I admit. "My uncle made me do it all."

The Der Hayr sniffs, and his mouth curves downward. "Still, it must not have been easy for you. Your father always said you were his favorite son, that you made him most proud. Armenian parents must be proud of their Armenian children."

"Weird. He told me that he was disappointed in me and my brother. In the end we return to dust, so who cares?"

The elderly priest raises an eyebrow and backs away, like I had just channeled Satan. He sighs, then ambles away without uttering another word.

Vonnie, Roupen, and Brent finally emerge from the church, and Vonnie walks over. She gives my shoulder a squeeze. "Hey, you okay?"

"Uh-huh."

"What's wrong?" She wraps her arms around me.

"That asshole. He doesn't know anything about Dad."

"First, never call a priest an asshole," Vonnie says. "Second, so what? We remember the dead in different ways. Okay, so maybe your father wasn't dad of the year. But other people don't have the same memories as you, and some of them might have good memories of him. Let them have their own memories and remember him how they want. You're under no obligation to feel the same way as them, but I don't know if shitting on everyone's parade is the right way either."

Vonnie's right, I suppose. Well, at least Dad won't become a shambling undead coke dealer.

Vonnie's eyes widen. Something in the distance draws her attention.

I follow her gaze and then my stomach sinks. Berj slowly approaches, his heavy boots bringing him up the church steps towards me.

"My condolences for your loss," Berj says. "You look fine, girl," he tells Vonnie with all the charm of a rotting animal. "You're working later tonight. Don't be late now."

"I'm not on the schedule," she replies.

"You are now." Berj waves his hand dismissively.

"This is a private ceremony." I direct him away from the mourners. "Immediate family and approved guests, only."

"Well, this is more of a business call," he says with a wicked smile. "I'm just making sure that you didn't decide to let pesky feelings for daddy get in the way of what you needed to do." The despicable man closes his eyes and faces the church, like he's sensing something. After a few tense seconds, he looks back at me. "You know, here I thought that you might not have the balls to actually do it. Your father will make a lovely host, I'm glad that you didn't disappoint me."

174

He says. He gives me a one-armed hug and I feel his other hand slip into my jacket and put a crinkling envelope in my inner pocket. "Can't arouse suspicion. But here, a little something extra for the *inconvenience*."

"That's very generous." I say quietly.

"Generous, yes. Remember how generous I can be, no? Make sure you remember it." Berj smiles, flashing those horrible gold teeth before leaving the same way he came, down the church steps and through the throng of mourners.

"What the fuck happened?" Vonnie asks.

"Bought myself some time," I say.

"What do you mean, Armand? You said that you didn't put the package in your father's body. Did you lie about the cocaine?"

"No. I destroyed the cocaine."

"Then what was Berj sensing inside?"

"The cocaine always came with a small cloth pouch filled with magical herbs, twigs, and stuff. That's probably what the cult was using to animate the dead. I figured that the drugs weren't magical so they were relying on the pouch. That's what Berj sensed."

Vonnie swallows. "You put that thing inside your ..."

"No! It's in the casket under the pillow."

"Won't this mean that your Dad will become a zombie?"

"I don't *think* that's going to happen, but just in case, I'm going to take the pouch out before he's put into the ground. I'll throw it in the San Joaquin River after the funeral so that it goes out of town. The pouch probably has to be *inside* the body for it to work."

Vonnie tilts her head. "What do you think will happen when the cult figures out they paid you all this money and you sabotaged their undead drug runner?"

What's the worst that can happen? I slip my hands into my pockets. "Vonnie, there's already a really high chance that they're going to kill me at some point, and I'm not sure that that's avoidable. So, if they're going to come after me anyways, then I'm not giving them another inch." I pat my jacket where Berj slipped in the envelope. "But I will take their money."

She wrinkles her mouth and squints. "Armand, that's reckless …"

"Now that Berj is gone, I've bought myself a day to think about it, because the other choice is to have my old man rise from the grave and peddle drugs. Dad will be buried and will rest in peace, with a bit of luck I can steal some time to figure out a plan."

Vonnie flashes me a look. "You are playing with fire, Armand."

"What else is new?"

We bury Dad in Ararat Armenian Cemetery, overlooking a rolling hill beneath a slowly spreading sycamore grove. I've attended hundreds of funerals over the years, but the ones you have for family members always feel different. They're personal. Everything that person meant to you in life feels like it starts to slip away from you.

The Der Hayr comes, vestments radiant in the late morning sun. He says a prayer and sings a dirge—a melody somber and mellifluous. Circling the casket, the Der Hayr gingerly touches each side with a small cross.

Vonnie stands next to me, her arm locked with mine. We watch, standing amid rows of gravestones and a carefully manicured lawn.

She brushes away the tears that run down my cheeks.

"I didn't tell you, but I watched my father's death. He was so alone and let himself die instead of calling for help. He felt that there was nothing left for him." I watch carefully as the burial continues. "Dad died without doing right and fixing the problems in his life. He died bitter and jealous of his brother. He died missing my mom. All he had when he left this world were regrets."

"That won't be you, Armand. You're not dying for a long time, you hear?"

"The cult will try to kill me. It's inevitable," I say.

"Nothing is inevitable." Vonnie squeezes my arm and leans her head on my shoulder.

"When you grow up Armenian-American, the church is everywhere in your life, it dictates obedience, and sears into your brain this weird idea of unity while rejecting outsiders. Our people were massacred, lied to, and excluded. We ensure survival by clinging to our community and church and embracing our cultural identity. That's why my family speaks Armenian, cooks Armenian, and lives Armenian. It's this sense of identity that I could never connect to—I had no direct experience with the horrors visited on my people in the past, but the aftershocks of history have been trying to consume me and stop me from being who I want to be."

"It's part of who you are. But it shouldn't govern you."

"Yeah … I used to think that I was stuck in this family. I was powerless to make a change, to confront my old man, my uncle, to change jobs, to get my own place to live … I let my family dictate the terms of my own life. After everything that has happened, I don't think that I *can* go back to that anymore. Too much has changed, and I know so much more than I did a few weeks ago."

Vonnie looks at me and gives me a warm smile. "Sometimes," she says, giving my arm a big squeeze, "you just have to hit the bottom for you to realize how much more there is to the world for you to grow into." She looks over the crowd of mourning people. "I think that I'm starting to see a different world too, one that's a little bit more magical."

"That's not pun-reasonable."

"Shut up, Armand."

"Yes ma'am." I say with a smile.

CHAPTER 21

SACRILEGE

After a funeral, Armenians hold a hokejash, or "soul meal" where the deceased's family share a meal and reminisce about the recently departed.

We all pack into a restaurant, sit at tables covered with linen, and drink Chardonnay from long-stemmed goblets. Everyone eats braised lamb and pilaf and waxes eloquent about Dad, pretending like he was more than he was. Maybe that's a side-effect of death—we immediately gain more stature than we deserve.

I fidgeted in my seat and prod the lamb with my fork.

Aunt Miriam leans over towards me, a little misty eyed. "Armand, you're not eating?"

"I'm not hungry."

"Why not? Lamb is the meat of your people. Try eating, sweetheart," she urges.

Vonnie raises an eyebrow. "Meat of your people?"

I shrug. "Armenians love their lamb chops. What can I say?"

Uncle George, exceptionally drunk, finishes delivering a eulogy that is so bloviating and pompous, that I wonder if he shouldn't have been a politician. When he's finished, Uncle George gropes my shoulder and insists that I say a few words about Dad. He doesn't ask Roupen. To him, like to his brother, Roupen and Brent were invisible.

I get out of my chair slowly and take a drink.

"Thanks for coming, everyone," I begin, unsure of what to say. "Dad was a complicated man. He was stubborn and obstinate. And now he's gone. Uncle George said enough good things about my father for both of us." I look over at my brother. Roupen has his arms folded across his chest. He looks up at me. "I have this memory of Dad. I don't remember how old I was, to be honest, but it was of me and my brother and him, all playing catch in the yard."

Some of the members of the family are smiling, nodding, and probably imagining that this was my father's nature.

"And it's the only fond memory I have of him," I say. "As we grew, my dad pushed against change and what the future brought. That's why the farm fell apart. That's why he couldn't talk to his sons. He drove everyone in his life away, especially his sons, and then he died, miserable, unhappy, and alone"

Uncle George tugged at my arm. "That's enough. You're embarrassing yourself," he hisses. I ignore him and continue.

"He thinks you all neglected him when he was alone," I tell the room. "He suffered, by himself, from self-inflicted emotional wounds. I'm sure that not one of you visited him either. Maybe that's all he really wanted, for things to be like they were before, for someone to pay attention to him. We're not supposed to talk ill of the dead, but if you all knew how much he spoke, and speaks, ill of the living sitting in this room, you'd probably spare a curse or two for that old man." I put my wine glass down on the table and pick my jacket up from where it was hanging off the back of my chair. "Come on, Vonnie. Time to go."

As we leave the restaurant, which is dead silent, I look over at my brother again. He gives me an approving thumbs up.

One foot in front of the other, away from the sour faces and through the parking lot, I put more and more distance between myself and everything that kept me feeling crushed and miserable. We climb into Uncle George's 1973 Cadillac Miller-Meteor hearse, and I jam the key into the ignition, flick on the radio, and drive. I stop at Camp Pashayan, a campsite and public park on the San Joaquin River. On the sandy riverbank, I reach into my jacket pocket and pull out the cloth bundle Berj gave me.

Vonnie smiles when she sees the pouch.

"You really fished it out of the casket?" she says.

"Sure did. I'm not letting Berj get his hooks into Dad." I throw it as hard as I can into the river. It lands in the water with a splash, and bobs gently above the surface.

Let the current carry it far away, I think. *Carry it across the state, for all I care. At least my father's body will be spared.*

"Damn. It's really gone." Vonnie watches the bundle float away.

I reach for her hand. She pulls me close.

"What now?" she asks.

"Now? We make like that enchanted pouch and disappear," I say.

We leave the park in the hearse, kicking up dust as I drive. AC/DC's "Highway to Hell" roars from the lousy speakers as we race down the Golden State Highway — windows open, scream-singing the whole way home.

It's dark and I'm thumbing through *Madame Opal's Guide to Seances and Psychics* when Uncle George and Aunt Miriam return. My thoughts have been drifting to Maddie Hinkle, Alvarez, and Dad, all lonesome ghosts that parted ways from life and had unfinished business. My father, at least, hadn't been murdered.

I hear Uncle George stomping through the house and up the steps. He opens the door to my room and bursts into the room like a hand grenade.

"You disrespect your father's memory," he seethes. "I took you in, gave you a job, and this is how you pay me back? By shaming the family?"

Aunt Miriam comes in and tries to soothe him. "He lost his father. He's not thinking straight," she tells him. The truth is that it's the clearest my head has been in years.

"Sacrilege! That's what it is," Uncle George rants. "Honor thy mother and father. It's in the Bible. Look it up."

I close the book and stand up, walking over to him slowly but my head high and shoulders arched back. I would not slink along anymore. The old man takes a step back, retreating slightly.

"My father cursed your success, and he hated that you were lazy," I tell him. "You skirted your duties on the family farm, passing your work off on others. My father stayed on the farm, and you did nothing for him or for grandpa. You went where the money was, not where the family needed you to be, yet you preach family obligations to me, like I'm not pulling my weight around here. When Dad died, you left the embalming to me because you're a coward. You couldn't even pay your own brother that last respect, so you made his son do it. I embalmed my father and put him in the casket. You greeted the family and played the role of bereaved brother."

Uncle George stares at me blankly for a second. His pushover nephew finally grew a pair.

He roars, "If you don't like it here, then pack your things and leave!"

I jerk my thumb over to my bed, where my trusty duffel, which in another life used to transport drugs and magic zombie-resurrection kits, is already packed. My uncle stares at it and then back at me.

"You're a lot like Dad, you know that, right?" I tell him as I pick up the duffel and sling it over my shoulder.

Uncle George smirks. "You're not really leaving. I'm paying your salary."

"Is that what it is? That meager pittance I get for working a dead-end job I'm overqualified for? The money I pay you in rent and

181

utilities for living under your roof? You keep me broke and dependent on you. And then you talk of family like you invented the word. I wonder how long ago my loans were paid off." George looks uncomfortable for a moment.

"Where will you go, Armand?" he asks angrily. "You've got no money, no prospects, no friends."

"I have friends."

"That Black girl? You're going to shack up with her? Go on, then! Leave your only family. Break your aunt's heart, why don't you?"

"You know something Uncle George? You're wrong about two things," I say.

"What's that?"

"First, that I have no money, no prospects, and no friends. I have every one of those things, but six months ago I was so deflated and depressed that I would have agreed with you."

"Yeah? And what's the other thing?" The veins in Uncle George's temple look like they might explode.

"That I'm breaking Aunt Miriam's heart. I don't think I am." I give her a small smile. She looks upset, but not angry—I think she knows my path forward is mine alone and that it cannot be dictated by anyone other than me.

I walk past Uncle George and out of the room, leaving them to bicker amongst themselves in Armenian. I head down the stairs and pass Dikran, who stands open-mouthed at my exchange with his father. I regard him for a moment, shrug, and exit through the front door.

Samantha is sitting on the front porch steps and looks up at me. I sit down next to her.

"Hi, Armand," she says a bit sadly.

"Hi, Samantha," I answer.

"Do you know where you're going?"

"Not really, but I have some choices."

"Dad's going to be pissed that he'll have to do the embalming himself again," she says, putting her head on my shoulder. I wrap my arm around her.

"He's a big boy, he'll get over it. Besides, it's only a matter of time before he notices that he's got a hard-working and brilliant daughter that can do the job. Just make sure that you don't let him cut your pay randomly or pay you less than you're worth. There's lots of funeral homes out there in the world, so make sure he pays you."

Samantha laughs. "Thanks Armand," she says.

"No problem, call me any time you want," I say as I stand up.

"Oh, Armand?"

"Hmm?"

"Here," Samantha stands up and fishes into her pocket, pulling out the keys to her Civic. "I want it back, but I think you might need it for a bit." I take the keys and give her a big hug.

"You're one in a million, cousin," I say. My eyes sting with happy tears. "Take care, I'll see you soon."

"Don't crash it. I want it back in one piece."

We laugh, and I walk over to the little blue hatchback, open the trunk and toss in my duffel and Madame Opal's book. I open the driver's side door, get in, close the door and take a big breath. I feel relaxed, truly relaxed, for the first time in a long time.

My phone rings.

I look at the number, and all the soothing feelings sort of disappear. It's Berj, and I'm sure he's pissed. I answer the phone.

"Hello?"

"Listen to me, you little shit," Berj hisses. "I don't like being lied to. We had an agreement."

"What's this about now?" I ask.

"Do you have any idea how much your bullshit cost me? That's the last fucking mistake you'll ever make. Disloyal Armenians are dead Armenians." The line goes silent.

I can't say that I'm surprised, but hearing an insane cult leader explicitly tell you that he was going to kill you is jarring. I take a deep breath and put the phone down in one of the cup holders.

A sudden chill fills the car, but it's not the air conditioner.

"I showed you these guys were dangerous," Maddie Hinkle's ghost says. *"I warned you, but now you're just going to wind up dead."*

"I never got to tell you that I'm sorry," I say.

"I appreciate it, Armand. You never took responsibility for what you did." Maddie is sitting in the passenger seat, her hair floats around her like she's underwater. *"What changed?"*

"I did."

Maddie smiles a bit. *"I told you though, you need to stop these assholes before they kill more people."*

"Yeah. If they don't kill me first."

"These guys are coming for you, so wise up and get your act together. This is no time to be a lamb. You better find something inside you that turns you into a lion, or something." I look at Maddie Hinkle long enough that she turns and looks out the window. *"What?"*

"You're wrong," I say. "This is *exactly* the time to be a lamb."

"Well, whatever you do, make sure you do it soon. I'd like you to give my spirit some amount of peace ... I don't want to be cursed to roam around this weird afterlife being jaded and angry," she pauses, and her features harden, *"I wasn't like that in life, and I don't like it in death, but it doesn't stop, it just consumes me. Please help, Armand."*

"Sure, I'll do my best." Maddie nods, apparently satisfied for now. "Oh, Maddie?"

"What is it?"

"Vonnie misses you."

Maddie's face softens a bit. *"I miss her too."*

And then she's gone.

I put the key in the ignition, start the car, and put the Tarkanian Funeral Home in the rearview mirror.

CHAPTER 22

TRIAL BY FIRE

I sit in the Civic with a cup of coffee and a Bavarian cream donut and wait. It's been ten minutes since I called the number on the card that Hank gave me. The conversation was brief but clear.

Hank had answered the phone with a curt and gruff, "Yeah?"

"It's Armand, the guy you found lying unconscious on the street?"

"Armand! What's up?"

"I need your help. Things are really bad and are about to get worse."

And that's all I need to say for the Legion of the Lamb to drop everything and come to meet me. Hank's old, beat up pickup pulls into the dark parking lot. Muskrat and Reece are with him. They all pile out of the truck and I meet them halfway.

Hank looks at me expectantly.

"Almost didn't recognize you without your hair," he says, eyeing my bald scalp.

"I'm ready," I tell him.

"For what?" Reece asks, looking at Hank and then at Muskrat who just shrugs.

"To get my hands dirty," I reply.

Hank roars with laughter and then gives me a shot in the arm. "Good man! Time to fill us in." Hank gestures at Reece and Muskrat to get closer as I start to go over everything that had happened since the last time I saw them. I finish my update at the point where Berj called and told me I was a dead man.

Hank tosses his keys to Reece. "You and Muskrat head to the funeral home. Keep an eye on it and call if anything gets weird."

Reece, all business, nods and walks over to the truck. "Come on Muskrat, we got shit to do."

"Okay, uh, Reece," Muskrat waves good bye pleasantly as he follows his friend, and they peel out of the parking lot.

"All right, man." Hank looks back at me. "Time to be really careful and start covering your ass. You got any other loose ends?"

"Vonnie," I say.

"The stripper?"

"Exotic dancer," I correct. I remember that the Legion has been tailing me for a while now, so of course, they know about her.

"Now is really not the time to get pedantic about job titles, kid."

"She's working at the club tonight."

"We should check on her." Hank says.

With a chill that shoots down my spine, I realize there's no going back now. Vonnie's life is in danger. Those bastards were playing for keeps and would kill her to hurt me. I can't let that happen.

"Gimme the keys," Hank says as we walk over to the Civic.

"Why?"

"I've heard how you drive," Hank says as I fork them over.

186

"It's my cousin's car, don't break it."

"Wouldn't dream of it."

Before we get to the Neon Oasis, we can already see smoke. My heart is in my throat the whole way, but Hank, much to my surprise, is a far better driver than I expected. We're in the parking lot moments later and I'm horrified at what I see.

Flames are devouring Vonnie's Airstream.

"You got a tire iron in the trunk?" Hank asks as he pulls up next to the trailer and gets out, hobbling quickly over to the door and tapping the handle with his hand. "Shit," he gives his hand a shake. I'm already digging through the back of the car for the long piece of heavy metal. When I find it, I sprint over, and we jam the tire iron into the door and start to pry it open. Between the two of us, we hear the latch crack loudly, and the door swings open.

"Here." Hank pulls off his leather jacket and gives it to me.

I put it over my head and go into the trailer, staying low. A woman's muffled and panicked screaming draws me through the fire.

Smoke obscures my vision, but I feel my way to the accordion doors to Vonnie's room. Vonnie is on the bed, thick rope binding her wrists and ankles. Flames shoot from the kitchen in roiling waves along the ceiling. I pull her off the bed, cover her head and body with Hank's jacket and drag her to the door and into the parking lot. Hank is waiting. I hand Vonnie over to him. My shoulders burn, and my chest feels like a million degrees. Flames lick the fabric. My shirt, which has sustained me through many workouts, is on fire. I rapidly pat myself down but it's no use, so I peel the shirt off.

Somewhere deep in the trailer a feeble smoke alarm beeps and a horrid groan of metal being warped fills the air. The trailer ceiling dips. I double over, coughing into my hand while Hank uses a pocket knife to cut through the ropes binding Vonnie. She looks back at me through half-closed eyes. The relief washing over me is palpable.

Tears run down her cheeks—I'm not sure if it is the panic or the smoke, but she grits her teeth and tries standing up. Hank holds her down, her back against the front bumper of the Civic.

"Berj," she murmurs. "He and his shitty fan club jumped me and tied me up. They drew a bunch of weird-ass symbols all over the trailer. Then they chanted, and suddenly symbols burst into flames. No matches or gas. It was fucked up, Armand." She coughs and closes her eyes.

Hank picks up his jacket, gives it a sniff, and then puts it on. "Been through worse," he says looking at me. "You got clothes? If so, stop being naked."

"Who's your friend?" Vonnie asks.

"Hank," he says. "Legion of the Lamb. You must be Armand's exotic dancer friend, Vonnie." He offers her his hand.

She takes it and gives it a weak shake. "Stripper, I ain't ashamed. A job is a job." Hank looks at me and smirks.

"Good to meet you, Vonnie." Hank looks over at me—I'm putting on a shirt from my duffel. "We gotta get outta here. If Berj's creepy little friends are still in the neighborhood, we don't want them thinking that Vonnie made it out alive. Gives us a few extra hours until they comb through the rubble and don't find her bones." I help Vonnie stand up and escort her into the confined back seat of the Civic before popping the passenger-side seat back in place and getting in.

Hank grabs the tire iron and my shirt from the ground, cleaning up any trace that we were there, and a moment later, we pull out of the Neon Oasis' parking lot.

On our way back to town, a couple of fire trucks and police cars scream past, their flashing lights soon behind us.

As we're driving up North Cedar Avenue, Hank's phone starts buzzing. He pulls it out of his breast pocket and answers, putting it on speaker and handing it to me to hold it.

"Yeah?"

"Hey, Hank," Reece says. "Muskrat is out doing a perimeter check, but this place is fucking cursed, man, things are going to get ugly at some point."

"Cursed?" I ask.

Hank ignores me. "What're we talking about?"

"Symbols mostly, beacons for malevolent entities, dark-sigil-type shit. Muskrat is wiping out the ones that he can find, but it's dark, and there are a *lot* of them."

"Good work, Reece. Thanks. Keep an eye on that place, and you call me the second that anything looks like it might go sideways."

"You got it, boss." Reece hangs up and I hold the phone for a moment before Hank takes it from me and sticks it back in his pocket.

"Looks like Berj's little scout troop has been busy tonight. They're leaving sigils around your family's house. It's like how the evil eye is supposed to ward off bad things, but, you know, the opposite of that. That asshole is trying to turn that house into a magnet for things that you don't want near your family."

"So, what happens next?"

"Well, first, we get you two to the clubhouse and start comparing notes. We haven't been sitting on our asses since the last time we talked. Reece and Muskrat are going to stick around your family's place just in case."

"You said that the house would be a magnet, though."

"Yeah, but things that go bump in the night have to be around first. Vampires and werewolves don't show up out of thin air. If they're in the area though, you can bet your last dollar that they're going to take Berj up on his invitation."

"What invitation?"

"Kill everyone and burn everything down."

Me and Vonnie stare at Hank.

"Don't worry," he says. "The Legion's got you covered."

"These are those lamb guys?" Vonnie asks.

"The Legion of the Lamb," Hank corrects.

"I swear I'll never make fun of your name again," she says.

Wanda sits on the wrap-around porch of the clubhouse when we park the car in the small lot at the side of the building. She smiles at me when we exit the Civic.

"I knew you'd be back." She taps the side of her head.

I take my duffel out of the trunk, and the three of us walk over.

"Vonnie, this is my lovely wife Wanda," Hank says as he makes his way up the steps slowly. Wanda wrinkles her nose and looks at Hank.

"You smell like a barbecue joint. Go get changed," Wanda tells Hank before turning to me and Vonnie. "And let's get you two inside and put some food into you." I help Vonnie up the stairs and smile at Wanda as we walk past.

"Thanks," I say.

"Don't mention it. I like having you around; you compliment my cooking. Vonnie, honey, we gotta get you some clothes," Wanda says.

As we walk into the clubhouse, I notice more details. My first time here, I had been beaten and almost concussed. This time, though, my adrenaline is surging, and I'm taking it all in. Vonnie sits down at a table.

"Something to drink?" Wanda asks us.

Both of us answer at the same time, "Beer."

"Water it is." Wanda fills two cups with water and brings them to the table—she sticks her head in the kitchen as she walks past. "Josie, go get an extra pair of jeans and a t-shirt or something." I can hear muffled talking coming from the back of the kitchen. "I don't care what you get, just make sure that it's clean." Wanda smiles at Vonnie.

"You and Josie are about the same size; we'll get you something clean to wear, though it might have a few motor oil stains."

"Thanks, ma'am," Vonnie says.

"Wanda," she corrects. "Come with me, we're going to make you a bit more comfortable." Vonnie looks at me suspiciously but I nod.

"Vonnie, we're as safe as we're possibly going to be right now," I reassure her.

Wanda gives me a smile and they disappear through a door at the back of the bar.

A little while later, Hank sits down across from me. He's wearing different clothes, but he still smells like a campfire. He puts a piece of paper on the table.

"I'm glad you called. Truth be told, we were going to be getting in touch with you soon anyways," he says.

"What for?"

"Well, like I said, we haven't been sitting here with our thumbs up our asses, we've been doing a little bit of digging." Hank slides the paper across the table.

"Kill Zombies for Kilos," I read. He nods, and I keep reading. "Feel the thrill of wasting the undead. Yeyo prize inside. Only $150K." A number to what I assume is a burner phone is scrawled at the bottom of the flyer. "This is insane," I say.

"Yup, your cult leader friend is making serious bank selling the experience of shooting supernatural creatures."

"Who can afford this?"

"Drug dealers, rich people, anyone who'd put a bullet into a giraffe so that they can make a chair out of it. You know. Assholes." Hank looks at the paper. "This is how he's been bank-rolling a lot of what he's been doing."

At that kind of price tag, it was no wonder that he had no problem giving me four or five thousand dollars at a time to fill corpses with cocaine and zombie fuel.

"Armand," Hank starts, "you and I gotta have a few words about what happens next." His phone rings and he frowns. He takes it out of his pocket and answers it. "Yeah, what is it?" Even though the phone isn't on speaker, Reece's voice comes across loud and clear.

"Boss, there's *something* running around the neighborhood, I'm not sure what it is, but it's definitely picking up on the sigils. You better get over here."

Hank hangs up and rises to his feet, grunting as he does so. "When it rains, it pours. Let's go."

CHAPTER 23

UNWANTED VISITOR

Reece goes in first, kicking in the door of the funeral home, his gun drawn. Muskrat is next through the door. Hank follows after them and I'm the last one to enter.

"You need to get to your family as soon as possible, but you leave whatever the supernatural critter is to us. We're trained to deal with it. Wanna be a hero? You'll only wind up dead—or worse, you'll get your family killed." Hank's voice on the drive over had communicated that there was no room for negotiations. My stomach has been in knots since we left the clubhouse.

The hulking creature stands on two muscular hind legs, its feet are reversed, the toes pointed backwards and heels at the front. A large wolf-like head with glowing yellow eyes stares menacingly down at us. Its long slender fingers end in sharp claws and when the thing raises itself up to its full height and opens its hideous jaws, revealing sharp fangs, I freeze. Pungent drool drips from its open mouth. The thing moves to strike.

Muskrat and Reece, their pistols drawn, flank the creature and start pumping bullets into it. Gore splatters the walls. I dive behind

Uncle George's armchair when the monster lunges at me. It hits the chair and tumbles over. For a frenzied moment we're a mass of fur, human, and chair. The beast swipes at me and nicks my jaw—a bit further to the left and I might have lost my head.

"Here doggie, doggie," Reece shouts as he puts a few more bullets into the creature.

Despite the stinging pain from the cut on my face I keep crawling away towards the nearby table. From there, I can see Uncle George and Dikran huddled on the other side of the sofa. Aunt Miriam, her head bloodied, is cringing in the corner near the kitchen. She points at the hideous thing and screams. Despite the stinging pain in my face, I make my way, inch by inch, towards Uncle George and my cousin.

A sudden burst of light hits the abomination with such force that it hurdles through a wall and into the dining room. Hank stands in the parlor's threshold with a shimmering object in his hands, a spear of some kind with a stone blade at its tip—white-hot light emanates from the old weapon. The monster's flesh sizzles from what I surmise is arcane energy.

The beast emits a shrill cry, a disconcerting mix of wolf howl and human scream, and topples over. Hank hurls the spear at the prone monster and it sinks deep into the beast's side. The creature thrashes around; one of its wild swings catches an approaching Muskrat in the chest and sends him into the sofa. Breathing raggedly, the thing collapses on the floor.

A pale, cold mist rises from the creature's body. The wispy shape shrinks in size and then starts to clear away, revealing a woman. She has a flat nose, broad chin, and dark shoulder-length hair that is braided. She rolls over as much as she can with a spear in her and sneers. I sit up carefully and wipe some of the blood from my face.

"What are you?" I ask.

"Purger of the lost. You are the nothing, the forgotten man I seek," she hisses, voice murky and distant.

"Why are you here?" Hank asks as he steps forward and wraps his fingers around the other end of the spear, pushing it in slowly.

194

The woman roars at Hank. "I am the claw, the blood-drinker, the walker between two worlds."

"Did Berj send you?"

She puts one hand over her eyes and another over her mouth.

"What's that mean? What are you doing?" I demand.

"More will come. More will feed. More will hunger. Flayed. Burned. Drained. Sup upon your meat. Your blood in my mouth. Your mortal bones my playthings."

"Not anymore, you spooky bitch," Reece says. "You're dead." One last round from his gun ends the conversation.

"You folks okay?" Hank looks at my family as he grabs the mysterious spear and yanks it from the body.

"What the hell was that thing?" Uncle George asks me.

"I don't know, but it's dead now," I tell him.

Hank looks at Muskrat, who is still sitting on the sofa catching his breath. "Muskrat, what was it?"

He stands up, rubbing his chest as he walks over and pushes the corpse with his boot. The once inhumane, wolf-headed creature was now a naked woman with bronzed tattooed skin, adorned with several swirling and ancient shapes. A wolf's pelt hangs on her shoulders.

"Uh, a mardagayl, I think." Muskrat puts his foot on the dead woman's head out of an abundance of caution, picks up the pelt, and gives it a sniff. "Yeah, it's definitely, uh, a mardagayl."

"Mardagayl? An Armenian werewolf? Those are real?" I apply pressure to the cut on my face and get up a little too quickly. My legs wobble a bit. "How did that thing get in here?"

"I heard a noise upstairs," Aunt Miriam says. "I found this horrible wolf crouching in the hallway. Its eyes. Oh, God, its eyes!"

"You're safe now, ma'am. That thing's pushing up daisies," Reece says as he and Muskrat holster their weapons.

Hank sighs. "The Children of Spandaramet put those sigils everywhere and probably sent it to tie up any loose ends, I guess. Figure that Berj Manoogian would want to send an Armenian monster as opposed to just a regular werewolf. Guy has a motif going."

"Where's Samantha?" I ask looking around in a panic.

"She went out with friends," Dikran says.

"Thank God for that," I say.

Uncle George grabs my arm and pulls me aside. "Who the hell are the Children of Spandaramet? Some kind of gang?"

"You've got to take the family and leave." I tell him. "Stay at the farmhouse. There's room now."

Uncle George shakes his head. "Hell no. I'm not going to live in the old house. We just buried Hagop. His things are still there. It wouldn't be right."

"The Children of Spandaramet ain't gonna stop until you're dead, old man." Reece says as he helps Aunt Miriam up to her feet. "They're gonna keep coming here until you're all D-E-D dead. Sucks, I know." He grabs a tea towel from the nearby kitchen counter and puts it against the cut on her head. "Put a bit of pressure here, you're fine, but better to not mess up that pretty apron." Aunt Miriam, in the aftermath of all the chaos, gives Reece a smile.

Look at you, you big softie, I think to myself.

"You've got ten minutes. Pack your stuff, whatever you need. Go stay at this place that Armand was talking about and don't tell anyone where you're going. We'll tell you when it's safe to come back." Hank tells my family.

"Who the hell are you?" Uncle George demands.

"We're the good guys. Trust us," Hank replies.

Uncle George looks irate, but also confused—it takes a lot to process the existence of a world you didn't know about—I can sympathize. Finally, my uncle nods and goes upstairs.

"My cousin isn't here. What should we do?" I say.

"Muskrat?" Hank asks.

"Uh, on it." He smiles pleasantly and salutes. "I'll make sure that she's safe, but you gotta tell her to get back here ASAP, Armand. The longer we, uh, wait, the bigger the risk of something else finding the invitation to ransack the place. Without anyone here, they'll probably just leave the building alone. No one to kill."

"All right," I say. I take out my phone and step out onto the front steps of the house to call Samantha.

"Sam?"

"Armand?" Her voice mingles with clinking glasses and several indistinct conversations. "What do you want? I'm actually having fun."

"Something bad happened. How soon can you come home?" I ask.

"Oh, my God," Samantha's voice cracks. "What happened? Are my parents okay?"

"They were attacked. They're shaken up, but will be fine. I think you should get back here," I say.

"Jesus, it's always something. This family is cursed, I swear."

After I hang up, I stand on the front porch of the house and stare out into the night.

A mardagayl.

Of all the fucking things in the world, a mardagayl. I first learned about these mythical creatures from one of Aunt Miriam's stories, but that's all they were. Stories. Until now. Hank had said that werewolves are also real. What else was there, out in the world, hiding from everyone?

Ghosts are real. Monsters are real.

I turn and look back into the house, Reece and Muskrat had moved the coffee table out of the way and were rolling up the dead woman in my uncle's favorite rug. These guys just went in and fought a literal monster—without fear and without reservation, and they did it to protect people.

I wanted to be like that. I wanted to be strong and fearless like them.

197

Muskrat pokes his head out the door. "You, uh, okay, Tark?"

"Tark …"

"Sorry," Muskrat says. "I, uh, could call you Armey if you'd like."

"No, Muskrat. I kinda feel like a Tark. Maybe more than an Armand, in fact." I say. "I told Samantha that you were going to be waiting for her."

"Thanks! I don't want to scare her." He peers at my face. "Hey! Congratulations!" He says giving me a big pat on the back.

"For what?" I ask.

He points at the cut on my face. "That's deffo going to, uh, scar. That'll be your first monster-inflicted scar!"

I touch the cut and wince a bit at the sting.

My first monster-inflicted scar.

Implicit in what Muskrat said was the idea that there would be more to come, and I was strangely okay with that idea.

I help Reece and Muskrat load the creature into Hank's truck.

"What'll we do with it?" I ask Hank.

"I know a few places out by Clovis that are pretty remote. We'll bury it out there," Hank says.

"You sound like you've done this before."

Hank shrugs and doesn't answer.

Uncle George comes out of the house and looks at Hank. Some of his bravado has returned, but not much of it. "I want compensation for the damage it caused."

Reece walks past my uncle as he carries Hank's spear and a satchel to the passenger side of the pickup.

"You gonna sue the dead supernatural wolf monster?" Reece asks him. My uncle looks chastened. "Look, old man, I ain't your nephew here, so I don't gotta be polite to you, but since you're his family, I'll make an exception. You ain't dead, and you have no idea—because people like you don't know what kind of nightmares go bump in the night—how incredibly lucky you are. Do what your nephew said, get in the car, go to wherever-the-hell he told you to go, and watch TV until we tell you it's safe to come back, got it?"

Uncle George stares at Reece for a moment, looks at me, and then nods. It amazes me that confidence has that much influence over people like my uncle. My uncle was a paper tiger, but I'd always been too weak to push him over. Miriam and Dikran come out of the house and pile into the minivan, my uncle looks at me and says nothing before walking over to the first call vehicle and getting in. A moment later, they pull out into the street and are driving away towards my family's farm house.

"So, what was that stick?" I ask Hank as he walks up to me.

"A Kaylxaz Spear." Hank says. "The flint blade is good for killin' our werewolf friend here. I had a guy track the spear down earlier this week after we learned a bit more about the Children of Spandaramet. The Legion always does its research when it can."

"Wow, you guys taking on new recruits?"

Hank looks at me, narrows his eyes, gives me a sniff, and then shrugs. "I'll think about it."

Muskrat is the last one out of the house. "All done Hank, there's, uh, nothing really left. Maybe it was a B&E, maybe it was vandals, but it wasn't no werewolf."

"Good man," Hank says as he flips his motorcycle key to Muskrat who fumbles them but manages to recover and snatch them before they hit the ground. "Make sure that Armand's cousin gets to their safe house."

"You got it. Uh, see you, Tark!"

"Tark," Hank repeats with a smile. "Well, *Tark*, we got a dead monster to bury, get in the truck.

"Can we stop somewhere first?"

"Is it important?"

199

"Very," I say.

"Where we going?"

"A bookshop."

We pack into the truck.

Roupen almost spits out his tea when he sees me.

"Hey Roupen," I say with a forced smile. "Surprise."

"Man, you went hard into rebellion after telling the family off at Dad's funeral, I see."

Hank and Reece walk past me and idle around, absently looking at books on nearby shelves as me and my brother talk. He looks at them and then back at me.

"Are you in trouble," he whispers as he eyes Reece. "Do you need me to call someone?"

"They're the Legion of the Lamb. Monster slayers. Occult researchers. They're sort of helping me now."

"Sort of?" Reece puts down a copy of *Pride and Prejudice* and snorts.

"Oh my God, Armand, did you join a cult?"

Reece and Hank both look over and speak in unison, "It's not a cult!" They look at each other, then back at Roupen and me.

"Look, Roupen …" I take a deep breath. "This stuff with the zombies, and Berj Manoogian, and everything is just going crazy."

"Well, you do need a bit of fun in your life," Roupen says, and sips his tea. "Most people would just get a hobby or something."

"They've already tried to kill Uncle George, Aunt Miriam, and Dikran. Samantha was out."

His eyes go wide. "Are they okay?"

"Aunt Miriam got a little banged up, Uncle George and Dikran are fine. They're going to stay at Dad's house. You need to skip town for a bit, I think."

"And go where, Armand?"

"Sonoma, Roupen. You go to Sonoma and make Brent happy." I give him a light shrug.

"God damn it. It's yuppie season. When do I need to go?"

"Tonight, if you can."

"Tark," Hank taps his watch and I nod.

"Tark?" Roupen asks. "Sweet mercy, you *are* in a cult."

"Again, we're not a cult," Hank interjects as he and Reece walk past me and out the door.

I fish out my wallet and pull out a few hundred dollars. "Have a bottle of wine on me, brother. Stay safe." I slip him the money.

He eyes me. "Are you going to do something stupid?"

"Everything I've done so far has been stupid, but I have to put an end to this, or I'm just another corpse rising from their grave. I don't want to end up like Alvarez, Roupen. We're ending this."

He walks out from behind the counter and gives me a big hug.

"Stay safe, Armand."

I hug him back.

"You too. Try to enjoy yourself. I hear Sonoma isn't nearly as bad as you make it out to be."

Roupen chuckles to himself and then squeezes my shoulder before going back behind the counter and punching a few things into the cash register.

"Twenty dollars," he says.

"What?"

"That's what you owe me."

"For what?"

"For that vintage printing of *Pride and Prejudice* that your little culty friend lifted."

Never in my wildest dreams had I ever thought I'd be burying the freshly-killed corpse of a shapeshifting monster in an abandoned field in Clovis.

Sometimes, you surprise yourself.

We dump the body, still wrapped in the rug, into the freshly dug hole where it lands with a heavy thud. I shine the flashlight Hank gave me on the corpse. The air around us is acrid and stale.

"We're just going to leave her here?" I ask.

"Yep. Now start filling in the hole." Reece says as he throws a shovelful of dirt onto the body.

This is the sort of thing that maybe happens in Las Vegas, but with gangsters burying the body of someone who owed them too much.

"Don't worry. We've done this before," Reece notes as he dumps more soil on the corpse and then looks at me expectantly. "Are you going to help, or not?"

"Sorry." I put the flashlight down and shovel dirt.

"We bury lots of things around here, Tark. Vampires. Ghouls. Werewolves. All of 'em bad. We put them down and then we bury them. People don't dig them up after the fact." Hank tells me.

I dump another shovelful of dirt onto the corpse. "Vampires are real, too?"

"Of course they're real." Reece talks to me like someone who's asked a stupid question. Maybe I had.

"Shut up, you two. Dig," Hank orders.

He burns the wolf pelt near the fresh grave. It smells of singed hair and blood. Despite the situation, everything around us is calm and peaceful—grass rustles in the wind, a coyote howls in the distance, and the stars flicker overhead.

Hank looks over at me as the pelt burns away to ash. "What you saw tonight is what a life in the Legion of the Lamb might look like. It isn't easy, it's dangerous. We do what we do to protect innocent people from the shadows of the world." As the pelt is reduced to nothing, Hank stomps out the embers with his boot. "If you want in, sure. But this isn't a decision you should take lightly, because there isn't really an option to go back and have a normal life after this. There's no white picket fence and retirement from this life."

"My life stopped being normal ages ago," I tell him. "This is the first time in a long time that I've felt like my steps are leading me somewhere. I'm in."

CHAPTER 24

FIGHT EVIL, SAVE THE WORLD

Vonnie is waiting for me on the front steps when we get back to the clubhouse. Reece and Hank walk past her, giving her a brief hello—she smiles at them—and then puts her hand on my chest when I get close. She turns my face with her hand to look at my cut.

"That looks nasty. You should get Wanda to look at it."

"I will. You okay?" I ask.

"Armand," she says. "Look, can I be honest with you?"

"Of course you can. What's wrong?"

Vonnie looks out into the distance past the road and leans against the porch's railing. "I've been talking to Wanda and Josie, and have had some time to think. I realized today that I hate being a victim." She looks back at me. "When Berj and his thugs grabbed me, all I could think about was dying in that fire, like …" She closes her eyes and stands up straight. "You have a family, it's clear that you want to protect them and that they're a part of your life, even though you have shit to work out with them. But I don't."

I'm confused. I'm not sure where Vonnie is going, but a cold pit is forming in my stomach.

"Okay…"

"I know that I'm still new to all this stuff, ghosts and magic and shit, but I can't go back to being a stripper after this. I can't go back to being the manager of a grocery store, either. What am I supposed to do with my life knowing what I know now?" Vonnie takes a deep breath. "Armand, I'm going to join the Legion. Wanda and Josie both said that it was a tough life, but it's one that I'm welcome to be a part of."

I give her a warm smile. "It's a good decision."

"You're not mad? I figured that you'd be annoyed or something that you just got a girlfriend and that she was going to join a biker gang."

"Not when her boyfriend is one of those bikers." I put my arm around her shoulder. "I'm happy that you told me, because I wasn't sure how to tell you that I'm also joining the Legion."

"You shit," she says. She laughs and slaps me in the face. Right on my cut.

"Ow!" I grab my face and she winces, patting me on the shoulder lightly.

"Yeah, sorry. I'm not used to that being there."

Reece sticks his head out the door. "Come on, lovebirds. Muskrat is back from escorting your cousin. We have things to do."

"Listen up, ladies and gents. We've got some guests," Hank tells the crowd gathered inside the clubhouse. "Armand and Vonnie. They're strangers in a strange land here. Be hospitable and give them a Legion of the Lamb welcome, would you please?"

Everyone in the bar hollers and raises glasses or bottles (and in Muskrat's case, both). My chest is tight now, but, for once, it isn't anxiety. It's anticipation. There is a new face in the room that I don't recognize, a handsome man with two scars on each of his cheeks—we make eye contact and I nod. He does the same.

"We're battling forces that are always lurking in the shadows—hungry things, hellbent on turning this world to dust. This is war, and in a war, you don't think of yourself. You think as a team. You act as a team. You fight as a team. Or you die. This isn't some drinking club and we ain't just bikers. We are the first line of defense against the armies of Hell. We are brothers and sisters in this fight." Hank raises his beer again. "Fight evil, save the world."

Everyone echoes back the saying.

"Tonight, both of our guests have come to us for their own reasons and want to be a part of our family," Hank says. The Legion cheers wildly. "Does anyone have any objections?"

Reece pipes up, "Tark is *very* scrawny; I'm not sure he's going to be much good other than as bait." Rancorous laughter fills the room and I exhale. Josie throws a chicken wing at Reece and it bounces off his face.

"Anyone have real issues?" Hank asks taking a swig of his beer. He waits for a moment, looking at me and Vonnie carefully. "Then it's settled." Hank nods towards Wanda who brings him two large candles. He puts his beer down, takes them, and then holds them out to us—we each take one.

Hank lights them.

"These candles are the light of the Legion. They represent the burning truth and cleansing purity. May your light illuminate your way through the darkness ahead. May it be held up for your brothers and sisters. May you use the light to conquer evil."

Big Earl steps forward and presents us each with a large hunting knife with a small lamb holding a sword engraved on the handle. "Welcome," he says, smiling proudly. "I'm happy that you're joining us. Let these knives protect you and serve you wherever they can."

"Bill," Hank calls over to the new face. "Bring the book."

The man with two scars walks over and stands next to Hank. He holds a large leather-bound book in his hands, opens it, and steadies it for Hank to read.

"Hear the Legion's Code and abide every tenant. Repeat after me, we will never stray from the light, we will not allow harm to our flock due to inaction, and we will never let evil seduce us."

Vonnie and I repeat it, stumbling here and there with the exact wording but getting it mostly right.

"Giving yourself to the Legion of the Lamb must be done with full measure and mental clarity," Hank tells us. "You bind yourself to the cause, to our fight against the dark ones sowing chaos. You are champions for righteousness and glory. Your actions will undo what evil hath wrought. Do you accept?"

"Yeah," I say. Vonnie nods firmly.

"Welcome to the Legion of the Lamb. We are one. We are united. We are unbreakable. Bring them their armor!"

I look around confused for a moment, and I see Muskrat and Josie approach us holding two black leather vests. They look new, but the patches that would mark us as part of the Legion were there. I guess that we have some discretion in terms of what patches we can put on the vest, but it doesn't seem like the time to ask.

"May our newest members, Vonnie and Armand, serve the Legion for the rest of their days, with humility and resolve," Hank announces. "Now let's party!"

The room explodes in applause and everyone drinks. Josie comes over and offers her a closed fist, Vonnie bumps it and they embrace. Muskrat and Two Scars stand nearby and give me approving statements of support. I feel in my bones that this is where I belong.

"I'm Bill, the librarian," Two Scars tells me. "I'm usually buried in books, and I'm not always around. It's good to meet you, Tark." I shake his hand.

"Good to meet you, Bill. So, do you guys just have extra leather vests kicking around?" I ask.

Bill laughs. "We honestly go through them fairly quickly sometimes, so we do keep a few extra ones kicking around. You should feel lucky, I got an I.O.U. at my ceremony."

Muskrat walks over to me and shakes my hand. "You should, uh, let Wanda take a look at that cut, Tark. Now that you're one of us, it'd be a shame if, uh, you died of an infection or something." He walks over to Vonnie and congratulates her next.

Hank has eased himself into a padded chair and is looking around the room. The group is a rag-tag troupe of wanderers and happy warriors, and he looks like a proud father. He beckons me over.

"Tark," he says, "you and me and Bill need to have a few words." I grab a chair and sit down in front of him. "Bill!" Hank nods at the young man who fishes through a large burlap sack and pulls out a blue book. He walks over, grabs a chair, and drags it over to sit with us. "Bill is our research guru. If there is something in an arcane book or some history text, he's the guy to ask. He's got one of those photographic memories or something."

"So, Hank said that you saw Spandaramet being summoned?" Bill starts flipping through pages covered in dark writing, runes, and drawings.

"Well, I didn't see Spandaramet, no."

"But you saw the ritual?"

"Alvarez," I pause, thinking of how long ago that felt. Almost no time had actually passed at all. "Alvarez had his heart cut out, and they did a weird ritual with it." I shake my head. "I honestly don't know what they did. I felt like something was wrong though, like in my bones."

Bill nods. "That sounds like the ritual. This look familiar?" He shows me a drawing on one of the pages of a dagger and a container of some kind, both looked like the ones that Berj had.

"Yeah, he used those."

Bill frowns.

"How bad is it?" Hank asks.

"Well, Berj didn't actually *summon* Spandaramet," Bill says. "He empowered her."

"Empowered how?" I ask.

"Well, summoning isn't just a 'wave your hands and things appear' kind of thing. You need to take precautions to summon something. Something like Spandaramet would just wreck Berj and the cult if not controlled properly. He'd need runes of power or a talisman or something like that to keep her under control." Bill keeps flipping through pages and checks at his watch. "Humans aren't always able to do all the bad things that they want. Berj wouldn't be able to summon larger and more dangerous things. No amount of preparation would let him pull that off, but if he was empowering Spandaramet, and using that dagger, odds are he's aiming for a bigger prize."

Bill turns the book around to show us an image of a round orb of some kind.

"So, he wants to summon a marble? What's the big deal?" Hank asks.

"It's called the Orb of Ancestors. You know those little packages that you've been stitching into corpses?" I feel my face get hot. "Well, the magic that those things use to reanimate the dead is the tiniest fraction of Berj's power, and only temporarily it seems."

"So, this orb would let Berj just, what, have more power?" Hank asks.

"Yeah," Bill replies. "Theoretically."

"So far this doesn't seem complicated; stop the maniac from getting the magic marble." Hank yawns a bit and takes a drink from his beer, holding it up and seeing that it's almost empty. "We've had harder missions."

"Well, there's a complication." Bill flips a few more pages and shows us a page with some kind of winged monster on it. Hanging around the creature's neck attached to a large chain, was the orb. "So, Berj isn't getting Spandaramet to bring an orb into the world, that's small potatoes level summoning. He's using Spandaramet to summon *this* thing. It's called a Vishap. It's a creature from ancient Armenian legends and the proverbial guard dog for the Orb of Ancestors."

"So, how big we talking? Wolf? Moose?"

"Dragon-sized." I look at Hank and then back at Bill.

"Like full-blown? Or those little Norwegian shits?"

"Full-blown, maybe bigger." Bill shrugs.

"Well that's just great," Hank says with a sigh. "Is there any good news?"

"Well, Spandaramet can only summon the Vishap when there is a Blood Moon."

"When's the next one?" I ask.

"Twelve days," Bill says looking at his watch again. "Wait, sorry, eleven."

"So, just to be clear. Berj Manoogian wants to use a death goddess to summon a dragon so that he can get an orb that has powers that can raise the dead?" Bill and Hank look at each other and then Bill shrugs and nods.

"That's about right," Bill says. "At least that's what I assume based on the things that he's been doing, anyway. I guess the option exists that he'll just unleash the Vishap on Fresno for kicks, but I don't know what he'd gain out of that."

"He must really hate Fresno," Hank says.

Hank is drunk.

Then again, so am I.

I've learned a lot about my new friends. Muskrat has a heart of gold, Big Earl can arm wrestle like a boss (I almost lost an arm), Reece doesn't hate me, but is generally a bit on the antisocial side, Bill is very good at remembering pages from random books, and Josie can take anything apart and put it back together.

And Hank is descended from monster hunters.

"My father, Walter Geist, was a Bible salesman from Rankin, Texas," he tells me. The more he talks, the more his breath makes my eyes water. "Years spent on the road selling Bibles for the Steadfast

Bible Company. Peddled the Good Book from El Paso to Abilene. He was a real churchy guy. Raised me and my brother Russ up to fear God, eat our vegetables, wash behind our ears." He leans back and rests his bad leg on a chair. "One night in 1957 he was ambushed by—for lack of a better word—a demon, out in Rankin. He told the town sheriff who laughed him out of the room. Rankin was an oil town with powerful interests pulling the strings. You couldn't pass wind in that place without the higher ups knowing about it, so when my father blabbed that he spied himself a demon in the oil fields, he attracted the wrong kind of attention."

"What kind of attention?" I ask, checking the row of beer bottles in front of me to see if any still have alcohol in them.

"Folks made life difficult for my old man. Restaurants wouldn't serve him. Newspapers branded him the town crank. Even the mayor told him to get lost. But my father was stubborn as a mule. He dug in. Bought himself a shotgun and hunting knife and investigated the oil fields himself. Amid the jack pumps and wells, he uncovered a network of tunnels dug out by some creature. He crawled through those tunnels for miles and found demons in them. He went back to town and told the people who'd listen to him. There was Rosie Ramirez, a waitress at Longhorn Diner, Burt Redberry, a high school janitor, and Mac Pearson, who was a truck driver and Marine. It didn't matter what you did, it mattered if you believed in the fight. They joined my old man and sent those demons, or whatever they were, back to Hell. Afterwards, they founded the Legion. My brother and I were brought in as members and sent out into the world to form our own chapters. During the 1960s, we hit the psychedelics, Vietnam happened, and we all did vision quests in the wilderness and shit like that. We ditched the Bible—the good fight wasn't about being Christian, it was about being a good person—and anyone can do that."

I force a smile. "Even people like me, I guess."

"Your talents aren't by chance, Tark. I stopped believing in coincidences a long time ago. They developed for a reason."

"You guys were already following me," I note.

"Sure, Wanda sensed something around Fresno and so we narrowed it down—Wanda didn't make you have an accident with Berj, or witness a ritual of Spandaramet, or even join us. You did that on your own, but all the pieces sort of placed themselves in the right position for it to happen."

I feel strong hands on my shoulder. Reece. "Mind if I borrow the neophyte, boss?"

"All yours."

"Come on Tark, I got a present for you." He pulls me out to the porch and the fresh air washes over me. Reece fishes into his pocket and pulls out a necklace. "Here. Wear this and don't take it off."

I take it and look at the simple silver charm and slip it over my head. "What's it do?"

"A bit of protection against the evil. It ain't foolproof, but it's better than nothing." He says. "A reminder though, bullets aren't evil. It doesn't make you invincible."

"Thanks Reece," I say as I tuck it under my shirt.

"I gotta go give one to your girlfriend now … so, glad to have you onboard and all that jazz."

"You needed to bring me outside to give me a necklace?" I look at Reece, feeling a little confused.

"No," he says. He grabs my shirt and pulls me in close. "I swear to everything good and holy that if you tell anyone that I lifted that book, I will put you in the ground so deep God himself won't find you." He lets go and I back into one of the posts.

"No problem," I say, his threat washing over me.

Reece turns around to go back into the bar and mumbles, "Thanks for paying for it, though." And then he's gone.

I'm outside for a while, I'm not sure how long. Vonnie comes out and rubs my shoulders. "Reece is a sweetheart, isn't he?" She stands next to me.

"I suppose so."

"Thinking about things?"

"It's been kind of a wild day."

"I've been having wild days for years now, *Tark*," she smiles. "You know, I think that I like it, sounds like a bit of a badass, this Tark guy."

"That so?" I smile.

"We're kind of like orphans, you and me. I think that this is our new family. I hope this is the right choice, but it's obviously better than what we were doing, me burning to death and you getting eaten by a werewolf or whatever it was." She leans against me. "Are you ready to save the world?"

"I think I am. But, like, tomorrow when I'm sober."

"We'll find out. Let's have a few beers and get crazy. Tomorrow they're going to turn us into soldiers against monsters. Tonight, it's only us, a lot of alcohol, and a high probability of sweaty sex."

"Okay," I laugh and take her hand.

After a few beers, we retire to the room we were given. Once inside, our eyes lock. I kiss Vonnie tenderly and pull her waist towards mine. She tilts her head and her lips touch my cheek. I shiver. "You really want to do this?" I ask.

"Yes," she whispers into my ear.

My heart races. We fumble out of our clothes. Shoes. Belt. Pants. Everything is off, garments shedding to the floor like dead leaves tumbling from trees until we're naked.

We melt into each other and fall asleep to the sound of crickets in a cool night breeze.

CHAPTER 25

FAMILY BONDS

Wanda's office looks like it belongs to a Coney Island fortune teller. A crystal ball rests on a small white pillow on a table covered with a black velvet cloth. Candles in brass holders light the room. I catch a whiff of incense and spot gemstones, crystals, and a worn Tarot deck.

Wanda sits in a high-backed chair, stroking a black cat. It's like she's trying to tick as many things as possible off her "I'm a mystic" bingo card. The cat hisses when I enter, hops off her lap, and wanders over to a small sofa nearby.

"Come on in, Tark. You'll have to forgive Fiona. She's always jumpy around people with gifts."

I slip into the chair opposite Wanda. "You wanted to see me?"

"I do. I think that we need to get you some answers about what's going on in your noggin. Maybe we can uncover what makes you tick. All we know so far is that you're a medium. A spirit-talker."

"You called me a Latent."

"That's right. There are different names for what you are. Latent is what Hank's old man called mediums, and given that he started the Legion of the Lamb, we sort of just kept using the term."

"Makes sense. I take it that you've met others like me?"

"Like us, yes. Our abilities are different, but we're both spiritual critters. Your abilities are far more refined, I just have a little bit of a gift for healing and tracking down things that have a magical presence, sort of like clairvoyance. Maybe more like a spiritual compass, I guess? That's why we were following you around—we were trying to figure out what the deal was with you. Turns out though, that you went and got yourself involved in all sorts of shit all on your own."

"Yeah. Hey, if you're also a Latent, how come your cat likes you?"

"She's my cat. Who do you think feeds her?" Wanda laughs. "Cats have a sense for this sort of thing. Lots of animals do, that's why sometimes they do things that don't make sense. Ever notice a cat stare at a blank corner or a dog bark at something that isn't there?"

"Sure."

"They're detecting residues of spiritual activity."

"Do they see ghosts?"

"Why don't you ask them and get a clear answer?" She smiles as she picks up a cup of tea and sips at it.

"Fair enough," I say. "How do you know this stuff?"

"I'm a witch. Also, I do a lot of reading."

"Okay. Wait, what? You said you're a witch?"

"Fuckin'-A I am. A practicing witch, right here. The rest is from books that the Legion has gotten a hold of, talking to other Latents, you know, a little here and there."

"Are there lots of Latents?" I ask.

"Nope, not really. The thing is that supernatural lives have a sort of magnetism to them."

"What do you mean?"

Wanda fills a mug with a heady amber liquid from a small metal pot and puts the cup in front of me. "Magical things have a habit of coming together. It's like there's a pull between these forces, like they're

215

pieces being put into position for events to happen. Doesn't happen with normal folk, but you think it's a coincidence that all these random events are happening to you?" Wanda shrugs. "Your accident with Berj Manoogian, your ability to talk to ghosts, finding us, meeting people that keep winding up dead, I don't think these things are coincidences."

"So, there's like some kind of grand plan?"

She shakes her head. "I don't *think* so. It feels more like the way that gravity and orbits affect each other, I think. I'm not a physicist, what do I know."

She gets up from her chair and walks over to the wall, pulling down a picture and handing it to me. I take the frame and look at the faded photo. It's Wanda in her twenties in an Army nurse uniform, posing with other members of the 44th Medical Brigade.

"Long Binh, Vietnam. 1970. I was mainly triage. That's around when my own abilities started to develop. Just a long day one day, and then *bam,* I started having woo-woo abilities. My ability to heal kicked in, and I was able to save people a bit better—only to send them out to die the next time. Saved some men, but lots died. That sort of stays with you forever. It gets locked into your mind and then these events sort of keep triggering your ability."

It was true for me, too. My own feelings had helped to trigger my abilities. "Did you meet Hank during the war?"

"Hank? He didn't get as much as a paper cut. Survived completely unscathed. Motor pool engineer. Hank fixed and maintained vehicles," Wanda says. "He wouldn't stop flirting with me. Kept asking me out. Finally, I relented. But this isn't about Wanda's romantic entanglements in Southeast Asia. This is about Tark and his penchant for chatting with spirits."

"I don't know how I got this ability," I confess. "It happened one day at work. I was just an embalmer trapped at his family's funeral home. Look, Wanda. All of this hocus pocus is new to me. I've seen magic since, but only the not-so-nice variety. Frogs bursting from bodies, worms appearing from nowhere, the dead rising from their graves."

"You know why?"

"No. Do you?" I ask.

"Nope." She laughs. "I got a theory though. Magic also corrupts. People are fundamentally not good or bad, generally. We're sort of a mish-mash stew of self-interest. If you give someone who is self-interested a bunch of power, they'll abuse people to better themselves."

"Why aren't you evil then?" I ask.

"We're not using magic, really. I guess that what we have is more of a *natural talent* as opposed to magic." She sips her tea again and leans back in her chair. "I don't know what Berj's plan is, but dollars to donuts it's something dumb like 'I want to be the ruler of such and such an evil arcane empire'. It's always something idiotic like that."

I chuckle a bit.

"Drink your tea," she says.

"What's in it?"

"Antioxidants."

"You're kidding right?"

"Guilty as charged. It's a special brew that'll put you in a trance-like state. Drink it."

"Chamomile?"

"Funny. You need to be in a deep, relaxed state. You're going on a journey."

"Where?"

"Don't know. You'll find out though. Exciting, right?"

"Sounds vague."

"It is. Very much so. But if we want to find out where your spooky powers come from, this is a good place to start. I'll be right here keeping an eye on things."

I give her a funny look.

"Don't worry," Wanda reassures me. "You're sitting in a chair, and I'm right here to pull your ass out of danger if anything gets too weird. Ten days to go before Berj Manoogian tries doing something stupid. Drink up. There isn't much time for you to be all 'overly cautious' about this."

The tea smells pungent and rotten. My first sip tastes earthy, like dirt and moss. I wince and wrinkle my nose.

"Bottoms up. All of it," Wanda says.

"It's kind of gross." I choke.

"No, it's *very* gross. Now drink up, you big baby."

I force myself to chug the whole cup, barely avoid retching and then belch. An acrid flavor lingers in my mouth. I feel my vision starting to blur—my stomach and head lurch and the world turns sideways.

"What's happening?" I murmur. Everything melts like a Dalí painting, a swirled and disjointed surreal dream. Then things get weird.

My eyes snap open. I'm standing in an ancient sandstone building; its portico of pillars and rising arches remind me of an Armenian church. Perfumed incense fills the air, and flames flicker from hidden niches.

I don't recognize this place, but it's familiar, like something in my bones is attuned to it.

A stone khachkar – an Armenian cross – resplendent with carved floral patterns and entwined vines, stands in a great hall lit by a thousand flickering candles. I wander silently through the space to an open door that leads out to a veranda overlooking distant snow-capped mountains. A solitary figure, wearing the white robes I'm now used to seeing on ghosts, stands looking at the mountains. The figure turns to me.

My mother.

She smiles —her face is kind, just like I remembered it. "My hokis. Barev, my brave boy."

Barev is *'hello'* in Armenian.

I reply, "Hi, Mom."

She frowns slightly.

218

"You didn't practice Armenian, did you?" She sighs before grinning and gives me a light shrug. "You never really did want to learn it." Her eyes shine. "It's been so long, Armand. Look how much you've grown."

I embrace her. Illusion, mirage, or hologram, I don't care. She feels real and warm in this place—that's all that matters.

"I see you haven't led a dull life." She touches my face where it's cut.

"You're dead, aren't you?" I ask.

"Of course, hokis. What else would I be?"

"Where exactly am I, anyway?"

"This is a place between worlds. Some call it the limbo, others the Veil, there are lots of names for it. This is the space that only people like us can visit."

"It feels *familiar*."

Mom turns away from me and looks out into the distance. "Those are the mountains of our ancient homeland. This church and everything you see is a place that no longer exists, but we can come here if we want. It is not in the mundane world, but also not quite the afterlife. Spirits come and go through these spaces, and a medium can feel their way through the ether to the threads of fate that connect everyone. That's why you can see me."

I touch the stone railing, which is cool under my fingers.

"I don't believe it," I murmur. "How is this happening?"

"It needs to happen, hokis. You came here for answers. You're not pulling the dead into your world now, you have come here because your spirit needed to come here. Your soul craves answers and you brought me here to hopefully give you those answers."

My gaze falls. "I don't know what I am or where I'm going. The dead started talking to me and keep asking me for my help."

"Our family is burdened with this ability, it has followed us across the generations." Mom folds her arms. "It began with your great-great-grandfather Hampartsoum Barsamian from Kharput in

Turkey. The one on my side of the family. This curse is of our blood-line."

"What happened to... Hampartsoum was it?"

"He made an infernal pact with an al."

"Who's Al?"

She laughs.

"No. An al is a demon from our ancient folklore, except they're very real. An al steals babies from a mother's womb and, as the story goes, your great-great-grandfather stopped the creature from taking his wife's unborn child. The trapped creature desperately promised fabulous wealth if it was released. Hampartsoum, a man of, shall we say *modest* education and sensibility, agreed."

"I'm guessing things didn't turn out well for good old Hampartsoum."

Mom pulls the robes tightly around her. "Instead of bestowing him with riches, the al cursed Hampartsoum with a second sight, and condemned him and all his descendants until the end of time to hear the complaints of the dead."

"How does this curse work? Why haven't we all had these close encounters with the spectral kind? Roupen thought I had lost my mind when I told him about it."

My mother's face beams at the mention of her youngest child's name. "Did he find a handsome man to settle down with?"

"You knew?"

"Of *course* I knew," she says. "I'm his mother."

"Yeah, he did. He owns a bookshop now."

"You tell him I'm proud of him." She pauses for a moment. "The curse flows, one person at a time. When the person dies, the curse moves on to the next first-born child in the line. My father had it, then I had it, and now you have it. Perhaps one day you will have a child, and then it will fall to them."

"Why didn't I see the spirits right away, after you died?"

Mom shrugs, "I do not know. Perhaps there is a reason, perhaps you were too occupied,"—she taps my head with a finger — "to notice what was happening. Whatever the reason, you have it and you cannot escape it now."

"Shit."

My mother frowns. "Language, hokis."

"Sorry mother."

"Do you believe that everything happens for a reason?" my mother asks.

"I can't," I say.

"A pity. Many Armenians believe that—all is preordained and God has his hands on the wheel, steering the ship. They have faith and that helps them get through life. Everyone finds a way to make it through life, for good or for ill. Our spirits crave connection. Some of us reach out to God, while others discover meaning in this world."

"How did you live with this curse? I was so unprepared, and I had no one to talk to, so it feels like I'm just being punished."

"I had hoped that ignorance from our family history would be a blessing. The Barsamians had a reputation in Kharput. So much so that they were shunned and eventually left for America."

"I hardly know anything about the Barsamians," I admit.

"And the Tarkanians do their best to make sure that the Barsamian side of the family is at arm's length. Your father married me, but he didn't want to marry into my family. He knew about the curse only in the sense that his wife was *troubled* at times." She smiled. "He could not understand, but he pretended to, he let me have my 'little fits', as he called them. But he couldn't see what I could, and he never understood why sometimes I just left."

"You left? What do you mean?"

"You asked me how I lived with the curse." Mom leans in close. "It wasn't a curse to me. People needed my help, and so I helped them where I could. To put a spirit to rest is like putting the body to rest. You already do one, why not do the other?"

I have a hard time thinking of something to say. My mother reaches up and strokes my cheek lovingly.

"I feel like I'm just accursed or something," I mutter.

"Do you know what it is to be accursed?" she asks.

"Yeah, it's like you're stuck with some punishment."

"No, hokis. That's to be cursed. To be *accursed* is to be detestable. You may not be able to decide the fate that your bloodline has given you, but you can control how you and others around you feel about it. I had your father, and you, and your brother. I was always loved and so my *curse* was never a punishment—perhaps that al was not as successful as it hoped. Fate always has its part, but it cannot control how you feel."

"Fate," I scoff. "My fate was to be working on the farm with Dad, or stuck in a cold room embalming bodies for Uncle George."

"Why would that be your fate, Armand?"

"Because of Agra Hadig. Dad wanted me to pick a garden trowel, but I wound up picking a knife." I kick the stone railing in front of me.

My mother laughs. "Aw, hokis. Agra Hadig isn't a gumball machine where you can keep trying until you get the flavor you like! It's the *first* thing you pick, not the second, or fourth, or eighth. When you were young, while everyone was so concerned with trowels and knives and needles, I gave you a toy."

"The motorcycle? You put that there?" I ask. "I thought that it had just gotten mixed in by accident."

"You loved that toy. I thought it best that maybe one of your options be something that you enjoyed that made you happy."

Tears sting my eyes.

"The Tarkanian in you is the pragmatist, and the part that tries so hard to please others by being a good son," she continues. "The Barsamian in you is the rebel. You are of two lines and where those two conflicting parts come together is where you exist. A foot in each world, but your own man."

I wipe my face.

"It's weird, Aunt Miriam always said that the family was cursed," I say. "I wonder if it's the Tarkanians that are actually cursed."

Mom looks skyward.

"Ugh! Your Aunt Miriam is great at making roast lamb, but lousy at giving life advice."

"So, what do I do?"

"Have strength and accept where you are in the world and in your life," she tells me. "But, be humble enough to know that you are not in this fight alone. Solitude is an actual curse."

I think of my father.

"Thanks, Mom."

"You have what you need."

"Yeah." My feelings about a lot of things are mixed, but my resolve is strong. I know more about myself than I could have ever hoped to learn, thanks to my curse. "Mom?"

"Yes, Armand?"

"I love you."

"I love you too." She smiles and hugs me again. It's a long and sad embrace, but oddly comforting. "Be good, and take care of your brother."

She shimmers, though I'm not sure it isn't the tears in my eyes, and then she's gone.

I jerk awake.

Wanda is sipping her tea with her eyes closed with Fiona purring in her lap. My head is fuzzy and pounding. I groan lightly and Wanda opens her eyes and smiles.

"Welcome back," she says. "How'd it go? Learn anything useful?"

"Ugh," I feel like I'm going to vomit for a moment as the world slowly stops spinning. "Yeah, I think so." I close my eyes and take a deep breath. "I saw my mom."

"Dead relatives should be listened to. They may or may not have information that applies to your situation and curse, but they'll *always* have something to say about your life and your emotional state. Moms especially. Did you get any clarity?"

"I think I did, yeah."

"Good stuff."

"Thanks, Wanda," I say.

"Not a problem, Tark."

It takes a little bit of time, but eventually I can get back on my feet without wanting to throw up. Wanda tells me that I should take a walk, gets some air, and maybe think a bit about what just happened. It's not every day, that you get to talk to one of your deceased parents (apparently I get to do this more often than most). I go outside and walk around the parking lot of the big building that serves as the Legion of the Lamb's clubhouse. As I near the back of the building, I can hear rock music and the clanging of metal. I make my way over to a large shed, about the size of a shipping container, and peek inside.

Hank is sitting in a chair, his feet up, listening to music. There's something large under a tarp and a number of different tool boxes nearby. I'm guessing it's a motorcycle, given the Legion's motifs, but I'm not sure. He has his eyes closed, but he gestures towards a folding chair against the wall which I dutifully set up near him and sit down.

"This here's Velma." He gestures towards the tarp with a thumb. "She's my pride and joy. A 1983 Harley-Davidson Willie G Special. She's a real beauty. Wanda always said why bother having a kid when I was already so in love with this bike."

"Why didn't you, if you don't mind my asking?"

"The Legion is my family, Tark. It wasn't possible to be a warrior against evil and also raise a couple of ankle biters. Wanda knew it too, at least she has that fucking cat." He laughs. "That thing has been around for ages. If it were any older it'd be claiming pension. This life is unique, it really is, and not everyone is parenting material. Teacher, maybe, parent? Nah."

"Ah." I'm really not sure what to say to that, I wonder how much of that was being resigned to the life chosen as opposed to what he might have wanted.

"You know how I got injured?" he finally asks. "I was shot in the leg by the Viet Kong in 'Nam."

"Wanda said that you made it out of the war unscathed."

He laughs. "Because saying 'I fell off my motorcycle' isn't cool, man. We're bikers." He rubs his leg. "Never really healed right, so I'm not particularly agile. Not as fast. Not as strong. That's why I rely so much on Reece and Muskrat. Those two really believe in what the Legion stands for, and belief is what makes us strong. That unity. Not just amongst Reece and Muskrat either. Josie, Bill, Wanda, hell, even me. We're a family and that bond is what has always made us strong."

"My experience with family has always been complicated."

"The family you're born into can mess you up for life, Tark. The family that you surround yourself with is the one that'll help you put yourself together."

That's twice in one day that I've gotten some good advice from parental figures. I guess I'm a part of this kooky family after all.

"Make sure you're not late for dinner," Hank says as he puts his feet down and stands up slowly.

"Yeah, boss."

I walk towards the clubhouse and leave Hank to work on his bike or reminisce about whatever it is that old bikers are introspective about when they're alone with their thoughts.

Between me and the clubhouse entrance sits a mutt.

225

The dog is the same one that I've been running into all over the place. Its pink tongue dangles from its mouth and the animal barks and spins playfully.

"Get away from me," I tell the pooch.

The dog barks again and starts to follow me. For a brief moment, I wonder if it was a mardagayl. The animal sniffs at my heels as I walk faster.

"What do you want?"

The dog barks again.

I turn on my heels to shoo the dog away, but when I look back, the dog has vanished.

CHAPTER 26

TARK

Sunshine streams through the window when heavy knocking on the bunkhouse door jolts me awake. Vonnie lays next to me, somehow still sleeping through it.

I slip into my pants and stumble towards the door. When I open it, Reece stands there, twirling a keychain around his index finger like a small propeller.

"Rise and shine, neophytes! We're starting training," he says loudly. Vonnie jerks up in bed and stares at me through bleary eyes. She groans, letting herself collapse back into the bed. "Let's go, lovebirds! We ain't got much time left. Downstairs in ten. Both of you."

I close the door and look over at Vonnie. She's glaring at me.

"You signed up," I say with a loud yawn and pull a shirt over my head. "Come on. Get dressed."

"Fine." She's clearly annoyed at being awoken at the crack of dawn, and I don't blame her. We kiss one more time, struggle into our street clothes, and haul ass downstairs.

We find Reece leaning against the bar. "Glad you rookies finally showed up. Ready to get started?"

"What're we doing?" Vonnie asks.

"A bit of hand to hand combat. We gotta make sure that you can throw and take a punch. Under normal circumstances, we'd be running you through a whole program—designed by yours truly—but with less than two weeks to go, it's not enough time to get much taught. We'll need to settle for a focus on breaking holds and throwing punches, and a bit of time working with firing practice. I guess I'll have a better chance to train you after we're done kicking the Children of Spandaramet to the curb."

"You're doing the training?" I ask.

"Unless you know of someone else with actual martial arts and combat experience, yes."

"Do you know karate?" I ask, smirking a little.

"Taekwondo, smart ass. I was a police officer for ten years, so I've got more than a little exposure dealing with aggressive people. Follow me."

"Why'd you quit?" My mouth feels a bit dry—I realize that I've never really been in a real fight. A few scraps here and there, but nothing as an adult, and certainly nothing where the other person might actually be trying to kill you.

"I got a little too overzealous one arrest. Broke a guy's arm. There was an inquiry. Mostly a lot of bad press. The yahoos at the Modesto Police Department thought it best if I took an early retirement." Reece chuckles.

"I'm sorry to hear that," I say.

"Don't be. It wasn't my fault. I was set up."

Vonnie finishes a yawn. "Set up?"

"Yeah, I was already doing a bit of moonlighting for the Legion back then, so more than a couple parties wanted to prevent us from having access to police records," Reece says.

He leads us through the kitchen and out a door to a side room that looks like a gym. Not a professional gym with equipment, though there is some of that. There are a bunch of mats on the floor and some boxing equipment at the back of the room.

The first part of the day largely consists of doing laps in the parking lot and then quickly throwing on some boxing gear and trying to avoid a few shots from Reece. He's obviously pulling his punches, but after getting hit more than a couple of times, I have to take a break.

Vonnie is doing much better than I am. "I had four brothers growing up," she says by way of explanation. I realize there's a lot about Vonnie that I still don't know. I'd need to survive everything, including Reece's training, if I was going to find out more about her.

Even though I jog frequently, my dexterity is rusty. I barely miss Reece's blows and kicks. One catches me in the side of the head and my vision explodes into darkness peppered with white stars. When my vision returns, I'm on my ass on the floor, Reece rubbing my shoulders.

"Atta boy," he says. "I was wondering how you'd handle that."

"And?" I ask, feeling a bit woozy.

"Well," he purses his lips. "Let's hope that no one tries to clean your clock."

"That's encouraging," I say.

"Well, the best way to not lose a fight is to not get hit," he says.

Vonnie laughs.

By the time lunch rolls around, I'm sweaty, sore, and sleepy. But I feel good. Vonnie looks like she's doing better than I am, I suppose that dancing keeps her fit. Reece shoos us so that we can go get some food, which Wanda has already set out for everyone. Josie and Muskrat are already eating.

"Hey guys," Josie says. "How's captain *I-know-all-the-martial-arts-in-the-world* treating you?"

"He's tough," I reply.

Josie nods. "Yeah, it's all right, you'll get used to it. Once you get a firm grasp of the basics, he'll start to lay off a bit. I guess next is ..."

"Me!" Muskrat says, clearly excited.

"Nope, it's me." Big Earl sits down at the table next to Muskrat. When he talks, he sounds like a drill instructor from a Hollywood movie. "Sorry bud, but they need a gun more than they need to know the difference between forty-three different kinds of werewolves." He gives Muskrat a pat on the back. "Your turn is coming soon."

Muskrat frowns. "It's always, uh, someone else's turn." He picks up a small bun and chews on it.

"I'm guessing neither one of you have handled firearms before?" He looks over at me and Vonnie.

"A couple of times," she replies.

Surprised, I look at her. "Really?"

"You think all strip joints have a major focus on work-place safety, Tark?" she says with a grin. The others around the table get a good laugh from this. Vonnie looks pleased at the sign of acceptance from the crew.

"You learn something new every day," I say.

"Don't worry. I'm going to go *real* slow, like you're a baby, so you understand me. The last thing we want is an amateur handling firearms." Big Earl now has me solidly in his sights. "After lunch we'll get started." He gives me a thumbs up.

After we eat he takes us to the firing range, an open swath of land behind the property with targets at the far end then presents us with a crash course on firearms and gun safety. Muskrat tags along for the practice.

Big Earl runs us through the basics: Treat every firearm as it is loaded. Develop a respect for the weapons. Show care when pointing a firearm. Practice trigger discipline, don't keep your finger on the trigger.

Over and over until it sinks in.

He starts us off with a .380 caliber —a Glock 42. Nothing fancy, it's a simple handgun. He teaches us where the safety is, how to load the pistol, and how to aim it properly. And, most importantly, how to shoot. We practice for so long that my hands feel like they're perpetually vibrating.

"Have you ever killed anyone?" Big Earl asks me.

"I'm an embalmer, Big Earl. The people I deal with are already dead," I tell him.

"Want a piece of advice?" he asks.

"Sure," I say, looking over at Vonnie.

"It's going to be hard for you to put things into perspective. You haven't really seen a lot of what is out there. But, you remember that thing at your family's house?"

"How could I forget that?" I say, recalling the mardagayl who nearly took my face off.

"That sort of creature is what we're going to be dealing with, but they often have human servants or take the form of humans. There's some horrible ones out there that'll hide themselves as children," He explains as he taps one of his hands against his chest, the signal for us to reload our pistols so that we're back to a full magazine and ready to fire. "All of us have needed to take a time-out here or there, it's a hard life, and it's a tough series of calls to make. Make sure that you aren't keeping shit bottled up, having someone break down on us can get someone killed, so if you're ever needing to talk about anything, make sure you talk to Wanda."

"Not you?"

"You can, but she's better at listening than I am. She also has a more soothing presence. Hell, even Muskrat is a great ear." He gestures to the big man who is loading shells into a shotgun.

"Uh, thanks!" Muskrat beams. "I do like to listen to people."

Vonnie narrows her eyes. "Won't the police see the same situation differently?"

231

"You know all those reports that you heard about police arresting people for the murder of a vampire? Or the time that several ghosts were blown away?" Big Earl shrugs. "We're not a gang, we don't just go around murdering folks, but we won't hesitate to put down a vampire or two if we need to. It's a hard thing to wrap your head around, Vonnie." Big Earl gestures to the paper targets we're shooting. "It'll all make sense soon." He picks up his ear plugs and pops them in.

We do the same and keep practicing.

The Glock in my hand feels awkward and alien. I am surprised by it—the recoil, the aim, and the sound. Earplugs in, goggles on. I grip the weapon, breathe, aim, and squeeze the trigger. Of the things that I found most surprising about practicing was that it was kind of addictive. Missing the target made me want to try again. And again. And *again*.

After several attempts, I finally hit the distant paper target. Not in the center, but I hit that sucker.

And practice continues.

Mornings I get my ass kicked by Reece for a few hours, and in the afternoons, I shoot firearms. It feels strange to not be embalming people—no more pumping false life into corpses. Now my sole purpose is to figure out how to make sure that a madman that is literally giving life to corpses is stopped. Three days into training I talk to Hank to let him know that I need to return my cousin's car. He seems less than thrilled at the idea, but finally agrees on the condition that I stay here to keep training. Muskrat and Josie can go drop the car off—besides, the more hidden I am, the less likely it is that Berj will take a shot at me.

I watch them drive off—Josie in the little blue Civic and Muskrat in Hank's old pickup. Soon enough they disappear down the road, and I realize that it's the longest I've ever been without having my family around. There's something both terribly sad but also liberating about it. I feel less pressure on my shoulders and in my chest—the anxiety has been consistently fading—and keeping myself busy has helped.

I'm leaning against the wooden railing that wraps around the porch of the clubhouse when Josie steps out and lights a smoke. She offers me one, holding out a pack of Luckys. I shake my head.

"Wise choice," she says. "How's the crash course going?" She takes a long drag and holds it in for a moment before exhaling through her nose.

"It's rough," I say.

"I'll bet. The rest of us had time to do our training when we were recruited."

"You did this too?" I ask, surprised. I rarely see Josie, and only ever when it's time to eat or drink.

"Sort of, I had a bit of experience already, but it's not really my *thing*," she makes air quotes, the cigarette hanging off her lips when she does. "I'm more of an under-the-hood kinda girl," she says. "I know how to fix the bikes, trucks, cars, the guns, and my ability to bullseye Reece's head with food is second to none. I'm not great with people, though."

"That's okay. I'm an embalmer, I literally used to hang out with corpses all day. I know what it's like to be bad at talking to people."

"Hmm," Josie mumbles.

We stand there quietly for a while, her smoking, and me looking off into the distance.

"Can I ask you a question?" I ask Josie. She takes her cigarette out of her mouth and nods for me to continue. "Am I insane for joining the Legion?"

"Probably," she said, taking another drag, the cigarette burning down almost to the filter. She flicked it out into the dusty sands in front of the building. "Not one person in this group has all their marbles, I think. Maybe Bill? He's just a big book nerd. The rest of us …" She shrugs, stands up straight, and dusts herself off. "You're here. You joined. You should know what it takes for a person to wind up joining a secret order that hunts down monsters and stuff." She turns around to back into the building. "Some people's stories are just more tragic than others. For what it's worth, your family seems nice. I can see how that would drive a person to fight. See you later, Tark."

"See you, Josie," I say.

Some people's stories are just more tragic than others.

I wonder if my own story is as tragic as I've built it up in my mind, or if an entire lifetime of feeling like I'm the victim of everything just makes it feel that way. Reece was framed and kicked out of his department, Wanda and Hank seemed to have been all in for years, Vonnie lost her family once already, and I get the feeling that Josie has some skeletons in her closet. Hell, even my dad spent most of his life jaded and miserable. Maybe this was the universe's way of telling me that I should be thankful for the things that I have. Maybe it was just my brain telling me to shut up. I'm not sure.

Maybe I just need to take a deep breath and keep moving forward.

"You hit me, and it's a hate crime," Vonnie shouts.

Reece freezes, stopping his punch mid-air, and Vonnie gives him a straight-shot, right in the nose. The bigger man stumbles and takes a few steps back, holding his nose.

"Nice work," Reece says. He's smiling.

Four days left.

While I'm no martial arts expert, Reece has punched me a few times. I've even managed to land a couple of shots myself. Reece called them lucky shots, but I wonder whether or not that's him making sure that my ego doesn't get out of control. But then again, maybe they actually were lucky shots.

I snap back to reality and I realize that the former cop is on top of me.

"Wait," I say. "I'm not going to …"

I take a padded boxing glove right in the gut.

"Pay attention," he says.

"Sorry, Reece, my mind is sort of all over the place." He looks at me and then at Vonnie. "Let's call it for today."

Vonnie stretches. "I gotta go take a shower, I smell like your blood," she says to Reece who laughs.

Reece peels off the boxing gloves and offers me a hand. I take it and he pulls me up to my feet. "You worried about what's coming?" he asks as he watches Vonnie disappear out the door.

"Yeah, man. I'm just a guy. I'm not a cop. I didn't fight in Vietnam. I don't have any particular set of skills. I'm just … me. I'm not sure I even see the point in learning to fight, I've never been good at it."

"I get that. But you're not just going to be able to grab a rock and hit someone with it. Knowing how to fight will help you to protect yourself, and those that matter to you. Some people in the Legion have more training than others. We'll figure it all out eventually." He picks up a towel and wipes his face with it. "Bill was like a university grad or some shit. Hank found him somewhere and the guy was totally all in so that he could get his hands on some cool books. Muskrat was a truck driver and hunter. Josie, shit, I don't think most people know why Josie is here, I sure don't. But we're all in here to try and do the right thing. You're just some guy? So what. We're all 'just someone', makes no difference to Chupacabras or whatever else is going to try killing people."

That seemed to be true. Everyone here was genuinely in it for the little guy.

"Who're you fighting for? Your girl? Yourself? Us? Your family? We all have reasons, just make sure you know what yours are," he says.

"Thanks, Reece."

"For what?"

"Reminding me to stay focused," I say. "Maybe you're not such a terrible sensei after all."

CHAPTER 27

WHISTLING PAST THE GRAVEYARD

Two days to go.

Vonnie and I stand next to the graves of my mother and father.

It's a strange feeling to be reminded that they're both gone. I read their tombstones and know that their time in this world has truly passed. While I might see them in the future—I suppose it's possible—they can't effect change in this world anymore. They're absent from my world forever, pale shadows moving across the face of my history.

Vonnie says nothing, and I appreciate the quiet.

I break the silence. "I wonder if I'll join them soon."

"Hush," she says. "We'll be fine. We're the good guys."

"So was Alvarez," I observe.

Masis Ararat Armenian Cemetery is beautiful. Charming and quaint, the graveyard is the final home for many prominent ethnic Armenians who eternally rest in burial plots beneath our feet. The writer William Saroyan has half of his cremated ashes buried here and the other half interred in Armenia. Actress Lucy Saroyan, decorated World War II Marine Captain Victor Maghakian, and writer and sculptor Varaz Samuelian are also buried at Ararat Cemetery. Our roots sink deep through this dirt and into our ancestor's Armenian homeland.

Vonnie, a stranger to this cemetery, looks over at an obelisk crowned with a gold-plated eagle grasping a snake in its talons. A chain encircles a slab beneath the monument.

"Who's buried here?" Vonnie asks.

"Soghomon Tehlirian," I reply, not needing to check.

"Who's that?"

"Armenians consider him a national hero."

"Oh." Vonnie bites her lip. "What did he do exactly?"

"Know anything about the Armenian genocide?" I ask.

Vonnie shakes her head.

I tell her, "During World War I, the Young Turk government of the Ottoman Empire eradicated Armenians from their ancestral homelands. The result was the death of a million and a half Armenians through massacres and forced death marches. The Ottoman Turks didn't just want to displace and kill Armenians; they wanted to exterminate our culture."

"That's horrible," Vonnie replies.

"The genocide resulted in a worldwide diaspora, as survivors relocated to other countries. Parents passed on the trauma to their children, educating them about tragic events from over a century ago and ensuring that the younger generations would never forget. If you're Armenian, you carry the genocide with you. It defines the culture and the shared experience haunts us even to this day. Nothing like shared trauma passed down from father to son," I recall.

"So it's kind of a big deal."

"You might say that, and Tehlirian played the part of avenging angel."

When I was young, Grandpa sung Soghomon Tehlirian's praises. Tehlirian was a soldier when his family perished in the genocide. After

237

the war he participated in Operation Nemesis, a campaign of revenge on the genocide's perpetrators.

"In 1921, Tehlirian assassinated Mehmed Talaat Pasha, the former Ottoman Grand Vizier, on a Berlin sidewalk. As the interior minister of the Ottoman Empire during World War I, Talaat Pasha was the mastermind behind the Armenian genocide, the mass executions that claimed Tehlirian's family," I say.

Vonnie leans closer. "So this Tehlirian dude had it in for Talaat. What happened to him? He go to prison?"

"No, he didn't. At his trial, Tehlirian admitted to killing the former statesman but didn't consider himself a murderer. The jury acquitted Tehlirian, deeming him temporarily insane due to the genocide's traumatic effects. He eventually moved to San Francisco, where he worked as a postal clerk," I tell her.

Armenian-Americans lauded him as the guy who put down one of their worst nightmares. All the pain the genocide caused—and continues to cause—and so Armenians throughout the world needed to be avenged. The Armenians needed to even the score. They needed a win, and Tehlirian delivered it with a single shot from a Luger pistol.

"My family told me stories about growing up in Fresno during the bad old days when Armenian immigrants faced discrimination," I tell Vonnie. "A developer who built the ritzy Fig Garden neighborhood kept out Armenians and other so-called undesirables through deed restrictions. You couldn't sell your house to Armenians, Asians, Blacks, Hindus, or anyone from the former Ottoman Empire. Fresno redlined sections of the city to keep us out."

"That sounds familiar." Vonnie rolls her eyes. "Some things don't change."

Turned away from the exclusively white neighborhoods, Fresno's Armenians settled in Armenian Town, a downtown enclave bordering Ventura Avenue, Van Ness Avenue, N Street, and San Benito Street. There, Armenian immigrants and their families built churches, businesses, and homes. They thrived in spite of elites restricting them from certain employment: Armenians couldn't work for the government, the newspaper, or financial institutions. But they grew fruit and vegetables and carved out a piece of the American dream as it was.

"History has treated my people like shit," I note. Vonnie gives me a side-eye and I immediately regret my choice of words. I clear my throat. "Yeah. I coulda phrased that better."

She smiles and puts her arm around me. "Both our people are children of pain. We cry harder and sing louder because we have to, right?"

The oppressed always sing the same song, one of hardship and longing for equality.

That familiar song has grown louder and more melodious over the centuries. This sweet melody drowns out discord and strife and preserves us despite the harshness we endure.

Starving didn't end us. War didn't end us. Hell, even pogroms didn't end us. We bounced back, partly because of pride and spite and anger. We willed ourselves awake. We exist and persevere because we choose to.

I will sing until those who despise me for who I am put me in my grave.

"For the longest time, I felt like an outsider, to this town, to my family, to myself," I say. "I never understood why, until you look deep into the past and realize just how prevalent the bigotry was."

"Things have changed, right? At least for you Armenian-Americans. You've got the Kardashians. You got System of a Down. Hell, you even got Cher," Vonnie says.

"My brother's favorite."

"You're a survivor, Tark. Whatever existential crisis you're facing, you got this."

I couldn't tell Vonnie the ugly truth. When townies called my grandfather a "dirty Armenian." When a large raisin grower intimidated Armenian farmers to join their co-op against their wishes. When they excluded immigrants hellbent on making it in this country, despite the unfair-as-fuck rules pushed by nativist bigots.

In addition to the hatemongers who derided us, Armenians also fought among themselves. There's some truth to the proverb Aunt Miriam once taught me: "One Armenian eats one chicken; two Armenians eat two chickens; three Armenians eat each other."

"Our community is fragmented. Those from the old country battle with those from America. Those from America detest those from the old country. Their memories are long. They never forget or forgive. If your grandfather transgresses, you wear his shame for the rest of your days," I say.

"I notice guilt is strong with you guys." Vonnie's flippant remark digs deeper than it should.

Everything that happened and the reason we're here is my fault. All of it. Alvarez's death. The family scared and scattered, all because I couldn't say no. Because what started as fear, turned into greed.

I focus on the words carved in stone before me, each letter etched in black granite:

THIS MONUMENT HAS BEEN
ERECTED BY THE ARMENIAN
PEOPLE IN MEMORY OF
SOGHOMON TEHLERIAN, THE
NATIONAL HERO WHO, ON MARCH
15, 1921, BROUGHT JUSTICE UPON
TALAAT PASHA, A PRINCIPAL
TURKISH PERPETRATOR OF THE
ARMENIAN GENOCIDE OF 1915
WHICH CLAIMED THE LIVES OF
1,500,000 ARMENIAN MARTYRS.

The words "brought justice" catch my eye.

Every Armenian living in America seemingly has their own genocide stories passed down from a relative involved. The terrible event impacted so many lives, splintered families, and left them irreparably broken and seeking justice that never comes.

I'm a grandchild of genocide, of displacement, of broken hearts. Unquenchable anger. The ultimate outcast in a family that has good reason for fearing outsiders.

Soghomon Tehlirian – buried beneath the stone slab at my feet – didn't take shit from anyone.

He would conclude it's high time for a reckoning.

"What Berj did to me, to my family, to you … he needs to be stopped," I say to Vonnie. "If he isn't stopped he'll destroy us all. But I can't do this alone, not without you or the Legion. We must bring justice to him."

"I've got your back." Vonnie smiles at me. "Consider that justice brought."

Her hand gently finds its way into mine as we leave.

CHAPTER 28

KNOCK KNOCK, MOTHERFUCKA

The old warehouse district runs past the train tracks, near the famous *Welcome to Fresno* arch on Van Ness Avenue. Even at a distance from the building where Berj is keeping his little cult, just being here makes my heart want to claw its way up to my throat. The last time I was here, the only person in the world who believed me died. My stomach sinks, and I wonder if any of my new friends will share that fate today.

We are a small group—Reece, Muskrat, Big Earl, Hank, Wanda, and me. Vonnie, Josie, and Bill are supposed to hold down the fort. There's genuine concern that Berj's lunatics could attack our clubhouse. Hank was clear that the three of them shouldn't be taking the night off.

An undulating squeamishness fills my gut.

I always thought my life would be mundane and boring — just like my mundane and boring family. But I'm Tark now, a member of a monster-hunting biker gang creeping through the darkness, ready to fight a magic cartel of zombie-creating drug dealers.

All in a night's work for the Legion.

Hank goes over the plan. We're beaching the building through the loading docks. A door that should be easy enough to pick open, into a storage area, lots of cover, and then into the temple proper. We make sure we callout anything that looks suspicious and keep our eyes peeled for Spandaramet.

"Okay, brothers. This is it," Hank says to us over the short-range radio we have connected to earpieces. "The big show. Be careful in there."

"Why can't we, uh, ask him to come outside and then beat him up in the parking lot like sensible people?" Muskrat's voice sounds annoyed.

"Because then we wouldn't have the element of surprise, you dope," Reece hisses.

"But it'd be, uh, easier and faster."

"Tark?" It's Hank," a voice buzzes through my earpiece. "Stay cool, follow the plan, and stick with Reece."

"Got it," I reply, my muscles turning into rubber.

We blend with the shadows next to the large metal door that leads from the docking bay into the building while Wanda picks the lock, manipulating the tiny metal picks with deft precision. After an audible click, she grins.

"Okay, boys. You're on your own. Good luck." She retreats to the parking lot. The plan is to have Wanda provide us with long-distance backup in case things get dicey.

Muskrat and Reece go in through the door and I follow behind.

"Clear?" Big Earl asks.

"Yup, we're inside," Reece says as we move quietly through the room. I see Big Earl slip in, move off to the side, and disappear.

Rows of large crates arranged around the room fill the space, giving us some cover, but obstructing our view of the room's far side. Small tables with trade magazines and pamphlets are arranged nearby. Various Armenian-inspired designs with sweeping angles and bold colors hang on the dark walls.

I realize that I miss Vonnie, but also that this is the last place I want her to be. My hands quiver as the adrenaline kicks in.

We reach a set of double doors with large glass windows. Reece holds up a closed fist. We freeze as he slowly peers from a corner.

"What is it?" I ask.

"Looks like a reception area," Reece says as he quietly checks the latch. "Listen. Someone's talking." There's a soft click, and he pushes the door open.

"Welcome to Spandaramet Enterprises, Fresno's number one shipping company," the TV on the wall announces. Berj appears on the screen, impeccably dressed in a suit and silver bolo tie. I recognize that tie from Maddie's vision. He's outside the building and cheery, upbeat music plays. "Whether you're sending a package to family overseas or need to send priceless relics to a museum, we can make sure that your products arrive on time and in one piece. If you look around our state-of-the-art showroom you can see our fleet of transports, ranging from trucks to boats to airplanes. Spandaramet Enterprises has you covered ..."

Reece unplugs the TV from the wall.

"Guy's a first-class asshole," Reece mumbles. "I hate pushy salesmen."

We move quietly, checking doors as we go. We're halfway down the hallway when we find our first cultist. He stares at us for a moment before his eyes widen. He's about to shout something when Muskrat shoves Reece out of the way and drives his fist into the man's face. The cultist's nose breaks with a snap and he collapses with a sickening thud.

"Tark, uh, your turn." Muskrat says, pointing at the man.

I reach into my satchel and pull out the duct tape. I wrap tape around the man's mouth, and then tightly bind his wrists and ankles. Reece and I drag the unconscious cultist into the room we've already cleared and dump him behind a desk. A dark, wet spot seeps down the man's pantleg.

"I don't like this," I say.

"Yeah. The dude, uh, pissed himself," Muskrat replies.

"Not that! It's too damn quiet here. Where's the ritual? Where are all the people? This building is off," I tell Muskrat.

"Don't ever say the q-word. That word is bad luck." Reece frowns.

"The q-word? What's wrong with saying it's too quiet?" I ask.

"Because that usually means the shit's gonna hit the fan. Trust me. I was a cop. We avoided that word like the plague," Reece explains.

"Keep your shit together," Hank says through our earpieces. "We don't know what we're up against."

"You got it, boss. We won't say it's too quiet." Muskrat pats Reece on the shoulder.

Reece shakes his head and mutters a string of profanities.

We continue up the hall in single file—Reece, Muskrat, and then me. I have no idea where Hank and Big Earl are, but they're in the building somewhere, prepared to cover our escape if necessary.

The halogen lights above flicker. We pause at a corner. The air is fragrant with incense. Footfalls echo down the hall. They're getting louder.

"One hostile approaching," I whisper.

"I see him." Reece crouches down, waiting for the unsuspecting cultist to come around the corner. A moment later, Reece pounces on the man, but misses the semi-automatic in his hands—the firing arc goes wide and he sprays bullets, floor to ceiling. Muskrat and me dive for cover.

As he goes down, the cultist mutters something.

Oh, shit.

I realize that this is the moment when things are about to go south.

Double doors ten yards ahead of us swing open and the room we're in floods with light. My reaction is to cover my eyes for a moment while trying to remember where the nearest cover is.

I hear Reece curse and Muskrat trips on something.

"What's going on?" Hank's voice pipes through the earpiece.

"We've been spotted, Papa Bear," Reece says as he pulls out his Glock and starts peppering shots in the direction of the door, getting the cultists to dive back into the room they just came out of. "Something's wrong here," he says, inserting a fresh magazine into his pistol. "This feels more like a trap."

Muskrat and Reece take turns alternating shots at the cultists while I make my way to a door frame nearby. I can give them a bit of cover, so I take a few shots in the direction of the robed servants of Spandaramet. Everyone winces as the shrill sound of feedback fills the room for a moment.

"Well, well, well." Berj's voice filters through the PA system. "If it isn't our little traitorous Armenian and his merry band of bikers."

Shit. Shit. Shit.

"You guys gotta bail," Hank's voice is authoritative—there is no room for discussion. "Big Earl, do it," he says.

"You got it." We hear Big Earl's voice through the earpiece and a spray of bullets rips into the crowd of cultists. I dive against a nearby door and cover my head. "You guys better start clearing out."

"If we don't stop him tonight, then who knows what he's going to do," I cry while leaning hard against the door.

"I expected that your smart little friends would figure out what I was planning to do, they do have a bit of a reputation after all. But, Armand, you really shouldn't have come—it's very much bad for your health." Berj laughs. His amplified voice reverberates through the building.

"Move it," Reece orders. Muskrat waves at me to make my way over. Bullets strike his cover. Muskrat grabs his arm and sinks to the floor.

Another spray of bullets comes from above and I think I know where Big Earl is firing from. His Heckler & Koch MP5 shows the cultists no mercy.

Reece pulls out a thin metal tube from his bag. "When I throw this sucker, get ready to haul ass!" I see him pull the pin and throw the smoke grenade towards the door where Big Earl has the cultists pinned. Another spray of bullets helps to keep them where they are.

My world spins wildly as the grenade goes off, but it isn't the billowing smoke. Someone has just opened the door I was leaning on and I fall backwards. My head hits the ground. My vision explodes into bright stars. Hands grab at me, pull me up by my shoulders, and wrestle the gun from my hand.

Berj's voice booms over the speakers.

"I told you Armand," Berj says with dark chuckle, "disloyal Armenians are dead Armenians."

Something heavy crashes against the side of my head and my world goes black.

CHAPTER 29

SACRIFICE CHOSEN

A splitting headache – a cross between a hangover and a migraine – wakes me up. I try shifting my weight, but I can't move. Ropes bind my wrists and ankles. Chewing through the restraints isn't an option, thanks to the cloth gag in my mouth.

I'm on the same stone altar where Alvarez died. The raised carvings hurt my back, so I try rolling over on my side. Dried blood cakes the grooves etched into the rock. I stare at it absently, lost in delirium and pain.

Heavy boots clomp towards the altar. Berj peers down at me and rips the gag from my face. He tucks the cloth in the breast pocket of his suit and runs his hand over a maroon necktie emblazoned with a gold lion.

"You should've let it go, my friend. You could have been making bank just keeping your nose out of everything," he says smiling at me, his gold teeth shine in the dim light. "Now you're fucked."

"Berj," I whisper. My mouth feels like it's full of cotton. "Where are the others?"

"The others? Oh, you mean your little friends? I killed them. That is how you deal with terrorists, right?"

"You're lying," I hiss.

"Sure thing." He gives me a pat on the chest. "We were going to hand you over to the cops. Give them that tape of you with that detective's mutilated body. We figured that it would be fun to see you go to jail."

"I'll see you in Hell," I said, channeling my inner Dirty Harry.

Berj laughs. "But in the end, Spandaramet thought that you might serve a *higher purpose* as it were."

"By all means, turn me over to the cops, you shit. I'll tell them my story and show them who you really are. I'll say you murdered José Alvarez and Maddie Hinkle and Stuart Newkin. That the Children of Spandaramet is a just a drug trade in disguise."

Armand Tarkanian would've cried and begged for his life, but Tark is different.

Tark feels nothing but contempt.

"You can't do nothing to me," Berj says.

"Cut these ropes and I'll show you what I'm capable of."

Berj's mouth twists. He grabs my throat with his stubby fingers and squeezes.

"Enough!" An ethereal voice fills the room, and I feel Berj's fingers loosen.

Shadows fall on the floor and approach, seemingly from all corners of the room. The shadows warp and take form. A statuesque woman in a towering headdress secured with headscarves approaches. Coins and golden adornment on her headdress hang over her forehead, and long robes cover her arms. Bangles, necklaces, and rings make her look like some kind of lavish queen.

Her eyes are pitch black, two pupil-less orbs that stare into my soul. When she speaks, her voice resonates with authority.

"You are mortal refuse for the taking," she says, extending her arms. "You will pay tribute to Spandaramet with your life, for your gifts are squandered on you."

249

My gifts? And then I realize it—Berj had even said it before. I was special. My gifts. Whatever Berj is going to do, he needed someone that wasn't just a normal human.

He needed someone like me.

"That *was* a trap," I say, the botched raid fresh in my mind. "You played the Legion of the Lamb. You knew we'd come here."

Berj releases me and takes a step back.

"If we could use anyone for this ritual, we would," Berj says. "But that won't do for Spandaramet here."

The woman still stares at me, her eyes shiny and black like obsidian.

"Spandaramet? As in the goddess?" I ask.

"Yes, mortal," the woman says. "I am Spandaramet."

"How is this possible? You're a myth." I say.

Spandaramet tilts her head back and laughs.

"The mortal called Berj Manoogian summoned me and bound me to this realm," Spandaramet says, her voice mellifluous. "I was promised the deaths of thousands to feast on."

I struggle, but the ropes are tight. "Why not just kill me then?"

"In time. You are a suitable sacrifice. You shall be offered as a tribute to the Vishap during the Blood Moon," she says, arching her back.

"I'm the sacrifice? Don't you need a virgin or something?" I ask.

"Virgin?" Berj chuckles. "Hardly. We were going to use one of the strippers at first, but turns out we need someone with a bit more spiritual oomph. You'll do just fine."

"Is that what Maddie Hinkle was? Just another sacrifice?"

"Armand, so much of this is beyond your feeble and limited brain. Why not use the remaining few hours you have to reflect on your life? You're our guest for a little while," Berj says.

"Answer me. What did you do to Maddie?" I pressed.

250

Berj sighed. "Poor girl overheard me talking about procuring an embalmer and certain inappropriate fundraising activities involving a popular recreational drug. When I saw her standing in the doorway, I knew I couldn't let her live."

"And you killed her. Broke out your junior occult kit and made with the mouth frogs," I reminded him.

Berj shrugged. "Frogs are khrafstra, creatures considered to be evil. I summoned them for assistance and they delivered."

"I suppose the worms that devoured Stuart Newkin are the same khrafstra?"

"Indeed!" Berj chirps.

"My friends will come looking for me," I say. "The Legion of the Lamb never leaves a brother behind."

Berj puts his hand on my shoulder and whispers into my ear. "And yet here you are. Left behind."

I try moving around, but the ropes dig into my ankles and wrists.

"Cocaine distribution using undead?" I ask Berj. "I know all about your zombie drug mules. Think selling a zombie hunting experience to a bunch of sickos is a great way to move your product? That's why you had me stuff those corpses?"

"It is, because those sickos pay out the nose to do it. My idea. All of it," he says, almost with pride.

"Why not provide the corpses yourselves? Why rely on a funeral home?" I ask.

"No one is going to ask questions about people who are already dead and buried. It's amazing to me that you haven't put this together yourself, you'd think that being my little patsy for so long would have given you some time to ponder this. Disappearances attract the law, and we didn't want the police digging around with missing persons reports—they'll never figure out how those corpses were taken, and that suits my needs just fine."

"Coward."

"Excuse me?"

I tilt my head up so Berj can see I'm not fucking around. "You're a coward. You're afraid to distribute your coke, so you create undead and market it as a game. These were real people with families."

"Armand," Berj sighs, "what, out of all of our history together, makes you think that I give a shit about any of those odars? Were you this high and mighty when you took my money? You're the coward. Afraid of your family, so you lied to them. Afraid of a private detective, so you lied to him, you brought him to my door, and he ended up dead."

My heart sinks. He has me dead to rights.

"Spandaramet is going to kill you," I say. "No death goddess would ever do the bidding of an asshole like you. She's got a plan, and you're just a puppet."

Berj laughs hard and wipes a tear away from his eye. "Spandaramet, honey. Answer me this. Who do you serve?"

Spandaramet coalesces in the shadows and looks down at Berj. "You," she replies. There is a pained look of annoyance on her face.

"Until?" Berj looks over his shoulder at the death goddess.

"Until I am no longer needed," she says. It's clear that she's been told to say this, Berj is surely the kind of guy that has had her repeat this every so often to satisfy his own ego.

"You see, Armand," he says, "Spandaramet is mine. I was careful, and there is no way that she can turn on me." He flashes me that horrible golden smile, and I finally put two and two together. His teeth—those runes that he showed me at the Donut King. That's how he's protecting himself against the vengeance of the bound goddess.

"We Armenians have assimilated here perfectly, no?" Berj tells me. "The odars regarded us as foreigners, but we worked the crops, sold rugs, and owned dry-cleaning shops. But we never quite fit in. When my grandfather came to America, he saw the Armenians treated like shit and marginalized. They treated us as criminals." Berj's face hardens. "This is the shared destiny for the Armenian people. We crawled our way through the bowels of history with nothing but determination and our survival instinct. We were exploited, displaced, put to the sword. And yet, we survived. For us, this nightmare will be over—the scattered diaspora will come together in a new world. What I do is for all of us."

"This isn't Armenia," I remind him.

"No, but it will be." He points towards Spandaramet. "The Children of Spandaramet will create a new nation for my brothers and sisters out of the ashes of America. Our beloved *Hayastan*," Berj uses the name Armenians use for Armenia, "will be reborn from the bones of this place. A nation where veneration of the ancient ways still burns, where we draw light from the natural elements and not a cadre of priests and bishops in an alien church. It will be a prosperous land where Mihr ignites the sun and Aramazd bestows us with blessings. Where our living mythology draws breath from sacred fire. And Spandaramet will rule."

"You mean *you* will rule," I say.

"And the people will never know it."

After gloating, Berj leaves. Spandaramet watches him go and then turns towards me. "You have a strong spirit," she says. "You'll make a fine sacrifice." The goddess reaches out, her skin almost glowing in the gloom, and she forces my head to the side. "Your blood will tempt the Vishap," she says.

"Should I know what that is?" I feign ignorance, I need her to give me something—anything—that might be of use.

"The Vishap was a fearsome creature slain by Vahagn the Dragon-Reaper."

"Vahagn the who now?"

"He's a god of thunder and war, one of the most lauded in my pantheon."

I pull against my restraints. "Forgive me, but dragon slayers and fire gods weren't discussed much in Sunday school."

"It matters not."

"I kinda think it does."

Spandaramet's nostrils flare. "You're an irksome creature."

"I've been called worse," I respond. "What's your role in Berj's little arcane shindig?"

The death goddess flashes a dark smile. "I will summon the Vishap, who will drink your blood. Berj will take the Orb of Ancestors, and I will use it to raise the dead. The Age of Mortals will end and the Age of the Dead shall begin."

"The Orb of Ancestors is a thing *you* want?" I ask. "Why didn't you just get it before when what's-his-name killed the Vishap the first time?"

Spandaramet raises an eyebrow. "I care little for it, but I am commanded to get it."

"Wait, what? You don't want it?" I turn my head back to the shadowy nightmare. "I don't understand. Don't you want to take over this place and kill everyone?"

"Such a talkative mortal." Spandaramet clenches her fingers into white-knuckled fists. "Why would I care about your Fresno?"

I blink. To be fair, she makes a good point. What possible use is Fresno to a goddess? Spandaramet must have been doing death goddess stuff long before Berj bound her to him.

"Do you want your freedom? If you help me, maybe I can ..."

"I serve the master, and my will is not my own," Spandaramet tells me.

"But ..."

"Be silent—you mortals will fall in line, or be destroyed." She squints her deep black eyes.

"And here I thought that someone like you was more powerful." When you're going to be killed anyway, you might as well piss off the death goddess on your way out the door. "What are you even waiting for? You have your dumb altar and the sacrifice you need. Why am I even alive?"

"This is not the place," she says. "You must die under the moon amidst the corpses of the past and the crops that will grow."

"What does that even mean?"

Spandaramet turns and returns to the shadows. Clearly, she's had enough of my questions.

Under the moon amidst the corpses of the past and the crops that will grow.

It isn't long before Berj returns, this time with Gor.

"Gor was just saying that he was really looking forward to this part," Berj says,

I turn my head as Gor approaches.

"What part?" I ask as Gor cracks his knuckles. "Oh. That part."

I close my eyes before the beast of a man drives a punch down into my face. The pain is intense, but after a week of getting punched in the face by Reece, I was surprisingly able to hang on to my consciousness, though I desperately wanted to sleep.

"Bag him," I hear Berj say. Gor's enormous hands lift my head and I feel a burlap sack slip over my face. I open my eyes and try to see though the fabric, but all I can see are lights and shadows. Someone hoists me off the altar. Gor slings me over his wide shoulders.

"Put him in the back of the van. We're going. We have a world to end," Berj says.

I hear the door of a van open and I'm, fairly unceremoniously, tossed inside. My head hits the carpeted floor of the van and I try not to make a sound. A moment later, the door closes and there is silence. There's no one else in the van, at least for the moment.

Under the moon amidst the corpses of the past and the crops that will grow.

Where is this place? Why do prophetic locations need to be so ambiguous?

This would all be so much easier if I could just have some zombie lead me to …

"Son of a bitch," I say quietly. I close my eyes and focus. If there was ever a need for a ghost in my life, this is it. After several tense seconds, a cold burst fills the back of the van around me.

"Man, what a pickle you're in," a voice says.

"Thank God. I was hoping that I'd be able to get ahold of someone." I turn my bagged head and look in the general direction of Alvarez's spirit.

"What do you want?" He sounds annoyed.

"Your help." I whisper, keeping my voice as low as possible.

"Last time I helped you, I wound up dead."

"I'm sorry, detective," I whisper. "I am sorry that you died, it was my fault."

"Tell me something I don't know," there's an awkward silence that hangs in the air for a moment. *"I accept your apology."*

"You were a good man," I whisper. "Really and truly, I wish that it hadn't played out the way it did."

"You know what a ghost wants?" Alvarez asks. I feel like this is not particularly the time, but given that I'm really short of options, I indulge him.

"What's that?"

"They want to be made whole again. I blamed you for what happened to me, and it was your fault … but also mine. I didn't want to die, and I wanted that asshole to pay. You too. But, you repent and that lifts some of the weight. I need the rest of it gone so that I can finally get some rest."

"How can I help you do that?"

"By making sure that Berj gets some justice."

"You got it, detective."

"Man, I miss my smokes. I could use a Lucky right now."

"Detective, they're going to kill me."

"Evidently. You're tied up and bagged in the back of a van. Promise you'll make sure that Berj gets some justice."

"How? You said it yourself. I'm tied up. Unless you're good untying knots, It's over."

"You're giving up, just like that? Typical. Stay with me. I need you to focus."

256

A chill tickles my spine and an audible *whoosh* yanks me from reality. Though I can't see Alvarez thanks to the bag over my head, I know what's happening.

"No! Don't! Please, don't!" I cry.

But it's too late.

José Alvarez is showing me how he died.

I'm pulled backwards in time, viewing Alvarez's last moments through his eyes. He lies on the stone altar, clad only in his underwear. Berj stands over him, knife held aloft, crowd of worshipful acolytes chanting around him. Strong incense stings his nostrils. He struggles desperately against his restraints, but he's trapped.

Alvarez screams. His view shifts to the gloomy temple. He looks straight at me. From this perspective, I can see myself cringing nearby, terrified while Berj officiates the ritual. Gazing into my own helpless face sends bile rushing into my throat. I'm about to vomit, but I can't look away. Through Alvarez's eyes I see Gor wrapping his thick hands around my head and turning me towards the altar.

Berj pushes the dagger into Alvarez's chest. I feel the blade penetrate the flesh, see the blood seeping out, and experience excruciating agony. Tears flood Alvarez's vision. Pain rushes through him as his whole body convulses. Berj reaches a hand into the open wound and roots around. I feel every move his hand makes violating Alvarez's body.

The chanting reaches a frenzied crescendo. Berj rips Alvarez's heart out and everything plummets into sudden blackness.

I'm back inside the van, bag still over my head. My skin tingles and I sense Alvarez is with me.

"Look familiar? That's what's going to happen to you if you don't think of a way out of here," Alvarez says.

"T-that w-was un-unnecessary," I stammer, my heart racing.

"Focus, Tarkanian. What can we do?"

If all this head-hopping works between ghosts and mortals directly, could it also involve a third party?

"Can you find someone for me?"

"*Living or dead?*"

"Living. I think. Her name is Wanda. She's got some ability to sense magic or ghosts, I'm not really sure, but if you can find her and tell her where these assholes are going maybe we can put a stop to it."

"*I can relay a message to her,*" Alvarez says. "*Where's this little party bus headed?*"

"The corn fields that me and my brother ran to when you got knocked out. That's where they stashed all the corpses from the killed zombies. That's where they're going to sacrifice me and summon the Vishap."

"*Vishap?*"

"Really not the time for exposition, detective." I explain where the fields are.

"*I'll tell this to your friend, Wanda, but I'll need you to concentrate. Think of her. Connect with her mind.*"

I close my eyes and clear my head. I focus on Wanda, on the clubhouse, and on my leather-clad Legion brothers. And then the chill in the van fades away. Alvarez is gone.

My link with the detective severs, and I slip into an uncomfortable and pained sleep. At the edge of my consciousness, I hear the doors of the van open and the engine start.

We're on our way.

CHAPTER 30

NOTHING GOOD EVER HAPPENS IN A CORNFIELD

Someone pulls the bag off my head.

I blink a few times, trying to focus and figure out what is going on. I'm seated on the ground, but tape binds my wrists and ankles together. I'm outside, in a clearing at the cornfield's center. The Children of Spandaramet gather in a semi-circle around me. A number of them illuminate the clearing with tiki torches, the kind you can buy at any hardware store. They're chanting in deep, guttural tones.

The moon slowly shifts from a rich orange to a foreboding crimson.

Berj wears the waistcoat of an ancient priest. An arevakhach, or circular Armenian eternity symbol, is stitched in gold thread on his maroon vestment. He stands at a stone altar, turning pages in *The Book of the Obsidian Way*. Berj finally finds the passage he seeks and reads aloud, reciting some eldritch incantation. Around me, a sinister communion with ancient forces unfolds, but I don't understand any of it.

Two stone monoliths flank the altar, each one carved with serpentine symbols. Brass braziers burn with heady incense near the monoliths.

Berj clutches a dagger.

This is it.

The ritual of the Blood Moon has begun.

I'm screwed.

A few cultists lift me roughly to my feet. They cut apart the tape around my wrists and ankles before dragging me over to Berj. He raises his dagger aloft, chanting at the moon while it slips into deeper and deeper shades of red. I struggle in their grasp, kicking my legs and pulling against them.

With great effort, they lay me down on the altar and restrain me. One cultist per limb, pinning me in place no matter how much I resist. Berj looks at me and smiles. He takes the dagger and cuts my shirt open.

"You know, Armand," he says. "I'm very much going to miss our little get-togethers at Donut King."

"It's never too late to change your mind," I tell him.

He snorts as he dips his fingers into a bowl containing some kind of thick black paste. Berj starts drawing symbols on my chest with one hand, while holding the blade aloft in the other.

He finishes and stares up at the moon; it's a horrible deep crimson.

"Spandaramet," he says, "it is time."

The death goddess appears from the nearby shadows and approaches the altar, standing at my head. She puts her hands on my cheeks and starts chanting. I shiver at her icy touch.

"I'm going to cut out your fucking heart, Armand," Berj says, putting his free hand on my chest and lifting the knife over my belly.

"Tark," I say.

"What?"

"My name is Tark." I spit in his face. If there was ever a moment to be completely defiant in the face of death, now is that time.

Berj steps back and wipes his face. "Call yourself what you like, you'll die all the same."

He lays his hand on my chest again, and lifts the dagger above his head. A sharp whistle and a spray of vibrant rich blood hits him in the face. For a moment, confusion reigns—one of the two cultists holding my legs just drops, releasing my foot. I immediately twist and kick the other one.

"No!" Berj screams as he brings the knife down, catching me deep in the side as I'm trying to roll off the altar. A sharp pain explodes through me when one of my arms pops out of its socket, but the other arm is free. That unlucky cultist also drops to the ground.

Chaos erupts around the ritual's perimeter. Shouting and gunshots fills the air. Brandishing firearms and clad in their leather jackets, the Legion of the Lamb arrives with a bang. Taken by surprise, the Children of Spandaramet drop their torches and scramble for their weapons.

Muskrat swings a baseball bat and strikes one bigger cultist in the face. I hit the ground and put my hand against the massive gouge in my side to try and staunch the flow of blood.

Shots ring out. Cultists fall dead. More sparks and gunshots. Figures emerge from the corn. They push their way through the cornstalks into the clearing.

Alvarez did it. He got my message to Wanda.

Berj is still chanting—delivering the last foul incantation. I look down at the fresh wound in my side—I guess that it doesn't matter if I needed to be killed for the ritual to work. Maybe sacrificial blood on the dagger is enough. Everything blurs and I feel faint from the blood I'm steadily losing. I'd be dead soon.

"Tark!" I hear Vonnie. She's out there, fighting her way to me.

If I could see her one last time that would be nice, but my vision starts to fade.

This is how I die, I think. *Right here. In a cornfield of all places. Bleeding out. In the middle of a firefight with an Armenian death goddess cult. Sucks to be me.*

I find myself staring into big brown eyes. I also see that long pink tongue hanging out of a smiling muzzle. My canine stalker sits in front of me, sniffing. As I slip down and lie on my back, the dog nuzzles my injury with its nose. Warmth spreads from the wound.

The dog sprouts a pair of large, feathery brown wings.

With its large pink tongue, the dog licks at my wound, lapping at it with concentrated determination. At first, it stings, but then it feels oddly soothing and my anxiety dissipates. I peer down at my injury and watch as it completely disappears. My dislocated shoulder miraculously feels better. The dog barks and curls its head into my neck, its wings folding inward, shielding me from the calamity erupting around us.

"You're an Aralez," I murmur.

After an elated bark, the dog licks my chin.

"Where'd you come from?"

The creature's head turns upwards and its nose points to the sky.

This mutt has been following me for weeks now, and here it is, helping me after I'd done nothing but shoo it away at every turn. Maybe I had someone looking out for me. Maybe it was my mother. Maybe it was fate. Whatever the case might be, I was deeply thankful that the dog had not given up on me. It barks. I see a bright light bathe me from above and the creature spreads its wings and vanishes up into the night.

"Anyone else see this dog?" I ask, still awestruck from my unbelievable encounter.

There's an incredible and almost blinding sharp pain across my face that immediately snaps me awake and back into the present. Vonnie is looking down on me.

"Who the fuck you calling a *dog*?" She looks angry.

"Vonnie?" I ask, my head swimming.

"Thank God," she says, wrapping her arms around me. I'm not next to the altar anymore, Vonnie must have dragged me away.

"What's going on?" I ask, sitting up. I grab my side and pull open my blood-soaked shirt. The cut is gone and I'm not bleeding out anymore. The Aralez had saved my life. People don't often get second chances, but here I am with mine. Time to make sure I don't squander it.

Berj holds the blade covered in my blood. Crackling electricity is forming into some kind of opening above the cornfield. It swirls violently, growing wider by the second. The undulating current that pulses above the altar challenges the fabric of reality.

"Jesus," I mumble. "We have to stop him."

"Hank!" Vonnie shouts. A moment later the older man hobbles his way over to us.

"We got anything big? Like a big rifle or shotgun?" I ask, pointing towards the portal. A clawed talon slips into this reality and pushes the entrance wider.

"I'll see what we can do," he says. "I don't know where this dragon is from or how tough it is, Tark. Guess we're going to find out." He speaks into the radio as he walks away.

I get up and steady myself.

"Vonnie, I gotta go put him down. This one is my fight and I'm not letting him win," I tell her.

"It's *our* fight, you mean." Vonnie furrows her eyebrows.

"Right," I say. "Let's finish this and get our lives back."

I turn and start running through rows of cornstalks to make my way towards Berj and Spandaramet.

I make it behind where they're chanting and emerge from the cornfield.

Right into Gor's fist.

The blow stings my face and I pitch backwards. I land on my back and see the horror of what's unfolding high above us. The portal yawns and a thing emerges from its chaotic depths. The creature resembles a gigantic reptile, with lustrous scales of several brilliant hues that gleam from nostrils to tail. Its four feet end in sharp talons and a pair of bat-like wings on its back spread wide. Two horns protrude from the dragon's sleek head, and around the beast's neck, amidst the fur of a lion-like mane, hangs an ornate golden collar with a large radiant pendant.

The Orb of Ancestors.

The Vishap's long neck dips towards the altar. It sniffs at the dagger that Berj is holding and turns its massive head towards me. I get up slowly and Gor grabs me by the shirt and punches me in the stomach.

"I've been wanting to kill you for a while, you bastard," Gor says.

"You know what, Gor?"

He punches me in the gut again, and I stumble back a few steps.

"What's that?"

"I don't think you're going to get the chance," I say as the Vishap raises its head, opens its maw wide, and comes crashing down towards us. I give Gor a shove and dive out of the way. The Vishap snaps its jaws shut on Gor. His legs flail wildly as he screams in the creature's mouth. There's a loud crunch and Gor's legs land on the ground nearby. The screaming stops.

I try not to vomit.

The Vishap turns back towards Berj and lowers its head. Berj reaches up slowly and grabs the Orb of Ancestors. He gives it a good yank and pulls it from the golden collar. Spandaramet watches, her face blank. I cannot tell if she's happy about what's unfolding or if she's just standing there, waiting for the right moment.

Berj holds the orb above his head and starts laughing. The Vishap's roar echoes through the cornfield.

That's it, I think. *It's over.*

For a moment, all hope fades from me. No more cards left to play.

Then the high pitch *thwip* of a bullet as it screams into the Vishap's snout. The creature snorts loudly and shakes its head. Berj looks up at the creature, confused. Another bullet finds the Vishap's neck, while another slams into its eye. The Vishap roars in pain and flaps its mighty wings.

I make a mental note in case I'm ever faced with this situation in the future; armor-piercing ammunition harms a dragon's natural armor.

The more you know.

The Vishap backs up a few more steps and I see something small and round bounce against its hind quarters. A large explosion rocks the air and the large creature's rear legs crumple. Apparently, someone brought a grenade to our little shindig.

I lift my head and find myself staring at Spandaramet, who looks at me—then at Berj, who still clutches the orb. I look back at Spandaramet and then I do what I've been doing my whole life—I run, full speed, away from my past and towards my future.

Berj, not expecting me to be alive, is caught off guard. I tackle him. The Orb of Ancestors rolls away from his fingers as we both hit the ground. We tumble a few times, each of us trying to get the upper hand. He realizes that it's me, that I'm still alive.

"You're remarkably hard to kill," he grunts, punching me in the side. The strike winds me, but I fight through the searing pain.

"You're not going to get away with this." I pin one of his hands and punch him hard in the chest. He coughs and looks over at Spandaramet.

"I demand that …" I shove my arm into his throat, cutting off his words.

"Cheater," I hiss. Berj frees his hands and hits me in the face, knocking me off and sending me onto my back. He gets on top of me and wraps his hands around my throat.

"I don't need her to kill you. I've been looking forward to killing you since the moment we first met, you whiny little coward," he tells me.

I try to break the grip on my neck, but I can't. Instead, I thrash my legs to try and get him off me, and drag my hands through the dirt in the field. My fingers close on a rock the size of a baseball. I take the swing like my life depends on it, catching Berj right in the mouth and knocking out several of his hideous gold teeth. He rolls off, clutching his mouth and bleeding through his fingers.

I stand up slowly and drop the rock. "You'd be surprised how many times people have said that to me recently," I say. Berj roars and starts running towards me, pulling his fist back to deliver a crushing punch, and then freezes, mid-swing.

For a moment, he looks confused—I am too, but then a look of panic sweeps across his features. Spandaramet walks between us, several feet away, and picks up the Orb of Ancestors. She looks at it, turning it over in her hands.

"Tsk, tsk, tsk." Spandaramet's pupil-less eyes stare at Berj. She turns and regards me for a moment before craning her neck over her shoulder towards the Vishap right as another grenade explodes near the monster's tail. Spandaramet raises the Orb of Ancestors in her hand and then holds her hand out, palm facing the Vishap. It flies skyward, retreating through the tear in reality from where it came.

"Spandaramet, release me!" Berj demands, his words muffled by gushing blood.

The death goddess grins as the Vishap disappears into the void, and then turns to face her former master. She leans in close and laughs. "No," she says. Spandaramet stands up to her full height and thrusts her arm forward, her fingertips passing into Berj's throat. "In fact, I think that you'll never see a moment of freedom ever again." The death goddess drags something out of Berj. Wisps of blue energy flow from his nose, ears, eyes, and mouth as she pulls his soul away from his body.

Berj's skin becomes brittle and is flaking off in large, desiccated chunks. His arms wither away, and then his body collapses into an ashen heap.

Spandaramet holds the energy that used to be Berj, and it flows into her body through her skin. She closes her eyes and smiles.

The Legion of the Lamb steps out into the clearing. With the Vishap gone, the cultists routed, and Berj a pile of ash, we can all take a breath.

Well, almost.

Vonnie walks over and stands next to me in front of Spandaramet, who finally opens her eyes. I feel my body tense up and Vonnie has a gun that she points at the death goddess.

"I guess now that Berj is dead and you have the Orb of Ancestors, you're the next in line to try and make your little empire?" I ask.

Spandaramet grins. "I have an empire. The underworld is my realm. Berj Manoogian discovered a path to control my powers and use them for his own wants. I was nothing more than a servant, much like you." She turns and eyes Vonnie's pistol. "You have no need for that, and it won't do you any good if you try to use it."

Vonnie lowers the gun and then slips it into a holster on her hip.

"Berj Manoogian's demise means my freedom, for which I thank you," Spandaramet says.

I regard her warily. "You're welcome."

"You shall receive my gratitude and be marked by me as a gift." Spandaramet reaches out and puts her thumb on my forehead. It stings for a moment and then the feeling is gone.

Hank makes his way toward her, gun drawn. "What're you gonna do with that orb?" He watches the goddess carefully. "I think it might be better if you gave that up and surrendered."

Spandaramet grasps the Orb of Ancestors. It disappears in a flash of light.

"This is the sort of thing that your kind cannot be trusted with." She turns and looks at Bill, who sneaks up to the altar towards Berj's book. "But, as a sign of good faith on my part, you may keep *The Book of the Obsidian Way.* I warn you, that it would be very unwise for you to attempt to do what Berj did … I will be taking *precautions* in the future and it would … end badly if you try to summon me."

Bill grabs the book and clutches it to his chest.

"Spandaramet?" I say.

"Yes, Armand Tarkanian?"

"Can you get rid of my curse?"

"I cannot. It can only be removed by your death or by the demon that cursed your bloodline. Before you ask, no, I will not find it for you, that task is beneath me."

I shrug. "Well, better than nothing, I guess."

"Yes, it is." Spandaramet turns and slowly looks over the Legion. "You all have so many more fights to come. I wish you luck." The death goddess turns back to me. "And *you* … I will see you again."

"Wait. You touched my forehead. What did you do to me?" I ask.

But Spandaramet doesn't look back.

With a swirl of shadows, the goddess of death departs, leaving the Legion of the Lamb standing in the field, tired and bruised, but victorious.

CHAPTER 31

THE WHEEL TURNS

After returning to the clubhouse, I shower, dress, and eat two bowls of Wanda's famous chili. I slurp the spicy stew down like a prisoner who hadn't tasted real food in decades.

Wanda treats our wounds. She marvels that I made it through with only a few bruises and scrapes. The Aralez had healed my grievous injury, and I try explaining that a winged dog mended me. Wanda chalks my account up to stress, while Vonnie tells me how relieved she is that I survived and plants a wet kiss on my cheek. Muskrat had gotten shot in the arm at the warehouse, but it's only a flesh wound and would heal just fine—especially with Wanda's gifts. He brags to everyone in the clubhouse about his latest battle scar.

Bill tells us that he's going to stash *The Book of the Obsidian Way* with the other arcane tomes the Legion has for safekeeping, and then disappears into his library.

Reece and Muskrat drink beer at the bar while Josie has one of Big Earl's machine guns taken apart on the pool table and excoriates him over the firearm's condition. It's amazing to see the big man crushed under the weight of Josie's words, but he chuckles to himself.

Wanda talks to Vonnie about the subtle art of healing spells. Everything here seems almost like nothing has happened, that the fierce melee with the Children of Spandaramet in the cornfield is just another mundane work day.

But the Legion of the Lamb is more than a monster-bashing biker club.

It's a family.

The next morning I find Hank in his garage, working on his motorcycle.

"Well if it isn't our hero of the week," he says with a smile as I approach. "Hand me that wrench." He gestures towards a wrench near my foot. I pick it up and give it to him. He tightens something and then puts it down.

"Look, Hank, I just wanted to say thank you," I tell him. "You believed me when almost no one else did, you took me in, you made me part of your family, and I really do appreciate everything that you've done for me and Vonnie."

Hank stands up, dusts off his jeans, and reaches into his pocket. "Sure thing, Tark. You're a welcome addition to the family." He tosses me a pair of keys. "I can't really mount the bike, but start her up for me."

I straddle the motorcycle. The black leather seat is comfortable. Hank tells me what to do and I turn the key in the ignition. The bike roars to life, sounding truly spectacular. I feed the engine some more gas and it roars.

"That's the right sound," he says as he turns the key and kills the motor. "She's all yours now."

"But this is your bike," I protest. "It's Velma. I can't take it."

"Tark, the Legion of the Lamb spends a lot of time hunting things down that go bump in the night. A werewolf here, a cryptid there, but we don't often take down death cults, banish a dragon and get a death goddess to back off. If this wasn't the best on-the-job interview, I don't know what else would be. Take the damned bike, say thank you, and keep being a good brother." He wipes his greasy hands off on a rag and smiles.

"Thank you, Hank." I throw my arms around him in a grateful hug. He pats my back awkwardly.

"Okay, that's good."

I let go and take a step back. "Hank, I need to get out of town with Vonnie for a while," I say.

Hank shrugs.

"Well, I don't blame you—I think we all could use a few days off to tell you the truth. After everything that's happened, and when we get all the leftover stuff sorted out, then we'll take a break too," he tells me.

"What's left to do? We took out Berj, Spandaramet is gone, and the Vishap isn't on this plane of existence anymore."

"Well, even though that corn field is out of the way, we made a bit of a mess out there. After Vonnie brought you back last night we made sure our handiwork disappeared. We don't want people to just run across a bunch of arcane nonsense and guns. Then we went to the warehouse with Bill, made sure that anything dangerous was gone, anything worthwhile was stashed, and gathered a bit of cash in suitcases that they wouldn't miss. Then we torched the warehouse to the ground."

"Jesus, Hank."

"We're nothing if not thorough," he says.

It occurs to me that being in a monster-hunting biker gang probably doesn't pay very well or have great benefits.

"We'll be back soon," I promise.

He pats my back. "Take your time. The road has its own special power. You're mesmerized at what's over the next hill or in the next town and keep riding on, hoping to find what you're seeking. At least, that's how it was with me."

"Did you find what you were looking for?" I ask.

Without missing a beat Hank answers, "Hell yeah I did. I found it." A chuckle escapes his lips and his eyes mist over. He stares across the lot at the clubhouse where his wife and Legion brothers wait. "I found it."

I'm a Legion brother, a warrior against evil, a bringer of pure light.

Or something badass like that.

Vonnie and I load up Velma with our belongings, putting them into the ample saddlebags and fastening them shut. Hank's nice enough to give me a few lessons on the bike, and I'm quick to pick it up. I'm fearless now, and for once in my life, doing something new neither scared me nor was difficult. It's like I was born to ride a motorcycle. Vonnie gives me my helmet and I hold it in my hands. The thing shines like a beautiful black egg.

Reece is the first one to bid me farewell. He shakes my hand, and stands almost at attention.

"Hey, Tark," Reece calls. "Here's a reward for you not mentioning a certain Regency romance book that I may or may not have lifted from your brother's shop."

He hands me a videocassette, one labeled with my name in handwritten letters. I'm familiar with this tape. It was inside a video camera Berj operated when he recorded me cutting Alvarez open.

"Don't know what it is, and I don't really care but the withering look on your face tells me it's something bad," Reece says.

"W-where did you get this?" I stammer.

"Me and Big Earl raided Manoogian's warehouse after our little dust up in the cornfield. Found some pretty interesting things including that tape."

My fingers grip the plastic videotape cover so hard it cracks. I swallow hard and try speaking, but the words bunch up in my throat.

Reece gives me a small hammer.

"Here you go, brother. Send that thing to Hell," he says.

I take the videocassette outside and smash it to smithereens with the hammer. Bit by incriminating bit the videocassette falls to the hammer's might. My destruction halts when the tape in the cassette spools out like shiny black noodles.

Not satisfied, I dump it in a metal bucket and burn a piece of the mylar videotape with a lighter. Flames consume the tape immediately and with it, my final act of defiance against the Children of Spandaramet.

"Thanks, buddy," I say to Reece. He's hanging around while the tape goes up in smoke.

"See you later, newbie," he says out of the side of his mouth, like he's a ventriloquist practicing his act. "I really enjoyed kicking the shit out of you."

"I know. Much appreesh, sensei." We shake hands.

Muskrat isn't as guarded with his goodbyes. The big doofus flings his arms around me and sobs, "I'm, uh, gonna miss you guys!" I guess he hugs Vonnie with the same bear-crushing grip because her eyes nearly pop out of her skull.

"We'll miss you, too, Muskrat," she grunts.

"I, uh, made something for both of you." Muskrat thrusts what looks like homemade necklaces at Vonnie and me. Two of Berj's gold teeth and a familiar glass nazar charm hang from the leather cords.

"Where did you get these?" I ask, turning the gold teeth in my hands and examining the detailed glyphs etched into each one.

"I, uh, found them in the cornfield. Since you lost the, uh, protection amulet we gave you, I felt that both of you, uh, should have them," Muskrat says.

"Don't know if I like wearing a dead dude's gold teeth." Vonnie slips the necklace on. "How do I look?"

I share Vonnie's reluctance, but the gold teeth and the glass evil eye are resplendent on her. Not wanting to be outdone, I put my necklace on. It hangs there like a gold pendulum, Berj's teeth and the lidless glass eye clack against each other when I move.

"Thanks, Muskrat," I say. "They're perfect."

Big Earl pats my shoulder.

"Take care, man." He eyes Vonnie, then me. "You've got a lovely lady there, Tark. Be good to each other, okay?"

"Will do," I reply.

While Vonnie hugs Big Earl, Josie fist bumps me, her candy-colored nails and gold rings dazzling against my fingerless black gloves.

"Have fun in Vegas, okay?" Josie says to me before looking at Vonnie. "I want all the deets when you come back. All of them."

"You know it," Vonnie says.

They hug. Josie wipes her cheek. "Damn, Vonnie. I miss you already, girl."

Bill shakes my hand and leans in for a hug. He thanks me again for helping him secure *The Book of Obsidian Way*. The Legion's librarian muses aloud about the power contained within that eldritch tome, and that he's keeping it under lock and key for now.

He gives me a small, leather-bound book emblazoned with the Legion of the Lamb's crest.

"All neophytes receive this handbook. It tells a monster hunter what they should know about identifying, investigating, and exterminating supernatural threats," Bill explains.

I flip through it.

"Hold on. Half of these pages are blank," I say.

Bill flashes a mischievous grin. "About that. We think Legion brothers should fill it in as they learn more. Take plenty of notes and record everything. After all, monster hunting isn't an exact science."

Vonnie and I say our farewells. Wanda joins us for one last round of hugs.

We embrace. Wanda whispers in my ear, "Goodbye, Tark. Don't stay away too long, you hear? There's a lot more to do."

She hugs Vonnie.

"We'll be back," Vonnie promises. "We're just going up to Vegas for a while. Who knows? Maybe we'll get lucky." She winks.

"You kids be good. And Tark?"

"Yeah?"

"Keep your ears open for things that might be trying to reach out to you. When you come back we'll keep working on figuring out how those powers of yours work."

"Thanks, Wanda. Looking forward to it," I tell her.

I turn the key. The motorcycle comes alive and growls, roaring like a turbo-charged tiger. I rev her up and Velma takes off like a shot. In the rearview mirror, the clubhouse shrinks until it vanishes in the distance. For the first time in my life, I feel sad to leave my home—and the Legion of the Lamb is my true home.

"You sure you want this? It's forever, you know," Vonnie cautions.

We stop downtown at Tokyo Palace on Fulton Street for some sushi and I spy a tattoo parlor. After a little deliberation, I find myself seated in a chair.

"Nothing is forever," I tell Vonnie. "But yes. I want this."

The place is immaculate. Framed pictures of tattoo designs line the walls. A boombox blasting heavy metal provides the background noise as I flip through several catalogs, looking for the right design. Getting a tattoo isn't something I planned for—but after everything I've been through, the death and loss, violence and love, I want a permanent reminder.

I find the perfect tattoo for an embalmer-turned-monster hunter.

"The Egyptian dog-headed guy? Why that one?" Vonnie looks over my shoulder at the catalog.

"Anubis. God of mummification and embalming. He sent pharaohs on their final journey. He'd judge the dead by weighing their souls against a feather," I explain with all the confidence of a seasoned Egyptologist.

The tattoo artist – a young man with a goatee and sleeve tattoos featuring skulls and cannabis leaves interlaced with roses – dons a surgical mask and rubber latex gloves. He gingerly shaves my upper arm, disinfects it, and sets to work with the stencil, outlining the mighty Anubis.

"Now this'll hurt," the artist warns.

"I can handle it," I say.

He mashes his foot on a pedal and the coil machine buzzes loudly. Carefully, the tattoo artist begins his work.

"You doing okay, buddy?" the tattoo artist asks through his surgical mask after ten minutes.

"Peachy, dude," I say, gritting my teeth.

Vonnie looks up from a tattoo magazine she's reading and smiles.

"That's a brave soldier," she says. "You show that needle who's boss."

Anubis starts to take shape. His slender limbs, jackal head, headdress, and skirt materialize in thin ink outlines. In his hand, a gold ankh symbolizing life.

The duality of life and death forever drawn on me.

Armand would never have gotten a tattoo. His family wouldn't have approved. He wouldn't have left the embalming room. He'd be paying his Uncle George for rent and bills. Making less and suffering for the good of the family. But Armand is long gone.

I'm Tark now.

CHAPTER 32

LOOSE ENDS

Roupen throws his arms around me and we hug for a long time. It's not like his usually brotherly hugs; this one comes with tears.

"Oh, my God!" he laughs in my ear. "I thought you were legit going to get yourself killed."

"Vonnie wouldn't let that happen, you should know better," I reply.

Roupen and Vonnie embrace.

"Are you crying, Roupen?" Vonnie asks.

"Guilty." He brushes a tear from his cheek. "You two safe now?"

"Yeah," I say. "It's all over. Is the family still at Dad's place?"

"Samantha called me and said they left this morning," Roupen says. "Uncle George couldn't stand the idea of people helping him."

"Can I ask for a big favor?"

"You need a place to stay?"

I nod.

"Of course, Armand! Mi casa es su casa," Roupen says.

He ushers us into his apartment. Brent is sitting nonchalantly at the kitchen table, sipping a mug of coffee. He blushes when Vonnie and I appear and clears away the dirty dishes.

"Sorry," he murmurs, and turns to his partner. "Roupen, you didn't tell me we were having guests."

My brother tenderly kisses Brent's forehead. "They came by. I wasn't expecting them. You know I make a fuss for company."

Roupen is always the most gracious host, even when he doesn't want to see you. He and Brent sit us down, then give us coffee, strawberry crepes, and bacon.

"How was Sonoma?" I ask. My brother rolls his eyes.

We eat, talk, and for the first time in a long time, we don't have the looming specter of our family casting shadows over our happiness.

Vonnie and I stay the night and sleep in the next day, while Roupen works in the bookstore and Brent teaches his classes.

That morning, Roupen knocks and pokes his head into the bedroom.

"Guys? You hungry?" he asks.

"I could eat a horse," Vonnie says with a yawn.

"Sorry, I can only promise you eggs and potatoes," Roupen replies, then ducks back into the hallway before Vonnie can hit him with her shoe.

We leave the guest bedroom, all bedraggled and bleary-eyed, and head to the kitchen. Brent sips coffee and reads *The Fresno Bee*. I'm not much for local journalism, but the front page catches my eye. My mouth drops open and I point at the lead story. Vonnie stops and looks at it too. Brent realizes that we're trying to read the paper over his shoulder, sighs and hands it to Vonnie. I lean over and read the story silently:

The remains of over a dozen people were discovered in a dirt pit in Goldleaf after the Fresno County Sheriff's Office received an anonymous tip yesterday.

Fresno County Sheriff Patricia Ruiz said the tipster left a message on her voicemail, pointing to a property off Peach Road. Deputies found the remains in a ditch behind an abandoned building.

"Obviously, we don't know any of the details, but my department is investigating. Once we identify these individuals, we'll notify their next-of-kin," Ruiz said.

Ruiz noted her office has the resources to comb through missing persons cases and identify the deceased.

The anonymous tipster also informed authorities of a warehouse fire off Van Ness Avenue in the early morning hours, according to Ruiz. The warehouse, belonging to Spandaramet Enterprises, was razed in the blaze that erupted two nights ago.

Asked if there's a connection between the fire and the bodies uncovered in Goldleaf, Ruiz wouldn't speculate.

"We don't know at this point whether this is the work of gang activity or a single individual. County, state, and federal authorities are combining their efforts on a joint investigation. This is a horrific discovery, and those responsible will be brought to justice," Ruiz said.

Vonnie and I look at each other after we're finished reading.

"Over a dozen?" Vonnie says. "Tark, what the fuck is going on?"

"I'll bet you dollars to Bavarian cream donuts that it's the Legion. When they told me they cleaned up the mess in the cornfield, they weren't kidding," I said, wheels turning in my brain.

"This have something to do with what you guys were doing?" Brent asks.

Vonnie and I shrug.

Brent picks up our reluctance and clears away the breakfast plates. "Whatever it is, please keep me out of it. Plausible deniability and all," he says before departing.

I slump down in a chair. Vonnie joins me, her head sinking to her chest.

"Anonymous tipster? You think that was the Legion?" she asks.

"Who else? They take the bodies and dump them into the zombie murder pit, then they burn Berj's warehouse. They're covering their tracks," I reply.

"You don't think this'll come back to bite us in the ass?"

My head is pounding. Nothing like a stress migraine now. "Some of those bodies – Maddie Hinkle, Stuart Newkin, José Alvarez – were handled by yours truly."

I fumble with my cellphone, my quaking hands dialing my only official contact who could make sense of this shitshow.

Chief Pathologist Dr. Lorraine Martindale answers on the second ring. After an awkward introduction, I tell her that I read the newspaper and inquired about the bodies discovered in Goldleaf.

"Doesn't George have enough for you to do?" Martindale asks, her voice strained.

"He wants to know if the coroner identified anyone there yet?" I ask.

"Jesus, Tarkanian. We're working around the clock. I've got thirteen people toe tagged and bagged in an overflowing morgue. I'm still putting the pieces together. I can tell you this. A few of them are familiar faces," Martindale says.

"Familiar? What do you mean familiar?"

There's a long pause, like Martindale cups the phone with her hand and is talking with someone there. After what seemed forever, she's back on the line. "That detective that's been reported missing? José Alvarez? He's among the deceased. You met the guy in the morgue. He was investigating the death of that woman you picked up a few weeks ago. Maddie Hinkle. Incidentally, we've got her again, too."

"Alvarez? He's been reported missing?"

"Like, weeks ago. It's been on the news. Where have you been living, under a rock?"

"What did he die from?"

"From what I can tell, homicide. He's been dissected like a frog from a high school biology class. It'll take some time on my end." There's a long pause. "Why's George interested in this?"

"You know my uncle. He wants a head's up in case we get some of those decedents. Needs to make room in the freezer," I say, impressed by my stellar bullshitting skills.

"I'm swamped, Mr. Tarkanian. Tell George that he's welcome to call me when we don't have a major homicide investigation, okay?" Martindale hangs up.

Roupen's bookshop offers little respite from my overactive anxiety. Imagined scenarios occupy my mind, distracting me from reality. Vonnie and I are free. We can leave Fresno anytime we want, yet the disturbing news keeps me here.

For two days, I wander the bookshop, check the newspaper, and scrutinize every online article about the warehouse fire and body pit.

Would the cops conclude some of those corpses were undead and had packages of cocaine stuffed inside them? Of course not. That would be madness. And yet, the thought stubbornly sticks around my brain like a squatter in an abandoned house.

Another article in *The Fresno Bee* sheds more light. Detectives working the case obtained a notebook from the late PI José Alvarez. They've learned that the detective linked the Maddie Hinkle murder with prominent businessman Berj Manoogian. Investigators are looking into the possibility that Berj might have been involved in criminal activity, according to Alvarez's notes.

How did they get Alvarez's coveted notebook? Then I recalled what Reece told me back at the clubhouse, that the Legion uncovered some interesting things in Berj Manoogian's place. Did he mean the notebook? Did the Legion of the Lamb forge Alvarez's writing to give the detective credit for exposing the truth behind Berj's cocaine operation and Maddie Hinkle's murder?

I learn the police are asking the public for any information on Berj Manoogian's whereabouts. Seems he's wanted in connection with the warehouse fire, where 200 kilos of cocaine, ten AR-15 rifles, and thirty stolen ancient Armenian artifacts were recovered.

That night, Brent made his special chicken mole. I poke and prod the meal with my fork but hardly take a bite. My appetite is shot. Insomnia grips me and I pace the floor until Vonnie tells me to get my ass back in bed. The following day, she and Roupen ambush me like a long overdue intervention.

"Okay, Armand. What's with you?" Roupen asks. He's seated at the register in the bookshop. It's a slow day with not a customer in sight.

"You haven't been yourself since we got here," Vonnie says. She's staring me down like a gunslinger in an old western, scrutinizing my face for signs of weakness.

"Don't give me those Lee Van Cleef eyes, Vonnie. Doesn't it bother you that the police are nosing around Berj's warehouse?" I ask.

"This is the bad dude who almost killed you?" Roupen perches on the edge of his chair.

"Tark, Berj is dead. They're not gonna find anything," Vonnie says.

"Then if the police are searching for him, why isn't he at the morgue? They found over a dozen bodies in that pit, mostly his followers. Where did his corpse go?"

The answer strikes me almost immediately. I remember that field in Clovis, the one the Legion plants the vampires, werewolves, and other creatures it exterminates. Berj Manoogian rests eternally, his rotting body moldering with monstrosities far more hideous than him. I can't think of a more deserving fate for that bastard. I keep this to myself and savor it. Some things are too delicious to share.

"Shouldn't you two get ready for Vegas, or is that not happening?" Roupen asks.

"The trip is postponed," I say.

Vonnie and Roupen give me that same open-mouthed, goggle-eyed face.

"Wait, what?" Vonnie cries. "Since when did you decide this?"

"Since we have unfinished business here. There's my father's will to settle and the aftermath with the Legion. We did some pretty shady shit in that cornfield, Vonnie," I tell her.

"Do I want to know this?" Roupen asks.

"No," Vonnie and I reply in unison.

"Okay. Well, stay here as long as you need to. My door is always open," Roupen says, returning to his reading.

Bookshops are self-contained madness. Left alone in one for too long, surrounded by all those words written by dead folks, it overwhelms you. I devour books on nearly every subject and restlessness plagues me over the next few days. Vonnie tries distracting me. We sneak in the bedroom in the middle of the day when Roupen is occupied with customers. Our carnal gymnastics, while amazing, fails to distract me from my restlessness.

I leave Vonnie in bed and head to the kitchen, strangely peckish. While digging around for something sugary, I find the latest *Fresno Bee* on the table and flip through it. José Alvarez's obituary screams at me in black and white, each word an indictment to my guilt.

According to the obituary, Alvarez leaves behind his wife, parents, and two brothers.

He has a widow now. I got a family man killed, I think.

I heave myself into a chair, my shoulders slumping, my muscles loose as rubber.

Whatever business we hashed out when I summoned him last wasn't enough. The Legion might have made Alvarez a hero to the public, but for me, my debt isn't paid.

A headache brews in my skull. I take a deep, cleansing breath and close my eyes. From within me, the murky shores of a distant place draws near, an ethereal realm of everlasting night and shadow. The temperature in the kitchen plummets to an all-familiar chill. When I open my eyes, Alvarez's ghost is in my brother's kitchen.

"You again? I'm not some genie you can summon whenever you like," Alvarez scolds. He crosses his spectral arms and hovers over the floor.

"Hear me out. I want to apologize again for everything I've done. I was reckless and you paid the price for –"

Alvarez waves his hand dismissively.

"Save it. Did you do what I told you? Did you give Berj some justice?" Alvarez asks.

"How come you never said anything about being married? If I'd known that, I never would've told you about Berj. I never would've gotten you involved," I say.

Alvarez lowers his head and bites his lip. *"Maria. Her name is Maria. We've been married for eight years. Best eight years of my life. I didn't talk about her because my private life is none of your damn business."*

"Had I known –"

"You didn't need to know," Alvarez snaps. His eyes dart from side to side like he's thinking. Finally, he sighs and says, *"Did you deliver Berj some justice?"*

I clasp my hands together like I'm a desperate drunkard minutes from death praying for salvation.

"Alvarez, from the bottom of my heart, please know I'm deeply sorry and I swear I'll make this right."

"Unless you've got resurrection powers in that little supernatural starter pack you have, you're wasting your time." Alvarez looks at the floor. *"I guess the reason I'm dead falls on me. I wanted to follow Manoogian that night. You didn't want me to, but I thought I had a break in the case. I got in over my head and paid the price. Play stupid games, win stupid prizes, right?"*

"I should've told you, but I was too afraid. Got myself tangled up in something I couldn't control," I admit.

"Back to my original question. Berj. Justice. You deliver any to him?"

"The world thinks you're a hero. The cops have your notebook. They're concluding you took down Berj Manoogian and the Children of Spandaramet," I tell him.

"So he's...."

"Dead. Berj and his cult are dead. The man who killed you is buried in a field in Clovis."

284

Alvarez cracks a smile. It's the first time I've seen him do this since he died.

"No shit? Well, that's something, I guess." He regards his translucent form with a disgusted grimace. *"Maria always said smoking would be the death of me. Boy, was she wrong."*

"Detective, you saved my life when you had no reason to. Let me help you now." I rise on wobbly legs.

"You really helping me or atoning for what you've done?"

Seeking forgiveness from his ghost is one thing. Been there, done that. Now I needed to make things right.

"You should be at peace. My uncle's funeral home has your body. I need to make sure you're taken care of properly. For your family," I tell Alvarez.

The ghost shakes his head sadly. *"I first met Maria at the Santa Monica Pier. I was working for my uncle in L.A. that summer after college, and went up to the pier one night. A mutual acquaintance introduced us. She stood by the gelato vendor, her raven hair flowing down her back, her brown eyes big as anything. Smitten wasn't the right word for what I was. Ever feel an electric spark strike you when you find the right one? It pulls you out of time and reality. A powerful jolt that lifts the best part of you to the surface. Time freezes. Everything falls silent. Nothing else exists except the two of you staring outside yourselves, witnessing the moment as significant, almost sacred. Only the two of you standing together, your true selves shining brazenly into the universe, into each other. For that moment, you know what all those poets and artists and troubadours have crowed on about for centuries. Love is enduring. Always."*

Alvarez vanishes into nothing, leaving a residual cold patch.

"Who are you talking to?" Vonnie stands in the threshold to the kitchen, wearing nothing but a large T-shirt that hangs past her thighs.

Without saying anything, I go over to her. Our eyes lock. I trace her shoulders with my fingers and draw her close. We kiss hungrily and fumble back to the bedroom, peeling clothes off along the way. I cradle her head in my hands and bathe her with kisses, on her cheeks, chin, and down her neck. My hands gently glide towards her breasts and around to the small of her back.

Her skin is supple, warm, and perfumed. Sex is a wild anarchy, a ripping apart of politeness and convention and rushing towards our truest, animalistic selves. Our lovemaking is so loud that Roupen bangs on the wall. "Hey! Quiet down, you two! I'm running a respectable bookshop, not a bordello."

Vonnie and I collapse into laughter. We kiss one more time and then fall asleep, our naked bodies intertwined in a blissful tangle.

I awaken an hour later and tumble out of bed. Carefully tiptoeing across the creaking hardwood floor so I don't wake Vonnie, I grab a handful of clothes. I shower, get dressed, and ride Velma to a familiar place I've dreaded for years, an old house that nearly broke me.

CHAPTER 33

A HARD GOODBYE

Tarkanian Funeral Home appears gloomy and drab, like a once-grand dowager gradually going to seed. A light in the downstairs window is on when I arrive. I wipe my boots on the welcome mat like I've done a hundred times before, but this time there's an unshakable feeling that I don't belong here.

I take a deep breath and ring the doorbell. Footsteps within the house approach, the lock unlatches, and the door swings open. Aunt Miriam looks tired; her hair is down (a thing rarely seen by mortal eyes), and her apron stained with tomato sauce. She beams when she sees me.

"Armand!" she cries. We embrace. She sobs with joy.

I gently push her away and smile.

"Hi, Aunt Miriam," is all I can say.

She leads me into the kitchen and plies me full of sweet date cookies, talking about how drafty and uncomfortable the farmhouse was and how Uncle George needed to return to the funeral home.

"We cleaned up all the broken plates and things. The insurance company says that breaking and entering and vandalism are covered, so they'll be paying for repairs. It was strange to see that there was no blood or anything from that thing in the living room." She shivers at the memory. "After that, Uncle George called the police and reported you missing. We hadn't heard anything for weeks, and now you show up."

"I didn't mean to leave things like I did," I confess, mustering all the sincerity I can.

"We were so worried. We thought you had died. Killed by something terrible," she says.

"Was Uncle George worried?"

"Ask him yourself," Aunt Miriam tilts her head towards the living room, where the TV is on at full volume.

I find Uncle George seated in his old recliner, staring blankly at the screen. He's slumped over, half asleep, perspiring beer bottle on the table nearby.

He shudders awake and regards me with tired eyes. Uncle George's voice wavers between full-throated scolding and whispered gratitude for my safe return.

"The family was worried sick, you son of a bitch." He presses the remote and the TV screen goes dark. "Where the hell were you?"

"I miss you, too, Uncle George," I say.

Aunt Miriam places a tray on the table and hands me a dainty cup filled with strong brown coffee.

"We thank God you're still with us." Aunt Miriam lovingly squeezes my cheek.

I tell them they have nothing to worry about and that the people who threatened the family are gone and will never return. Uncle George demands I explain what happened, and I politely decline.

"It's better for everyone if you don't know." I force a smile.

Uncle George frowns.

"I'm sick of this bullshit! If you don't come clean about where you were and why we had to live in Hagop's farmhouse, then you're fired," he says.

"Fine by me. I'm here to give you notice that I quit. I figured the least I could do would be to tell you in person." My words ring like sweet poetry.

Uncle George scrunches his face and turns crimson.

"Quit? You're going to quit? What the hell will I do now? After everything I did for you, taking you in, giving you a place to live. How ungrateful!"

"I'm not ungrateful. Truthfully, I appreciate a lot of what you did. If you hadn't, I wouldn't have realized what I really needed." I stand my ground, but unlike the past, I'm not angry at him. "I'm leaving Fresno for a while, after I get things squared away with the farmhouse."

"Leaving? Where are you going?" Aunt Miriam asks.

"Vonnie and I are taking a trip, one long overdue. This is my goodbye," I tell them.

"I should call the goddamn cops and have you arrested. Worrying us like that. Hanging out with those undesirables," Uncle George rants.

"You can't have someone arrested for worrying you, Uncle George." I sip from the demitasse cup and smile at Aunt Miriam. "This is *really* good coffee."

"What am I supposed to do? Advertise for another embalmer? They don't exactly grow on trees." Uncle George peevishly folds his arms like a child.

"You have a smart daughter who wants to learn the family business. Teach her and stop putting all your chips on Dikran. You have two kids, not just one," I tell him.

"Samantha?"

"Samantha actually wants to work with you. Maybe you should realize what an enormous gift that is," I say.

Uncle George stands there, stupefied that anyone would stand up to him. He's making that same bewildered face when I head downstairs to my old workspace.

The embalming room is colder than usual, so cold it raises gooseflesh on my arms. The sterile table, floor tiles, and the tools of my trade arranged on the worktable are distant and alien to me now. My old gown, mask, and box of latex rubber gloves are next to a clipboard with records of the decedents.

I check the list. Alvarez's name is among those in cold storage. Though Alvarez's body is a few feet from me behind a metal door, I'm not interested in seeing him. One talk with his cranky spirit is enough for today.

Samantha leans against the embalming table. She's in full Goth mode; black nail polish, blood red makeup, T-shirt from some death metal band I don't know.

"When did you get back?" she asks, a big smile on her face. "I thought I'd never see you again. When your friend showed up with my car I thought that something had happened. He just dropped it off in the parking lot and was gone, the keys were in the mailbox."

"Hey, Samantha," I say. "Who's doing the embalming?"

"Uncle George. He's pissed about it though. He actually has to do work!" She laughs.

"What are you doing down here?" I ask.

"I like to imagine myself embalming. Maybe if I look like I'm familiarizing myself with this stuff, Dad will see that I'm interested in learning," she says.

"Samantha, you've got to tell him yourself. You've been obsessed with this business since you were a kid, even more than me. This is your passion, so don't be afraid to pursue it, you spooky weirdo."

Samantha blushes.

"Fight for it. Study hard and don't give up." I give her shoulder a squeeze. "Where's Dikran?"

"Holy shit, you're not going to believe it," she says. "Dikran is going back to school."

"Wait. I heard 'Dikran' and 'school' in the same sentence. Are you kidding?"

"No, I'm not. After everything that happened, he calls me one day and is all like 'we need to talk'. I think that he's going to pull some dumb bullshit like he always does, but he takes me out for lunch and apologizes. He tells me that he's not good with bodies, but that maybe when Dad decides to retire he can do the front office stuff and I'll handle all the embalming stuff."

"That's shocking," I admit.

"Yeah, I guess almost getting eaten by a monster will give you a new perspective on life."

"You know?"

"I think that he really wants to do better. Mind blown, right?"

"Well, life has been crazy recently, so what's one more thing?" I admit. "Tell your brother that I'm happy for him, and that I hope the two of you can run this place better than Uncle George."

"We got it, Armand. Just you wait," she says.

I confess my plans with Vonnie and our long overdue vacation. While Samantha is disappointed that I won't stick around, she understands. Samantha possesses more resolve than Uncle George gives her credit for.

"You really love this Vonnie chick, huh?" Samantha asks.

"I do. Vonnie will help me make sense of myself," I say.

"You don't let too many people in. I guess that's our family's mistrust of outsiders. You know my father. He doesn't trust the odars as far as he can throw one of them. For Armand Tarkanian to put his trust in a stranger and open his heart to another? That's pretty big," Samantha replies.

We hug one last time.

"Goodbye, cousin. Study hard and kick ass. Let the world see what you can do," I tell her like a reluctant mentor dispensing worn advice. I try repressing my tears and fail. We both stand in the embalming room and have one last cry. It's both cathartic and hilarious.

Aunt Miriam packs a plastic container with paklava and nazook. Though my sweet tooth has been sated, her pastries comfort me so I eat a couple more and take the container. She agrees to send my remaining belongings to my new address, wherever that might be.

"Thanks, Aunt Miriam," I tell her.

"Your mother and father would be proud of you," Aunt Miriam squeezes me tightly. "Armenians say that a traveler's departure lies in his own hands, and his return is in the hands of God. Do you believe that?"

I think for a moment.

"Maybe," I reply.

"Don't tell me you lost your faith!" Her eyes widen and her face turns ashen. If Aunt Miriam wore pearls, she'd probably be clutching them.

I'm the farthest thing from devout right now, and maybe that's for the best.

"It's complicated. Life, death, the universe. I think we weren't meant to know everything," I reply.

Aunt Miriam looks down and nods to herself. "You know about the Martyr's Vow, Armand?"

"Is this one of your folk tales?" I ask.

"Whoever gives their life willingly to save another shall be rewarded in abundance ever after. Our ancestors were martyrs in the genocide. In our family, my grandparents sacrificed themselves to save their children, who were spirited out of Turkey. Taking the Martyr's Vow is a sacred tradition in our family. Anytime we lay our lives down, it must be for a higher purpose."

"Why are you telling me this?"

"Because I want your life and death to mean something, Armand. I don't want you mixing with the wrong crowd and paying for your impetuousness. Promise me you'll stay away from those odars." She looks at me like my grandfather did, with an unwavering stubbornness born from generations of groupthink.

"I won't promise that," I tell her. "I can't."

Aunt Miriam looks disappointed, but pats my shoulder.

"You're welcome here any time, Armand. We love you," she says, her voice cracking.

"I love you, too." I sniff.

"No matter where the road takes you, remember that this family will always love you," Aunt Miriam says.

Uncle George walks over and thrusts a check into my hands. It's for two thousand dollars and made out to me.

"Let's call this your severance pay," Uncle George says. "You're not working here, so I'll work downstairs until Samantha graduates. Or I'll hire someone part time. Anyway, we're fine without you. But, family is everything—my brother would curse my name if I just let you go out into the world with nothing. Armenians don't have much in this world and there aren't that many of us left. So you've got to sacrifice for your family."

"Thanks." I say, giving him a thin smile. "Funny you should talk about sacrifice. I need you to do something for me."

Uncle George raises his eyebrows and grits his teeth. "What? I just gave you money —"

"You have José Alvarez downstairs."

"The PI? What about him?"

"I'm requesting you give him the works for free. His widow will not pay for his funeral. You will give him the best casket, offer the best service, bend over backwards for his family. There will be plenty of police officers at his funeral and it wouldn't do you any harm to be magnanimous for once," I tell him.

Uncle George scratches his head, as if he's postulating a philosophical conundrum.

"You've got balls, kid. I'll give you that. You want me to give this PI a free funeral?" he says.

"José Alvarez was killed investigating criminal activity in this city. He wanted nothing more than to be remembered for his sacrifice. I think we should give him the best sendoff we can with respect and dignity," I say.

Uncle George puts his hands on his hips. "And how do you know what a dead man wants?"

"Because I spoke with him after he died," I reply.

Uncle George and Aunt Miriam turn pale. They look at each other, then at me. Aunt Miriam's lips tremble and she clasps her hands together.

"He's got the Barsamian curse, just like his mother. Lord have mercy," she says.

"I knew you were a little off." Uncle George points an accusatory finger at me. "But I didn't want to see it."

"Neither did I. It frightened me when it first happened, but I learned that it wasn't a curse. It was a gift. The way the Tarkanians behaved towards my mother was shameful. You alienated my mother and treated her like an outcast. The way I see it, you owe me an apology. That's why you're giving Alvarez the send-off he deserves," I tell them.

Uncle George and Aunt Miriam argue back and forth in Armenian. Aunt Miriam makes the sign of the cross, while Uncle George splutters a few choice profanities I understand. They settle down and agree on a compromise.

"We'll bury your friend, the PI," Uncle George relents. "But you cannot mention this to Samantha or Dikran. Keep my children out of whatever hocus pocus you do."

"Agreed." I shake Uncle George's clammy hand.

I say my goodbyes, tuck Aunt Miriam's pastries under one arm, stuff the check in my pants pocket, and leave the Tarkanian Funeral Home for what I hope is the last time.

Alvarez would've enjoyed his funeral.

Fresno's law enforcement community – the police chief, sheriff's deputies, and private investigators – all turned out, joining Alvarez's family for a graveside service. A priest from St. John's Cathedral delivered the eulogy, commending Alvarez for his service in exposing one of the city's largest drug rings. Zombies and ritual sacrifices weren't mentioned, proof the Legion is skilled at burying all supernatural loose ends.

Uncle George and Dikran stood by the hearse, hands in their pockets. Both begrudgingly acknowledged Vonnie and me.

I straightened my black suit and necktie and removed my sunglasses. Vonnie squeezed my hand, silently reassuring me that we'd get through this.

After the ceremony, we pay our respects to Alvarez's widow. She's a demure woman, standing at a little over five feet with short brown hair and eyes red from crying. Her hand grazes the metal casket and drifts toward the flowers adorning the top.

"Maria Alvarez?" I ask.

"Yes?" she replies softly.

"I'm Armand Tarkanian. I worked with José as a consultant," I tell her.

She smiles faintly. "Tarkanian? You're with the funeral home?" She takes my hand. "I appreciate what you've done. This has been so hard for me. José left a lot of unpaid expenses and planning all of this was too much."

"I just want to tell you that your husband was a hero. He put himself in harm's way, but his investigation saved the lives of many people," I say.

Maria Alvarez purses her lips and a tear runs down her cheek.

"Yes. That's what the police detectives told me. Without José's notebook, they wouldn't have connected the warehouse fire and that terrible place he was found with all the others." She winces and then sobs before composing herself. "Thank you for telling me this, Mr. Tarkanian. And thank you again for this lovely service. When your uncle called and told me the funeral home wouldn't charge us, I thought it was a miracle. You gave José the respect he rarely got in life."

Vonnie offers her condolences before we leave, skirting the mourners making their way to the casket. A profound lightness fills me on the way out of the cemetery, a sensation that hovers between relief and contentment. It's as if the darkness plaguing my life has finally lifted, revealing brighter hues and a clearer path forward.

José Alvarez, that chain-smoking private eye with a penchant for quips and one-liners, is finally at peace.

CHAPTER 34

THE GREAT OPEN ROAD

Dad's attorney tells me about the wonderful opportunities of home ownership, but I'll never have the coveted all-American house with a white picket fence and back yard swimming pool. I inherited an old farmhouse with too many complicated memories, a sour monstrosity anchoring me to Fresno. The attorney slaps the keys down on his desk and has me sign some documents and the house I've lived in most of my childhood is now legally mine.

Going back home fills me with a weird sense of déjà vu—the uncomfortable feeling that this house is like another member of the family, quietly dying and slipping away.

I imagine how Dad, in all his sadistic glory, must be cackling at me from beyond the grave.

"Now you're stuck in Fresno, my boy," he'd say. "Plant some roots and live the rest of your days here, where all your trauma began."

But his ghost doesn't appear. Perhaps he's found some peace as well.

Instead of chaining myself to my childhood home, I gift the property to Roupen.

My brother and Brent put the bookstore and their apartment up for sale and move into the old farmhouse, which they plan on renovating and turning into Fresno's newest (and best) bed and breakfast. The two of them plan to take the time off to fix up the old place. Hopefully it'll be unrecognizable by the time they're done.

My brother and I demolish the old grape arbor and clear away the dead vines and rot from decades of neglect. Tearing down the trellis and snapping each beam gives me a perverse satisfaction, like the past will never govern me again. Roupen shares my sentiment and outlines his plans for the property. Instead of a moldering, dusty farmhouse it'll be a warm and inviting place — like those distant and fleeting memories from our youth.

I hope that Dad – wherever he is – can see Roupen. He might roll his eyes eternally, knowing his gay son is living in the family home with another man, serving kickass galettes and waffles and loving each other with tenderness and passion, but at least he'd know what real happiness looks like.

About a week after Roupen and Brent move in, they get an offer on the bookstore. They give me a check for one hundred thousand dollars, a goodbye gift for Vonnie and me. We celebrate with a bottle of Sonoma wine. I smile reading the label and my brother warns me to keep my mouth shut. Brent makes me blueberry pancakes (a food that I am incapable of escaping it seems) and expresses his gratitude with a big hug.

"Thanks for everything, brother," Roupen brushes away his tears. "If you're ever in the neighborhood, you'll have a place to stay."

"You guys are going to have this fixed up in no time."

"So," Roupen says, walking over to a drawer in the kitchen and taking out a small box, "me and Brent were cleaning up and I thought that you might want this." He offers me the little box, wrapped in blue paper with a white bow.

"Mm … A book," I guess as I give the box a shake. The box is incredibly light and might as well be empty. "What is it?"

"A part of your history, I guess." Roupen shrugs. "Maybe something that reminds you where you came from."

I carefully remove the ribbon, unwrap the box, and gently open it. Under white tissue paper sits a small toy motorcycle. The die-cast frame and plastic wheels are tarnished and scuffed, but it's unmistakably the same toy motorcycle I chose long ago. My hands shake as I take it out of the box.

"I found it with some of Mom's things. I thought that you might want it, what with the whole 'I'm in a biker cult' thing that you've got going on," Roupen explains.

I wrap my arms around my brother and squeeze him tight.

"Thanks, Roupen," I say. "I love you and so does Mom, by the way."

Roupen freezes, then playfully swats me and returns my embrace.

"That money I gave you. Don't spend it all in one place. I know Vegas is one seductive bitch," he says.

"It'll help us get settled. For now, the road calls," I tell him.

We speak outside for a bit and I notice that large dog curled up on the front porch. It lifts its head and looks at me with big brown eyes and its tongue flops out of its mouth.

I know.

"That guy has been coming around here the last few days." Roupen walks over and scratches the dog's head.

The dog yawns, stretches its back, and barks. It walks down the front steps of the house and over towards the motorcycle. The dog barks and stares at me soulfully.

"I think he likes you," I tell Roupen. "Okay, time to go. I gotta pick up Vonnie from the apartment and then we're out. I'll call you soon."

"Ride safe, Armand," he says and goes back into the house.

As I walk over Velma, the dog backs away and winks—actually winks—at me. It sits down and extends a paw. I reach down and shake it.

"Thanks, my friend," I say. "Thank you for everything you've done."

The animal winks again and two huge feathered wings sprout from its back. The Aralez bows its head. It beats its wings and rises until it's gone, leaving a large solitary feather, brown and mottled, drifting slowly to the ground. I bend over and pick it up and put it into the box with the little toy motorcycle that my mother kept. I pack the box carefully into one of the saddlebags and get on the motorcycle.

The ride back to the apartment is quiet and the warm air feels nice as it whips around me.

"What's that? A condor feather?" Vonnie asks.

"It's a present," I say. I'm waiting for her to get the last of her things packed up. I tuck the feather into my vest pocket, next to my heart, and hope that one day my soul will be light enough to be weighed against it.

Vonnie straddles the bike behind me, sidles close, and wraps her arms around my chest. I rev up Velma and we ride, roaring down the street and kicking up dust behind her.

We don't look back.

The Everafter Cemetery is deserted this late in the afternoon. My biker boots sink into the soft mud the whole way to the gravesite. We pause at a small but familiar headstone. Vonnie kneels and places a bouquet of red roses on the ground. She drapes her arm around me and we stand silently for several minutes.

After the police found her body in the ditch near the cornfield, Maddie Hinkle was reinterred. Fresh sod covers the area where weeks before, the disturbed grave yielded a horrific find.

We soak in the afternoon sun and pay our respects, muttering condolences and awkward prayers, or as close as we can muster to a prayer. A slight breeze shakes the grass, and for a crazy instant I think Maddie has returned.

"She misses you," I tell Vonnie.

"You can see her? She's here now?" Her eyes get wide and her tone excited.

"No. But she did say that she misses you a while ago."

Vonnie's shoulders slump.

"It wasn't supposed to happen this way. Maddie should've grown old. She should've gotten married and had a house full of rug rats and a husband from Madera who sells used cars. Not end up like this." She waves her arms over the grave as if to accentuate her point.

"We did it, Maddie. It's all over," is all I say to the grave under my feet.

"Yeah, kid. We did it. You can rest peacefully now," Vonnie tells the headstone.

We stand there silently for a few more minutes before Vonnie kisses my cheek.

I hope that Maddie, Alvarez and Stuart all saw what happened in the cornfield. I hope they found consolidation from Berj's demise and the cult's downfall.

I also hope that I did right by them, and that they can get the rest and peace that they all deserve. Maybe other ghosts would come in the future, but for now, I hope those three stay in my past.

For now, my life is traveling with Vonnie wherever we want. The roads are long and accommodating if we never stop.

"Had a conversation with my aunt recently," I tell Vonnie. "She was so worried that I was losing my faith. I told her, after what I've seen, everything is complicated. Life, death, and everything in between. The answers aren't that simple now that we know what we know."

301

"It's certainly a brave new world. Monsters, magic, mythology. All of it real." Vonnie's hand scrabbles for my vest. She holds on tightly.

"We witnessed things most humans can't imagine. How do we return to our regular lives?"

"That's not a problem."

"Isn't it?"

"No way. Life is a fool's journey with interesting bits thrown in. It might not be perfect—but, then again, it doesn't have to be. Take the mundane with the magic." Vonnie tugs at my vest. We hug.

"A fool's journey? I like that."

"We just want the good feelings to continue for as long as they can and ride happiness out forever." Vonnie looks at me. "But we're not built for forever. Only the here and now. Good parts, grimy parts, joy and pain. The whole shitty enchilada."

I spent my life trying to make my way to the grave, buried by obligations and misery. Yet the grave only punctuates the end — it's only a conclusion, not our entire story.

In her darkest hours, my mother told me I should embrace and celebrate life, realizing every day is a new chance for joy, for apologies, for redemption, and for reward. It's taken me decades, but I understand what she meant.

"Life will surprise and annoy you, and that's why it's a beautiful paradox," I say.

Vonnie showed me what I've been missing all of these years: a true connection. Together, we'll bathe in life's waters, soak in the sunshine and stand in the rain. Life is finite, but our potential infinite.

We witness a mere sliver of time in history. Glimpse it all around. Maybe it's just a Thursday. Or a birthday. Or the most special day of our lives.

I used to think I would be alone forever, trapped with the dead in a cold embalming room. But I was never alone. Not really. There were always kindred spirits all around me, helpful strangers seeking a similar connection. People hurting. In pain. Afraid. Maddie Hinkle helped me leave that basement and transform into a better version of myself. A ghost made me less afraid. For this, she'll always have a special place in my heart.

Vonnie and I don our helmets and straddle Velma, both of us smelling like leather, oil, and sweat. Vonnie hugs me from behind, her body melts perfectly against mine.

I lift the kickstand with my foot, pull the choke lever, and turn on the ignition. Gripping the handlebars, I squeeze the clutch and press the start button. Velma purrs like a cheetah about to pounce. I carefully close the choke lever and open the throttle. The bike's low purr switches to a beastly metallic growl. She's a pulsating vixen, a roaring temptress feeding on my adrenaline and wanderlust.

We ride southeast along Highway 99 towards Bakersfield, screaming past Visalia and Tulare, wind slapping against us, engine roaring in our ears. By the time we reach Bakersfield my pain is a million miles away. We head east, up Highway 58 then Interstate 15, Vegas-bound.

The California sun beats down on us, a harsh observer splashing the asphalt with a shimmering heat haze. Miles of emptiness and stark beauty, a peaceful desolation enticing us further down the highway, past rusted filling stations, sweeping vistas, and truckers hauling freight. America spilling out in all her ruinous majesty.

Vonnie tightly nuzzles my back.

"When will we get there?" she shouts into my ear.

I don't care about the destination. This is our moment. Our slice in time.

On this motorcycle, we're completely and unabashedly alive, two fools making their way along the great open road.

I lean back and say, "Just hang on and enjoy the ride."

ACKNOWLEDGMENTS

Between writers and readers, I think readers get the sweeter deal. The heavy lifting is already done, because readers only see the finished book, the end result of a writer's creative endeavors. What they don't see are the hours writers pour into writing, editing, and rewriting. They don't see nights spent pacing the floor, drafts bloodied with red ink, crumpled pages hurled into trashcans. They don't see the horrible anxiety, dizzying self-doubt, and the feeling your dreams are running faster than you can catch them.

Readers also don't see the people behind the scenes who help cultivate the writer's vision. Without the assistance and encouragement from the following people, this novel would've languished unread on a hard drive. Their kindness and expertise closed the distance between dream and reality, for which I'm immensely grateful:

To Jessica Moon, Mandy Russell, and Dan Fitzgerald of Shadow Spark Publishing for believing in this macabre little novel and giving it a home.

To my editor Susan Floyd for wading through a shambolic manuscript, killing the darlings, and making everything shine.

To Derek McPhee and Michelle Hauck for their superior editing skills and nudging me in the right direction.

To Charles Barouch, Jeni Chappelle, Clay Harmon, Ralph Walker, and Tim Zatzariny for their suggestions on arranging these stubborn words into the right order.

To my beta readers Alex Geffard, Laura Kincaid, Tyler Meyerhoff, Tova Seltzer, Ellen Symons, and Rachel Luann Strayer for your patience and feedback.

To Ace Tilton Ratcliff for answering my questions about the funeral industry, embalming, and a bunch of other stuff related to death.

To my former Writing Arts professors Megan Atwood, Ron Block, and Lisa Jahn-Clough for their developmental notes when this was a painfully awkward first draft.

To François Vaillancourt for a marvelous cover illustration that perfectly captures the Legion of the Lamb's patch.

To the #5amwritersclub – Twitter's mega-awesome writing group – for inspiring me to continue sitting at that keyboard every morning and holding myself accountable.

To my parents, who introduced me to me the local public library, fostered my appreciation for books at an early age, and unknowingly started my journey as a writer.

To my wife Elnie for supporting me throughout this whole maddening process and tolerating my eccentric writerly ways more than anyone. Sorry about the dirty coffee cups scattered throughout the house.

To my Armenian family who provided me with stories, nurtured my imagination, and are probably mortified by this book.

And to those acquaintances and strangers who motivated me to continue writing when things looked bleak, or who offered advice or kind

words. Thanks for jumpstarting the muse.

ERIC AVEDISSIAN

Eric Avedissian is an adjunct professor at Atlantic Cape Community College in New Jersey where he teaches English composition. He has an MA in Writing from Rowan University and is a member of Science Fiction and Fantasy Writers of America (SFWA).

When not writing, he wastes time on Twitter (like writers do) and participates in the writer's groups #5amwritersclub and #WritingCommunity

You can find Eric On Twitter @angryreporter or on his website, www. ericavedissian.comw

Made in the USA
Middletown, DE
14 December 2022

18463218R00176